Read 2024

Eva

By

Diane Solomon

Eva

ISBN 978-0-9989949-3-2
Printed in USA

Chapter 1

Summer, Pine Hill,
near Stonington, Connecticut

Tucked amidst the pile of spam and solicitations, Eva spotted a formal-looking envelope made of heavyweight cream paper. She recognized the name of a well-known law firm in the center of New London from the embossed corporate logo and address.

What does a law firm want with me?

Ripping open the envelope, she tossed it on the half-table by the foyer wall and scanned the contents of the brief cover letter. Waffly and full of legalese, the gist was she should have received this letter five years ago on her twenty-first birthday. Then came vague apologies and explanations.

Mystified, she unfolded the two pages to which the cover letter referred. This paper was blue, like old-fashioned personal stationery, for handwriting. No address at the top, just the date, from eight years ago. At the bottom of the second page, it was signed,

Love you forever, BG, Sophie.

Her heart began to pound. *Aunt Sophie has been dead for eight years.* In Sophie's letter, she apologized for not telling Eva earlier but had thought it best to wait until she was twenty-one. *Tell me what?* Sophie wrote that she assumed Eva's mother would have told her eventually if she hadn't passed suddenly. And then there it was. William Hastings III. Eva stared.

The front door opened and her roommate burst in, the screen door slamming behind her.

"Damn," Jamie said, "It was busy in town. Jean agreed to do my hair at 7:30 this morning. What an angel. And I went for bagels..." Her hands were full, so she kicked the door shut with her foot. Laying the bags and coffees down on the table, she whirled around. "Check it out. You like?" Her jet-black, pixie cut now sported a green streak down one side, dramatic against her brown skin and almond eyes. Framing her hands on either side of her head, she posed. "Ta-da!"

Eva couldn't speak.

Jamie dropped her hands and her eyes widened. "Eva? What's going on? You're as white as that wall."

Eva just held out the pages and watched in silence as her friend scanned the page from the law firm.

Jamie drew in a sharp breath. "What the hell?" Then her eyes raced back and forth over Sophie's letter. Her mouth dropped open. "Oh my God... Seriously? This is huge. But why didn't she tell you?"

Eva shook her head, still wordless. Time had stopped. She simply stood there, in the foyer, with her best friend staring at her, while fragmented thoughts jockeyed for attention. *So, not an orphan after all.* She repeated the name in her mind: William Hastings. *The third, don't forget that.* From Boston. He attended Harvard University. That's all it said. But that was enough. Mom had never told her anything about him. Eva never knew his name, what he did for a living, or why he and her mother were not together.

For that matter, she never even knew if he was still alive.

"I didn't even know Aunt Sophie knew who he was," Eva finally answered.

Jamie held up the firm's cover letter. "Can you believe this? Some BS about the lawyer in charge of the case dying suddenly and his cases handed out to various other partners and attorneys in the firm. Blah blah blah." She glanced down and read, "'Got overlooked.' Overlooked? Seriously? For five years? They're a law firm for God's sake. I mean, 'fiduciary responsibility,' and all that?"

Jamie glanced up at Eva. Her face softened. "Come on, you look like you're going to fall down. I got you a decaf latte—but now's one of those times I wish you could drink. Like a large brandy."

"It's 8:30 in the morning... And I'm due at the shelter."

"They can wait. It's not every day you get news like this!" Jamie took her arm and pulled her toward the kitchen. "Sit," she instructed.

While Jamie collected plates and cream cheese for bagels, Eva sank into a wicker chair at the old farm table. She always loved this spot, especially when the morning sun streamed in. She stared at the blowsy pink peonies she'd cut a few days ago which were now dropping petals all over the pine planks. The mess would normally have bothered her, but now she just swept them aside and spread the letters out in front of her. She read through them again. But she couldn't focus, as if someone had stuffed her brain full of cotton wool.

Her little golden cocker spaniel leaned against her leg, head on her knee, gazing up with worried chocolate eyes. She reached down to stroke the silky ears.

"Oh, Cookie, you're such a love," Jamie said. "She knows something's up."

Eva closed her eyes. She was thrown back to the days just after Sophie died, remembering the phone call from a neighbor, the race home from college, the visit to the funeral home. How she'd existed in a dazed stupor, for God knows how long. Aunt Sophie, who was, in fact, her great-aunt, had been there for her after her mom died.

Took her in and raised her. Sophie, who called her Baby Girl, or BG.

Sophie hadn't told her of her illness. Eva had been away in her freshman year at UConn, and by May of that year, had suspected something was going on. Sophie had sounded tired on the phone, and when pressed, explained she was having some tests done. It was probably nothing, maybe a bit of anemia. She'd insisted she was fine, that Eva must stay and complete her exams. Sophie ended the call by saying she looked forward to seeing her when Eva got home in six weeks.

Sophie didn't last six weeks.

Her aunt's death spun around and around in her head. Eva learned that Sophie had decided to forgo treatment for a fast-growing abdominal cancer. Refusing to allow her treatment to consume her last dollar, she left her savings to Eva, hoping it was enough to pay for another year of college.

Eva didn't even get to say goodbye.

Jamie put a plated bagel in front of her. "You want anything else?"

She shook her head. The thought of eating anything made her slightly queasy. But thank God for Jamie. She wasn't sure how she'd have survived the months after Sophie died without her. Jamie cheered her up, distracted her, and made her laugh. She was as close to a relative as Eva had after Sophie had gone. There was no other family.

Well, wait a minute. Maybe there was, now.

Jamie sat down across from her and sipped her espresso. "Let's research him." She crunched up a bit of bagel and her brow furrowed as she thought. "The third, huh?" A small smile formed on her face. "Do you think he's rich? That would be cool."

Eva shook her head. "No idea." The latte felt good going down, warming her. But why did she feel so chilled? It was already a warm day, and humid. "I'll Google him later when I get home." Starting for the door, she added, "Thanks, Jamie, got to run."

"Wait, take your bagel." Jamie wrapped it in a paper towel and plopped it in her hand.

Eva smiled her thanks. Trying to shove the entire episode from her mind, she hurried out to her faithful, if ancient, SUV. Wending her way down the familiar wooded lanes of Connecticut, everything looked strange. She felt as if she were looking at the world through the wrong end of a telescope. Now, everything was different somehow, out of kilter.

What do I do with this?

Focusing on breathing deeply, she remembered what Aunt Sophie used to say. "Relax, Baby Girl. If you can't figure something out, don't think about it. It will come clear in time."

When her mom died, Sophie tried to help her the only way she knew how. Eva's great-aunt was a spreadsheet sort of person, extremely organized and logical. Nothing ever flapped her. Sophie's British upbringing had instilled a degree of calm and restraint, which rubbed off on Eva. Not control, exactly, but certainly never histrionics or dramatics. The old stiff-upper-lip approach.

Still, if ever there was a time, this was a fitting moment for a dramatic response. A father she didn't know might be living a couple of hours away.

She turned her mind to the animal shelter. Seeing and holding that little Maine Coon cat would help. Her hours at the shelter were a haven, most of the time. The cold sterility of the hard floors, the concrete, the cages, were offset by the amount of unconditional love pouring from the dogs. They were of all sizes and breeds and mixes. It made no difference; they rushed to the kennel gates, barking or whining for attention, eager to lick a hand if it was offered. A few were fearful or damaged, but she usually got through to them. Even the cats, so many of them reserved or downright prickly, needed affection and love. And of course, there were often cases of seriously injured or ill animals, or cases of abuse, which were almost impossible to fathom or to bear.

She parked outside the low, nondescript building of the shelter. As she shut the front door behind her, she called out to Jake, the resident veterinary tech.

"Yo," she heard him holler, from the treatment room in the rear of the building. "Back here."

He was always there. First thing every morning, Jake dug in with one of the volunteers to clean cages and feed all the dogs, cats, and occasional rabbit currently in residence. That completed, he could be found preparing any necessary meds. She would assist with that, then they'd move on to hosting the potential adopters as they arrived. But her favorite part was just being with the animals.

He was filling metal food bowls in the dogs' cages. Perfect for the job, Jake was efficient, professional, and compassionate. Double-wired, a wiry physique, and wired on caffeine most of the time. How could he drink double espressos the way he did in the morning, then switch over to strong coffee for the rest of the day? Did he ever sleep at night?

Emptying a large kibble bag, Jake folded it up and shoved it down into the recycle bin. "Now, the first job. I'm going to bring the new orange male cat—let's see, he's in here, cage four—I need you to hold him while I re-test blood sugar."

As she watched him unlatch the cage, the big-framed cat rubbed against the door and then against Jake's hand.

"We got him in yesterday," he said. "Someone found him behind their barn. His blood sugar is way high."

"Poor guy. Hope he's not diabetic, it'll be hard to get him adopted."

Jake brought the cat to the metal table and shook his head. "Never say never." He paused, sipping from his travel cup, his constant companion. "He sure is handsome. Maybe..."

Eva grinned. "How many more will Trina be OK with? I know you guys have the best marriage ever, but... What is it now? Five? Or is it six?"

Jake grimaced. "Enough, I guess," he muttered. "But none of us can match Gabby—I think she's at eight cats right now."

"I'd take him, but since I rent a room in Jamie's house, I can't take home a cat. She's allergic. But she loves Cookie—doesn't seem to be allergic to dogs."

"You got lucky there. I don't think you told me—is she a rescue?"

"Sort of," she replied. "I adopted her when a hunter found she was gun-shy. He didn't want to keep her as a pet."

"His loss. Your gain, I suspect."

"Definitely." As Eva held the cat still, in deft movements Jake collected the small blood sample from the cat's ear.

"There, Pumpkin, all done," she said, as she scooped him up.

"Pumpkin?" Jake grinned.

Shrugging, she said, "We have to call him something..."

While Jake set up the blood, using the glucometer, she focused on the cat, as he purred in her arms. Soon she felt the familiar sensation she experienced so many times with animals. There it was again; as she sank into that peaceful place, there was warmth, then the slight vibration. An internal hum. A tone you feel rather than hear. It was a connection, a bonding, a resonance. Something like that. And a huge darkness, almost like floating in deep water. She'd never tried to explain it to anyone—she wouldn't dare, they'd think she was nuts. She needed to prove her scientific focus and professionalism and the veterinary world was not somewhere to expose anything that might be seen as flaky or "woo-woo."

Jake checked the sugar count. "Yup, 385." He glanced up at her. "And what should it be?"

"80-120," she replied promptly. Online courses covered that early on.

"Right." He studied a nearby computer screen. "Let's see, Dr. Michael is on at the clinic today and available for us. Have you met him yet?"

She shook her head.

"Nice guy. And a 'hunk,' my wife says. 'Real GQ with an IQ', was how she put it. Honestly, the expressions nowadays. But you might get lucky there."

She rolled her eyes. *Would people ever stop trying to set me up?*

"Anyway, I need you to go right away." Jake glanced at his watch. "I don't want to wait—this boy needs insulin."

While he wrote up some notes, Eva grabbed the opportunity to wander among the large steel cages of abandoned or rescued dogs and cats. The little Maine Coon was still there, but Jake had said someone was interested and the center was now reviewing their application. Fingers crossed. She knew that young cat would steal someone's heart. What a gentle, affectionate creature, with big bright eyes and a meow that was more of a chirp.

Her heart fell when she saw the old black Labrador. So, still here after last Saturday's open sessions. "Hey there, sweetie," she said as she fondled his ears. She refused to call him by the name his people had named him. Booger. *I mean, seriously?* She had renamed him, Jeremiah. His eyes drooped and his muzzle was gray. He was a sweet dog, and it turned her stomach that people could abandon an old pet, a family member. Just like that.

As she headed off for Wood Lane Veterinary Clinic, the orange cat gave a couple of stressed yowls but settled down soon after she held her hand to the grid-like door of the carrier. She felt the little nose touch her hand and he quieted when she talked to him in a soft voice. As she waited in the reception area of the clinic, she gave in to her own need for comfort and pulled the cat out of the carrier onto her lap. He began to purr, a deep throaty sound that reverberated against her chest when she cuddled him close.

"Such a good boy," she whispered. He rubbed his silky head against her chin. She closed her eyes and settled into that experience of connection once more. She tried to shove the discovery of her father's identity out of her mind, but there remained a gray shadow over everything. She'd have to Google him when she got home.

But then what? Her stomach clenched and jumped whenever she thought about it.

Chapter 2

"Room Six, Dr. Michael. A cat from Coastline Shelter."

"OK, good Nina, thanks," Michael replied, as he took the clipboard from her.

He smiled at her. Nina was a stylish sixty-something African American woman who somehow managed to make scrubs look good. A vet tech with long experience under her belt, she was completely indispensable as manager of the clinic. "If in doubt, ask Nina," everyone said. The place ran like clockwork when she was there, and Michael wondered what the partners would do when she wanted to retire.

He sure hoped this next appointment would be a quick one. It had been one of those hectic mornings and he was behind already. He read through the notes from the shelter, then opened the door to the exam room.

"Hi, you must be–" He glanced down at the notes Jake had sent. "Eva? Oh, right, Jake has mentioned you. Sorry I kept you waiting. I'm Michael Lowery."

He strode across the sparkling clean room to the stainless-steel table, where a young woman stood holding his next patient, a long-haired orange cat. The woman was tall, maybe five feet nine, slender, in white t-shirt and jeans. Her dark blonde hair, streaked with sunshine, was twisted up into a casual knot on her head and secured by a tortoiseshell clip. He couldn't see her eyes well, hidden as they were by large, gray-rimmed glasses.

"Good morning," she said. "Thanks for making time to see him." She placed the cat gently on the table.

Michael reached out slowly, allowing the cat to smell his hand, then began to examine him. Thin. Ears were clean and his fur wasn't matted. Plus, he was gentle and friendly, so not likely to have been abused.

Michael thought out loud. "It doesn't appear he was out in the wilderness too long. No one's come forward?"

She shook her head and tucked a loose strand of hair behind her ear. "He was just found yesterday. We've posted on social media and neighborhood apps and we're hoping someone will come forward. I've been calling him Pumpkin."

"Hey, Pumpkin." Michael stroked the cat's head.

"The main issue is elevated blood sugar. Jake took it last night and again today."

"Yeah, I see that. Some people dump cats who are diabetic. Makes me furious." He shook his head. "We're seeing more diabetes and we're not sure what's causing it. Often, it's obesity, but that's not this guy's problem. Well, not now, anyway."

The cat's teeth were in good shape, he was maybe six or seven years old. While he continued his examination, Michael kept up friendly chatter with Eva. "You're volunteering at the shelter, right?" At her nod, he added, "You new?"

"I've been there a couple of months. I'm on the vet tech track. I've done the first year and have been volunteering at the shelter about ten hours a week."

"Studying online?"

"Right. And hoping to do my clinical work here, or at one of the other nearby vet hospitals."

"Jake said you really have a way with animals. He called you a 'natural.'"

"I love them," she said simply. "Working with animals is all I've ever wanted to do."

"You like them better than most people?"

"Yeah, I guess," she said and smiled.

That smile... what a transformation, Michael thought. Aloud he said, "I hear that a lot. Some say human beings have been a bit disappointing."

She grimaced. "You could say that..."

"Animals have no agenda and are true to who and what they are. Ever thought about what animal you'd want to be? If you could?"

She turned her head to one side. "Huh. Great question."

He stood up straight and studied her. The answers to that question always told him so much about someone. "Let's see, Pumpkin, what do you think? I know, maybe a doe?"

Eva gave a quick shake of her head.

"Nope," said Michael, "on second thought, you're too confident. I don't see the fearful flightiness... And I'd hate to wish all those ticks on you. Or deer flies."

"Not to mention hunters."

"Ah, yes, there is that."

She said, "I know, maybe a dragonfly. Or a cardinal."

"Hmmm... OK. Or a heron. I'd love to be a heron. Or better still, how about a dolphin?"

Her face lit up. "Perfect. Oh, yes, a dolphin. I'd like to be that playful and trusting. But it must be a wild dolphin, even as risky as that is, not one in a rescue center or aquarium that has no freedom. I'd just have to stay away from boat propellers. And nets..."

As she spoke, she took her glasses off and grabbed a tissue to give them a quick clean. While her attention was on the lenses, Michael found himself studying her long eyelashes, the high cheekbones, the golden tan, the perfect skin. No makeup, but she needed none. He imagined what it would be like to touch her cheek.

With a sharp movement, she glanced up at him, as if something had alerted her. Her eyes were a rich brown, with flecks of gold in them. He stood silently, suddenly lost for words.

He saw those eyes widen, then she withdrew. That's the only way he could describe it. She covered herself over and disappeared. She slid her glasses back on and stood up straight.

"I'm holding you up," she said quietly.

Collecting himself, he reached into a cabinet for a glucometer. "We'll have to double-check blood sugar," he said. "Sorry, not that I don't trust Jake's findings, but for legal purposes, we have to confirm the test ourselves."

"Right, of course."

She held the cat while Michael did another quick stick into the cat's ear. Pumpkin didn't seem to notice, didn't even stop purring.

"Jake's requested tests for Feline Immunodeficiency and Feline Leukemia, too," he said, "so we'll take him to the back and do a blood draw. Come on back. You can meet Nina and assist." He pressed the blood drop onto the test strip. "OK, let's see." Michael waited while the little device determined the sugar levels. He frowned. "That's weird." Holding up the device, he showed her the reading.

"95. Wait, what? 95? Is that a mistake?"

"Perhaps I didn't get enough blood on the strip." Michael scooped up the cat and led Eva to the large open space at the back of the clinic, where there were work areas and operating tables, and a line of sturdy metal cages holding pets in various stages of treatment or recovery. While Nina brought him up to speed on two other cases in the clinic, he noticed Eva visited several of those animals, petting a head here, stroking ears there, and murmuring to each one.

"Thanks, Nina," he said, as he glanced at his watch and headed for the next treatment room. He needed to catch up on his day, if possible. But at the doorway he couldn't resist turning for a moment, to see Eva standing next to Nina at a treatment table, holding Pumpkin. He was struck by the look of tenderness on her face. She stood with her eyes closed and it washed over him, the realization he was in the presence of someone different, someone special. There was just something about her. Beautiful, yes, in a natural understated way, but it was more than that. She was calm, self-contained, didn't spout the usual chatty nonsense. Most people are uncomfortable being still, so they move, smile, fuss with something. Not Eva. She stood still, quiet. Her composure was authentic.

After finishing a lengthy initial visit with a family of five Siamese kittens, he went hunting for Nina again.

"What did you get on the blood sugar test for that orange cat? You know, the one Eva brought in?"

Nina didn't have to look at the notes. "That cat's not diabetic! We did the test two more times. Poor guy, he had to put up with all those sticks in his ears. We got 92 the first time, 94 on the retest. And you got normal too, right? Well, it can't be the glucometer—we used a different one. They can't both be broken."

Michael shook his head. "Not to worry, I'll call Jake. Maybe something's up with their meter. But good news for the cat!" He paused. "And Eva, she's gone, I assume?"

"Yes, she took Pumpkin back to the shelter." Nina gave him an odd look. "She has a great way with animals—sure but gentle. We should think about hiring her when she's qualified."

Now there's an idea.

Chapter 3

Eva glanced at her phone again. There was another text—the third—from Jamie.

> Looked up William Hastings
> yet? I found him. O.M.G. Call me!

A possible family after all these years, on the one hand, was enticing. But what might she be getting into? There must be a reason her mother hadn't told her about her father. She remembered a strange kind of vibe from her mom whenever Eva asked about him.

In the small, dormered bedroom she used as an office, with Cookie curled up at her feet, she sent off her final email of the day, a reply to a client who wanted a new theme for her website and changes to the header. Work came in consistently, thanks to referrals from Jamie, and from her current clients. Creating and maintaining websites kept the bills paid, just, while she found time to study and volunteer at the shelter. All part of the overall plan: to become a veterinarian. To spend as much time as possible with animals and get paid for it. It's what she did anyway, now, for free.

Now, having finished work for the day, she grabbed Cookie's leash from its hook and headed out with the pup around the lanes near the house. Although too hot and humid to qualify as fresh air, she hoped a bit of exercise would clear her head. Not only of the morning's shocking letter but of Dr. Michael's face. Those warm eyes, that thick dark hair, his height, his wide shoulders. She'd found herself studying his hands, gentle but sure, as he examined the cat and felt a stir, a melting inside. Since when was she attracted to *hands?* Why had he made such an impression? She was immune to overtures from guys, even "hunky" ones, as Jake's wife had described him. Yes, he was certainly charismatic. Probably sure of himself and his attractiveness to women. Not a bad thing, but she would just have to keep her guard up.

Leave it alone, BG. She just didn't want to get involved. She had her reasons.

Taking a deep breath, she opened a new Google tab.

OK, focus. I have a father, after all. Come on, how bad could it be? There's nothing to lose... This man doesn't know about me.

A chill ran up her spine. Wait a minute, what if he did? What if he had known about her and wanted nothing to do with her?

She was going to talk herself out of this if she wasn't careful. But the bottom line, for better or worse, she had a family. And she simply needed to know.

Into a fresh Google page, she typed: "William Hastings III." Then added "Massachusetts" and "Harvard." That's all it took. Up came pages and pages of links with his name connected to dozens of companies, and organizations both political and philanthropic. Could there be more than one William Hastings? The years he attended Harvard included the year before she was born. Seemed unlikely to be more than one William Hastings achieving an MBA at Harvard that year.

Her phone chirped.

Jamie's excitement raised the pitch of her voice, tinny anyway from the tiny speaker. "Can you believe it? Remember I said it would be cool if he was rich? Man, oh man!"

Eva scanned the webpage. Will Hastings was from one of those wealthy New England families, political and connected. These were Massachusetts elite, almost celebrities, with William

Hastings III being the CEO and owner of a well-known pharmaceutical company.

"Hastings Pharma," Eva said. "I've heard of them." There had been some controversy in the media recently over the price of their drugs.

"I know, he's *that* Hastings! He has properties all over Massachusetts. And you've got brothers and sisters!"

"Yes, I found him. The corporate headquarters of Hastings Pharma is just south of Boston... And the family compound is in Plymouth County."

Jamie cut in. "*Compound?* As in one of those Kennedy-type places?"

Eva could detect a touch of awe in her friend's voice. "Yup." She kept reading. There was also a stately mansion in Boston's Beacon Street area. That was just the beginning. There were holdings all over New England and even manufacturing facilities in Ireland.

As she ended the call with Jamie, she realized she was sweating. Her office wasn't air-conditioned, but it wasn't usually this bad. The trees shaded the house on one side and the room benefited to some degree from the two AC units in the main bedrooms. But now feeling flushed and overheated, she reached for her yoga towel to wipe her forehead.

Digging deeper, she learned William Hastings had been married three times, but there was no mention of her mother, Marianne McGrath. Not surprising. And other children? Eva didn't have to hunt to find references to them. There were hundreds of images of well-dressed young elites at parties, on boats, at graduations. This lot sounded like members of the trust fund brigade.

She found plenty of pictures of William Hastings III, too. Judging from the number of staged photo ops and press conferences, he'd shaken hands with everyone who was anyone in

New England politics and business. Images showed a tall, lean, gray-blond man, fiftyish, in impeccably tailored suits. There was a still shot from an interview with a well-known TV news journalist. And then there was the head-of-the-company photo, well-lit and posed, showing his square clean-shaven face, strong jaw, and golden-brown eyes. She looked closely. Her eyes.

This was her father. Her *father*.

Jumping up, she hurried to her bedroom and stood in the cool air blowing from the window air conditioner. She turned slowly, letting the icy wind flow over and around her. If only that could straighten out this reality rip.

From back in her office, she heard her phone pinging. A text. Probably Jamie again.

She kept turning in the cold breeze. She figured she might as well spin in circles. It would match the spin her mind was in.

—◆—

"Oh, come down, just for a little while," Jamie pleaded on the phone. "Jake and Trina are here. And I won't mention William Hastings, I promise. We'll talk about it whenever you're ready. But the food's great, everything from Thai spring rolls to tapas to grass-fed steaks."

At the mention of Thai spring rolls, Eva's mouth watered. She couldn't remember when she'd eaten last. She could almost taste the chicken, the crunchy vegetables, the tangy sauce. At dusk, she had dodged clouds of mosquitos and taken Cookie out again, but now she was antsy and restless. Couldn't focus on work, couldn't focus on her studies. Not even on what to do next about William Hastings III. Food and a bit of company might take her mind off it.

Driving slowly through Stonington, she felt her usual rush of pleasure at the eclectic boutiques, restaurants, and historic seaside homes of this picturesque New England village. She couldn't resist heading down Water Street for a quick stop at Dubois Beach. This late, it should be deserted. She stood on the sand, gazing out at the spectacular view across the Sound toward Fishers Island. The air was humid and warm, but still, as if preparing to rest for the night. Breathing in the salty tangy fragrance, she scanned the water's surface for dolphin fins. Although Eva knew it was highly unlikely she'd ever see them this near the shore, she never stopped searching.

As the door to Million Corks wine bar swung shut behind her, she spotted Jake with his wife Trina at a table near the bar. And there was Jamie, vibrant in a bright red tank top with black jeans. Red and black looked great on her, setting off her black hair, now with a bit of green, and her brown skin. She was leaning in close to an elegant-looking woman, a red-head who looked a little older than Jamie, perhaps in her mid-thirties. When the woman threw back her head and laughed, Eva wondered if this was a date. Had she missed something? Jamie hadn't said anything... Of course, Eva had been so distracted by the morning's discovery, Jamie could have told her it was raining toads and she would've missed it. She hoped this one might work out. Jamie met so many women, but for one reason or another her relationships never seemed to last very long. It was as if she expected too much.

She glanced around. Granite and wood, with golden hardwood floors and leather stools and chairs, gave the place a warm inviting feel. Over the bar hung a string of wine bottles filled with lights, casting a soft glow. Eva drew in a deep breath, and the fragrance of seared beef and roasted vegetables set her mouth watering and her stomach growling. She didn't eat much meat, but it sure smelled enticing. A guitar player at one end of the room was singing close into a microphone. It was an Ed Sheeran song, about how his woman was perfect.

She was suddenly glad she'd come. The whole father issue could just go hang for the rest of the night.

She plopped down on the other side of Jamie, who introduced her to the redhead, Clare. Clare explained she needed new marketing materials for her distribution company and she'd heard great things about Jamie's talents. Eva still couldn't tell if this was just a good example of a graphic designer cultivating a client, or if this was a potential girlfriend. Maybe both.

Jake spoke from across the table. "Eva, about that orange cat? The one you call Pumpkin? Did you hear? He's not diabetic after all. We figure it must have been a misreading or something."

Before she could respond, a voice spoke over her shoulder. "Hey, Jake, good news, huh? Except for your broken glucometer."

Eva looked up to see Dr. Michael Lowery standing just behind her. Her stomach jumped, just a little. She reminded herself he wasn't there to see her.

Jake jumped up and shook his hand.

"Anyone sitting here?" Michael pulled out the free chair next to Eva.

She felt her face get warm. Why was she so aware of this man? *Honestly, I'm not a teenager, what's wrong with me?*

Jake introduced Michael to Jamie and Clare. "This is Dr. Michael Lowery, a vet at Wood Lane Animal Hospital."

"Ah, Lowery?" Jamie asked. "You related to Luke Lowery?"

"He's my cousin—how do you know him?"

"From Lowery Construction."

"Oh, right, that's my dad's company."

"It was Luke and one of your dad's teams that did my mom's new kitchen last year," Jamie said. "They did a great job, too. Now she tells everyone about them. Soapstone countertops, I'd never heard of them... who knew?"

Michael grinned. "I'll tell them she's pleased." He signaled to the waitress nearby and took a menu. "My dad wanted me to join the company, got my cousin Luke instead. I think he got the better deal. And believe me, my summers working for my dad have paid off. I bought an old colonial last year that needs a ton of work. I can do a lot of it, and for anything I can't do, I get cheap help."

"Have you met Eva?" Jake asked Michael. "She's working toward a career as a vet, too."

Michael turned to Eva. "Tech's a great place to start. Lots of people do it that way." He asked the server for a glass of old vine zinfandel.

"Well," she replied. "I have to save up, big time. My dream, as long as I can remember, is to be a vet." She gave a rueful smile. "Eventually," she added. "Who knows how long it's going to take me to get my degree."

Trina groaned. "I hear you. School loans are a bitch. It's been fifteen years and Jake and I still haven't paid ours off."

Jamie looked up from the menu she was studying. "I got really lucky. My parents paid for me to go to RISD."

Trina looked puzzled. "What is 'Riz-dee?'"

"Oh, sorry, Trina. Rhode Island School of Design, it's in Providence."

Eva said, "And you got a scholarship, too. You're just that smart."

"For some of it," Jamie said. "But affirmative action played a big part, I think. I mean half black, half Chinese, and a woman? Tick off three boxes. Add gay and they should have paid *me* to go to college!"

Everyone laughed. Food arrived and they all dug in.

Her friend Jamie. Eva was happy just to glide through life in the wake of Jamie's personality. Though physically small, just a bit over five feet tall, she was usually the most vibrant personality in the room. She was, by nature, a people person, extroverted. Eva wondered, not for the first time, what that was like. By comparison, people had always worn her out. She'd rather pound nails in her temples than endure a cocktail party, where each brief encounter took a bit more energy and soul. She ended up feeling like a balloon flying around the room, falling limp and damp and flat in the corner. Wishing she'd just stayed home.

Eva tuned back into the conversation around the table. Jake was talking about Jeremiah, the old black lab at the shelter.

"He's such a sweet old boy," Jake said. "How could they have dumped him? How could people be so heartless?"

Michael said, "I know. It's hard. But humans are flawed. We believe we've been made the custodians of the animals but look at the things we've done. The cruelty, the abuses... Human beings are the only creatures on this planet that don't know their place in the scheme of things. In the cycle of nature."

Eva stared at him.

"Sorry about the rant," Michael said. "It's one of my pet peeves."

Jamie was shaking her head. "Wow. I've never heard anyone say that but you, Eva. 'Human beings don't know their place in the scheme of things.' Those are your exact words."

Eva felt Michael watching her.

It was a powerful realization, that she and Michael were on the same wavelength about this. She turned to him, studied his face, found she wanted to know what made that square jaw soften into a smile. What that thick hair would feel like...

She met his eyes. And was held there, somehow, in that deep brown. Behind them lay a vortex that tugged at her, like a powerful magnet. It drew her in, deeper and deeper. The voices, the music, and the clatter of plates and cutlery all faded. There was nothing but his eyes.

Michael said gently, "You're staring at me."

Eva jerked her eyes away and grabbed her iced tea, fussing with it and her napkin. "I'm sorry," she said.

His eyes didn't leave her face and his voice was hardly above a whisper. He leaned close to her ear and replied, "I wasn't complaining."

Heat rushed to her cheeks.

She felt other eyes on her and glanced around quickly to see Jamie studying her. Emotions were racing across Jamie's face.

Then Jamie leaned close and spoke quietly. "Sorry, looks like I'm interrupting... But you might want to know there's an older guy at the bar who's been watching you for a while now. I wonder what his deal is."

Eva swung around to see a man, solo, at the bar, wine glass in front of him. Sporting a buzz cut of graying hair, he was maybe fifty. He appeared a touch out of place. He looked more like Whiskey Guy than Wine Guy.

"How do you know he's looking at me?"

"When you went to the bathroom a while ago, he watched you all the way there and back..."

Eva stared at the man. When his eyes met hers, he turned away sharply and busied himself with his wallet. Nonchalantly dropping some cash on the bar, he strode out.

"Huh," she muttered. "That was weird."

———•• ◆ ••———

The man strode down the street a few paces, then ducked into a doorway of a closed retail shop. He watched the door of the wine bar behind him for a couple of minutes. Then put his phone to his ear.

"Bad news. I think I've been made. Better not take any chances. Want to come and replace me?"

He listened.

"OK, well, ask him what he wants me to do."

Chapter 4

"I can't believe this is the same dog!" Michael bent over to greet the Golden Retriever as she pranced from her cage.

Friday was the weekly shelter day to examine the most recent animals found or turned in. It was Michael's week. As he passed the full cages which lined the walkway, he had to steel himself. Although the animals were treated with kindness here, he struggled a bit every time he saw all the unwanted pets. Nothing could soften the effects of the concrete beneath his feet, the aromas of litter pans, the whines and meows of the caged animals, and the hollow clangy feel of the place. Every visit, he had to remind himself of the potential good he could do.

"When I saw her just last week, she didn't even want to stand up," Michael said. "Now, when I palpate her hips and legs, she doesn't even flinch."

"I know." Jake shook his head.

"You sound dismayed."

"No, no, of course not. Don't get me wrong—it's wonderful. She's doing great. I mean, it's hip dysplasia, and the outlook was awful. We put her on glucosamine and chondroitin, but that was only—" Jake checked his clipboard "—four days ago. In a perfect world, it would take two to three months before we noticed improvement. I can't figure out what helped her so much, so quickly. The x-ray from last week showed severe arthritic changes in the joint. If you remember, she was turned in because the owners couldn't, or *wouldn't*, pay for hip replacement or osteotomy."

"What about showing the owners how improved she is?"

Jake shook his head. "Someone who turned in this sweet dog because they didn't want to treat her? Give her back? That's not going to happen."

He made a good point.

"Golden Rescues, up in Mass," Jake said, "thinks they've found a potential foster, but after that, who knows? People willing to adopt a dog with hip dysplasia are in short supply."

"But look at her!" Michael fondled the big dog's ears, and she licked his hand. "Sweet Nellie." His heart went out to this gentle, beautiful dog. Jake led her back to her cage, where she curled up on an oversized dog bed and plopped her muzzle down on her paws.

"It doesn't matter," replied Jake. "Her file says hip dysplasia. The x-rays show hip dysplasia." He paused, an odd look on his face. "You know, Dr. Michael, I just don't know what's going on. I've been here for almost fifteen years, and I know what I'm doing. Or thought I did."

Michael waited.

"So many weird things happening! You remember the orange cat with the high blood sugar that then *didn't* have high blood sugar? Well, we've checked and rechecked that glucometer. It's functioned just fine since then. And now, this Golden. But there've been a bunch of other oddities. We had a cat with hot spots all over her skin—one of the vets at your office recommended a short course of prednisone. But she healed up in a day or two and we hadn't even picked up the drug, yet. Allergy to something where she was living? Maybe... But the skin to heal over? In two days? We fostered her out two weeks ago and haven't heard she's had any skin issues at the foster home."

Michael shrugged. Identifying the triggers for allergic reactions was often impossible.

Jake continued. "Here's another one: a basset hound mix with otitis, diagnosed by Dr. Jacobs, which recovered overnight. Literally overnight. Ear infection gone. Now I know antibiotics still work well for some minor infections, but not that fast. So maybe it wasn't an infection?" He shook his head. "I feel like I'm losing my mind."

Michael clapped him on the shoulder. "Well, it sounds like a great problem to have."

Jake grinned. "OK, I'll get over myself."

Michael looked back at the cage again with the Golden Retriever. It was a bit miraculous, he had to admit, but there must be an explanation. Or was this one of those flukes that life offered up now and then? "Well, is there a common theme running through these cases? Anything you can identify?"

Jake chewed his lip in concentration. Then chuckled. "They're all Eva's favorites. She's always a sucker for the sad-sack hopeless cases." He read something on his clipboard, then continued along the walkway, opening a cage holding a young-looking black cat. "OK," he said, gently picking up the cat. "Here's a new one."

"Looks like a Bombay, or Bombay mix," noted Michael.

"Probably. Needs checking out. He was turned in, probably out on his own for a while. Too thin, but besides that and his matted fur, we hope he's OK."

"Right, let's do it."

As Michael drove away from the shelter an hour or so later, he just kept thinking of that Golden Retriever. This might be the right dog for him. This wasn't a puppy needing a ton of work and training. A great companion, now he had the house with the big yard, and if anyone could deal with a dog with hip dysplasia, it would be a vet. He might just do it.

All thoughts of the dog and the shelter were banished from his mind that afternoon as he tackled myriad jobs in the clinic. With a vet tech's help, he performed neutering and spaying in two young cats, then a dental operation to remove teeth in an older one. Plus, there were two new patients, a first exam for a twelve-week-old puppy, and then a duck with a fungal infection. Rural people often kept chickens and ducks, and it was amazing how many people turned these birds into pets, with the emotional involvement this entailed. But he grinned. It was a sweet duck.

Then there was the family who couldn't bring themselves to butcher their chickens for the freezer when they stopped laying. He told them, with a laugh, they were keeping a chicken nursing home, looking after them all lovingly until their natural death. Most of the staff at the vet clinic thought it was madness, but Michael could find no fault with growing compassion toward animals. It was better than history's alternative.

The final job of the day wasn't one he was looking forward to. He had to deal with the small calico with a tumor on her jaw. In the furthest cage in the back room, the little cat lay, unmoving. Kurt, one of the older vets on the staff, had examined her and given her pain medication. The x-ray revealed the depth and invasive quality of the tumor. The cat's owners were coming in at 5:00, and Michael had to inform them the cat should be euthanized. He made himself focus on the best interest of the suffering animal, but he dreaded it, every single time. It never got any easier.

He was grabbing a water bottle in the break room when Nina came in. He gulped back a few swallows.

"Michael, the calico cat's owners have arrived," she said. "They're in Room Four. You ready for them?" She studied him, then touched his arm. "I know," she said.

Her compassion choked him. He took a deep breath and headed for the exam room.

The anxiety in the room was palpable. The cat's owners were a young couple, mid-thirties, with a pre-teen daughter chewing her nails. The mother, eager and polite, nodded frequently, birdlike.

The husband was taciturn, stern-jawed, as if he knew the bad news even before it was delivered.

Michael told them the diagnosis clearly and kindly. The tumor had invaded the jawbone and now even the sinuses. He explained it wasn't a good prognosis for their pet. The husband said they'd been to a previous vet who suggested a lengthy and extremely costly operation that held no guarantee of success. Couldn't even promise the procedure might grant the cat some quality of life. Wanting another opinion, they said, they'd come to Wood Lane Veterinary Clinic.

As hard as it was, Michael had to tell them. "I'm afraid it's progressed too far even for that option. Your little cat is in pain. And there's no guarantee the operation would be successful." He paused. "I'm sorry to tell you, but the kindest thing to do would be to put her to sleep."

The young daughter wailed and burst into tears.

"I know you'll want to say goodbye. I'll have her brought in."

When the tech carried in the little calico, the small girl, who couldn't have been more than eight or nine, reached for her pet. She held her close and buried her face in her cat's fur.

"Come on honey," her mother said. "Let the doctor look at her." The mother gently took the cat and placed her on the examination table. She bent over to study the animal's face. "Wait a minute... Charles, look," she said to her husband. "Isn't the tumor on this side? But, hang on... I can't see it now."

Michael stared in surprise at the cat's face. He physically examined it, while it stood quietly on the table. There was no swelling.

"This *is* your cat?" he inquired.

The couple nodded.

What on earth was going on? The file described a large squamous cell carcinoma on the left side of the animal's face and neck, invading the teeth, the jaw, the sinuses. But there was no tumor. He felt carefully. Nothing. With effort, he kept his face still, without expression. How to explain this? He looked again at the file, again scanned the x-ray.

The owners confirmed again it was indeed their pet.

Speechless, Michael excused himself and turned for the door, with the image of the little girl's full eyes seared into his mind.

Two hours later, after several vets and techs had examined the little calico cat, they were all stunned, but no one had any answers.

Kurt, the vet who had first examined her, was adamant that yesterday there was a large growth, an SCC. And he kept referring to the x-ray. "The x-ray doesn't lie," he repeated for about the third time, clearly feeling defensive.

"No one's claiming you're lying, my friend," replied Jerry, the clinic's founding vet. An older man with a full head of silver hair, he had the respect of everyone at the vet clinic for his knowledge and lengthy experience.

"But what the hell? How is it *possible*?" Kurt asked.

Jerry patted his colleague on the shoulder. "There must be an explanation..."

But no one had one.

Most of the staff headed home, but Michael just couldn't leave. At this rate, he knew he was not going to be able to give a rational explanation to the owners of the cat. He had simply told them he'd like to keep her another night until they figured out what was going on. He said he'd call them in the morning. They were fine with a reprieve from euthanasia but Michael knew he was just buying time.

Bottom line, there was no tumor anywhere on that cat.

Like Kurt had asked, how was that possible?

The only thing Michael could think of to do, because he needed to do *something*, was to watch the closed-circuit TV camera footage from the back room, to see what had happened since the cat was brought to them yesterday morning. What, if anything,

anything at all, might explain this "miracle?" Damn it, he hated to even use that word. It didn't mesh with the practice of science.

The veterinary practice had recently installed three cameras in the back room, two over the operation tables, and one for the line of cages housing the animals in their care. They ran 24/7 for insurance reasons, liability, and security. He didn't think anyone had yet needed to view them, but now he logged into the app which controlled the cameras and hunted for yesterday's date. He chose to view the camera focused on the line of cages. Fortunately, there was a fast-forward selection in the digital app, and he systematically plowed through many hours, sped up. He watched the assistants, vets, and vet techs as they moved in and out of the cage area, taking animals out and returning them, cleaning the cages, and adding food to bowls. He saw an assistant lift the little calico from the cage and return her half an hour later, and glancing at the file, he confirmed this was the logged time of the X-ray. Scanning through a few more hours of normal behavior, he was beginning to think he should just bag it and go home.

Wait a minute, isn't that...? He slowed the images to normal speed. Yes. It was Eva. Why was she there? Four in the afternoon of the previous day. He watched as she slowly moved past the cages, touching a Rottweiler through the bars, then opening the cage door of another dog, a little terrier mix, and stroking its ears. When she reached the last cage housing the Calico cat, she stood and stared, her head slightly to one side. She reached into the cage and gently scooped the cat into her arms. Sinking down onto a small metal stool at the end of the line of cages, she closed her eyes. As she held the cat close, Michael could see her lips moving, although he heard nothing. There was no sound, just this image of a young blond woman holding a small multi-colored cat. The look on her face was the same as the day he saw her holding the orange cat, Pumpkin. It was an intense, all-consuming tenderness and focus.

An idea struck him. "No." Michael spoke the word aloud. "*No*," he repeated. "That's ridiculous." He shook his head.

But he continued to stare at the screen.

Chapter 5

The shelter was closed to visitors since it was after 6 p.m. but two long-term volunteers were on clean-up shift, and Jake and Gabby, the town's animal control officer, were just finishing up for the night.

"We had a good day here," Gabby said to Eva. "You'll be pleased to hear the Maine Coon went this afternoon, like we hoped, with the retired couple you met last week."

Gabby was a magician, with a spectacular record for placing animals. She handled her work with strength and passion, as if it were more of a calling than a job. A large, muscular woman, she exuded alpha energy. Jake always said even aggressive or anxious dogs simply gave it up and became submissive in her presence.

"Two other cats and a young dog found homes too," Gabby said, "and we took six or seven more applications."

"But the old black Lab is still here?"

"Sadly..."

Eva headed for the cages, wanting to spend a little time with the abandoned or turned-in pets, especially Jeremiah. He wasn't having any luck finding a forever home. She opened his cage and invited the old Lab out to greet her, and as she sat cross-legged on the floor, and leaned against the wall, he sprawled across her. "Hey, Jeremiah. You think you're a lap dog, big guy, don't you?" He shoved his nose under her hand so she would stroke his face and ears.

"Did you hear about Wood Lane's miracle?" Gabby laid her clipboard down and her fingers whipped across the keyboard as she typed data into the computer.

Eva shook her head. "No, what do you mean?"

"They had a cat with an invasive tumor on her jaw. X-rays confirmed it. They determined euthanasia was the only option."

She knew the cat. "Oh, right, that beautiful little calico. I saw her, a couple of days ago, when I picked up that prescription for you."

"Well, the tumor vanished. No one can believe it, everyone is blown away over there." Gabby shook her head. Then, at the sound of the front door opening, she disappeared into the lobby.

Eva was stunned. She had seen that cat and she had seen that tumor. It had broken her heart, that cancer could take such a gorgeous young creature. That was the hardest part about working with animals. But what, now the tumor was gone?

Eva heard Michael's voice in the front lobby, talking to Jake and Gabby. Her heart sped up. She couldn't seem to escape this man.

He appeared in the back room carrying a crate.

"Thanks for bringing them, Dr. Michael," Jake said. "Sorry to inconvenience you. You could've called me—I'd have come over."

"Not a problem, I was going right by." Michael shook his head. "Can you believe this? Someone left this little family on the front steps of the clinic. They were there when we opened, in a cardboard box, a mama cat and four kittens."

When he lay the carrier gently on an examination table, Eva could hear a chorus of mewing.

Gabby peered inside and said to Michael, "Why didn't they bring them to us? Then we'd know something, at least, about them. Why did they leave them with you guys?"

"Trying to escape your judgment," Michael replied. "The parking lot to our clinic is hidden from view. They might've been spotted if they'd left them here at the shelter." He scowled. "Cowards."

"Well, at least they didn't just dump them in the woods," Gabby said. "But no problem, we never have any trouble finding homes for kittens."

"Cage three's empty," Jake said.

Gabby handed the cats over to Jake, who carried them to their new home. Hopefully, their temporary home. "I'm off. Night all," she said with a wave and disappeared into the lobby.

Michael turned and saw Eva sitting on the floor. "Hey, I didn't see you down there. That old guy's getting some love, is he?"

"So am I," she said. "Not sure who's getting more out of it. Probably me."

"Can you make them younger, as well as heal them?"

"Excuse me?"

"I know you heal them," he repeated, with a grin, "but can you also make this old guy younger?"

Eva suddenly couldn't breathe.

Truth.

The shock was like a physical blow, felt in every cell. She scrambled up off the floor and guided the Lab back into his cage. Now, with her back to Michael, she knelt on the floor in front of the dog, petting his face and ears. She couldn't face eyes on her. The hair was standing up on her arms and the back of her neck.

Feeling naked and exposed, yet knowing she had to respond, she spoke over her shoulder. "Yeah, right, wouldn't that be amazing?" She clambered up from her knees, then turned to face him, forcing a laugh, but she knew it sounded strained.

She watched as realization dawned on Michael's face.

"Oh my God...," he said quietly. "I was kidding, mostly. But it's true, isn't it?" He studied her, eyes widening. "Wow. You didn't know, did you?"

She swallowed. Couldn't find words.

"OK, guys, I'm going home," Jake said as he returned from the cages. "Promised Trina dinner out. I owe her lobster for all the late nights here." He stopped and looked back and forth between Michael and Eva. "Uh, what's going on?"

Attempting to appear nonchalant, Eva managed to put a smile on her face. "I have to go, too. See you soon." She needed to get away, immediately.

Jake gave them one more odd look, then grabbed his coffee mug and headed off through the lobby.

As Eva reached for her handbag and keys from the counter, Michael said, "Wait. Don't vanish. Please?" When she paused, he added, "I'm sorry, I didn't mean to embarrass you."

Eva shook her head, hard. "No, no, that's fine, I'm not embarrassed. It's a good joke..."

"Eva, it's not a joke."

She froze, then slowly met his eyes. Could she trust him?

"You can trust me," he said.

It was as if she had spoken the question aloud.

"Your secret is safe with me." His voice was grave. As he watched her, his face softened. "How about we go get some dinner? We don't have to talk about this if you don't want to. But God, I need a drink."

--- ◆ ---

They ordered fish and chips at Cutters, a casual seafood joint near the water, taking their food to a rustic picnic table overlooking the boats in the harbor. Eva didn't eat much, just picked at the fish and the fries. Michael asked if she wanted a drink, suggesting it might help. When she told him she didn't drink, fortunately, he didn't press it. She couldn't relax and she suspected he couldn't either. The situation was just too bizarre, with the impossible becoming possible.

The impossible, on her mind, needed addressing.

"I'm not healing them," she said, finally. "It's ridiculous." She hunted for the right words. "I think it's just something to do with the love and care I give animals... Maybe it speeds their recovery, to some degree. Somehow." She realized she was just pushing the fish around her plate and set down the fork. "I don't believe for a second I'm *actually* doing it."

"What about the orange cat with high blood sugar? Or the Golden Retriever which suddenly had no pain at all from hip dysplasia?"

Eva shook her head and looked away. And what about that sense of truth, of rightness, that had flooded through her? That must have been her imagination. Must have been.

Could it possibly be true?

No. Stop, BG. Don't be absurd.

She didn't know what to make of any of it. It felt as if someone had taken sandpaper to her nerves.

He went on. "And the miracle of all, the tumor that disappeared overnight on that little calico cat." He gave her arm a light touch. "It's all too much of a coincidence, don't you think?"

"I don't know, I really don't." She shivered and pulled the light cardigan around her shoulders. "Forgive me, but I just can't talk about it anymore." She smiled, to soften the demand.

They sat together quietly in the sea breeze, in the fading light, for a few minutes.

But she knew she couldn't leave it there, after all. She had to know, to confirm it somehow. "I want to test it. To consciously attempt a healing."

"May I be there? As an observer? I can help—organizing that will be simple."

"A witness."

"I won't laugh if it doesn't work, Eva."

As bizarre as this moment was, she was grateful for his kindness, his understanding.

But after that test, if she could do it again, intentionally, then what? She couldn't even begin to think about what this would mean in the greater scope of things. If she could truly heal animals... Seriously, what do you do with that?

———••◆••———

Eva swam in hazy, blissful ocean dreams. Deep in the water, where she could breathe, where she often saw dolphins grinning at her, she floated without a care in the world. It was Sunday morning, and as consciousness grew, she tried in vain to go back to sleep. To return to the peace of the dream again. Cookie was nestled beside her on the bed, and as she stroked the silky fur, she stretched and snuggled closer to her little dog. Something awaited her in the waking world, she knew. It circled, looming, a dark shadow, just out of reach. Then it hit her like a punch in the gut. *Healer.* She cringed. The idea she had healed those animals seemed even more ludicrous in the light of a new day.

And then, there was Michael. Sitting next to him last night, near the water, the attraction was certainly strong, but that part she thought she could ignore. She'd certainly had her share of this kind of appeal. Dark hair on a wrist, the confident easy smile, lean strong legs. Oh yes. It was an instantly recognizable sensation: chemistry.

Most of the people her age didn't date, but hung out, or hooked up. Sex was treated so casually that sometimes it came first. As her friend Kelly from college used to say, "Our generation does it in reverse. Sleep together to get sex out of the way, see if that works, then get to know the person." Once Eva had even heard her say, "Sex isn't a big deal. Essentially, it's just bits of skin touching someone else's bits of skin. Existentially, it's as meaningless as holding hands."

Eva didn't agree. Meaningless sex seemed no better than drinking, doing drugs, or overeating junk food. She wasn't interested in scratching an itch with some guy. Or even taking part in the whole thing as Aunt Sophie had suggested, with her usual dry sense of humor, "Women just need to lie back and think of England."

She wasn't sure about good ole' England, but whenever Eva thought about sex, she thought about Zach, the only long-term relationship she'd had. She wasn't in love with him, as she understood "in love" to be. She had concluded all that "in love" stuff was just hormones and pheromones, anyway. He was fun, easy to be with, and he made her laugh. Their comfort with each other grew along with their friendship, and they tried sex one night. Quite frankly, Eva wondered what the fuss was all about. A rather speedy affair, it didn't work for her all that well. But she figured she didn't have anything to compare it to, nor even the desire to try it with someone else.

When Eva wasn't willing to take the relationship to the next level, living together, Zach turned out to be surprisingly harsh. *When people don't get it or feel hurt, why do they have to get nasty?* He'd said some cruel things. Maybe they both did... She couldn't remember, now. But she did remember his words, the things he said, in anger. That she was closed, cold, that she had used him. It worried her. Had she?

But when she was near Michael, it was different. When he touched her, she felt things she'd never felt around a man before. Sensual, warm, with the threat of passion and fire.

And what was even more powerful than the attraction, was the connection. His kindness, his strength, those eyes. She leaned on him last night. And she never did that.

Chapter 6

Michael woke that Sunday morning with his mind full of Eva. He lay there, slowly drifting up from warm, peaceful sleep. From floaty dreams. Sitting up, he stretched and leaned back against the bare wall. *A headboard, must get a headboard. Add it to the list.*

He was comfortable in this room, even though it was an eyesore at this point. He'd stripped away three generations of unbelievably garish wallpaper, peeling his way down to the bare plaster. Now the walls looked rough. And there were no blinds or curtains yet. *Must get to that, too.*

But there was no need to jump out of bed. It was Sunday. Luke would be there in a couple of hours, but he could laze around for a while.

He wondered how Eva was feeling this morning. The whole healing thing must take some absorbing. It did for him. He still found it a complete contradiction to all his scientific training. Miracles fit more in the realm of Catholicism, which he'd managed to escape. That's how he thought of it. There was a particularly fraught period in his teenage years when he challenged his Italian-Irish upbringing and culture, at least regarding religion. His parents hadn't fought him. They hadn't insisted on his honoring the Catholic faith, but his grandparents were adamant. He'd had to walk a fine line, as he made his own path into spirituality from what he considered to be the dogma of religion, without deeply offending his grandparents.

But the truth of the matter was simple. It didn't matter one iota if he found it hard to believe Eva could heal. Reality eclipses belief. There was simply no other explanation for those animals recovering so dramatically.

This was a truly profound discovery, which had the potential to rock her world. His primary goal was to protect her. No, more than protect. The word that fit best was 'cherish.' It wasn't that he felt Eva needed cherishing, exactly. She didn't come across as remotely fragile or helpless. But he wanted to cherish her. He needed to.

And rock her world? Yes. But *he* wanted to rock her world. Him. He grinned. And reminded himself he'd known her for only three days. He shook his head. Three days. Time is surely irrelevant in moments such as these. He knew she felt the connection, as he did.

As for being able to get to know this woman, to become a part of her life, he pondered his next step. Clearly, she wasn't married and didn't seem to have a boyfriend. She'd come to the wine bar on her own and lived with a roommate, Jamie, the vivacious Afro-Asian woman he'd met that same night. And he was sure Eva wasn't gay. The way she'd looked at him...

He thought back to the previous evening, sitting by the water with Eva in the gathering dusk. Seagulls had cruised overhead, like floating gray shadows against the glowing red and orange sky, searching for their last meal of the day. This peaceful spot should have been a perfect location for a first date. But it didn't feel like a date.

When he asked about her family, Eva told him, shortly and without detail, of the death of her mother, Marianne, and her aunt, and that she was on her own, with no family to speak of. There had been a strange moment when she talked of family, or rather the lack of it. He sensed there was more to that but didn't question her further.

"Losing your mother at eleven...," he said. "That kind of grief is hard to get over. I know this isn't the same, but when I was seventeen, my best friend died on a motorcycle. A birthday present from his parents. He was gone a week later."

"Oh, Michael." She shook her head.

"I was lost. We'd done everything together since we were six. He was as close to a brother as I had." He paused, thinking. "I didn't know how to get over it. I scabbed it over and tried to leave it alone, not to pick at it. But even years later, when something did tear the scab off, it felt just the same, just as urgent, just as vivid. Maybe that's true of all grief. Maybe emotion doesn't age, and if you sink back into the memory of that moment, you feel exactly the same emotion, even many years later."

"I think you're right. I don't know if I've completely recovered from losing my mom. How do you know? I've just learned to live with it, somehow."

Michael said, "Maybe we don't get over grief, we just get past it. We grow around it... we surround it with time and new experience and distance. But it's still there."

He wanted to cheer her up. "As for me, there's a multiplicity of family to go around. I have five sisters."

"Five?"

He nodded, enjoying her surprise. "They all live close by, within an hour's drive. We get together often. If it's family you want, you should borrow some of mine." That elicited a rare smile from her. Her quiet stillness changed in an instant, and she glowed. It occurred to him he'd do a lot to see that smile again. "That's nothing," he said. "Wait till you get a load of the slew, the plethora, the *avalanche* of aunts and uncles and grandparents and cousins I can barely keep track of." Her smile grew. "Italian mom, Irish dad, kind of typical. But that's the end of typicality. My family's weird." He grinned.

"You're crazy about all of them."

"Yup," he said softly. "You'd like them. They're all unique. And strong. Oh my God, are they strong. They don't let me get away with anything. Five older sisters... sometimes it's been hard work." He was hoping he'd get the chance to introduce them to Eva.

He found himself aching to wrap his arms around her. To lift that clip out of her hair, to let it fall, feel it all around his face. To gently slip those glasses off and learn the world in her eyes. To feel those full lips under his, until they start to burn...

Slow down, buddy. One step at a time.

By the time they'd finished eating, she seemed tired and fragile. She'd had quite a discovery, a jolt to her world. He dropped her back at her car, offering to follow her to make sure she got home safely. She assured him she was fine, but he did manage to program his cell number into her phone.

That brought him back to the present. Grabbing his phone, he checked for a text from her. Nothing. Climbing out of bed, he threw on work clothes and headed downstairs, once again blessing his parents for most of the down payment for the house. It was a fixer-upper, but there was nothing wrong with that. So far, last year, he'd overhauled the ancient HVAC system, then put on a new roof, complete with solar panels. That had pretty much wiped out his savings.

As for the kitchen, there was a ton of work still needed to haul it into the twenty-first century: set porcelain floor tiles, install stone countertops, remove the dropped ceiling, and add recessed LED lighting. He could see it all now, and one thing at a time, he'd get it all done. He did have a great toaster and coffee maker already—*priorities, you know.*

After a leisurely espresso and English muffins, he headed over to the barn, which he'd turned into a workshop. Flipping on the lights, he surveyed his current project with satisfaction. He couldn't wait to pull out those tattered kitchen cabinets, beat up and misaligned as they were. He'd found ancient, but high-quality cherry cabinets, for a song, at a local salvage house. All it was going to take was refinishing, which he was tackling evenings and weekends. So far, all the effort looked like it was going to be worth it.

As he sanded, he focused on the grain of the wood under his hands. He loved working with wood, the feel of it, the smell of it. There was something organic about it, something comforting and grounding.

His phone pinged. It was a text from Eva.

> Dr. Michael, thx for your support last night. And your kindness. Apologies if I was short or remote. Shock, I guess.

Dr. Michael. She felt she needed to use "Dr.?" And nothing about her being able to heal animals or about getting together to do a test. As for the apology, he couldn't imagine this graceful woman needing to apologize to him for anything.

He resisted the temptation to dial her number.

Chapter 7

"That's what I've found out about him so far." Eva took a sip of her now lukewarm tea. There in Dr. Chin's new kitchen, she'd relayed all she had learned about Will Hastings III. She looked around. What a kitchen it was, designed and created by the construction company Michael's father owned. What a coincidence.

Jamie shook her head. "I read a lot of that online. I still can't believe it—all this time you didn't know who your father was, now you find out he's this one-percenter..."

Eva waited for Dr. Chin's response. Jamie's mother had been there for her since her mom had died, in all kinds of ways. She was kind, if not overtly motherly or affectionate. A tiny Chinese-American woman, she was highly educated, and Eva wanted her rational take on this situation.

But she couldn't bring herself to tell Jamie or her mother about the idea that she was actually healing animals. It would sound preposterous.

Dr. Chin pushed her chair back from the table and tucked a lock of her shiny black bob behind her ear. Reaching for a tissue, she blew her nose. "Damn cold. Or maybe it's the flu. Anyway, it's threatening to go down my chest." She absentmindedly fingered the asthma inhaler beside her coffee cup on the kitchen table. She'd listened intently, as Eva spoke, nodding occasionally throughout. "So, do you know what you're going to do next?"

Eva gazed out past the new soapstone counters, through the bay window. Dr. Chin's manicured lawns were flanked by rhododendrons and roses, the latter now in full peach and pink glory. She could almost smell the aroma from here, in the warm morning sun. "Right now, I'm just trying to find the right place in my brain for this information. I have to figure out how... or *if*... to approach him."

"I know, it's too weird, isn't it?" Jamie was shaking her head. "But you know, it might be wonderful."

Jamie's mom coughed and cleared her throat. "It certainly is a shock, Eva. And before you need to ask, no, Marianne never said a word to me about this. Neither did your Aunt Sophie. You have no reason to believe he knows about you, do you?"

"I don't know what to think about it. Why didn't Mom tell me?" Eva shook her head. "This morning I just feel punch-drunk. Didn't sleep well last night..."

"Yeah," Jamie said, "but that could have been from that *moment* you had with Michael. What was *that*?"

When Eva didn't respond, Jamie turned to her mom. "Eva has a not-so-secret admirer—Dr. Michael Lowery, a vet at the Wood Lane clinic." To Eva, she said, "He sure is taken with you."

Her mother was firm. "Don't tease her, she has enough on her plate right now."

"Good point," Jamie replied. "Just messing with you, Eva."

"We should go," Eva said to her. "You told Clare we'd pick her up at eleven, right?"

Jamie turned to her mother. "You want to come, Mom?"

"Thanks, honey, I'd love to, but no. I have to look after this cold. You guys go ahead, have fun. Who's Clare?"

"Just a new client I'm wooing."

Eva kept her face still. It might be wooing in more ways than one...

Dr. Chin's face was serious as she spoke to Eva. "This thing with your father. I understand you need to think about it. But it *is* family."

"Thank you for listening," Eva said.

Jamie stood. "OK Mom, see you later." She started toward her mother, who held a hand up.

"No, don't hug me, you don't want this bug. I don't know if I'm going to even make it to work on Monday."

"Feel better, Dr. Chin." Eva grabbed her handbag from the back of the chair.

"Alice, please. You're twenty-six, for goodness' sake, call me Alice."

"Thanks... Alice." She found it hard to say. Jamie's mom would always be Dr. Chin to her.

Eva hit the brakes for what she was sure was the four hundredth time. I-95 was choked with traffic heading north for Rhode Island, Cape Cod, and even further points like New Hampshire and Maine. Like a flock of birds in flight, it was a slow-motion murmuration of vehicles as far ahead as she could see. Summer in Connecticut. It was necessary to plan when to be on the road, and weekend mornings were not a good idea.

"It's ages since I've been able to get away from work to come with you." Jamie poked her head through the front seats, from behind Eva. "So, where today? Narragansett or Watch Hill? We haven't been to Napatree either for a long time. Or East Beach either, for that matter."

"Rip tide danger looks minimal at Watch Hill today. And it's always clean there. Might be busy, though." Eva glanced over at

Clare, in the passenger seat. "I prefer to come off-season—like early May. That's when I sometimes have the place to myself, pretty much."

"Isn't the water still cold in May?" asked Clare.

"Well, I have a wet suit, but I don't swim alone. The rip tides aren't safe."

Clare asked, "Why do you drive all the way up here? Connecticut has some great beaches, like Hammonasset."

"Yeah, but you aren't usually going to see dolphins in the Sound," Jamie answered. "Connecticut beaches are all on Long Island Sound. Rhode Island beaches are open Atlantic. Cleaner, more wildlife. And even dolphins sometimes."

"And sharks?" Clare's tone was wary.

"No," Eva said, "Thankfully, sharks aren't often seen off the coast of Rhode Island. More often off Massachusetts. Something to do with seal availability, which is their main diet."

"I wouldn't be able to tell them apart. Sharks from dolphins, that is," Clare said. "Sounds terrifying."

Eva explained. "Dolphin fins are curved, whereas shark fins are straight. That's one way to tell them apart. And a shark swims back and forth like this." She waved her hand from side to side in a wavy motion. "Dolphins swim up and down."

"Yes, but by the time you figure that out you're dead," Clare said.

As they laughed, Clare asked, "Have you guys ever seen a shark? Or a dolphin?"

"Yes," said Jamie. "On one incredible occasion—dolphins, that is. I've never seen a shark." She touched Eva's shoulder. "Do you want to tell it or can I?"

"You go ahead. I'll focus on not driving into the back of that Tesla."

Jamie said, "I think it was 2008..."

Eva figured quickly. "It was 2007. I was twelve. The summer after my mom died..."

"Oh, Eva," Clare said, "I'm so sorry. That's awful, to lose your mother so young."

Eva had experienced nightmares for months. On that horrific day, she'd ridden her bike home from swim practice and found her mother lying motionless on the cold tile floor of the kitchen. She'd thrown herself down to touch her, shake her, wake her up. Eva didn't think she'd ever get over the shock of feeling cool flesh. Her mother just wasn't there, no matter how much she called to her.

And would she ever be able to smell the fragrance of lilies again without that image searing into her mind? Her mother had cut yellow lilies from her garden that morning. The vase was cracked and lying empty on the counter, and the lilies lay abandoned, under and around her, broken yet filling the room with their spicy aroma. Water had dripped from the counter to the floor and pooled all around her mother's body.

Eva found the presence of mind to call 911, then her Aunt Sophie, who came running from down the street.

She returned to the present as Jamie told the story.

"My dad took us out on his boat," she said. "It was a steaming summer day, even hotter than today. He lived in Charlestown, kept a motorboat up there, and took us out sometimes. We learned to water ski—"

"Not very well," Eva interjected. "But it was fun."

Jamie nodded. "And this was after the divorce, so Mom wasn't with us. And my dad wasn't living with his new girlfriend yet. She wouldn't have come anyway—little Kimmy-babe might have broken a fingernail on a rope or something."

So, no reduction in the anger. Eva glanced in the rear-view mirror and caught the grim set of her friend's face.

Jamie went back to the story. "Anyway, we anchored, and Dad was fishing while Eva and I swam off the side of the boat. It felt great in the water—it must have been in the nineties that day. Then Dad shouted and pointed, and we saw, in the distance, a pod of dolphins. They were leaping, racing around, playing. About ten or fifteen of them."

Clare glanced at her. "And you knew they were dolphins?"

Jamie answered, "Oh, yeah, Dad confirmed it. We looked them up later, too. Short-beaked common dolphins are distinct looking, mostly dark gray, but in front of the dorsal fin their flanks have a flash of yellow, and there's white behind it. As they leaped through the air, we could just make out the colorations. Dad took a thousand pictures... I haven't seen those photos for years—I wonder where they are. We should hunt for them, Eva."

"Then," Eva said, "as we watched—believe me, we were beyond excited to see them—three of them broke off from the pod and approached us. They swam all around us. Two full-grown dolphins and a smaller one which was about half the size of the adults."

Jamie added, slowly, "I've never experienced anything like it. Before or since."

"You never saw them again?" Clare asked.

Eva shook her head. "A one-off experience. And one of the adults had a big scar on its fin, remember? Like a gash that had healed."

"Like a propellor hit it. Or a shark bite, or something," said Jamie. "They stayed for quite a while, swimming around us. They even let us touch them."

Clare gasped. "Wow. I'd give anything..."

"We were a bit scared, at first," Jamie said. "They're wild animals, after all. My dad kept warning us to keep our distance, but they were so gentle. We were just kids—it's like they knew that or something. The whole thing was thrilling! And, I don't know, it was kind of..." Jamie's voice trailed off as if she were searching for the right word.

"Spiritual." Eva finished the thought.

"Yes," answered Jamie. She sighed. "Exactly. But that's what you said at the time." She touched Eva's shoulder. "You said,

'Swimming with wild dolphins was an act of spiritual generosity on their part.'"

••◆••

Fortunately, Watch Hill Beach wasn't as busy as Eva had feared—there were some thunderstorm warnings for the late afternoon and that may have put visitors off. While Clare picked just the right spot, Jamie dug into her backpack for sunscreen, books, and drinks. They spread out giant beach towels and stripped down to the bikinis under their shorts and tees. To get some sun, first, before swimming, Clare had said. Not much, she hastened to add.

"My ancestors crawled out of a peat bog in Ireland," Clare said with a laugh. "We're not used to the sun—in fact, it's a bit of an enemy. I get sunburned just watching the travel channel."

Jamie chuckled and pointed to her own brown legs. "You guys are just jealous."

"Too right!" Clare grinned. "Your skin is gorgeous."

The contrast between them was marked. Clare had the fairest skin Eva had ever seen. With her long red hair, she looked like one of the 'Celtic Women.' Clare and Jamie would make a glamorous couple, and Eva was sure now there was interest beyond business between them. At least on Clare's part. As Jamie opened a can of sparkling water, Clare's eyes were fixed on her. Eva could feel the energy zapping through the air.

Three's a crowd.

Eva ripped off her cut-offs and tank top, then headed for the water in her two-piece suit, calling behind her as she jogged. "I won't go in far—see you in a bit."

It *was* spiritual. That was the right description for that once-in-a-lifetime dolphin experience. She repeated those words to herself as her feet hit the water. The cold was always a shock, for a few seconds, but she soon adjusted, and it felt wonderful after the eighty-five-degree air. She waded out waist deep, then sank down to her neck. As she floated there in the cool water, arms swooshing back and forth, she could just feel the surf pushing gently against her body. She watched for jellyfish, such as Lion's Mane or the rarer Portuguese Man-O-War, and of course, the stinging sea nettles which are common in Rhode Island waters. And as always, she endlessly scanned the horizon, watching for those telltale fins.

Eva let go of everything. She lost herself to the floating sensation, to the smell of briny water, to the gentle spray against her face. To the distant sound of waves as they rhythmically hit the shore, muffling the voices coming from the beach. The vastness of the ocean eclipsed her worries, made them feel unimportant in the scheme of things. The stress evaporated out of her pores and disappeared into the chasm of the sea.

And there was the tingle of hope, always present when she was near or in the water. Hope that they might come again. She knew it was highly unlikely she'd ever see dolphins this close to the shore— after all, they were deep-water animals. When they came this close to shore it was often a mistake, one that could leave them stranded. Nevertheless, she swam every chance she got, since that summer. But since Jamie's dad had sold his boat, they weren't able to access deeper water. Now her dream was to own a small motorboat to fulfill the only item on her bucket list. To swim again with wild dolphins.

As far back as she could remember she'd heard about dolphins. Her mother told her stories about her internships at New England Marine Institute, up near Fall River, for two summers before Eva was born. Her mom offered to take her to an aquarium, but dolphins in aquariums were captives, prisoners, and Eva would never agree to go.

Those dolphins, that summer when she was twelve, had seemed to seek her out for twenty minutes of joyous play. She was with Jamie, but she always felt they were there for *her*, somehow, although she certainly never shared that with anyone. And when she touched the dolphins' smooth gray skin, it was the first time she had ever felt the vibration, the hum, the connectedness, those sensations she experienced regularly now, when she focused on an animal. Ever since that day.

She didn't know it at the time, but later came to realize the dolphin experience gave her some measure of healing from losing her mother. Two different counselors provided by the school didn't help at all. They wanted her to sink into the grief, to experience it, to talk about it. She refused. Aunt Sophie had removed all pictures or memories of her mother, tried to distract her, suggested she not think about it. So, that's what she tried to do. But it was numbness by day and nightmares by night. For many months. She remembered knowing for sure she didn't belong anywhere... not even here on this earth. She gazed up at the stars and longed to "go home." But she had no idea where home was.

After swimming with the dolphins, the nightmares became less frequent. And less intense. They changed from a painful reliving of the horror of finding her mother, that afternoon, to dreams of floating in deep water with the silky feel of dolphin skin. With those open mouths curved in giant smiles, and with a feeling of connectedness that was unlike anything else she had ever experienced.

Chapter 8

Sunday evening seemed to go on forever. Eva tried to focus on studying, tidied up a website she'd created, and played with Cookie.

She had no clue what to make of the healing situation. It still didn't feel real. How could it? It was as if she had discovered a superpower, that she could fly, just by intending to. Or was invisible. *Hah!* How was she going to share this with other people?

As for the other matter, a father she didn't know existed, she didn't know how to approach that either. Would he want to meet her? If he didn't already know, how pleased would he be to learn he had a daughter who lived so far outside his elite world?

There must be advice on the web. It turned out to be easy to find articles by people who'd met their birth parents. The internet was full of advice: what to ask them, what to ask yourself, how to prepare yourself. To Eva, this was useless. There were as many different stories of meetings as there were types of people and surely no one protocol covered them all. Add to that, the fact that most of these people were meeting birth parents who had given them up for adoption. Eva had no idea if her father even knew she existed.

Then she found a New York Times article entitled, "I found my birth parents and wish I hadn't." That chilled the blood and put a dead stop to her internet research. There was enough to go wrong in the situation, without reading horror stories.

She longed to jump in the car with Cookie and just drive somewhere, anywhere. To find a little Airbnb near the beach and escape completely. She could hear an echo of Sophie's voice in her mind, *"Now, that's not logical, Baby Girl. How's that going to help?"*

On Monday morning, after a night of tossing and turning, she'd decided what to do.

Just get over yourself. Enough of waffling. Make your destiny, BG.

Knowing she could catch up on her work that evening, Eva grabbed her phone and googled directions to the headquarters of Hastings Pharma. It was almost due north, an hour and forty-one minutes, to be exact. Although she knew she needed some sort of a plan, all she could think of was to park in front of the place and check it out.

And what's that going to tell you? Not a lot.

So, then maybe simply march into the building and see if he's in the office.

Wait, then what? What to say?

"Oh, he's in? Well, then, thanks very much. Bye now."

That wasn't going to work. What if the receptionist asked if she had an appointment?

"Well, no, but please tell him it's his daughter."

Hmmm. There didn't seem to be an easy answer.

It was going to come down to winging it.

Jamie had suggested putting it off for a few days until she could clear her schedule and come along, but Eva didn't want to wait. She didn't want to be gee-ed up, or distracted, or made to laugh about it. She didn't even want to talk about it. In this situation, she knew Jamie meant well and wanted to help, but she had to do this alone.

Hastings Pharma turned out to be a well-tended campus on the outskirts of Boston to the city's west, tucked amidst suburbs and more rural areas. Turning where the GPS instructed, she drove along an elegant avenue, between arching dogwood trees. This opened into a series of newly paved parking lots, with leafy landscaping and bedding plants interspersed. Not a weed in sight. Prosperity glowed. The peace and beauty of the place did nothing to slow her heart rate.

The four-story main building directly in front of her was graced with a pond, fountain, and a beautifully designed gold and black sign announcing "Headquarters." This was the place. It looked like the only building of several which allowed visitors. At the buildings on either side, she could see turnstiles and manned checkpoints. These must be R&D, laboratories, and the offices requiring higher security.

Eva parked in the shade of an oak tree at the edge of the lot, where, from about 50 yards, she could watch the giant double glass doors of the headquarters.

She took a deep breath. *Is he there?* It couldn't hurt to go in and look around. She concocted a story about an appointment to see... She made up a name. John Wazinsky. He'd told her he worked there and suggested she drop in to see him on a workday as he needed some website work.

Wait a minute, if he worked there, for a pharmaceutical company, why would he need website design? She shook her head. *You'd be the worse spy ever, girlie.*

Stepping out of the car, she noticed two men coming through the front doors. Deep in conversation, they stopped at the edge of the parking lot, as if headed to different cars. She studied them. The taller man looked familiar, but she couldn't fully see him as he was in profile. Then he looked up and away from his colleague and she saw his face clearly.

It hit her. She knew where she'd seen him. That buzz cut of graying hair. She spun around and dived back into her car, keeping her face turned away. She hadn't thought her heart could beat any faster or harder, but she was wrong. The man who had gestured in her general direction was the man from the wine bar the other night. The same older man who sat with wine glass untouched, who'd sauntered out when he saw her watching him. Still ducking down, she kept her face averted but stole occasional careful glances his way.

It seemed he hadn't seen her, or if he had, didn't recognize her. He waved at his colleague, then headed to a large black sedan parked half a dozen vehicles to her right. He jumped in and drove the few yards to the front of the headquarters, where he sat, engine idling.

He works for Will Hastings. It was too much of a coincidence. And that meant he was following her, checking her out, for her father. It took her a few moments to process that.

A part of her longed to run into the building, find this man who was her father, and scream and rail at him.

If that's what she wanted to do, she didn't have to enter the building to find him. For there was the man himself. He'd just swept through the huge front door and was approaching the waiting sedan. Easily recognizable, even at that distance, this was the elegant man she had seen in the photographs. His brisk walk spoke of complete confidence, of power.

Buzz Cut jumped out of the car and hurried around to open the back door for William Hastings III. She watched the car drive out of the campus and disappear.

The fire of rage cooled to a steady burn on the drive home. How long had Will Hastings known he had a daughter? Her whole life? If so, then why the interest now? No, she decided, as she thought it through. The most logical explanation was also the simplest. Perhaps he had received a similar letter from the law firm and Aunt Sophie. In the end, it didn't matter. He knew about her and had chosen to have her followed. As sleazy and tacky as that was.

Some of her anger was aimed at herself. Why didn't she march straight up to Buzz Cut at the wine bar, ask him who he was and why he was watching her? Or jump out of the car right now, go straight up to Hastings, and accuse him of spying on her?

No. She shook her head. It's all very well wishing she'd done something differently. That was typical. Thinking of what she should have done after the fact. What she should have said.

Give yourself a break.

Women just don't go up and get in the face of strange men. Doesn't happen. If they did, it would be stupid, maybe even dangerous. She forced herself to relax the death grip on the steering wheel.

But where this new development left her, she had no idea.

Arriving home from Boston, she pulled into the driveway of Jamie's small Cape Cod. What a great home. Eva doubted she'd ever be able to buy a house. How could she ever save enough? It was a good thing Jamie had bought it when she did, before the sudden run-up of house prices in the spring and summer of 2021. Jamie's dad had given her the down payment, and she complained he was trying to buy her off and assuage his guilt with money. He had cheated on her mother, divorced her, and then to make matters worse, was living with a woman fifteen years younger. It had left Jamie struggling to adapt and determined not to become angry and bitter. She said if her mother could rise above it, she should be able to as well. And she tried to view the whole thing in a positive light. She said, with her usual good-natured grin, at least she got a house out of it.

Eva spotted Cookie through the living room window, dancing back and forth from one leg to the other on the back of the sofa. This is always where the little dog stood, waiting and watching for her return.

But she saw something else. There, tucked into the screen door, was a letter-sized white envelope. Her stomach jumped. Wait a minute, since when did she start being nervous about an unopened letter? Recent events had made her inordinately jumpy. But then, it hadn't arrived in the regular mail. Someone had been there.

She hurried up the steps to grab the letter, which was addressed simply, Eva McGrath. No address. Yes, hand-delivered. The return address was a large hotel in New London.

What now?

She opened the door to let Cookie out, and after a quick exuberant greeting, the pup raced over to the edge of the woods to do her business.

Eva ripped open the envelope.

Dear Eva,

What a complete delight it is to discover your existence.

I took the chance on finding you home after Will gave me your address last night. Sorry I missed you.

Give me a call at the hotel, Room 232. We can meet here or at yours if you're more comfortable.

I hope this is not a shock. I assure you, I wish to welcome you and am so looking forward to meeting you. I hope you feel the same, my dear niece.

Chloe Hastings

Eva poured a glass of raspberry iced tea, put Eva Cassidy on the old CD player, and curled up in a wicker chair on the little stone patio behind the house. She read the letter again and again.

Scooping up Cookie, she snuggled the little dog on her lap. Holding her close, she focused on letting go of the stress of her trip to Boston. Eva Cassidy was crooning "Fields of Gold," and she lost herself in the melody. For her, music was the silver thread between the human spirit and heaven. And the universe. Perhaps the creator. The longer she sat still, with the music, with her dog in her arms, the more her heart eased. The letter had helped, oddly. Warmth rolled right off the page, and she hoped this wasn't a game, a ruse, a gambit, a veneer. What did it say about her, she wondered, that she was this skeptical, this suspicious?

Even with these doubts, the letter had managed to counteract, somewhat, the crassness with which Hastings had behaved. The fiery anger burning her stomach had been doused by her new aunt's words.

Chapter 9

The New London Grand boasted a coffee shop, and as Eva approached the doorway, she spotted a woman standing outside on the sidewalk. She looked to be in her fifties, a slim figure in a soft silver linen shirt, one of those long, elegant things that smacked of class. She wore matching capris, high wedge sandals, and her blonde hair was swept up in a French knot. Elegant sunglasses hid her eyes. But Eva could tell straight away this was her aunt. Glamorous, but low-key. The word "stately" came to mind, but, no, on second thought, that wasn't right. This woman didn't seem intimidating. Maybe "aristocratic" was a better fit. In any event, it looked as if wealth lay easy on her.

Eva slowed, nerves building.

Her aunt saw her, whipped off her sunglasses, and hurried forward to meet her.

"Eva," she cried. Her smile was huge, her expression open. Beautiful skin, with hardly a line on her. Confidence, kindness, openness. *Mom would have loved her,* Eva thought, out of the blue.

The warmth flowed from this woman as it had from her letter.

Chloe studied her. "You're beautiful."

Eva flushed. "I look like you."

"Well, then, I'll take that as a compliment."

Eva grinned. "Me too!"

They headed into the coffee shop, which turned out to be a personality-less place. Booths and tables, all in gray and blue. Completely unmemorable, like American hotel coffee shops she'd seen in movies. It smelled like new plastic and old coffee.

Chloe said, "Come, let's grab a booth. You must have a million questions and I know I do!" She laughed, a light bubbly sound that made Eva want to laugh as well, for no good reason she could think of.

After ordering tea and scones, Chloe took a breath. "OK, first things first, has he been in touch with you?"

"Not... directly."

Chloe gave her a questioning look.

"He had me followed." Eva rolled her eyes. "Sent some guy to watch me in a restaurant a few nights ago."

"Oh, for God's sake. I knew he'd screw it up. So, I'm glad I got in touch fast to try to redress that. But that's worse than I thought." It was her aunt's turn for an eye roll.

"But that explains how he knew my address."

Chloe cocked her head to one side and gave a small smile. "He's just a man, you know. Powerful and wealthy, and that's how they do things. But he's still just a man."

"As excuses go..."

They both laughed.

Eva asked, "And what about the rest of them? Now I know I have a half-brother and sisters. How did they react?"

"I don't know, yet. I was so excited to hear about you I didn't ask Will about them. I think they mean well when you get to know them, but they're a bit spoiled. It didn't help that my brother went through wives like chiclets, chewing them up and spitting them out at some point. It's sad, too, he seems to be making bored noises again, and I fear he may be dumping the latest one."

Eva didn't know what to make of this. This was her *father* they were talking about. It sounded like someone in a movie.

Chloe waited while the waitress delivered their tea and scones. "Anyway, he told me he'd received a letter from your aunt. Said he was 'gobsmacked.' That was the word he used."

"I got a letter, too. It was a shock, I can tell you."

"I bet! Gobsmacked sounds like a good word for it. Anyway, my first thought was to jump in the car." She grinned. "Impulsive? I just had to meet you."

Eva spoke slowly. "You're not what I expected."

Chloe's face softened into a small smile. She leaned in, across the table. "I'll take that as a compliment, as well."

"It's just that you don't seem like you come from a wealthy family. Oh, I'm sorry, is that presumptuous on my part? I don't know any rich people."

Chloe put down the knife she had been using to smear butter on her scone. "Well," she said slowly, "My upbringing was a bit different from Will's. There was more focus on him—I skated under the radar a lot." She paused. "But I confess I wanted it that way. I just didn't want the money, the material things. I know, easy to say when you have it. But I don't spend my life trying to get more of it, if you see what I mean. Give it away, like JK Rowling—she's a great role model."

Chloe sat up straight. "I'm getting off track…" She studied Eva, her eyes kind. "I want to know about *you*. Will spent some time researching to find out what he could about you—"

Eva started to protest, feeling invaded.

"—but so did you, right?"

Her aunt had a point.

"I know you lost your mother when you were young," Chloe said. "And your aunt, too… I'm so sorry. That's rough."

Eva gazed out the window. There was that numb sensation inside, again.

Chloe continued. "But tell me about your other family. Do I get to meet your grandparents, your other relatives?"

"There's no one left but me... My grandparents are long dead—I never knew either of them. My mom's mother died young, a heart issue. And my grandfather died when I was about two in a helicopter accident."

"Oh, Eva." Chloe reached across the table and squeezed her hand. "Well, you have grandparents on this side." She paused, then grinned. "They're not the warmest people in the world, I'm afraid, but you do have them. You know WASPs, and they're rich WASPs."

"My mom's side is also English and Scottish," Eva said, "so I guess I can relate."

"So, you understand. If an emotion is discovered, it's to be stamped out as quickly as possible. Certainly never expressed. Oh my, is that a feeling? Quick, catch it. Kill it, kill it!" She covered her mouth as she acted out shock and dismay.

Eva laughed.

"Dad was a force of nature," Chloe said, "but he's changed a lot... He had a pretty severe stroke a couple of months ago." She sighed. "You can meet them, too, whenever you're ready." She gave Eva a knowing look. "A bit daunting?"

"A bit. And exciting, too. Did you ever hear about my mother? Marianne McGrath?"

"Yes, I did. I liked her."

"Seriously? You knew her?"

"Well, I met her one night. We were in college, it was the summer of '94, or maybe '95. A bunch of us sailed to Cuttyhunk Island. It was a glorious sunny day, with sunburn, seafood, laughter and somehow a sense of magic in the air." She laughed. "And Tequila... oops, we all had a bit too much I remember. Marianne was warm, and funny, studying marine biology, as I recall. We had a great chat, and she told me about her work with dolphins. I didn't see her again, but Will seemed very taken with her."

"What happened?" Eva hoped she didn't sound plaintive.

"He said it didn't work out. Told me he broke up with her, that she moved away. But then, oddly, he kept on talking about her for months... something didn't seem right about that. I never got the whole story."

"My mother moved down here from Fall River to be near Aunt Sophie, the only family member left, really. I was born here. After my mom died, I lived with Sophie. But Mom never told me what happened, just that my biological father wasn't going to be in my life."

Chloe chewed on her lip. "Guess we may never know. My brother can be closed. Now, I could be wrong, but I don't think he knew about you, until recently."

They talked for almost two more hours. Eva told Chloe about her love of animals, her veterinary ambitions, the animal shelter, Jamie. Her aunt was a good listener and easy to talk to. But Eva didn't tell her about her apparent ability to heal animals. She didn't know what to do with that, yet. Hadn't even told Jamie about it.

Eva looked down at Chloe's ringless left hand, holding her cup. "Do you have kids? Have you ever married?"

"Nope, never did either this lifetime. I guess I had a load of kids in a previous life, so I didn't get to this time around."

There was more to it than that—there would have to be. Eva couldn't believe this woman didn't have a guy knocking at her door. Or a line of them around the block.

Chloe stared off, out the window, then seemed to pull herself back. "But I'm not lonely—I love my life, with my friends, and my dogs, music, and my garden. Music is a big part of my life, and I travel, I read. What about you, Eva? Is there someone in your life?"

Eva shook her head. "I don't have time for a relationship. Too much on my plate, between work, volunteering at the shelter, and studying." This was the standard answer she always gave, and yet this time it felt wrong, somehow, saying it to Chloe.

Her aunt didn't dig. "So, my dear, come visit me? I have a cottage near Newport. And no," she added, with a wry grin, "not *that* kind of cottage. It's in Jamestown, it really is a cottage—small and cozy, but with plenty of room for me and my two springer spaniels. What I like most are the three acres—that gives me tons of room for herbs and vegetables and perennial gardening. I do have a guest bedroom or two, and you're welcome anytime! Come see me."

Eva found herself agreeing. "I swim from time to time in Narragansett or at Watch Hill."

"Oh, I'd love to come with you sometime." Chloe's expressive face frowned a little. "Unless I'm being pushy...?"

Eva couldn't imagine anyone taking offense at this lovely woman. "I'd love that," she replied.

Chapter 10

Michael shot off a text.

> Eva, a perfect test case for you. Stray cat with FP. North East Feline Rescue brought her, no owner. Rescue center won't pay to treat–we have to euthanize. Urgent. Can you come?

> I'll be there in half an hour.

When Eva arrived at the clinic, Michael handed her disposable nitrile gloves and a lab coat. Sensing she was nervous, probably feeling put on the spot, he decided on the professional approach. "Feline panleukopenia is nearly always fatal," he said. "Especially in such a young cat. She's only four to five months old. Her fever's very high and she's vomiting. Blood tests show extremely low white cell count and dehydration. As for treatment, all we did for her is inject saline to help with the dehydration..."

Eva didn't respond, so Michael stopped talking. Had she heard anything he said? It seemed the fact this was a test was now forgotten. She'd already put on the protective gear and approached the young tabby cat, lying still in the carrier. Opening the door, she gently scooped the creature out into her arms, perching on a nearby metal chair. She closed her eyes and held the cat close, murmuring to it.

Several minutes passed and Michael knew he too was forgotten. Watching the exquisite tenderness on Eva's face, as she was lost in the revery of connecting with this small animal, he was profoundly moved. His eyes began to sting, and he had to turn to gaze out the window to collect himself.

When she finally opened her eyes, she drew in a long breath, then let it out. She stood, and as she lay the cat back in the carrier, said, "There you go, little one." She turned to Michael. "I guess we won't know anything for a while."

"Is that tiring for you?"

"No. It's deeply peaceful, actually restful." Her brow furrowed in thought. "Then, at some point, it's as if I have to come back from somewhere... Doing this isn't new to me, I've done it for many years. But I've only ever thought it helped me. It never occurred to me I might be helping them."

He nodded. He wanted to hold her.

"I'm thirsty," she said. "The cat's thirsty, too, I think. Let's give her some water."

She stripped off the disposable lab coat and pulled off the nitrile gloves, keeping them inside out, being careful not to touch the surface of the gloves with her bare hands. She'd learned early in her course the importance of aseptic procedure, to keep from spreading contagious diseases.

"OK, now let's get some coffee," he said. "And we can give the cat some time."

The staff's break room was comfortable in a lived-in kind of way, complete with a TV on the wall, veterinary magazines scattered around, a single-serve coffee maker, even a long couch where Michael grabbed a bit of shut-eye from time to time when on call. The room wasn't plush but offered a casual, relaxed atmosphere, and it smelled less like disinfectant than other parts of the clinic.

Most of the other staff members had gone home, leaving an assistant and a vet tech on clean-up duty and handling the required feeding and meds. The place never really slept. Sick animals took attention to detail and a good deal of looking after.

"You should think about applying for a job here," said Michael, sniffing the milk from the fridge, then pouring some into his coffee.

She didn't answer. She stood near the counter, with a teabag in her hand, staring off into space.

"Earth to Eva?"

"Oh, sorry, what was that?"

"Where were you?"

"Just dreaming."

"About what to do if it works? If this is a... what do we call it? Skill? Technique? A *gift*?"

"How do you do that?" She shook her head. "You pluck thoughts right out of my head."

He reached for her hand and spoke slowly. "You really don't get it?"

Eva's eyes widened. "Michael...?"

Their eyes met.

He couldn't wait any longer. He pulled her to him, never taking his eyes from hers. One arm went around her, and the other hand gently stroked her hair. She started, just a little, then drew back.

"Michael," she repeated. She shook her head ever so slightly.

He pulled back but kept her hand. "Why? You must feel the connection, don't you?"

She nodded, almost imperceptibly. "It's just... I'm sorry...."

"Dr. Michael, Dr. Michael!"

The voice was calling from the hallway. Hurrying out into the hall, they saw Roxanne, the vet tech on duty, staring through the open door into the isolation room. They heard a mewing sound from inside the room and Roxanne held the door back so they could see past her.

There, in the carrier, the young cat was sitting up, cleaning herself. Once again, the cat cried, "Mrrowww?"

"Oh, my God!" Michael was stunned. He hadn't believed, *truly* believed, until that moment she could do it. On demand. Intentionally. Heal an animal in a matter of minutes simply by holding it. How on earth? He stood shaking his head.

Michael took the cat's temperature, and it was now normal. There simply couldn't be any doubt Eva's focus and concentration had done this. Somehow.

Roxanne had, of course, known of the Feline Panleukopenia diagnosis for this cat, knew how dangerous this illness was in cats. Her eyes were wide in her round face and one hand was covering her mouth. This woman knew and loved cats. As well as working full-time here at the clinic as a vet tech, she also volunteered at a local feline rescue center.

"I checked her a couple of times since we got her settled in isolation, and there was no change," said Roxanne. "Now, suddenly she's a lot better. What did you do, Dr. Michael?"

"I didn't do anything, just continued subcutaneous saline, but Eva—" He stopped short. Behind Roxanne, Eva was shaking her head. "I'm not sure. Maybe we just got lucky." He knew it was lame but understood that Eva wanted to lay low.

"Well, this is wonderful," Roxanne answered, slowly. She studied Eva for a moment, then said, "I was afraid the poor little girl was a goner. I can hardly believe it... I hope this means she'll recover completely. Of course, she'll have to be in isolation for weeks. If she's still this well tomorrow, I'll get in touch with the rescue center—see if they will take her and see her through the isolation."

Michael had the distinct feeling Roxanne was suspicious. Perhaps suspected.

Giving Eva another odd look, Roxanne left them.

"I get it," Michael said to Eva. "Hard to know where we go from here."

She looked startled. "Excuse me?"

"I was talking about your healing, Eva."

"Oh, right." She paused. "Yes. I need to think about that."

"Yes, for sure. Think about it with me? Have dinner with me? Tomorrow night?"

She looked away. "I can't tomorrow, I'm sorry. A lot on my plate at the moment. Maybe another time?"

As Eva reached for her handbag and car keys, it flashed through Michael's mind: *She's going to vanish. What the hell am I missing here?*

———•••◆•••———

At home, an hour later, Michael took out his frustration on the cherry cabinets. Hand sanding the cabinet doors worked up quite a sweat and he paused to wipe his brow and stretch his back.

His mind was in a whirl. *She is a healer—so much for the empirical scientific approach. What must it feel like to heal a creature? With your intent, with your mind? So easily?* He couldn't imagine. He'd wanted to be a vet as long as he could remember and took pride in helping animals. Years and years of studying, and thousands of dollars later, he did succeed. Some of the time. But what Eva did... *How is she doing it? How is it even possible?*

I can't stop thinking about her. About a woman who doesn't want me.

Maybe he needed to back off.

A horn blast brought him sharply back from his contemplations, and he popped his head out the barn door. He waved to his cousin Luke, climbing down from his truck. Luke dropped the tailgate and pointed inside.

"You got it?" Michael took off his leather work apron and headed around to the back of the truck, where he peered in. "It looks in great shape."

"Yeah. It's only a couple years old." Luke reached for his leather work gloves on the floor of the truck, beside a huge hot tub. "The guy actually asked us to get rid of it. I said, 'Yes sir, not a problem.' We were tempted to charge him extra for the disposal." He grinned.

Michael climbed into the truck bed and surveyed the hot tub, complete with its keypad and entire electrical system. "Can you believe he wants to replace it?"

Luke said, "I know. For a bigger one. Wants to rip out the entire bathroom—to create a giant tile grotto, of slate, no less. So, give me a hand. Where do you want it?"

"For now, at the back of my workshop, thanks, Luke."

Luke was five years younger than Michael, at twenty-seven, but looked older. Already balding, he said he was damned if he was going to cut whatever hair he had left. So, he grew a long dark ponytail from the back of his head, which hung down almost to his shoulder blades. He heaved the big tub to the end of the truck bed. What Luke lacked in height he made up for in width. This was the guy who once said, in his best Tony Soprano voice, "You don't know from heavy. You weigh 200 pounds? Hah. My right arm weighs 200 pounds."

Luke wiped his brow with his sleeve, then, between them, they carefully transferred the tub to the far end of the workshop.

Michael said, "I guess I'm going to need a plumber. I should give Nate a call."

"Yeah, he's good. I wouldn't suggest wiring and plumbing this sucker yourself."

"Nah, horrible job, no one likes plumbing."

"Ask any plumber's wife," cracked Luke. He grabbed his gloves and set to work sanding one of the cabinets.

Luke was well-paid in the construction company. In fact, very well. But working on Michael's house was different, Luke said. They were family, best friends. "You don't charge family," were his exact words. But Michael knew Luke's three rescue dogs were all going to need vet services and Luke was going to get the Lowery family 100 percent discount.

"Hey, Mom was picking up takeout at Cutter's last night. She said you were there with a woman," Luke said.

"Why didn't she say hi?"

"She said you seemed quite engaged. Nod nod, wink wink." Luke threw him a knowing glance. "She said it was a hot babe."

"Your mother, my aunt Jill said '*hot babe?*'" Michael raised an eyebrow and stared at his cousin.

"Her actual words might've been something like 'sweet and lovely.' I translated... So sue me."

"Actually, she's interesting. Different. There's a definite connection, but she turned me down when I asked her to go out with me again."

"Ah..." Luke said.

Michael stopped sanding. "What's that mean?"

"That means, now you know how the rest of us feel. All the time."

Michael stared at his cousin.

"Well, you know, Mikey old boy, you're used to women lining up to throw themselves at you. Now you know what it feels like to be a regular schlub." He turned his attention back to the cabinet door.

A bit of an exaggeration... But maybe there was some truth to his cousin's statement. He'd had it pretty easy, where women were concerned, being six feet two, outgoing and personable. Some said he was good-looking, but he didn't see it. His attractiveness was something to do with confidence and magnetism, his sister Tia told him. Although magnetism remained indefinable.

Yes, he had plenty of opportunities to be with women. But he certainly didn't enjoy the dating process. He'd thought long and hard about it. Covid lockdowns and social distancing had given him an excuse to take a break from the "game." He liked women, and appreciated who they were, how they thought. He was particularly drawn to their nurturing and compassionate natures. He went so far as to think women should run the world, especially since men had made such a colossal mess of it for thousands of years.

But the women he met so often seemed a bit shallow. More interested in fingernails and heels than in really getting to know him. Or, he suspected, they wanted to find a husband. Or find a father for their babies. He frowned inwardly. He had felt almost *objectified*. He shook his head and grinned when he realized how ironic that sounded.

And when he ended relationships, no matter how gently he tried to do it, women got hurt. He hated that part.

The best relationship was the most recent. Lauren. Older than he was, by about five years, she had matured beyond the shallow materialism he so often encountered. He wanted it to work, but somehow it just wasn't deep enough or strong enough to last. She was feminine, sweet, kind. The way she would lean over a daffodil, completely engrossed in stroking and admiring the beauty of the petals, as if it were her child. He loved her love of nature, he loved her love of beauty, he loved her laugh. But somehow, he just didn't love *her*. What was missing? She was a remarkable woman, a teacher, a painter, a gardener. She taught art in high school and the children adored her. Sex was a gentle and tender experience, unlike the unsatisfying experiences he'd had before, which turned him off and left him feeling incomplete. It was sweetness with Lauren.

But he'd begun to realize that what was missing was fire. With the woman who met his heart, with the woman who matched him, was his equal, there would be sizzle as well as silk.

With Lauren, it didn't sizzle. It fizzled.

But Eva was different. There was a spark and potential fire. And a deep undercurrent of connection. Understanding. Potential partnership. He hoped he would be allowed to explore all the layers of it. Of her.

His sister Tia often reminded him that patience was not his strong suit. Well, he'd have to make it his strong suit.

Chapter 11

I can heal animals. Repeating it to herself didn't make it any more real to Eva. If anything, it had the effect of sending her more and more into denial. If it sounded crazy to her, imagine how it would sound to anyone else.

She felt stretched, pulled, in all directions.

It was odd, but even with the mind-blowing realization that she could heal, just with her energy, what was uppermost in her mind was the memory of Michael's arm around her. She could still feel his skin touching hers. She'd been paralyzed, unable to move away, like her will was not her own. If it hadn't been for Roxanne calling them, she knew he would have kissed her. She'd never responded this way to a man, and now she was off-balance, nervous in case she made a wrong move. She should have stopped him sooner. But a part of her just wanted to let go, to be in his arms.

Would you listen to yourself? Get a grip, woman.

Gravel crunched under her tires as she pulled into the driveway. Jamie was on the porch, paying a pizza delivery guy, and Eva's mouth began to water.

Cookie came rushing to meet her, jumping and dancing.

"Enough for me?" She called to Jamie as she waved hello to the pizza guy and knelt to greet Cookie.

"Of course! I got half plain and half with every vegetable imaginable."

"So, I owe you, what? Ten bucks?"

Jamie waved a hand. "Nah."

"Jamie, I owe you so much already, let me pay you for my share!"

"It's nothing," Jamie said, as she carried the pizza inside and went for plates and drinks. Breathing in cheese fumes, Eva followed her into the living room, where the air conditioner in the window whirred, keeping the room almost an icebox.

"I just have to get central air installed," Jamie muttered, "these window units are hopeless. We're either roasting or freezing. Plus, they waste electricity and they're noisy as hell. I've heard heat pumps are the answer—that's what Clare has. Something about a 'mini split,' whatever that is."

Eva pulled apart the pizza slices, cutting the long strands of mozzarella cheese as they stretched across the box. "How is Clare? Is that working out?"

"Oh, too soon to tell. But she's great fun." Jamie handed her napkins.

Jamie chatted on, about Clare's family up in Maine, about her love of skiing, but Eva found it hard to concentrate. The first bite of pizza was heaven, full of melted cheese, peppers and onions, and a crunchy crust. But after a few mouthfuls, she felt full, and her stomach was upset.

"You're not listening." Jamie's voice was accusatory.

"Oh, I'm sorry. I have a lot on my mind."

"I can see that. Finding out you have a father you didn't know about is heavy stuff. I hope your new aunt will be able to help with that."

"Yes... oh, I don't know. He had me followed for God's sake. Who does that? Meeting him, or not meeting him, it weighs on my mind. Every time I hear my phone, I'm afraid it's him."

"He has your number?"

"I'm sure with his money and connections he could get my number."

"Yeah. But you knew all that yesterday, has something else happened?"

Jamie knew her so well.

"There's something else, isn't there?" Jamie asked again.

Eva shrugged. "Like finding out who your father is, isn't enough?"

Jamie waited.

Eva took a deep breath. "OK, don't laugh. I'm not kidding about this. I've just found out something." She paused. How was she going to say this? Every way she tried it in her mind it sounded ridiculous. "Turns out I can heal animals, just by holding them in my arms... with focus... with intent."

Jamie grinned. Then the smile vanished from her face. *"What?"*

Eva told her roommate everything. She described the vibration, the connection, the floating-in-water sensation she experienced when she held an injured or sick animal. She told her about the animals she had recently helped, which had completely recovered without any other treatment after she held them and connected with them in that way.

Jamie stared at her.

"Then, today, we did a test. I did a deliberate, conscious healing."

"We?"

"Michael," Eva replied. "Dr. Michael—you met him at Million Corks."

"Yes, I remember."

There was an odd expression on Jamie's face and coolness in her tone.

"I didn't know for sure until today that I'm actually healing them." Eva described what had happened that afternoon, with the young cat with FP. "It's pretty much a death sentence. This cat was at the exact age where they can't fight it off. She was already terribly ill, vomiting. There's usually no coming back from that."

The pizza was forgotten.

"We left her for half an hour," Eva said, "and when we came back, she was sitting up, cleaning herself, and the fever had broken." She waited. After a minute, she said, "It's just too much of a coincidence."

Jamie took a deep breath. When she spoke, it was slowly. "OK... you know what you're asking me to believe."

"It's impossible, I know."

Jamie paced across the living room floor. "OK, let's think about this for a minute. Well, your Cookie has never been sick."

"That doesn't mean anything."

"And remember the cat that was hit by a car outside my parents' house, when we lived on Lyndborough Place? We were about fifteen. You held it in your arms in the backseat of the car all the way to the vet and then we were all surprised it was OK. We thought it just wasn't hurt that badly by the car, remember? But what if you *healed* it on the way to the vet?"

Eva threw her hands in the air. "I just don't know..."

Jamie shook her head. "So that's why you're distracted. Oh my God, what do you do with that? What does it mean? This is *huge.*" Jamie stared at her. "Holy shit, Eva. You're serious."

"I need you to believe me. I know how it sounds, but I'm not making it up."

Jamie chewed her lip. "Have you told anyone else?"

"No, just you. But, of course, Michael knows."

"You told him first?"

"He's the one who figured it out! He told me."

Jamie's eyebrows went up. "God, I wish I still smoked—I need a cigarette. OK, so what now?"

"Absolutely. No. Freaking. Idea."

"What does Michael say about it?"

"We haven't talked much about it..."

Jamie said slowly, "Why not?" When Eva didn't answer, she said, "OK, now, spill it. Please. There's something there, isn't there? With him? I saw that moment at the wine bar. I know I teased you about it, but... What's going on?"

Eva shrugged. She tried nonchalance but doubted it would fool Jamie—they'd been friends since middle school. "Probably nothing."

"Why the hell not? You finally meet someone you have a real connection with, and you're just going to ignore it, turn your back on it? What are you so scared of?"

Eva felt punched in the stomach. "Hang on a minute. I'm not scared."

"Oh really? Then what's the problem?"

She stared at Jamie. Why did she look angry? "Why are you being like this?"

"Because if you're freaked out about him, it's your own fault."

"Ouch, Jamie." She couldn't believe her ears. "You know why I can't."

"You've told a few people..."

"Just close friends."

"You told Zach. Why is this different?"

She searched for words to explain something impossible to explain. But why was Jamie so upset?

Jamie watched Eva, her face working, then suddenly burst into tears. "Oh, God, Eva... For years I never even worried. If you went out with somebody I didn't worry because I knew you weren't going to... You weren't going to find someone... Oh, what am I saying? So, all these years, even with Zach, when you ended it with him, I wasn't surprised. You've never really been interested in anyone."

"Jamie, what is it, what are you talking about?"

Jamie was pacing back and forth and not looking at her, but still crying. "Let me finish. I always thought with the guys you went out with, that you were just being nice, or you wanted a friend, or you thought you *should* find someone. Or you wanted to see what sex was all about..." She gasped and wiped the tears from her face with a napkin. "I never took any of that seriously, never worried about any of your male friends... because..." She hiccupped. "Because..."

"Because?"

Jamie sobbed and put her hands over her face.

"Oh honey, what?"

"I thought you might realize... you were in love with me!"

Eva was dumbstruck.

Jamie barreled on. "I didn't see any of them as competition. God knows there've been enough of them—you're gorgeous, you don't even know it..."

"Jamie—"

"And then I saw the way you looked at Michael."

Jamie ran from the room and out the front door.

Eva groaned. So much, oh yes, so much suddenly made sense, now. All the years Jamie had dated woman after woman, she never found the right person, someone she could love and be with. Eva had always thought her friend just hadn't found the right person. But Jamie thought she already had. And all this time, when they talked about their love lives, Jamie was hoping, as irrational as she must have known it was, that Eva would realize she was gay.

How the hell did I not see it? Or did I? But chose not to deal with it?

When Cookie whined and pushed her nose against her leg, she scooped up the dog. And sat there, on the couch in Jamie's living room, for at least an hour. Even with Cookie asleep on her lap, she felt more and more chilled but didn't get up to turn down the air conditioning unit. Cold pizza dried up on the coffee table, and the sun was low in the sky, casting a reddish glow on the opposite wall when she heard the front door open. Jamie appeared in the living room, with swollen eyes, blotchy face, but calmer.

She spoke slowly as if the conversation hadn't been interrupted, "But the moment I saw you and Michael... I knew. I just knew."

It hurt to breathe. Eva said, softly, "I'm so sorry. I'm so, so sorry."

"No, don't be nice to me. Don't want to cry again." Jaimie headed for the dining room, where she kept a small selection of what Jamie called medicinal liquor. "I need a drink."

Eva followed her. She couldn't think of anything else to say.

Jamie gulped down some scotch. She grimaced. "Why do we have this stuff around? Tastes like you could run the lawn mower on it..." She turned and faced Eva. "Here's the deal. Don't blow it. You may never find this again—it doesn't come around that often." She rolled her eyes. "Take it from me."

"But Jamie..."

"What?"

"You're forgetting something."

"What?"

Eva took a deep breath. "The aneurysm."

"Oh, come on, why don't you just tell him about it? You told Zach. Or wait a while and have a few dates with Michael first. You guys don't really know each other at all, yet."

Eva kept silent. She'd never been at a loss for words with Jamie. But now there was a chasm to cross.

Jamie flopped down on a dining room chair as if suddenly exhausted. She swallowed another gulp. "And besides, the way you look after yourself, you'll probably outlive us all, anyway."

"I told Zach because I didn't really care if he ended it. That sounds awful. But I thought it might make it easier. Let him off the hook, or something."

"But this is different. This time you're actually scared he'll walk away." Jamie stared at her, a clear challenge on her face.

Chapter 12

Michael, can we talk? Coffee?

> Sure, come by 5:30-6?
> Never know when I'm
> free. Or I can text when
> done.

I ll be there, 5:30. I'll visit the
animals.

> Sounds good. See you
> then.

When Eva arrived at the clinic, Michael was finishing up in an exam room, but Nina welcomed her and introduced her to Jerry. "I think we should offer her a job," she said. "When she's qualified. We're losing Beth soon."

"Hi," Jerry said, shaking Eva's hand. "Michael says you have quite the touch with animals."

If you only knew.

"That's nice to hear," she said out loud. "But it will be a while before I'm qualified. I'm just finishing the first year."

Jerry gave her a wave. "OK. Let us know. Night, Nina."

Nina turned back to her. "Make yourself at home—are you waiting for Dr. Michael?" Nina gave her a knowing look, and Eva felt her face get hot.

I'm doing it again. Acting like a schoolgirl.

"I helped him with a case yesterday," Eva said, "and wanted to know how it worked out. The cat with FP? Do you know if she's still doing well?"

"Oh, yes, that was amazing... never seen a recovery like that. We're all flabbergasted. And a feline rescue association from up in Cheshire is coming tomorrow to look after her 'til her quarantine time's done."

An assistant called out for Nina, asking for help back at the cages, and Nina turned to go. "Go see her if you like," she said. "She's isolated in Room Nine. Dr. Michael will be out soon. I'll tell him where you are."

Eva found the room and donned gown and gloves she found on a rack, near the door. The cat was in a large cage, with litter pan, food, and water, and meowed a greeting when she entered the room.

"Hey sweet thing, how are you feeling?"

"Mrrooowww." The tabby rubbed against the door of the cage, started to purr, and Eva soon had her out and in her arms. Her heart filled up, as she connected to the simple energy of this little spirit. It was like a meditation, of two living beings combined.

When the door opened, and Michael popped his head in, she was ready to gently put the cat back in the cage. He looked wonderful, in black shirt and blue jeans, and she felt an electric tingle of pleasure from just looking at him. New territory. It seemed as if everything lately was new territory.

Michael drove them to a nearby restaurant, on the main drag. On the way, he told her the tabby cat's fever had stayed down, and she was now eating normally. No more vomiting. And that all the staff at Wood Lane were thrilled but surprised. Shocked, even.

"This kind of recovery is unheard of," he added. "What do I tell them?"

"I don't know, Michael. It was one of the reasons I wanted to talk to you. I need to figure that out."

They were shown to the bar section of a Texas Steakhouse, a big chain restaurant, with steer horns on walls and beef on plates, and plush booths conducive to relaxation and conversation. Adele was singing, and Eva found herself thinking it should be Lady A. She asked for iced tea and Michael ordered lager and a plate of chicken wings.

"Starving," he said. As soon as they were alone, he shook his head. "Oh, hell, I forgot. Meant to ask you to visit a dog we took in today. But I saw you... and it went right out of my head." He grinned. "Will you have time tomorrow? Heartworm infection. Do you think you can help with that?"

She looked at him helplessly. "You're asking me? What do I know?"

Michael grinned and threw his hands in the air. "I'd laugh if it weren't so serious."

"What do I do with this?"

"Well, the first thing that comes to mind is you help as many sick animals as you can."

He sounded almost envious.

"This little cat... I saved her life," Eva said. "I know it. Do you know how hard it is to say that out loud?"

Michael watched her for a few seconds, then shook his head. "I can't imagine."

Eva closed her eyes and the feelings flooded back. "When I realized that I'd done it... Oh Michael, being able to heal a creature, to take her from almost certain death to a healthy life with a loving family..." She stopped, opened her eyes. "Well, the..." She hunted for the right word. "...*reward*, it's hard to describe."

Michael reached for her hand across the table. "Yes."

She looked down at their fingers entwined. "And when people find out about this?" she asked. "They will, you know. Then what?"

"Let's deal with that when the time comes." He paused. "I want to tell Nina. And Jerry."

She shook her head. "Not yet..."

"I get it." He squeezed her hand. "So, are you staying for dinner? Can I call this a date?"

"I'm sorry about last night, Michael. I owe you an explanation. There's... uh... something I have to tell you."

The waitress chose that moment to deliver wings and drinks and take their order for dinner. Pasta wasn't what people usually ordered in a steakhouse, but Eva listened to her body. Pasta was what she wanted. Comfort food. Like Sophie's Shepherd's Pie. That would have been even better, but pasta would have to do.

Michael had let go of her hand when the waitress arrived, and now she kept her hands firmly in her lap.

He was waiting.

Eva dove right in before she could change her mind. Or chicken out. "My mother died of a burst aneurysm in her brain when I was eleven. It turned out the specific kind of aneurysm she had is congenital. A Familial Intracranial Aneurysm, it's called. I have the same genetic anomaly."

He looked stunned.

Eva felt a sharp stinging in her palms and realized her hands were clenched, with nails digging in. Consciously, she made herself relax them. "I don't mean to presume you want a long-term relationship with me, Michael, but—"

He held up a hand. "You don't need to do that, Eva. Thank you for taking me seriously."

"I could die in three days, three years, or thirty years."

His face warmed and softened. "Then we will have to make the most of the time we have, won't we?"

It was Eva's turn to be stunned. That was the last thing she expected him to say.

"It's not operable?" he asked.

"It doesn't seem to be," Eva replied. "Sophie didn't have the money to even pursue it—we had no money to see surgeons. But the neurologist said it was dangerous to consider an operation. He also said I could live forever. But my mother died when she was thirty-one, and her mother died at thirty-four. So, I may only have a few years left."

She swallowed and studied his face.

Oh, what is he thinking?

"What an incredible burden you've been carrying," he said. "All this time."

Eva let out the breath she'd been holding. It was such relief that she'd told him, but this was still territory she didn't want to revisit.

"How did you find out?" Michael asked.

"About six months after my mother died, Aunt Sophie took me for an MRI, then started to act weird. She told me I had to be careful of my health. In particular, I should avoid extreme exertion. I loved swimming, was on the swim team. I was good, completely at home in the water, and just didn't understand why I couldn't compete. Then, out of the blue one day, I asked if what had killed my mom would kill me. Sophie went pale—I'd caught her out, I guess. When I kept pushing, she told me, reluctantly, about the aneurysm. From that day forward, for the first year or two, I wondered if I was going to die in the very next minute."

How she wished she hadn't pressed Sophie about it. She wished all kinds of things. She wished Sophie had kept it from her until she was old enough to handle it. But when would that be? Or, better still, she wished her great-aunt had never told her at all. Was it better to know, and have it affect every aspect of existence? Or better not to know, and have the chance to enjoy life in blissful ignorance? Well, pointless even to ponder. It was a waste of wishing.

"It's a shame, in a way, your Aunt Sophie told you about it," Michael said. "If there was nothing to be done about it. That's a heavy load for an eleven-year-old."

He'd done it again, spoken her thoughts. She reached for his hand, this time. "You're amazing. Thank you."

There was a pause while he just held her hand. And her eyes. "I'm not like other men, Eva."

She was surprised. Hubris? No. He was being truthful. She felt a twinge of shame that she had thought him arrogant. But seriously, she had never heard anyone say anything like that and not be bragging.

She slowly nodded. "I think I can see that."

"I live life more deeply than some. I carry honor and integrity as my guiding lights. I don't play games and I won't ever lie to you."

Eva saw him wince. She asked, "You ever been hurt?"

"Everyone has. I've suffered breakups that didn't go well. With hard words. You, too?"

She grimaced. "Yes."

"And I learned fast the hook-up thing is not for me," Michael said. "I've been on my own for some time." His eyes took on a faraway look and he absentmindedly squeezed his chin between his thumb and forefinger. Then he met her eyes once more. "But I haven't been heartbroken, and seeing what other people go through, I'm glad. My poor sister—the oldest, Caroline—her marriage has broken up and it's really hit her." He shook his head. "No, I love and admire women, but I hadn't met the spirit that touched mine..." He smiled. "Till now."

Eva's eyes were stinging. He was lyrical, even poetic. New territory again. "You don't know me."

"If you mean I don't know the side of the bed you sleep on, you're right. I don't know how grumpy you can get when you're tired or hungry. How to make you the perfect smoothie. I want to correct all that. But that's not *knowing*. I've seen you hold an animal. I've seen the tenderness and compassion on your face, I've seen the dignified and quiet way you carry yourself as if older than your years. I know that part of you."

He squeezed her hand and leaned forward. "I want to know what your dreams are... if you dare to have them."

Eva sat quietly, lost in his words, in his gaze, in this moment.

"I want you to get to know me," he said. "Do you want to do that?"

She didn't trust her voice to speak.

He grinned. "OK, enough heavy stuff. When's our food going to get here? My stomach thinks my throat's been cut."

She smiled. As for her stomach, it was settling down.

"Oh, and Eva? Thank you. For telling me."

They talked until the managers of the Texas Steakhouse nearly threw them out. She learned of his dream of owning his own veterinary clinic, his desire to travel and see all of Europe, especially Vienna and Florence. Of the colonial house he was fixing up.

And she saw that he listened, really listened, where in her experience, many men did not. Although opening up was never her default position, she plunged in and told him she had just learned who her father was.

"I know Hastings Pharma," Michael said. "They have a generic division and some of the antibiotics we use, like doxycycline and amoxicillin, are manufactured by them." He stopped, brow furrowed. "But Eva, you must be full of questions. Didn't he know about you?"

She swallowed and made herself say it. "If he did, he chose not to have anything to do with me."

"Then it's his loss."

She studied her hands. "All Mom told me was that he wasn't going to be in my life. She wouldn't say more than that."

There was a pause. Michael said, "I'm wondering why not."

"Me too. Believe me. She may have intended to tell me when I was older, but she never got the chance. And here's another piece to the tale. Remember that night at the wine bar?" She told him about Buzz Cut and her trip up to Hastings Pharma. "I recognized him—the same guy who'd been at the restaurant."

"Oh, man." He shook his head. "He had you *followed*?"

Eva shivered. Why was it so cold in there?

Michael's face was hard. "Maybe you don't want to know your father. What a jerk. So, what are you going to do? Do you want to meet him?"

She could only shrug. "I guess," she said. "I don't know."

"Well, let me know if you want me to go with you, or if you want to talk about it..." He grinned. "Or if you want me to beat him up for you."

She laughed. So, the father discovery was out in the open. It made it less weird, somehow.

But opening up was a rare event. Even with Jamie, especially now. She had decided to give her roommate some space after her recent revelation, since Jamie might be uncomfortable, or even embarrassed. Perhaps some recovery time was in order. For both of them.

As Michael drove her back to her car, Eva asked, "This healing thing... What exactly am I doing? Where does it come from?"

He shook his head. "I've been wondering the same thing. The one thing I *am* sure of is you're a rare breed. Tons of charlatans claim to be healers." He paused for a moment, brow furrowed. "Do you think it comes from you? Or does it flow through you?"

She chewed her lip. "I don't know. When I hold an animal, it's hard to describe... There's a fleeting intention to heal and then I let that go, then I feel compassion, then a connection, not only with the animal I'm holding but with something greater, I think. Can't explain it. It feels like a vibration, a warmth, a comforting. Mine, as well as theirs. Then somehow an ending of, or deliverance from, their pain. I don't ask, it's not like I pray for it to happen."

Michael was quiet. "Is it God? Or from God?"

"I don't know, Michael. I really don't know. I've never tried to describe it before. The experience has always felt, somehow, beyond words. But I'm beginning to trust the feeling."

Back at the clinic, he parked his car next to hers. "I did some reading. I was wondering how faith communities view healing. Whatever it is.... spiritual healing? Energetic healing? Whatever. Anyway, the Catholic Church calls it superstition."

"*Funny*. And ironic, since I think most of *their* beliefs are superstition. So, I'm not sure I care very much what the Catholic Church thinks."

Michael grinned. "My family's Catholic. When you meet them, do me a favor and don't voice that opinion."

"When I meet them?"

His face grew serious. "I'd like you to."

At her car door, she felt his arms come around her and turned to look up at him. Bending his head, just barely, softly, he brushed his lips to hers. She felt a shiver run up her spine, and an answering tingle deep, low down in her belly. He stroked her hair, the back of her head, then bent in again and brushed her lips a second time. Then pulled away again. *Why did he go away?* She heard a tiny sound, almost a whimper, and realized it came from her. She gripped his back and pulled him tighter.

"Eva." He said her name and took her mouth. To her surprise, her world opened and encompassed him. There was nothing but Michael. His smell, his taste, his tongue. All that strength and spirit... It combined somehow with hers. The sensation grew, and grew, and grew some more.

She had felt connection before. With animals. But this connection, with this human being, was different. The kiss and the feel of his body against hers fueled a simmering heat. Electricity. The threat of fire.

As she drove home, an irrational thought plagued her. She would have to be careful. That fire might consume her.

Chapter 13

"He's agreed to drive down to my place." Chloe let out a small groan. "Will's funny—you'd think we were negotiating the Middle East peace talks. Anyway, 11:00 a.m. Saturday, for brunch? I texted my address."

Eva's heart sped up. Maybe not peace talks, but still momentous to her. She knew her aunt understood that and was just trying to add a little lightness to the situation. They'd spoken a few times on the phone about this potential meeting. Having decided she was going to meet her father, putting it off any longer made no sense. And as a go-between, Chloe was perfect. Eva was beginning to feel comfortable, even safe with her, which was odd, considering she'd only known her a few weeks.

Chloe said, "It'll be fine Eva, he does want to meet you. I can tell."

Eva repeated it in her mind: *It will be fine. You can do this, Baby Girl.*

As she ended the call it hit her: This was it. Three days from now she would meet her father. But then, the same evening, she was going to a concert with Michael. She decided to focus on that, and even if the meeting was a disaster, Saturday evening would be fun. They'd discovered a mutual love for The Wailin' Jennys, a three-woman folk group who created an achingly beautiful sound. Three-part harmony from angelic voices.

Her workdays were racing by, packed full. A few times, at the end of the day, she'd swung by Michael's clinic to work with a dog or a cat, once even a rabbit. Reveling in the realization of how much she was helping these innocent animals, she took a break from wondering how she was doing it, where it came from, and what it meant. She just enjoyed it.

She had focused on the dog with heartworm and was awaiting a lab result to see if her efforts paid off. As for her being there at the clinic regularly, Michael explained it to the others as a sort of internship, that Eva was doing extra hours to add to her vet tech studies and experience. But it seemed to her that Nina saw right through that.

Saturday dawned clear and sunny. Eva hadn't slept well, anticipating the meeting. It hadn't happened in years, but she dreamt again the same old terrifying dream of finding her mother lying on the kitchen floor. When she awoke, her jaw ached from clenching her teeth.

Trying to decide what to wear didn't help. Her clothes in the summer consisted of cropped jeans, loose t-shirts, or short-sleeved cotton Henleys. Winter clothes were turtlenecks and jeans. Never wanting to draw attention to herself, she dressed casually, and not in the sexy outfits so many other women her age wore. She scanned through the closet, then stood, her hands on her hips. *For goodness' sake, BG, be yourself.* Deciding on a green tee and cutoff jeans, plus sandals, she twirled her hair up on her head and held it fast with a green clip that matched her t-shirt. She grinned. *That's at least a bit of color coordination. Jamie would be so proud.*

Normally Eva would ask her friend's advice about what to wear. But Jamie's dramatic confession had put a bit of a wrinkle in their relationship which they had yet to iron out. Eva squirmed every time she thought of it, still kicked herself for not seeing it. In any event, she'd decided to act as if it never happened. Say nothing.

What was it Aunt Sophie used to say? "Least said, soonest mended."

With Cookie harnessed in the back seat, Eva headed north on I-95. She slid Yola's new CD into the slot in the car's out-of-date sound system and relished the singer's powerful vocals on the way to Rhode Island. She didn't mind being alone, she was used to it. There was always wonderful music for company. Man's redeeming feature, she thought to herself. Music. To her, music inspired passion, a flow like a river of emotion, harnessed in sound.

It was one of those splendid summer days in Connecticut, where the humidity level was low, a breeze kept it comfortable, yet the sun was in full glory. Directions showed Chloe's home situated near Jamestown, just across Narragansett Bay from Newport. Eva had driven up to Rhode Island many times, to various beaches, but had never crossed the Jamestown Verrazano bridge toward Conanicut Island. The island boasted old forts, a historic windmill, and unbelievably upmarket houses tucked along the coastline. The kinds of houses with eight-car garages. The sea glinted everywhere, it seemed. Everywhere Eva looked, another opening to the water beckoned.

Once past Jamestown, she headed down a quiet road lined with red maple trees and white pines. At random intervals, granite columns with wrought iron gates offered brief glances down long driveways. Sometimes she caught a glimpse of a stately mansion— just for a split second—tucked back from the road. Then it vanished again, hidden by arborvitaes or flowering hydrangeas.

Turning onto a small lane, Eva found Chloe's house, nestled behind flower beds and a low stone wall. A coastal cottage, typically New England, it was inviting, with its gambrel roof, cedar shingles, and long covered porch. Not ostentatious, the place was warm looking but elegant. Like Chloe herself.

She unfastened Cookie's harness, and they headed up the stone path to the front door. With each step, the fragrance of the thyme growing between and over the steppingstones drifted up to greet her. The glass multi-paned front door opened and Chloe, in white slacks and a long blue peasant shirt, stepped out on the porch.

"You found me! Is this Cookie?" Chloe knelt on the porch to greet the dog, who bustled around her legs, in pure joy at meeting another human.

"Thanks for letting me bring her. It's been a busy week and she hasn't had as much attention as usual."

"She'll have fun with my two. Come on out to the courtyard, they're out there."

Chloe gave her a quick hug then led the way across the wide planks of the hickory floor in the foyer, through an expansive great room, to glass French doors. Through them, Eva could see the enclosed stone courtyard with wrought iron benches and terra cotta pots of begonias and geraniums scattered around. It beckoned like a photo spread in a home and garden magazine. A haven. A well-tended grassy pathway snaked its way between elegant beds of shrubs and perennials and flowed seamlessly into a wildflower meadow. Beyond the meadow, a mini forest stood guard against the outside world.

Chloe raised a hand to shield her eyes from the noonday sun. "I bought the place a few years ago. It was a clean slate—the previous owners had planted nothing. I mean *nothing*. Just gravel right up to the foundation. So, I've had fun. As for the cottage itself, it was in good shape, just needed decorative changes."

Eva pointed to a large glass room that made up one side of the "u" of the cottage. "That's gorgeous."

"That's new—I had it built on."

Floor-to-ceiling glass windows revealed a grand piano at one end and at the other, a spiral staircase up to a loft/balcony area.

"It's large enough for house concerts," Chloe said. "I haven't even told you about my passion, yet. I help young musical artists— singers and songwriters and musicians. Scholarship to Juilliard, or funding for recording... it's different depending on the artist. Sometimes I hold a small concert to present someone new."

As Cookie nosed her way around the courtyard, Chloe put two fingers in her mouth and let rip with an ear-piercing whistle. "My two springers, Juliette and Jesse, are in the woods. The whole place is fenced, so they're safe. And my gardens are off limits for hordes of munching deer!"

Two chocolate springer spaniels came bounding through the grass from the woods, and all the dogs started their sniffing, getting-to-know-each-other routine.

"He'll be here soon—let's go have a cup of tea." Chloe gestured back to the house. Before Eva followed Chloe into the kitchen, she glanced back to see Cookie racing off to the meadow after Juliet and Jesse.

Eva perched on a high stool next to a large butcher block island. The kitchen was white with pops of blue and green, giving off almost a beach feel. The room embraced utility without entirely surrendering its elegance. The aroma of freshly baked bread mixed with that of the mint tea Chloe was stirring in a flowered teapot.

"Are you nervous?" Chloe looked up from pouring tea with a smile.

Eva figured her expression must have answered that question.

"Of course you are," Chloe said. "I can't imagine what you're feeling right now."

Before Eva could try to tell her, she heard the sounds of a car engine, tires on gravel, then the slamming of a door. Her stomach jumped into her throat.

Here we go.

"He's actually on time," Chloe muttered. "That's a first."

"Chloe!" Eva heard a voice calling, then the front door closing, and footsteps in the foyer.

Then he was in the room with them, the tall gray-haired man from the pictures and from the headquarters of Hastings Pharma. He stopped a few feet away and stared at her. Chloe began to speak, introducing them, but Eva didn't take in what she said.

Impressions whipped across her mind. Serious. Cool. Charismatic, as a politician is charismatic. A smile on his face that didn't reach his eyes. Sunglasses dropped carelessly down on the butcher block. Matching light gray polo shirt and slacks, black loafers, and a belt of some exotic leather. A disjointed thought hit her: his belt and shoes cost more than everything she owned, combined. But then his hand was out to shake hers and all thoughts flew out of her head.

He gripped her hand, hard, and she almost winced. He held it and studied her. "You have a beautiful face. Why don't you wear contact lenses?"

She pulled her hand away. "We couldn't afford them... besides, I like my glasses."

"Well, anyway, I guess I don't need to order a paternity test, after all. You look like Chloe. Not so much like your mother."

Eva couldn't find the right words.

Chloe sounded shocked. "Will! For God's sake!"

"Of course, I can hardly remember," he added. "It was many years ago."

"Twenty-six, to be exact," Eva said. Of all the things she had thought of, and worried about, it hadn't occurred to her that he might not believe she was really his daughter. This wasn't a great start. He'd just said her mother could be a liar.

"Do the test," she said firmly. "You mustn't have any doubts." But as she spoke, she told herself she didn't care. Why did she need to prove herself to this guy? The desire to make a great impression vanished. She would deal with the disappointment later.

Chloe gave a bright smile and reached for the teapot. "I have a fresh pot of tea here, Will."

"Nope, coffee. Thanks."

His words were brusque. Chloe rolled her eyes and turned to open a cupboard where she selected a coffee canister.

Will pulled out a stool by the center island. "Eva, listen. This is a strange situation. I'm sure it's stressful for you, too. Look at it from my point of view. I learn, all these years later, that I have a daughter. I'm sorry, but I think it's normal to be skeptical. Especially considering my position. That of my family."

"So now we're *gold* diggers?" Eva shook her head. "For God's sake, my mother didn't get—or *ask* for—a penny from you. Ever."

"Good point," Will said.

"And you didn't know?"

"Pardon me?"

"About me. Why didn't you know of my existence? You broke up with my mother, Chloe said, and it was amicable."

"That's right."

Eva couldn't read his face. "Then why on earth didn't she tell you she was pregnant?"

Will shrugged. "Pride?"

"Pride? My mother did everything she could for me until she died when I was eleven. Why didn't she ask you for help? She struggled so... For all I know the stress of that contributed to her early death." Eva felt her throat closing and her eyes burning. She took a breath, her hand shaking slightly as she lay her cup on the counter.

"I would've helped, of course," Will said. "If I'd known. I don't know why she didn't tell me. All I can think of is that she might have been embarrassed after I ended it."

Chloe cleared her throat. She placed coffee by Will's hand. "This is not how I imagined this meeting... Come on. let's go sit outside. It's lovely out there."

"It's too hot, I prefer it in here," replied Will. "Let's change the subject and lighten up. Chloe, tell me how you're doing with your music prodigies. Having fun?"

"Yes, absolutely. I've discovered a wonderful young singer/songwriter—and he's a fine guitar player. I'm sending him to publishers and producers I know in Nashville. And I found a young girl in Old Saybrook with the most spectacular voice. She wants to study classical music, so I think she's in line for a Juilliard scholarship."

As Chloe spoke, Eva realized the man was only partly listening. He kept stealing glances at her, where she stood on the other side of the island from him. She could feel him studying her, but she steadfastly watched Chloe and didn't meet his eyes.

"I don't know why you don't just relax, travel, have fun," Will said to Chloe.

"Oh, right, and go shopping with a little dog in my bag. Get my nails done. Have a masseuse come to the house. Have lunch with vapid spoiled women." Chloe placed a large stainless-steel sauté pan on the stove and reached for olive oil. "I love what I'm doing. I'm supporting creativity and the arts. And I get to be involved in all that joy. OK, now to food... A French mushroom omelet with Boursin cheese, with a new loaf of bread out of the oven. Sound good?" She opened the refrigerator to collect what she needed.

"My clever sister," replied Will. "Which reminds me, I've booked Gerard Toussaint to cater the party next weekend. You remember? The chef you liked from Block Island? I hope you'll come, Eva. It's my birthday. At our family home, south of Boston, next Sunday." He turned back to Chloe. "You're coming, right?"

"Of course," Chloe said. "Your fiftieth, a big one! Why wouldn't I?"

"So often you don't show up."

Chloe raised an eyebrow. "Oh, come on, Will, I'm there for all the real functions, birthdays, anniversaries. I just don't come every time you snap your fingers."

Will didn't respond to that. He turned to Eva. "What about it, Eva, you can meet your half-sisters and brother. Mom will be there. Hopefully Dad, too. Chloe told you, I'm sure, about his stroke? Anyway, can you make it?"

"I'll check. Thank you for the invitation." Eva knew polite convention required she smile at him. But she didn't. She stood from the stool. "Can I help, Chloe?"

Before Chloe could respond, Will said, "Eva, you seem irritated." He grinned. "We've only known each other five minutes, I can't have done something wrong already."

She stared at him and spoke quietly. "Why was it necessary to have me followed?"

Will's eyebrows went up and he laughed. He turned to Chloe. "Oh, she's feisty. I like that."

Eva turned and collected her bag from the wicker chair. She did her best to give Chloe a real smile. "Thank you for the invitation, but I'll have to take a rain check. It's been great seeing some of your lovely home. I'll go find Cookie." She strode to the courtyard where she called out to her dog.

Behind her, she could hear Chloe's voice.

"Will, what's *wrong* with you? Why are you being such a jerk?"

Eva started to shake. She had only driven for a few minutes when she pulled off onto a side road. Even the baroque string quartet playing on the classical station wasn't calming. How she wished she could cry. She knew women, Jamie included, who could have a good cry in times of stress and feel decidedly better. As if it were a relief valve. Ever since her mother's death, crying had eluded her. She just had to be alone, hold an animal if possible, and let time and stillness work their cure.

In retrospect, she was now a little embarrassed she had hightailed it out of there. And wasn't quite sure why she had. Escape? Was she that much of a wuss? Just wanted to get away from the strange harsh energy she felt from him? Or was she so angry she was afraid she might say something she'd regret?

Her phone dinged with a text from Chloe.

> Eva, I'm sorry. He's always controlling but he can be charming. Not today, don't know why. So sorry you're hurt or angry.

> Not your fault! The apology should be mine—the way I left was rude. Thx for all your trouble. Lunch sounded great...

No sooner had she sent it off than another came in, from Michael. He simply asked how it was going and if she was OK.

> Disaster.

> WTH? Come over, we can talk... or I'll divert you—my workshop, the house renovation, seduction...

> LOL Shoot me your address.

On the drive home, Watch Hill Beach called to her. She needed time, and the beach, to calm down. It was cooler by the water, and she tramped along the sand, with Cookie, for over an hour. Off in the distance lay sand dunes and tall grasses waving in the breeze. Nearer, on her other side, waves broke into white froth and raced toward her feet. Seagulls swooped and called while the gray sea churned. Putting one foot in front of the other and breathing in the tangy sea air was a tonic. She wished she could swim but had checked rip tide warnings and it wasn't safe. She scanned the water, endlessly searching.

She couldn't count the times she had walked this beach, or another in Rhode Island, hoping for a sign of the dolphins. She never gave up hope.

Chapter 14

Michael made Eva tea, gave Cookie some kibble, then stood with his cup of coffee, leaning up against the kitchen counters, watching Eva.

"I stopped at the beach for a bit, to get rid of the stress," she said.

He focused on her fingers drumming incessantly on the wood plank table.

"So, not all of it, huh?" He smiled.

She looked up at him, questioning, then followed his look toward her restless fingers, and stilled them. Rolled her eyes. "Guess not."

"Before I forget, I have a bit of news to cheer you up. You were wondering if you could rid a dog of heartworm?"

She nodded.

"Well, kudos to you. That pup is now clear."

"Oh Michael," she said, clapping her hands together.

"It's getting weird at the clinic, though. Don't know how long we can keep the lid on this thing. We have coincidence after coincidence, inexplicable cure after inexplicable cure. People are talking. I think Roxanne suspects."

Eva stared toward the kitchen window, but he knew she wasn't admiring the oak tree beyond it. He could almost hear the gears churning.

"The time is coming where we will have to trust the staff with the truth," he said.

"You're right." She sighed.

He was quiet for a couple of minutes. There was something about this whole healing thing that rendered a guy speechless. It was so *big*, and so seemingly impossible, that talking about it out loud sounded crazy. If he hadn't seen it with his own eyes, he wouldn't have believed himself.

"OK, tell me about meeting your father," he asked. "Didn't go well, huh?"

Michael listened as Eva relayed what happened. He grimaced. "I was kidding about the beat-him-up idea. But it's sounding better and better." He shook his head. "What a piece of work."

She sighed, then stood up. "Show me around. Please. I'm done thinking about it."

"Come on, Cookie," Michael said, ruffling the dog's head. He led Eva out to the rolling lawns, where the fragrance of the newly cut grass filled his head. Cookie liked it, too, he thought, watching the dog race around, then roll, then leap up and tear around again.

Michael turned to look up at the house and she followed his gaze. "It needs a lot of TLC. But Dad says it has 'good bones.' I have lots of plans... paint job, black shutters on the windows, and I must get to the landscaping. The list is much longer than that for stuff that needs doing inside." He grinned. "But there's no hurry, it's livable."

He loved the setting. He found himself hoping she loved it, too. Rolling lawns separated the house from the road, and a towering maple tree, far enough from the house not to shade the solar panels on the roof, lent a sense of timelessness to the property. He pointed off to the side toward a fenced garden area, overgrown with weeds. "I must clean that mess out. Jules found asparagus plants hiding in there."

"Jules?"

"My sister—the gardening sister." He grinned. "It'll take you a while to get them all straight."

He grabbed her hand and led her into the barn/workshop, where he showed off the newly refinished cherry cabinets, now fully stained and drying. Once back in the house, he asked her opinion on the living room walls. "What color would you paint this? This dark blue has got to go."

"Perhaps... it's a bit of a cave in here." She smiled. "But the wainscoting's gorgeous, and I love those built-in corner cupboards. I can see them all in sparkling white. Of course, Jamie's the one to ask—she's the graphic designer. But for the walls... how about celadon? My Aunt Sophie used that for her main room."

"Sounds terrific. I *love* it..." He cocked his head to one side. "What's celadon?"

She laughed. "It's a light green that almost has a bit of gray in it. Very elegant."

He was just detailing his plan to break through the wall connecting the dining room to the kitchen when he heard a car pull up outside. He glanced out the nearby window. "It's my folks." He called out the open door. "Hey Dad, Mom!"

His mother hugged him, looking like a fashion plate in cream summer linen. Her dark shoulder-length hair sported a wide silver steak down one side. This was the Italian mother who'd born six kids? She looked too young and fit. His dad looked smart, as well, in an open-necked shirt and slacks, and his jovial face was quick to smile. What hair he had left was blonde with tinges of red, his skin was pale, and Eva remembered that Michael had said his father's ancestry was Irish.

"Sorry to interrupt," said his dad, eying Eva. "You have company."

"Mom, Dad, this is Eva McGrath, a colleague, a vet tech. She is helping me with several cases."

"Uh, huh." His dad looked skeptical. "What's wrong with you? I taught you nothin'? This is a beautiful woman."

Eva blushed. "Nice to meet you," she said.

"Richard." Michael's mother said, "Stop it, don't embarrass her."

"No, no, that's fine," Eva said.

"I'm sorry, Eva. I'm Michelle, everyone calls me Shel, except him." She elbowed her husband lightly then shook Eva's hand.

"I call her Shelly Belly." Richard took Eva's hand and with a sweeping courtly gesture, kissed the back of it. Eva grinned.

Michael asked, "Dad, why are you here?"

"Can't a father visit his favorite son?"

"Since I'm your only son, that's not saying much..."

Richard raised his finger in the age-old, wait-a-minute-gesture, went back to the car, and pulled something long and metal from the back.

"We found something for you," Michelle said.

His dad said, "Look at this. Your mom and I found this at the auction in Manchester this morning. We think it's an antique—or else we got taken, what do you think, Shel? Anyway, it'll look great on your barn." He held up a six-foot-long weathervane with the green patina of aged copper. Complete with a sculpted rooster twirling at its top.

"Oh, great, thank you, guys," Michael said, turning it in his hands and studying it.

Michelle said, "We're heading to the Brass Door for dinner." She gestured to her husband. "I made your father put on real clothes."

"Hey, wait a minute!" Richard said. He winked at Eva.

She laughed and won a grin from Richard.

"Want to come?" Michelle turned to Eva. "You're welcome to join us."

"Thanks, Mom, another time," said Michael. "We have tickets for a concert."

"Ah..." His dad said. "Well, enjoy!"

After his folks had bustled off, Michael said, "I tried to warn you about the energy of my family. And that's just two of them. My dad keeps us all on our toes, that's for sure. Come on, let's get inside away from the skeeters."

"Your dad's fun."

"You ain't seen nothin' yet."

Once inside, he turned to her. "I'm glad they dropped by. I knew she'd love you."

Eva stared at him. "You speak so... directly, sometimes."

He reached for her hand. "Well, here I go again: Was it too soon to meet my mother?"

Eva's eyes grew wide. "Michael..."

He pulled her slowly to him, never taking his eyes from hers.

"Michael," she repeated.

He looked down into those eyes. Those eyes... Then he kissed her as if he had been doing it for twenty years. It was right, somehow, and exciting at the same time. So, this is what kissing can be. He realized he'd never experienced kissing in quite the same way. Other kisses had felt like work. He usually had to concentrate to figure out what to do next, or how to respond to what the woman was doing. Not this. Not work at all. Give and take. Just a flow of natural sensation and response.

Much too soon, he made himself pull back.

During the Wailin' Jennys concert, Eva seemed rapt, throughout. At one point she whispered in his ear, "Divine." He agreed. After the disappointing meeting with her father, he knew she needed this music. He understood that, on a deep, almost cellular level. Music had always moved and filled him, was a magical and essential part of his life.

He took her hand early in the concert, lacing his fingers through hers. From time to time, when he glanced over at her, her eyes were closed, and he wondered if she was floating on the waves of delicious sound, as he was.

On the way home, she said, "The sound floods through me. Like waves of internal chills. It's like nothing else on earth."

"You're right. It's not of earth, it's of spirit. Art, music, creativity. Humanity's redeeming qualities."

"Exactly." She looked surprised. "That's funny, I've always said that, too."

"And simply put, it's so beautiful it hurts."

"Yes," she replied with a sigh.

How he wanted to be a place to lean for this woman. He had a foreboding feeling when word got out about her healing, things would get hard for her. She kept to herself and didn't like attention. But he feared attention was what she was going to get. He wanted to give her a place to trust, even to fall, if necessary.

As they approached Jamie's house Eva said, "Thank you for a lovely evening, Michael. You should let me pay my share."

He shook his head, dismissing that idea, then touched her forearm gently. "It was my idea... Here's another. Can I take you away for a weekend? Vermont? The Cape? The Berkshires?"

When she didn't answer immediately, he said, "There's no hurry, Eva." He put the car in park and turned to her. Their eyes met and hers held that smokey fire. "God, I want you, but you need you to be ready."

She looked down at her lap, where her hands were clutched together so tightly her knuckles were white. Michael reached for a hand and enfolded it in his own.

When she spoke, her voice was strained. "I love our friendship, Michael."

"Friendship? Is that what you want?" He studied her. "Have I been reading this all wrong?"

There was a pause, and he waited.

She cleared her throat. "Let's just take it slow, OK?"

He held her gaze, sinking into the golden lights in her eyes. She was honey, summer, spiced wine. Irresistible. He lifted her hand up to his lips, kissing her palm. She shivered.

She leaned over to give him a soft kiss, then reached for the door handle.

"Wait," he said. He tapped the volume button on the steering wheel and the music that had been playing softly in the background swelled. It was Christina Perri singing *A Thousand Years.*

"I love this song," Eva said.

"Me, too," he replied, turning it up, even higher. "Wait right there."

He jumped out of the car and was around her side in a flash, escorting her from the passenger seat. He gave a flourish, almost a bow, then took her hand and pulled her close into his arms, and began to dance. His lips grazed her ear as he swayed to the music. He nearly groaned in pleasure, feeling her body move against him, feeling her hand stroking his back.

"Ow!" Michael pulled back sharply and slapped the back of his neck. "Damn skeeters..."

"Maybe I should say good night."

"Nah, let's ignore them." He pulled her close again. Humming along with the tune, he put his lips next to her ear. He sang along with the lyrics.

She snorted.

"You mocking my singing?"

She laughed. "No, no, I'd never do that," she said. "You have a breathtaking voice."

"Yeah yeah, breathtakingly bad... Well, I'm deeply hurt, I want you to know. OK, you show me how it's done. Come on, sing with me."

She shook her head, still laughing under her breath. "Not in a thousand years."

He chuckled, gave her a squeeze, and sang louder.

"You'll wake the neighbors!"

They twirled and swayed around the grass until the song came to an end. But he carried on dancing, unwilling to let her go.

"Song's over," Her voice was muffled, as her face was buried in his neck.

"Is it?"

All he could think about was this woman in his arms, filling his senses, filling his heart. The moonlight and stars lit her hair, she smelled like jasmine, and he was infused with a sense of magic.

This moment. He would never forget this moment. Michael stopped dancing and pulled back just enough to bend his head and kiss her. He wanted to kiss her until she loved him. Kiss her until she got it. That they belonged together.

Chapter 15

As Eva locked her SUV in the shelter's parking area, two young teenagers climbed out of a nearby pickup truck. The boys looked about eleven or twelve, with the unkempt hoodie and droopy jeans that being that age seemed to require.

One of them carried something in his arms, wrapped in a towel. He spoke hesitantly. "Are you Eva?"

When she nodded, he asked, "Will you help us? Mr. Gleason told us to ask you..."

She asked, "Mr. Gleason?"

The kids pointed behind them to the truck. She could just make out a figure in the cab.

She studied them. "You know my name. What's yours?"

"Jason," said the dark-haired boy.

She looked the question at the other boy, whose red tufts of hair stuck out, in random fashion, from under a Yankees ball cap.

"Kyle," he replied.

"OK, Jason, Kyle, what do you want help with?"

Jason pointed back at the car. "Uncle Roger told us you heal animals... Will you? Please?"

Eva gestured to the gray cat peeking out of the towel in Jason's arms. "Him? This cat?"

"Yes," he said, "This is Shadow."

She looked again at the car. *How did this person, their Uncle Roger, hear about me?*

She reached for the cat. "What's wrong with him?"

Jason offered, "He's old—Mom says there's nothing else we can do."

Kyle sounded derisive. "No, stupid, it was the vet who said there's nothing else we can do. Not because he's old. Because he has bad arthritis—he can hardly walk. Dad wants us to put him to sleep..." There was a plea in his voice.

Eva led them to a rustic bench near the door of the shelter and sat with the cat in her arms. "I'll try. But, boys, I need you to be quiet. Will you do that?"

Eyes large, the two agreed.

Helping the cat was straightforward. His energy was strong and easily available. She drifted into the connection, and in a few minutes, when she floated back up, it occurred to her it was getting easier every time.

She heard clicking sounds and opened her eyes. A man stood in front of her with a fancy Nikon camera pressed to his face. About forty, she figured, he was skinny, wearing nondescript khakis and safari shirt, with rimless glasses like a John Lennon wanna-be. He approached her, coming too close, right into her personal space. He was verging on creepy, and she tried not to cringe.

He held out his card and said, in a high-pitched, slightly nasal voice, "Eva McGrath? Roger Gleason of GsGs.com. I'm writing a blog about you. You call yourself an animal healer. Would you care to comment?"

As she took his card, she wondered with his abrasive attitude how he ever got anyone to comment, much less confide in him. Then she saw his website name on the card. Gleason's Gleanings—she'd heard of this site. This guy was a local blogger, who called himself a journalist, but who often dabbled in Fake News.

She handed the cat back to Jason. "I don't call myself anything. Who said I'm an animal healer?"

He smirked. "Not going to reveal my source."

"Oh, for goodness' sake, Mr. Gleason, you sound like you're in a B movie."

Kyle spoke up. "Uncle Roger, it was that guy—"

Gleason cut him off. "Boys, wait in the car for me. No, go on, take the cat, I'll be there in a minute." To Eva, he said, "I can pay you for an exclusive."

She shook her head, headed for the shelter door, and heard his voice behind her. "I can make it worth your while, Eva. 500 bucks? And you talk to no one else?"

"No, thank you, Mr. Gleason."

"Well, you think about it, and check out my blog on GsGs.com. Sunday morning."

Eva hurried into the shelter, slamming the door behind her and leaning against it. Her heart was pounding.

Jake looked up from the counter. "What's going on?"

She shook her head.

"What the hell, Eva? You OK?"

"A news guy, or blogger, or whatever. Gleason of Gleason's Gleanings."

Jake waited.

"He wants to do a story..." she said, "about me."

He looked a question at her.

She paused and took a deep breath. And plunged in. "About my ability to heal animals."

Jake stared at her.

It took quite some time to share the whole story with Jake. But oddly, after his initial disbelief and shock, he accepted it.

He shook his head and muttered, "I knew there was something up..." He confessed he'd been confused by the dramatic improvements, over and over again, in some of the animals. He said at least this made sense, in some weird way.

Eva was glad she'd told him. It made it more real, somehow, but it felt odd saying it. It sounded not only impossible but self-important. But she was going to need all the understanding she could get if, no, *when*, this thing became common knowledge.

And who talked to Gleason? Michael knew, of course... Now Jamie knew, which meant Clare must know... Did Roxanne or Nina or someone else at the clinic now suspect?

It was going to be hard to keep a lid on this. Maybe it was already too late.

Chapter 16

Eva woke the next morning to frantic texts from Jamie, who'd been staying with her mother since Dr. Chin had taken a turn for the worse. The cold or flu had worsened rapidly and was now deep in her chest. Now she was having a hard time breathing. Her asthma meds were helping somewhat, but Jamie was getting frightened and sounded beside herself.

Eva found herself chewing on her thumbnail. Then her phone dinged again.

Might be pneumonia.
Fever's higher... 103.

Call 911?

She says no.

What? Why not? I'm on
my way.

Why didn't Dr. Chin want to go to her own hospital? Although she'd been in private medical practice early in her career, she was now an administrator at one of the big hospitals in Norwich. It didn't add up.

Arriving at Dr. Chin's, Eva hesitated at the big front door. Not wanting to ring the bell in case she was sleeping, Eva tested the door, found it unlocked, and let herself in. In the marble foyer, guitar music, with floating keyboard pads and strings, drifted through the system. Dr. Chin loved New Age music. She said since her job was so often busy as hell, she wanted it to sound like heaven at home, with music from artists such as Mark Isham, Tim Janis, or Enigma.

Jamie beckoned to her from the archway to the living room. Her face was tense as she led Eva toward her mother, who was lying on an overstuffed couch. Uneaten chicken soup and tea sat abandoned on the coffee table with inhalers, bottles of vitamin C, and acetaminophen.

"Oh, Eva, she got worse so fast! Listen to her!"

Dr. Chin's breath came in wheezing gasps, interspersed with deep wracking coughs.

"Since I texted," Jamie said, "her fever's even higher—104. So never mind what she said, I called 911. They said twenty minutes."

"Why doesn't she want to go?"

"Pride I think." Jamie shook her head. "Mom said she didn't want to endanger anyone there. But I think the truth is she didn't want any of her staff to see her sick. She's never sick. Either that or she's just stubborn—you know how she is."

Alice moaned and her eyes opened. Between short hard breaths, she whispered, "Chest hurts... Hard to breathe. Water.... So dry..." Her words trailed off into a deep hacking cough.

Jamie jumped up and disappeared into the kitchen.

Eva drew a chair up next to Jamie's mom and took her outstretched hand, at which point Alice closed her eyes again. She looked terrible. Her straight black hair, cut in a bob, was usually glossy and perfectly groomed, but now it lay, stringy and limp.

Jamie came back carrying the water and knelt beside the sofa. "Mom? Mom?"

There was no reply. Jamie tried again, shaking her mom's arm gently. Nothing. "Oh God, she's unconscious."

Eva stroked Dr. Chin's hand and felt a hard-edged lump in her throat. Heart racing, she closed her eyes and tried to relax.

For a moment, a soaring string line from a film theme caught her attention, and her mind floated with it. Guitar, high violins, soft percussion, and a deep cello line. It reverberated through her and the energy of it seeped into her bones, filling her with chills.

Her heart lifted. She began to feel that familiar sensation, not unlike when she held an animal. The vibration began, the hum, an energetic connection. Even as the feelings began, the thought whipped through her mind: *Is it possible?* Then the sensation disappeared. That had never happened with an animal. She focused on Jamie's mother, who'd always been good to her, feeling the compassion she had for the woman whose hand she was holding. *Dear Dr. Chin.*

She made a conscious effort to open. To find that connection again. As she did, she felt, rather than saw, a dark gray wall in front of her. She touched it, probed it, pushed it with her energy, and it began to dissolve. But another wall was behind it.

She felt Jamie touch her shoulder, then squat on the floor at her feet. Eva reached out one of her hands to her. Jamie grasped it and held on.

"I'm so scared," Jamie said, her voice cracking.

Eva squeezed her hand and concentrated on dissolving that second wall. Each time the connection started to fade, she consciously connected once more. She felt her hand, the one holding Alice's, grow warm. She went deeper, felt the dark space widen and grow. She wondered if it was her imagination, but she felt Jamie's love for her mother pulse through her hand, and on through her to Alice.

The second gray wall dissolved and behind it was the open, expansive feeling she was used to with animals. With it came a feeling of dropping, a deepening sensation, a widening of reality inside her, dark and floating. As if she were submerged in fathoms-deep water, but was able to breathe.

Minutes passed. Jamie didn't speak.

Eva was lost in this world, where there was power and passion, but also deep silence, almost reverence. It was bliss, and no fear of illness, no fear of loss, no fear of the future, or of life, invaded her. Everything flowed and whirled and pulsed.

Then the sensations gently and slowly faded.

She had no idea how much time had passed, but when she opened her eyes, Alice wasn't moving, her eyes were shut, but her short gasps of breath had eased. Eva touched her forehead. Still warm.

Too soon to tell. Could she do it? Could she heal a person?

Turning to meet Jamie's eyes, Eva saw tears overflow and stream unchecked down her friend's cheeks. Jamie shook her head, as if unable to speak. Eva sat unmoving, for long minutes, feeling inexplicably drained.

The doorbell chimed.

Jamie leaped up. "Finally," she said, as she rushed to let in the EMTs.

Eva moved her chair back and stood out of the way, as the two men and a woman, covered head to foot in personal protective equipment, hurried into the room. She sank down on an upholstered chair in the corner, away from the bustle of activity. She was weary to the bone. And cold, suddenly. Wrapping her arms around herself, she stroked her upper arms. She had never felt like this after holding an animal.

She heard Jamie tell the EMTs about her mother's asthma, unresolved cold symptoms, and the possible pneumonia complication, but she couldn't hear the paramedics' replies or questions. They took Dr. Chin's temperature, checked her pulse, blood pressure, and listened to her heart. Jamie stood nearby asking questions, but Eva felt too wiped out to inquire. She figured she'd know soon enough.

Jamie approached her. "They've persuaded Mom to go to the hospital to get checked out."

Eva looked up. "She's conscious?"

"Yes, and her fever is now ninety-nine degrees. Her breathing sounds better. They think I exaggerated. Any chance my thermometer is broken?"

"Seriously? It's ninety-nine now?"

Jamie nodded.

"You didn't exaggerate—I heard her breathing. That horrible cough. And she was definitely unconscious."

"I'm going with them." Jamie looked at her oddly. "Are you OK?"

"Just tired. You go, honey, I'll lock the door on my way out."

When the paramedics had carried Dr. Chin out on a stretcher, and Jamie had followed in the car, Eva stood up, feeling suddenly aged.

Why am I so exhausted?

She headed out the door, longing for fresh air.

Outside, she drew in long breaths. Once in her car, she sat still, aching in every muscle and sinew, as if she'd run a marathon. Did she help Dr. Chin? Was that what had wiped her out? She was too tired even to think about it.

She woke up with a start, sweat dripping down her back. The car was in the sun and the interior was blazing hot. Eva hadn't even started the engine but had just fallen asleep. Glancing at her phone she saw she'd slept for an hour, right there in Dr. Chin's driveway.

At home, she let Cookie out for a few minutes, promised her a walk, then went upstairs to try to catch up on assignments. But she couldn't concentrate. She flopped down on her bed, Cookie by her side, deciding to rest her eyes for just a few minutes. She woke when her phone dinged a couple of hours later and had to climb up from sleep, out of a deep, deep mist.

She reached for her phone, to find a text from Jamie.

> Mom's good. They've admitted her, but temp is normal now! WTH? Was that you? You heal people, too???

> IDK. But good news, such good news.

> She doesn't remember seeing you–she was so out of it. But she had a dream about floating in deep water.

Eva drew in a sharp breath. Dr. Chin had felt the floating, even the sense of deep water. What did this mean? Had she healed her? Or was the fever going to break anyway and this was all a coincidence?

Her heart began to pound. *Am I really doing this? Healing human beings?* Suddenly the reality of it struck her, with all its ramifications: If it was true, word would spread. She would be in constant demand, her life wouldn't be her own.

She wanted to run somewhere, anywhere.

Chapter 17

"So, about Jamie's mother. Do you think you helped her?" Michael waited while he heard rustling through the phone.

Eva said, "Hang on a minute—Cookie's digging a hole under a tree." He heard her shout, "Cookie, stop that. Come on, let's go, it's a million degrees out here!"

Then she was back. She replied, with a sigh, "I don't know. Maybe. Unless it's all a coincidence and she was getting better anyway."

Having witnessed the power of her gift firsthand, that didn't ring true to Michael. "Unlikely," he replied.

"I don't know what to make of the whole thing," Eva said. "It felt the same as when I hold an animal. But it took a whole lot of conscious effort. I was wiped out afterward. Why, Michael? Why would it take this much more work to heal human beings?"

"I don't know..."

"With animals, it's effortless. I feel better afterward, even invigorated. This time I felt drained."

"That bit doesn't make sense," he said. *As if any of it made sense. I mean, what must it feel like to heal like that? With your intent, with your mind?* Years and years of studying, and thousands of dollars later, he did succeed. With animals. Some of the time.

She was quiet, and he couldn't imagine what she was thinking. "Eva?"

"Yeah, I'm here. Just thinking... Perhaps humans have a bigger spiritual footprint than an animal. Maybe that explains it. Maybe when I'm healing a human being, I'm faced with a spirit that's the same size as mine, more or less. So, it takes more out of me..."

"Isn't that giving human beings too much credit? Are people really more spiritually advanced than animals?"

Eva gave a guffaw. "No idea."

"So, when can I see you? How many days do you have to isolate?"

"I should know by tomorrow. The techs said four days to be sure, with viral pneumonia. Jamie and I were stupid to be in contact with her mom without masks. I can't believe we didn't even think about that."

"OK, when you're clear, which I'm sure you are, how about the weekend? Let's do something fun."

"I can't this weekend. I've got Chloe's house concert, and then Sunday we're going to my father's birthday party. At the Hastings 'compound.' Not sure that qualifies as fun. And imagine that, 'my father.' That's the first time I've said those words out loud."

"Congratulations," Michael said.

"Not sure congratulations are in order. He's strange, *my father*. There, I said it again." She laughed. "And a little on the difficult side, I think..."

"All that wealth."

"Does that automatically create narcissism? Well, on second thought, no, it can't, because Chloe isn't narcissistic."

"I'd like to meet her." When Eva didn't respond, he realized it sounded like he was fishing for an invitation. He quickly changed the subject. "It's a shame about your isolation, for another reason. We have a kitten here—he's about twelve weeks old—with terrible diarrhea that's just not responding to meds. We've tried everything. The little thing is fading fast."

"Oh, no, that's awful."

"We have him on IV antibiotics and saline, and he's in the isolation room, just to be safe. If he makes it through the night, we have to decide in the morning whether to euthanize him."

"Oh, Michael." Eva groaned. "You know I don't dare go."

"Even if you kept your distance and were careful with masks and gloves?"

"Damn, I feel like a pariah..."

There was a pause.

"I shouldn't have told you. Forget I mentioned it," Michael said.

"The poor little thing. But I'd feel awful if someone got viral pneumonia from me."

Michael ended the call with "I miss you," and was surprised and thrilled when Eva answered, "I miss you, too." As he shoved the phone into his pocket it occurred to him she'd spoken without thinking. Was that the only way he was going to get close to this woman? Surprise her?

---•• ◆ ••---

"I miss you," Michael had said. Eva had said it back, and realized, as she tossed the phone on her desk, that she did. She really did. But she wished she hadn't said it. It was moving too fast. And she wasn't sure where. Oddly, she appreciated these few days of forced isolation, to collect herself, to figure out how to handle the new conundrum that was Michael Lowery. What was it he wanted, marriage and kids? Wasn't that for other people? How could she have children, not knowing if she'd be there to see them grow up?

She didn't know the answers. And it was no use thinking she could return to the life she had before she had met him, before she learned of her healing gift, back to the life where she knew "alone," and did it well. Everything had changed.

As she tried to work, a question kept haunting her, relating to this ability to heal. A persistent question that demanded an answer: *Why me?* But there was no answer, and if she'd expected God to appear from the heavens to explain it to her, she was out of luck. There was just silence. A silence ringing with hollowness, like a shout in a canyon between two mountains.

She felt jumpy and out of sorts, as if someone had poured a mild acid on her nervous system.

And she couldn't stop thinking about that poor little cat at the clinic. Now that was something she believed she could do something about. She simply couldn't let the kitten die if she could prevent it.

At six o'clock, as she drove to the veterinary clinic, she reviewed her decision. Creep in, covered in protective gear, help the young cat, and creep out, without being discovered. She knew most of the staff at Michael's clinic went home between five and six o'clock, leaving just a skeleton crew. She also knew that the back door, which led directly to the exam rooms, was open until the facility was locked up by the last person there.

The plan held. The back door creaked ominously when she peered through it so she waited for a minute, but it seemed no one had heard. Creeping down the back hall, she pulled on a disposable gown and gloves and found the kitten in the isolation room. The little cat was terribly thin and lay still on the floor of his cage. She didn't even see his chest rising and falling with his breath. Was she too late? The mat under him was stained with the diarrhea dripping from him.

Her heart ached as she scooped him up and held him gently against her body. She knew he was near death, she could feel it. His spirit was hardly perceptible. The dehydration, exhaustion, and pain had taken a tremendous toll.

She crooned and murmured to the little cat, treasuring the weary little creature. "Come on back, little one. Come on back to us. You can do it," she whispered. For many minutes she focused, feeling the connection, the vibration. And floating in the deep, dark space.

It was quite some time before Eva came back from wherever she'd gone with him. But she thought she brought him with her. The kitten's energy seemed better, stronger.

But something drew her attention. Glancing up quickly at the door, she saw Jerry staring at her through the glass. He was holding an N-95 mask to his face, which he pulled into position. He pulled open the door.

When he spoke, his voice was grim. "You've been exposed to someone with viral pneumonia, Michael tells me."

She began to speak but he cut her off.

"Then what are you doing here, girl? I know you know better. It's airborne, like colds and flu. What are you thinking?"

She stood up and carefully lay the young cat back in the cage and closed the door, grateful, oddly, for the face covering, to mask the heat in her face. "I'm completely covered as you can see and have not touched anything without gloves." She held up her hands.

"OK, not enough. You're supposed to be isolating. Aren't you?"

"Yes, but—"

He repeated, "You know better. But even so, why are you here? In this room?"

Eva looked back at the kitten, who lifted his head and gave a small meow. She kept quiet, knowing nothing she said would make sense to Jerry unless she told him the truth. And she couldn't do that. That would *certainly* not make sense to him.

"I'm sorry," she said. "I shouldn't have come. Please, step back, away from the door, and I'll leave immediately."

After a pause, Jerry muttered something she couldn't quite hear and stepped back a few feet to let her pass. Hurrying down the hall, she disposed of the gloves and paper gown in the receptacle by the back door. Wiping the handle of the door down with an alcohol wipe, she turned to see Jerry watching her. He shook his head, his brow furrowed.

———•••◆•••———

"I tell you, it's amazing," Jerry said, the next morning, shaking his head. "Last night this kitten was near death. I thought we should euthanize him, but you talked me out of it, Michael. You were right. Did you change the antibiotic?"

Michael shook his head. *Eva. She must have come after all.* Now, how was he going to get through this without betraying her confidence? And without lying? The "when" about telling other people had to be her decision.

He'd arrived at the clinic to find Jerry, Nina, and Roxanne in the isolation room. As desperately sick as the kitten was, last night, now he was sitting up, a hind leg straight up in the air as he washed it. Then he rubbed his head against Nina's hand when she reached in to pet him and he began to purr. Michael could see he'd eaten—the food bowl was empty.

"It's *beyond* amazing, Jerry," Nina said. "It seems impossible. And this is not the first 'miracle' that's happened around here lately." She looked up from the cat, at Jerry, then at Michael, eyebrows raised.

Michael looked away, uncomfortable. He could feel her eyes on him.

Jerry turned to Michael. "By the way, I saw your friend, Eva, here last night, and I confess I was upset with her. Isolation does not mean it's OK to endanger everyone here..." To Roxanne and Nina, he added, "Did either of you see her?"

Roxanne looked up sharply. "Eva was here? Last night? Why?"

"Damned if I know," Jerry replied. "Yes, in this room. I was checking on the kitten before I went home, and there she was, bold as brass, sitting and holding him."

Nina spoke quietly. "You know, Jerry, Eva is the common denominator in this situation."

"What do you mean?" Jerry asked.

Nina turned to Michael. "You saw Eva holding that calico cat the day before its tumor vanished, right? And remember the orange cat she brought over that suddenly turned out *not* to be diabetic? And it's not just happening here. Jake tells me there have been similar things happening recently at the shelter. Things he can't explain. All coincidence?" She took a deep breath. "Now, don't scoff. You'll think I've lost my mind, but could Eva be healing them... somehow?"

Jerry gave a whoop of laughter that trailed away when he realized no one else was laughing.

"I've been wondering the exact same thing," Roxanne said, slowly.

Jerry stared at them. "You guys are serious?"

"Is there another explanation?" Nina turned to Michael. "Could she have given them something...? Care to chime in?"

Michael said nothing. He had no idea how to navigate this.

Jerry stared, then laughed again. "Wouldn't that be just awesome?" He shook his head, and still chuckling, headed for the door. "Sign me up for lessons in how to do *that*. Now, I must get on."

Michael, too, made for the front desk, to start his day. For the next couple of hours, he saw pets, took notes, prescribed meds, and tried to focus fully on each task. But he couldn't stop thinking about Eva. She must have helped the kitten. Nothing else made sense. Each time she performed these amazing feats of healing, it sank in further. She was indeed doing it. She was responsible for these miracles. If he was this blown away by the reality of it, how must Eva be feeling? He couldn't wait until her isolation period was over.

Michael was stirring cream into coffee in the break room when Nina came in.

"There you are. I called Eva and asked her outright," she said quietly.

Michael waited.

"She described what she does when she holds an animal." She paused. "Just with her energy. But she didn't sound 100 percent sure."

"Well, *I'm* sure." Michael sipped his coffee. "There've been numerous miraculous recoveries. She goes in and out of denial. Understandably. But there's no doubt, Nina."

"But wait, you *knew*?"

"Sorry. But it wasn't my secret to tell. She was hoping to contain it."

"But, Michael, how?" Nina's voice was incredulous.

Michael threw his hands up. "I have absolutely no idea. Neither does she, by the way." Relief flooded through him that Nina now knew. He realized how much he had wanted to share this.

"I knew there was something special about that young woman... But still, it's hard to get my brain around. I mean, it's unbelievable. Could we get her to work here? Can you imagine what we could *do*? Do you think she'd do it—come work for us?"

"I think she'd love to. Not sure how the rest of the staff would feel."

Nina paused, then looked up at Michael, her brow furrowed. "The implications, Michael. My God. Spiritual, philosophic, even religious... Do you realize the *enormity* of this?"

Michael sighed. The enormity had been weighing on him for days. He didn't speak.

Nina stopped suddenly and looked at Michael. "What?"

Michael spoke slowly. "I'm concerned about Eva, what all this will do to her. What about when the press and social media catches on? It's going to be a zoo—it will go viral."

"Ah. So, it's true." Nina smiled. "I thought so. You two are an item." She paused. "Serious?"

"Yes. Certainly, for my part. But she's had it hard, no family, really. She's somewhat closed off... Sometimes I can get through, and then other times she shuts me out, sort of disappears into herself." Michael stopped himself. "Sorry. It's just that I'm worried about her. Especially when the world finds out she can also heal people."

Nina stared. "You know this for sure?"

"We believe so. Just once, her roommate's mother. But there's no other explanation that makes sense."

"Oh, my God." She spoke slowly. "If it's true, you do realize her life is never going to be the same again?"

Michael had been trying not to think about that.

Chapter 18

Eva breathed a sigh of relief. Friday morning, after four days of isolating at home, she was clear. No symptoms. She felt like celebrating and planned on doing just that with Michael that evening. He had asked her to dinner at the Brass Door, which she'd heard about, but she'd never been. Way too pricey.

On a whim, she ventured out to the outlet mall, where she hunted through row after row of dresses until she found just what she was looking for. It was perfect: a soft, flowered, summer dress, which clung to her waist and flared gently to her knees. Pretty, but not ostentatious. Splurging, she bought a pair of blingy sandals to go with it.

As she lay in a warm bubble bath early that evening, she thought about the plans for the next couple of days. She had toyed, briefly, with asking Michael to accompany her to the weekend's events. But only briefly. The house concert at Chloe's was one thing. But her father's 50th birthday party the next day? She didn't know what kind of madness she was going to be facing or how to handle it. She didn't want to put him through it.

There was something more, something she certainly wouldn't share with Michael. She hardly knew how to handle the new situation—was it a relationship? —with him yet, let alone add in the stress of her new family. For the very first time, she was going to meet her grandparents, her half-brother, and two half-sisters. One challenge at a time.

But there was tonight. And she planned to make the most of it.

The bath water was almost cold when she realized it was later than she thought. She heard Jamie greeting Michael at the door and chatting to him in the living room. And Eva was just stepping out of the tub. She quickly slid into her new dress and sandals, brushed her hair until it shone, in long soft waves, and even used a bit of mascara and lipstick for the occasion. For Michael.

It paid off.

When she came through the doorway of the living room, he saw her, jumped up from the couch, and his eyes grew large. "Wow. You look sensational."

"Sorry. I kept you waiting."

"Not to worry. It was worth it."

"Michael and I were getting to know each other," said Jamie, with a grin.

Just looking at Michael took Eva's breath away. Black silk shirt and slacks with a gray blazer, those long legs, and all that dark hair.

He hugged her, buried his face in her hair, and groaned softly. When he kept his arms wrapped around her and held her close, she reveled in his warmth, his strength. He smelled male, of soap, and a bit like wood shavings. He pulled back and grinned, then kissed her again and again, as if he hadn't seen her for weeks. Her whole body began to tingle and hum.

"Get a room, you two, for God's sake," Jamie said.

"You're just jealous," said Michael.

"You better believe it," shot back Jamie.

"Uh, wait a minute..." Eva was dumbstruck. "What?"

"Like she said, we've been getting to know each other," Michael said with a grin.

Jamie's secret was out?

"Oh, hell, Eva, I just decided it was time to get over myself," Jamie said. "Michael made me laugh about it." She punched him lightly on the arm.

Then Jamie gave Eva a quick hug. Softly, in her ear, she whispered, "We're good, Eva. And this guy's a keeper."

Eva let out a breath. Until that moment she hadn't realized how uncomfortable she still felt around Jamie since her revelation. But she couldn't help but wonder... Michael had learned about Jamie's feelings in the twenty minutes it took her to get dressed? It never failed to amaze her when people were so open about personal things. It was as if Jamie had released steam off a pressure cooker with her confession, from which she'd been suffering for years.

In the car, Eva told Michael about the blogger at the shelter. "It'll be nothing. I only knew of him because Jamie found a blog he'd written about one of her clients. He's small potatoes as media goes—I'm sure it won't amount to anything. And I'll talk to Roxanne and the others at the clinic and ask them to keep it to themselves."

"Hope you're right," Michael said. "What's the name of the blog?"

"GsGs.com. For Gleason's Gleanings."

"Cute."

"He has a biggish Twitter and Tiktok presence. Real extreme. Hyperbolic hair-on-fire stuff. And he's a born-again type, too. Hellfire and brimstone. Wait, I have his card." She dug through her purse until she found it.

Michael pulled into a parking spot at the restaurant. He studied the card. "Roger Gleason. OK, I'll check it out."

"Good. Now let's stick it on a shelf and forget it, OK?"

The Brass Door surpassed expectations and reviews. For that matter, the evening itself surpassed expectations. Michael shared stories of his family's camping trips to the Berkshires in the summer, of drool-worthy steaks over an open flame, of trips hiking along the Appalachian Trail. She told him how she'd become close friends with Jamie in middle school. The conversation ebbed and flowed. They chatted about their love of scuba diving, her experience swimming with dolphins, even the new stainless-steel pans he wanted for his kitchen.

They avoided the topics of a new father and healing.

Full of buttery scallops and cheesecake, she floated on the drive home. But peace evaded her, as did the answer to a question hovering in the back of her mind. What to do about the end of this evening? Maybe she should just have sex with him, now, tonight. Maybe then this overwhelming need to be close to him would ease. Maybe he'd stop wooing her heart because he'd think he had won it. But her armor would still be intact.

However, it could throw her in the deep end, and bring up the whole commitment question. That had tanked her relationship with Zach. As good a swimmer as she was, part of her now longed to stay in the shallow end. Now she was just sitting on the steps with only her feet wet.

Zach had wanted more and she knew Michael certainly wasn't in this just for sex. But it was clear he wanted it. He was a man, after all. She grinned. And the way she responded to him, to his kisses... *Tell the truth, it's hard to think of anything else when he's near.*

And Jamie was away for the night. She had the house to herself.

She had no idea how or if lovemaking would be different with Michael. But with this man, there was something... indefinable. Power in the touch, power in the sensation, power in the connection. For right here and right now she wanted to experience that power. Perhaps life was too short to pass some things up. Especially for her.

Oh, there was that flock of tiny birds flapping around in her stomach again... *Hang on.* That swoony feeling was just a symptom of sexual attraction, of arousal, not undying love and devotion.

She didn't have to be in love to have sex, she thought with a grin.

Chapter 19

It turned out her nerves were not necessary. As they left the restaurant, he simply asked, "My place or yours?" She heard herself say, "Mine."

Inside her front door, he just took her hand, led her upstairs, and said, "Let's go to bed," as if they had been married for a lifetime. But that's where the similarity to an old married couple ceased. What happened in that bedroom was unlike anything she'd ever experienced. Or could have even imagined.

He drew her toward her bed, slipped off her glasses, and lay them on the nightstand. Running his fingers through the long waves of her hair, he then gathered it up in one hand and pulled her close with the other. His lips met hers in soft kiss after soft kiss, each becoming deeper, longer, more searching.

Icy fire raced through her.

Sex, in Eva's experience, had always felt hurried. This lack of haste, this measured action, was so contrary to her expectations that it achieved the opposite. She wanted him, right now. "Hurry," she implored him.

He whispered in her ear. "We have all night."

His actions were magnificently slow, his touch magnificently gentle. In slow motion, he undressed her. After slipping the straps of the new dress off her shoulder, he reached around to unzip it, and it dropped to the ground. He ran his hands down her shoulders, down her arms.

"You're so beautiful," he murmured.

She clutched the front of his shirt, near his waist, and he stripped it off over his head, not bothering with the buttons. Looping her arms around his neck, she kissed him, deeper and deeper, marveling at the heat, even the sizzle, his flesh created where it touched hers.

Had she been dead before tonight? Or numb? She'd never felt much in early caresses, but now these light touches set her squirming. Scooping her up as if she weighed nothing at all, he lay her down on the bed. She relaxed into his tempo, closing her eyes, slowing everything down. As she did, every sense heightened. His touch created fire, everywhere. Eva never knew what was coming next. It was a dance, but unchoreographed, natural, organic. As if connected to electricity, as if plugged into a low-grade power socket.

She could feel his hunger. It was fierce, but his actions were controlled. He pleasured her in every possible way, with what seemed to her to be a conscious awareness of her, of her wants, of her needs. As they made love, she didn't speak, made no sound at all. She couldn't. She was held in a deep ocean of warm water in a timeless, weightless age.

She could sense his eyes on hers, and looking up, her eyes met his. He held the gaze. "Stay, stay with me," he murmured. "Don't let go, don't look away, don't close your eyes, stay with me, float with me." She was lost in sensation, lost in his eyes, lost in the deep pool of warm pleasure.

As she at last let go, a shower of sparks filled her. She cried out, spinning and melting, as she heard Michael breathe her name.

He cried out, collapsed onto her, but almost immediately began to lift himself up.

She held on tight. "Don't go, it's fine. Stay."

"I'm too heavy."

"Stay."

They lay, just breathing, for a long time. His heart pounded against hers. As if it longed to join with hers into one huge heart. He was doubly connected to her by a lake of sweat between their chests and stomachs.

This was the first time she had ever had sex. She nearly said it aloud, stopping herself just in time. It would have been a ridiculous thing to say. But it certainly was the first time she *got it*. Why sex seemed to control the world.

He rolled onto his back and pulled her into his shoulder. Nestling into him, she buried her face in his neck.

He kissed the top of her head. "I love your hair," he said.

"I usually wear it up, it's hot in the summer."

"And you attract less attention to yourself."

She smiled.

They lay quietly for several minutes, regaining their breath. She felt as if she had to come back from somewhere. Somewhere she had been with this man.

"You ever been in love?" Michael asked.

"I... don't think so."

"Well, from everything I've read and seen, I think if you had been, you'd know it."

She chuckled into his shoulder. "So, the answer is no, then. How about you?"

"Not since I've been an adult."

"Excuse me?"

"When I was nine," he said, "there was Becca Barlow—doesn't that sound like a movie star? Talk about bowled over. Trembling, absolutely speechless in her presence. Then one day she enticed me back behind the gym, kissed me, and asked me if I wanted to see her panties. Thought I'd pass out from the bliss—thought my love was complete. Until I found out the next day, she'd taken Timmy

Wilson behind the gym, too. So basically, she was just a flasher in training."

Eva laughed. "You poor boy."

"And then when I was fourteen, it struck again. Mrs. Ackerman, my English teacher. Oh my God. Petite, gorgeous, the most beautiful thing I'd ever seen." His voice grew wistful. "She had long chestnut hair she wore on top of her head in huge curls and waves, held in place by clips and pins. She looked like she should be wearing a velvet band around her neck, with a cameo, like those paintings of Edwardian ladies. Oh, and she smelled like magnolia blossoms." He sighed. "I'd grown up from the nine-year-old passion, so I didn't tremble or shake this time, but I was pretty much struck dumb around her."

"But you've escaped the whole in-love thing since, huh?"

"Jury's out," he said.

He climbed out of the bed, saying, "Back in a minute." Naked, yet with a complete lack of self-consciousness, he headed for the bathroom, bringing her back a glass of water, and her terrycloth bathrobe slung over one arm.

She watched him walk back. He looked great in clothes... *that black shirt and jeans, oh my.* But naked he was a sight to behold. His confidence, that comfort in his skin, the way he moved. Yes, everything about him was superb.

He tossed the bathrobe on the end of the bed. "I hope you won't wear that, but it might make you more comfortable." He climbed under the sheet, drew her back to him. "Ah," he breathed.

That was the last thing she remembered. In the middle of the night, she stumbled to the bathroom and was touched when Michael woke and asked if she was OK. On her return to the bed, he pulled her close again.

The next thing she knew, dawn sunlight streamed in, painting his torso with pale light. She lay quietly on her side, waking up slowly to the beauty of this man. He lay on his back, his head and face turned toward her, and she studied the long eyelashes resting on his cheek with its deep summer tan. His hair fell onto his forehead in a thick wave. She raised up on one elbow. The sheet only covered him to his waist, so her eyes were able to feast on his body. The sanding and other construction work kept him in great shape, his chest muscles were certainly impressive. The black hair on his chest tapered down to lean waist and hips, then disappeared beneath the sheet.

She longed to touch but didn't want to disturb him, or the moment.

In her mind, she said his name.

Michael.

His eyes opened and she saw the pleasure on his face. He smiled and his eyes crinkled. He yawned. "Good morning."

"Hi."

"Did you say something?"

She shook her head and when he lifted his arm in invitation, she slid over to rest her head on his shoulder. She reveled in the warm, soft touch of his skin next to hers and the sensual musky fragrance of recent sex. She felt a frisson of arousal. *After last night, how is that even possible?*

Was last night real? The slight burn of rarely used body parts told her it had been. As did the whisker burns on her breasts and chin. Plus, that dull pressure deep down.

Morning kisses usually left something to be desired. Like a thorough brushing of teeth, for a start. But not this kiss. It was tender but filled with renewed energy from a night of sleep. It was intensely sweet, intensely intimate, intensely connected. He wrapped his arms around her. Everywhere their skin touched they fit as if they had been together for years, not hours.

This kind of arousal was new, though. Completely new.

The gentleness of his hands as they held her head, the strength of his body as it pressed against her, sent a thrill through her. She remembered the bliss of last night and it was not far away. Michael growled low in his chest, then his lips took hers once more.

She burst into flames as the sudden peak of heat and passion took her. She pulled him into her as if he belonged there, belonged inside her. It was almost a continuation of last night's experience, as if they hadn't been asleep at all. They moved together as the intensity of the feeling grew and grew and this time she stayed lost in his eyes.

A sense of expansion. A sense of opening. He was everything and everything was him. She was drawing all of him into her. No, it was as if she were pulling *everything* inside her—all of nature, all energy, all life. It filled her and she grew and grew until she merged with all there was. Deep, deep water, like the universe below the sea, surrounded and filled her. She was the water. Her heart grew, her body grew, her mind grew, like a sea flower opening.

Once again, the electric energy coursed through her veins, through her cells, and yes, through her heart.

I can't tell him this... This sexual experience with Michael Lowery was feeling all the love she had for her mother, for Sophie, for Jamie, all the love she had for all the animals she had ever held.... It held the shadow of the healing energy. It held her affinity for deep water. It carried the beauty and bliss of divine music. It was all wrapped together in this expansion of her spirit. Triggered and sparked into fire by this man.

As one they peaked. She overflowed and melted, and believed, for a long moment, that the universe had flooded all its power and mystery into her.

When he slowly pulled away and lay on his back, she floated.

And she wondered.

This was a new type of connection.

Long minutes passed.

Then, right by her ear, his voice was deep and throaty. "What are you thinking about?"

"Nothing, I'm just basking, just floating." She couldn't tell him. She had to put all those thoughts away in a tight plastic container at the back of the shelf to be brought out and examined at another time. When she was alone.

"Eva." He stroked her waist and hip. She shivered. He pulled the sheet up to cover her. "You're cold. But I want nothing between us... I envy that sheet." He smiled.

His eyes were above hers and his face just inches away. He bent down and kissed her again in a long, open kiss. He stroked her hair out across the pillow, kissed each eye, then the tip of her nose. "Are you OK?"

She nodded.

"For me," Michael said, "with you... it's a little like scuba diving. That first dive, when you go deeper and deeper, into that endless volume of water. It's dark, it's warm, it's silent. Everything of the world disappears. There's nothing but the water. And you and me."

He is using some of the same images.

"You communicate better than most men," she murmured.

He chuckled. "Remember, five sisters. To get a word in edgewise I had to learn to compete."

"You learned well. You're doing great."

Suddenly she heard words, in her head. *But I'm not. Oh, wait, did I say that out loud?*

"It was like being in a deep, warm, pool," he said. "Safe, erotic, connecting us with everything."

"All that? So, I take it this was not just a quick lay?" She laughed. It sounded a little shrill to her own ears.

His eyes shuttered and for a few seconds, he didn't reply. Then, in a quiet voice, he said, "No."

He turned back to lie flat, but then sat up and headed for the bathroom. "Got to shower, get this show on the road. Luke will be at my place soon."

She heard the shower start to run.

Turning on her side and staring at the wall, she blinked a few times, hard. Her eyes were stinging. For some reason she couldn't explain, she felt like weeping.

She didn't have to fall in love to have sex. That's what she said.

But she hadn't encountered Michael Lowery before.

Chapter 20

Why did I say that? A quick lay? Seriously?

Eva had meant to just lighten the mood, but she knew immediately she'd hurt him. Or made him angry. She wasn't sure which. And she couldn't take it back.

Kicking herself, she made her escape while Michael was in the shower. She didn't know how to face him, so left him a note that just said, "Gone for a walk with Cookie..." She tucked an x and o at the end, called her dog, and took off on a speed walk around the country lanes.

I mean, what was that?

She needed to get back to normalcy, to her life as she knew it before. Before everything had spun out of control.

Arriving home, she saw Michael's car was gone, and her phone dinged with a text from him.

> My exquisite lover. Sorry I didn't get to
> say goodbye. A kiss for each of your
> beautiful eyes. xx Call when you can.

She was clutching the phone so hard her knuckles were white. Shoving the phone back in her pocket, she groaned. Cookie whined, and she reached down to fondle the pup's head. "Sorry, Cookie."

On the way north to Chloe's, Eva couldn't resist a brief stop at Narragansett Beach, but as she suspected, it was jammed, as all the beaches must be on this perfect Saturday. There would be no peace amidst all the people and mp3 players and kids shouting. She let Cookie have a quick run, then kept driving.

"You get to stay with Juliette and Jesse tonight, Cookie, it will be fun. A doggie sleep-over!" Eva was staying at her aunt's that night, then they planned to go together to her father's party on Sunday. Eva had struggled with the decision to go, but eventually decided it was as good an opportunity as any to meet the rest of her family. There'd be other people around to act as a buffer and the focus would be on her father for his fiftieth birthday.

Maybe the rest of the new family would not be as difficult as Hastings himself.

She helped Chloe make veggie burgers and salad and they ate on the patio in the softness of the late afternoon sun. Three pairs of dog eyes followed every bite from plate to mouth like synchronized staring.

"Ignore my two, Eva. They'll look piteous and try to get you to think I starve them." Chloe shooed them, pointing to the woods. "Go, go on, go play. No begging." The springers gave them a last pitiful look from big brown eyes, then wandered off toward the meadow and woods, with Cookie trailing after them.

Chloe turned back to Eva. "Good about Jamie's mom. Glad to hear that. Being asthmatic makes her vulnerable to things like pneumonia."

Gazing down, unseeing, at her plate, Eva spoke slowly. "I think I might've had a hand in that."

Chloe cocked her head and her eyebrows raised in a question.

"You're going to think I'm crazy," Eva muttered.

"I doubt that."

Pushing her salad plate away, Eva slowly, hesitantly, told her aunt about the first couple of times healing animals in Michael's clinic. How this had become more and more obvious with each healing. Until any chance it was a coincidence had been put to rest. Until there was simply no doubt about it. Unlike the reaction she'd had from Jamie or Jake, Chloe didn't express shock or disbelief. Her eyes grew huge, and she just drew in a long slow breath. Then the corners of her mouth turned up in a tiny smile. "Yes," was all she said.

Eva said, "I don't understand it..." The floodgates opened, and the words poured out thick and fast. She described the vibration, the connection, the deep floating state, as best she could. And she finished with the recent experience with Jamie's mother. "It's like a miracle, every time, and I don't even know how it's happening, Chloe. Why me? I don't understand!"

Chloe touched her arm gently. "It doesn't surprise me at all, Eva. I knew the moment I met you..." She leaned back, and Eva could see her searching for the right words. "You were special. You are special. There's just something about you. You have a... a presence, yes, that's it. Presence."

Eva stared at her.

"And really, my dear," Chloe continued, "what a gift." She studied Eva, her face animated. "A spectacular gift. I've always believed people could heal. We've lost touch with our spirituality... But this is no different than a great surgeon saving lives. You just do it differently. With energy." She clasped her hands together. "That I lived to see this, I'm grateful. And excited for you. How do you plan to handle it?"

Eva shook her head and let out the breath she'd been holding. "I haven't got that far. I have to learn to deal with the fact that I couldn't... that I didn't... help my own mother. Or Aunt Sophie." Her stomach cramped and a slight queasiness rolled over her. She lay down her fork on the plate with a clatter. "So, what good was I?"

"Sweetie, you were a child! And you didn't know what you could do. You can't blame yourself, you just can't. That would be too cruel."

"If I can heal people, and I still don't know about that, then how is it that I couldn't help them? Maybe you're right—Jamie said the same thing—that maybe I was too young, or the ability hadn't kicked in yet, or something."

"Or it's something to do with intent..." Chloe said slowly.

"What do you mean?"

"You said you've felt the vibration, the connection for a long time with animals."

"Yes," Eva replied.

"OK, and then you said this time you had to focus, to work at it, with Dr. Chin. Right?"

"Right."

"Well, you didn't know there was anything wrong with your mother. So, you never tried. And the same with Sophie."

Eva closed her eyes, taking that in. "Ok," she said slowly. "And there's something else." She told her aunt about Roger Gleason snapping her picture outside the shelter.

Chloe shook her head. "Invasive... But I guess that's to be expected. How could word not get out?" She pursed her lips. "But don't let anyone run you around or push you. If there's anything I can do to help... Or if you need to escape, come here." She gave Eva's arm a comforting squeeze. "You said 'Michael's clinic.' Who's this Michael? Someone you work with?"

"He's a veterinarian in a local clinic."

"And...?"

"And we're spending some time together."

"And...?"

Chloe was just too intuitive. Eva had to chuckle as she gazed out at the meadow beyond the flower beds and gathered her thoughts. "He is not like anyone. I react to him differently... I've never met anyone..." She gave up and shrugged. "My friend Jake's wife called him 'a hunk.'"

"Is he?"

"He is."

They both laughed this time.

Chloe's face grew serious. "What about him makes you hesitant?"

"This guy is so different So direct. Most men play mind games and dance around and flirt, and I've always hated all that." She sighed. "I can't figure him out. He's in my mind, knows my thoughts. But he's full of opposites." Eva searched for the words. "He's like a poet who plays fierce football... Or a construction worker who paints divine images." She shook her head. "Nope, none of that's right."

Chloe said, "A devastating combination of virility and tenderness?"

"Huh..." Eva thought. "Wow, yeah, that. Thank you."

"I've experienced it. But isn't that a good thing?"

Eva said before she thought, "It's dangerous."

"Why dangerous?"

She shook her head. Shrugged again.

"Does he have a dark side?"

"I haven't seen it. But he must of course. But it isn't that. He's super easy to be with. Fun. Kind. Sexy as hell."

"And he's crazy about you."

"Well... let's just say he's pretty interested."

Chloe was silent. Then she spoke softly. "Then there's something else."

Eva looked up and met her aunt's searching eyes. She spoke slowly. "My mother died, at thirty-one, of a burst brain aneurysm. I have the same aneurysm, it's hereditary. Confirmed by an MRI a few months after my mom died."

"Oh... Oh no. Oh, Eva." The shock was clear on Chloe's face. "I'm sorry. I hate it, I hate that you're living with that." She shook her head. Quietly, she asked, "You've told Michael?"

"Yes. He said we have to make the most of the time we have."

"Well. All I can say is 'Oh my.' He sounds amazing, Eva."

"I keep thinking I should end it before it gets out of hand."

"Why?"

Eva searched for words. "I don't know. I'd... rather be alone, I don't want..." She trailed off.

Chloe watched and waited. "You've told him about the aneurysm. Isn't it his choice now? That is, if you like him, and want to keep seeing him?"

Eva sighed.

Chloe leaned over and patted her hand. "You don't know yet. Then my suggestion is, don't overthink it."

An hour later, after cleaning up in the kitchen, while Chloe worked with a couple of volunteers setting up chairs for the concert, Eva stepped through the glass doors of the solarium. It was now transformed into a concert venue. A large room, it held about 50 chairs, the front row of which stopped just before a small, raised stage. More of a dais. Candles cast a soft glow from wrought iron sconces, which graced the wall spaces between the huge windows.

About seven o'clock, people began to arrive. Chloe knew most of them, greeting many by name. The room was soon full. The light dimmed, and there were a few moments of anticipatory silence, and darkness, except for flickering candlelight. Then a spotlight lit up a young man, who looked to be in his early twenties, as he approached the stage. She heard Chloe's voice over a mic, announcing: "Please welcome, Kip Ryan!" The audience broke into applause. He picked up an acoustic guitar, perched on a stool in the spotlight, tossed his shoulder-length hair back from his eyes, and began to play and sing.

By the second song, Eva felt this might be an important debut of someone of the caliber of John Mayer, James Taylor, or John Legend. Here was a significant talent, with a sweet but soulful tenor voice, and masterful skill on his instrument. But it was even more than that. He was charismatic, intense, hard to look away from, with his big brown eyes revealing a sensitive soul. His face was a screen, on which emotions played. He seemed to lose himself as he sang each poignant song, unaware of the people watching him and listening. In between numbers, he connected with his audience, with his quick bright smile, his warm, self-effacing chat.

There was one song in particular, near the end, which gave her goosebumps. The chorus returned again and again to a soaring hook line that followed her all the rest of the evening. It was a plaintive cry: "Let me love you tonight." Her mind was drawn to Michael. She could smell him, taste him, still feel him. She could feel the warmth of his body, skin to skin, as he held her. She could still see his eyes, the way they had looked at her last night, so warm, so open to her. Open for her.

What do I do with the feelings this man stirs in me?

---◆◆◆◆◆---

"EVA: A MIRACLE HEALER?"

There it was. Sunday morning, on her phone, Eva spotted the headline on GsGs.com. The landing page held the image of her sitting on the bench in front of the shelter, holding the black cat, Shadow, in a towel. She scanned down to read the short article. Someone, according to Gleason, had waxed lyrical about her "mysterious and powerful ability to heal." So, Gleason had kept the source's name out of it. But not her own. He'd included her full name and the name of the shelter where she volunteered, but at least her home address wasn't there. She scrolled down to the bottom of the blog—there were already eighty-four comments. And they ran the gamut.

"Bullshit, fake news!"

"There's no such thing as energy healing."

"Amazing, could it be true?"

"Blasphemy! Only Jesus can heal."

Icy cold ran through her blood.

She flipped over to Twitter, found the business profile of GsGs, listed there as Gleasons Gleanings, and found there were more than 58,000 followers. Not huge, but big enough. What if this story was picked up and slammed around the internet?

"So, you've seen it, then." Chloe stood, holding an iPad, in the doorway of the guest bedroom. Her phone dinged in her hand. It was Michael, asking if she was OK, telling her not to worry. Wishing her luck for the party. Then Jamie, expressing shock. Then Colleen, another friend from college, who lived in Fairfield County and wrote "WTH?" Then Jake from the shelter offering support.

This Gleason guy must have a wider following than I thought.

Her secret was out.

Chapter 21

"Oh..." Eva gasped, involuntarily.

By noon, after an hour's drive, she and Chloe had approached the coast of Massachusetts and turned onto a mile-long private road through forests and meadows. This culminated in high stone walls and giant wrought iron gates, behind which she could see a mansion. That was the only word for it. She stared. It looked like images she had seen of chateaus in France. Elegant and rustic at the same time, it was built of beige stone, with various steeply slanted roof lines, tall sash windows, some of which were arched to match the oak door. A matching arch adorned the porte-cochere which stood guard over the entrance. The imposing structure reigned over a collection of smaller buildings: stone gatehouse, guest house, garage, servants' quarters. She had no idea what anyone did with all that space.

Chloe said, "It is rather grand, isn't it?"

"Understatement?" Eva muttered.

Chloe grinned. "They call it French Provincial style. Imagine growing up here... It was my norm until I realized other people didn't live the same way. My parents had this place built in the seventies when we were kids. Before that, we lived in Boston. They've been adding to it since then—tennis courts, the conservatory, the walled vegetable garden back there." She pointed beyond the porte-cochere to the back of the property.

Taking a breath, Eva shook her head in amazement. "How did you escape it?"

"Escape it? The weight of wealth?" Chloe asked, with a smile.

"Yeah, I guess."

"Well, I always found it something of a burden. Now it's a blessing, now that I know what to do with it. My dad always reveled in it all. Until the stroke, that is. He's discovered all the money in the world doesn't give you back your health." She paused. "Anyway, I think he always thought he'd been born in the wrong time. He'd have been right at home in the Gilded Age, Robber Baron and all that, rubbing elbows with Astor or Rockefeller." She waved at the mansion ahead of them, and gazed around, as if seeing the estate for the first time, through Eva's eyes.

Chloe smiled at the security guard at the gate, who waved them through. Driving through the porte-cochere, Eva took in the rolling lawns, pavilion-sized tent, garages, and a line of cars parked neatly to one side. Closer to the house Eva could see a pool and veranda area where at least fifty or sixty people milled about, drinks in hand. Caterers in white moved through the guests, with champagne and hors d'oeuvres. A waft of some heavenly savory aroma got her mouth watering, and she could just make out the sounds of a string quartet playing something baroque. Beyond the tent stood a commanding ten-foot stone wall, which curved away and disappeared from view.

Chloe pointed in the direction Eva was staring. "That's the walled kitchen garden. I'll show you later. And the greenhouses are over there." She smiled at the uniformed valet who saluted her as they climbed out of the car.

"Greenhouses? Plural?"

"Yup." She grinned at Eva. "Come on, let's go find the family."

They headed toward the people, the music, and the caterers. Eva's heart was beating fast, although she kept telling herself it didn't matter. That she didn't care what the man who was her father thought of her. But although she was not impressed with Will's behavior when she met him, she didn't have any preconceived notions about her half-siblings. Or her grandparents. Maybe she'd find a friend.

Chloe had filled her in. Eva was the oldest, and next was Jared, at twenty-three. He worked with her father in the pharma company. Then came Olivia, who was almost twenty-two. She'd flunked out of college but currently didn't seem to care. And her youngest sister, Samantha, was nineteen, and was in her second year at Boston U. Then there was her grandfather, William, (the second, Eva assumed), and her grandmother, Angela. She allowed herself to hope they might be welcoming. If indeed her grandfather was well enough to meet her.

A woman, who looked to be about ten years older than Eva, approached them from the stone path, with one hand up in a restrained wave. She was avoiding the grass, probably because of those perfect high-heeled pumps.

Chloe murmured, "Latest wife, Susanna," in Eva's ear.

Too thin, Susanna seemed a bit brittle, with perfectly coifed dark hair and long pink fingernails. She wore a beautifully cut skirt and cream-colored jacket. So overdressed for an outdoor party in the peak of summer, Eva thought, but then she noticed quite a few of the women wore what looked like cocktail dresses. Chloe's light green linen shirt and slacks with sandals looked right for the occasion, by comparison. And although she kept telling herself it didn't matter at all, she was glad Chloe had convinced her to wear the pretty new dress again today. She'd twisted her hair back up on her head, and wore flats, to not draw attention to her height. Five feet nine inches was already noticeable enough.

"Chloe, dear, lovely to see you!" The woman pulled Chloe into a stiff, brief A-frame hug, kissing the air near her sister-in-law's ear. Then she turned to Eva with a fixed smile, and said, "You must be Eva. I'm Susanna. What a pleasure."

The words had a hollow ring to them. They shook hands briefly, then Susanna slid her arm through Chloe's and led them up the stone path toward the pool and veranda.

"Is that *her*? Is that the infamous *Eva*?"

It was a strident voice, from a young woman whose arms were thrown wide as if planning an all-encompassing hug. And unaware—or didn't mind—that she was sloshing champagne from her glass. She sauntered toward them, a stunning beauty in a clingy black and white dress. Her thick chestnut hair hung in waves past her shoulders, and she wore dramatic, cat's eye sunglasses.

"My new *sister*!" the woman cried, drawing looks from the crowds of people on the veranda. Eva detected a slur in her speech. It was slight, but noticeable. It wasn't quite noon, and she was already half-drunk?

Once again, Chloe whispered a name in her ear. "Olivia. And oh, dear, she's had a few, already. And that's Samantha, just behind her."

Little Samantha trailed along in Olivia's wake. Eva wondered if the young girl knew what a sharp contrast she made to the stunning Olivia. How could she not? That must be tough. Short and rather plain, with snub nose, freckles, and nondescript sandy hair, Samantha was a shy little hedgehog next to her glamorous sister. Just nineteen, but appearing younger, she still sported baby fat, and hadn't yet found her way to any degree of style or self-confidence.

As the charismatic Olivia drew near them, all eyes were on her. Eva suspected they usually were.

"Don't you just *love* my hat?" Olivia twirled in a circle, showing off the huge black and white feathered hat. "I had to have it, I tell you, I just *had* to have it. Just like Princess somebody-or-other in England!" She slipped off the huge sunglasses, slung her free arm around Eva's waist, and gave her a squeeze. "A new sister. How thrilling." She peered closely at Eva. "And you're so *gorgeous*." She waved her sunglasses in the air and called out to the guests, now staring. "Isn't she gorgeous?"

Samantha took Olivia's arm. "Livvy, I think you should slow down on the champagne. Come on, let's go get some food."

Olivia shook her arm free. "Don't call me Livvy! And oh, yes, of course, food. That's your raison d'etre, isn't it baby sister? *Food!*" She threw her head back and laughed, a raucous sound that turned the few remaining heads in the crowd.

Samantha flushed. A flash of rage sparked in her eyes but was instantly suppressed. She muttered, "I'll be in the tent. Cooler in there.

She's trying to act nonchalant, Eva thought, as the young girl turned abruptly to walk away, plucking self-consciously at her clingy sleeveless top.

Olivia called after her. "Sorry, Sammy. Oh, come on, don't be offended, I didn't mean anything." Turning back to Eva and Chloe, but not lowering her voice, she said, "Well, honestly, if she'd stop *eating*..."

Chloe said, in a soft voice, "Olivia..."

Susanna motioned to a waiter who brought champagne and soft drinks and Olivia disappeared into a crowd of friends, having apparently forgotten all about her new sister.

Susanna said, "I'll find Will. He asked me to let him know when you two arrived." She headed for the veranda and disappeared amongst the throng of guests.

"Glad you kept your expectations low?" Chloe said to Eva with a wry grin. She gestured to the French doors leading to the house. "Ah, there's Jared, now, just coming through the doors, see? Will should be nearby."

Will Hastings was right behind his son, in animated conversation with an attractive couple in their sixties. He touched the man's shoulder and said something which set the couple laughing. Eva could see the charm for which her father was famous. He had been gifted that magnetic quality some people could switch on, to draw people like night bugs to a candle.

Her brother Jared was a younger rendition of his father. Blonde and tall, she noticed his walk was the same, his clothes were the same, his gestures were the same. How much of this was innate, how much copied? His eyes remained glued to his dad.

Susanna spoke to Will, who looked up sharply, saw Eva and Chloe, and excused himself from the couple he'd been entertaining. He strode toward them, with Jared in tow.

"Happy Birthday, little brother," Chloe called out, as he approached.

"Thank you, my dear. And Eva, thank you for coming. I didn't know if you would. I owe you an apology, Chloe tells me. I didn't mean to be a tease when we met. Just over-compensating for the stress of the situation, and I apologize. How can I make it up to you?"

Eva said, "Happy Birthday," and held out her hand to shake his, but he grabbed it and pulled her into a brief, hard hug. Then he kissed her forehead. She stiffened.

He didn't seem to notice or indeed, wait for a response from her. He released her and turned to Jared.

"This is your brother Jared," her father said. "We've all been looking forward to getting to know you."

"Hi, Jared," she said, shaking his hand.

"Hey," he replied. His eyes were wary.

"And here comes Mother." Will called back down the path, "Mother, come meet your new granddaughter!"

They started toward Will's mother, a tiny older woman, impeccably dressed and turned out, and rather imperious. Soft peachy skin was set off by the dusky gray of her dress and the fine silver jewelry at neck and wrist. She didn't come across as grandmotherly to Eva.

"Oh, my, your father's cranky today," Eva's grandmother said to Will. "He keeps telling me not to fuss. But then, he does have a lot to contend with. I think he's afraid this is as good as it gets. That it'll always be this bad..." She sighed, then saw Eva. Recognition dawned on her face. "Oh, I'm sorry, here I am, blathering on... You must be Eva. I've heard so much about you, welcome. I'm Angela Hastings." She reached out a hand.

Eva shook the offered hand and was surprised at her new grandmother's firm grasp. Not a weak, submissive old lady, at all. She smiled. "Thank you for inviting me."

"It's a pleasure to have you here. And I hope you'll be able to meet your grandfather. If not today, then soon."

Chloe asked as she kissed her mother on the cheek, "Where is Dad, can I see him?"

"I hope you will be able to say hello. I left him in the library—he's asleep, I believe," replied Angela. "Give him some time. I think the excitement of today has worn him out. I'll check on him in an hour or so." She turned back to Eva. "Well, Eva, you must feel a bit like cameras are on you, with everyone focused on you. We must find a quiet corner later and get acquainted."

Jared spoke up. "We've heard a lot about you, Eva, from Dad. But he didn't tell us you're a miracle healer."

"What, Jared? What are you talking about?" Will asked.

Eva's heart missed a beat. She heard Chloe, beside her, draw in a quick breath.

"Miracle healer? Whatever do you mean?" asked his grandmother.

Eva tried to remain calm, or at least not to show her discomfiture. The others were staring at her, then at Jared, then at her again.

And she'd wanted not to draw attention to herself.

"Jared, this is not the time or place—" Chloe said but was cut off.

"She's famous, Aunt Chloe. She's been healing animals." Jared said. "Or at least that's what you claim, right Eva?" He held out his phone, with the GsGs.com website for all to see. He handed it to his father, then he reached into a back pocket and drew out sheets of paper which he unfolded and handed to his father and grandmother. "It's fascinating, I must say, impressive. I printed out copies so we could all learn about you."

"How did you find this?" Will scanned the page.

"Our PR firm. They set up an algorithm to monitor the web. For any mention of us. Or of her. It notified me by email this morning," Jared said.

Eva longed for a chasm to appear beneath her, so she could drop in and vanish. She considered turning on her heel and escaping to the car.

Everyone grew quiet.

"Well, of course, this is a joke," said Will, looking up at Eva from the printed page.

Eva decided which tack to take. She glanced at the website header. "I've heard of that guy—he's famous for fake news and hyperbole. I help out at an animal shelter near where I live in Connecticut. So, it's true I do help animals. He must be short of real stories."

She could feel Chloe staring. Well, what she said wasn't a lie. And she wasn't ready to share her secret. These people were still strangers, family or not.

Eva's grandmother spoke firmly. "Honestly, Jared, were you trying to embarrass her? Why? What on earth were you thinking?"

Jared flushed.

Eva could feel Will's eyes on her.

Chloe spoke quickly. "I must tell you all about this fabulous young singer/songwriter I've discovered. At my house concert last night, the audience loved him. Tomorrow we're flying to Nashville to introduce him to a couple of publishers and producers that I know. He's talented, isn't he, Eva?"

The conversation shifted to music. Thanks to Chloe. But when Eva gave a surreptitious glance at Jared, his face was tense. He'd tried to catch her out. He wanted to mortify her, make her uncomfortable. What a strange and sometimes nasty group of people. Her relatives.

"I'm going to find the restroom," Eva said softly to Chloe.

"First door on your left as you enter the foyer," Chloe said.

As she made her way up the path to the large stone patio, Eva could feel the stares. When she met eyes, most looked quickly away. Two or three smiled. One man raised his glass as if in a toast, grinned, and took a big swallow. It was clear they knew she was the new daughter/sister/granddaughter, and as such, was worthy of inspection. She was a curiosity. Her cheeks flushed with heat.

She took her time in the elegant powder room, resplendent with roses in a Waterford crystal vase, heavy gold fixtures, and a crystal chandelier (in a powder room?). Splashing water on her face and taking a few deep breaths helped to restore some degree of calm and balance.

She stood hesitantly in the enormous foyer. The sweeping marble staircase reminded her of the old 1940s movies from Hollywood that Aunt Sophie had loved. Several doors opened off the foyer, and she wondered which of them might lead to the library.

An elderly man in a black suit approached from a side door.

"Can I help you, Miss?" He stared and recognition dawned. "Oh, you must be Miss Eva. My name is Roberts, I am the butler. If I may say, you look just like the pictures I've seen of your grandmother when she was a girl. That is, Mrs. Hastings."

"Hello, Mr. Roberts. I'm hoping to see my grandfather."

"He's in the library, Miss Eva."

He pointed to double oak doors, intricately carved, at the far edge of the vast foyer. "He may be sleeping. He's not been well, you know. But he indicated earlier he wished to meet you."

Eva smiled her thanks and pulled on the weighty doorknob. As the door swung open, the fragrance of lilies filled her nostrils, sending a chill up her spine. Would lilies forever hurl her back in time to a montage of dripping water and broken glass?

She stood quietly, taking in the room, with its floor-to-ceiling bookshelves of some luscious dark wood. A stone fireplace lay unused on this hot summer day but was adorned with a giant vase of lilies in its hearth. The wrought-iron spiral staircase at the far end of the room gave access to a balcony of upper bookshelves. Couches and leather chairs graced the large space.

It was empty of people, save for one small man in a leather recliner.

He slept, his head back on the headrest, his legs covered by a plaid throw. She'd seen pictures of the elder Hastings online, and there was little resemblance to this shrunken shadow of a man. His pale skin was almost translucent, revealing the veins and ligaments of his gnarled hands which lay unmoving on his lap. The one sign of health and vigor was the full head of thick gray hair, like his son Will's, atop a sagging, wrinkled face.

She slipped into the room and closed the door noiselessly behind her. Her feet on the thick rug made no sound as she approached her grandfather.

As if she had spoken, or as if he had felt her presence, his eyes opened, and he jumped a little.

"I'm sorry, I didn't mean to startle you."

One eye flew wide, the other, in the drooping side of his face, remained half-open.

His mouth opened and he slowly croaked out, "Angie?" It was a long word, more of a breath, or a sigh.

"No, Grandfather, it's Eva. Will's daughter. I'm Eva."

He stared, then raising his good arm toward her, he beckoned her to him. He managed to spit out, after a degree of effort, the single word, "Come."

She hurried to his chair, knelt in front of him, and took his hand.

He reached forward and stroked her hair. He worked to form every word. "Pretty." He stroked her hair with his good hand. "Talk... tell me..."

What to say to this man she'd never met? She knew nothing about him. There was only their familial connection, and what she'd read of his reputation for building successful businesses. Quietly, she told him what she could of herself. A bit about her mother, her aunt, about being left alone. She didn't share her newfound ability to heal. And she said nothing about Michael. Just her own small story, as she saw it. How she loved animals, how she was studying to be a veterinarian, how she volunteered at the local animal shelter. Even about swimming with the dolphins, which seemed to delight him. His rheumy eyes studied her, and he nodded a bit from time to time. She could sense his frustration when he tried to ask a question or respond. She could also see, after fifteen or twenty minutes, that he was tiring.

"Just rest now, Grandfather. I'll stay for a bit. Just rest."

His eyes closed, his mouth fell slightly open, but his hand stayed snugly wrapped in hers. She felt the beginning of the familiar vibration.

She closed her eyes, and as the darkness and sensation of warm water grew, she spent a few moments in wonder. *What is this thing?* This... ability. This skill. Was that what it was? She hadn't learned it. Where had it come from? She hadn't been hit by lightning or had a near-death experience. It was just *there*. To be able to help this way, to heal... Could she call on it at will? If so, where was it leading?

Not able to answer a single one of these questions, she gave a mental shake of her head. All she was sure of was the feeling. She knew it. Recognized it. And although she couldn't yet see where the path led, she was beginning to trust the path itself.

She settled deeper into the dark space. And came upon a wall. Which gave way easily, dissolved. Then another, a thicker, harder obstacle. It was no good trying force or strength against it, she intuited. She had to dissolve it, not break it, using her own gentleness, her own calm strength, her own energy and spirit. She needed her own sweetness and nurturing. Not force, but persuasion, almost as if she had to convince the wall to let her through, not overpower it.

She didn't know this man, but he was her blood, her genetic link. With effort and focus, she felt the wall of energy dissolve around its edges, then collapse. But immediately she saw (or was it felt?) another wall behind it. And she could already feel her strength draining away.

What if I can't do it? Who am I to think I could undo the ravages of a stroke?

As she drew in two or three deep breaths to prepare to refocus, she heard the door open behind her, then whisper-soft footsteps across the carpet, stopping at her side. Eva didn't need to open her eyes. Chloe.

She focused again on what felt like a wall of concrete before her, in this man. It was a vast wall of energy, and she wondered again if she was strong enough.

At that moment, she felt Chloe kneel at her side and slide her arm through hers. Empathy and compassion flowed into her, and Eva drank it in, nourished by it. Then refocused to try to get past the obstacles. There was softness there, deep down inside, she could feel it momentarily from time to time, but it was covered by layers of hardness. As she refocused, she was aware her aunt remained beside her, close and warm, quiet, still. New energy poured into her. It flooded from Chloe, through her own arm, through her own hand, and into this hard energy that was her grandfather.

As the final wall fell, at last, she felt it, the openness. Unencumbered energy. There was a connection, a blending of her energy with this new one deep inside her grandfather. They floated in deep space, like the deepest of dark water.

Time stood still as the energies blended, rolled, combined. Then, slowly, the vast open spaces began to fade.

She felt herself falling, and everything went black.

Chapter 22

Eva floated up from a place of swirling shadows. *Where am I?* She could smell something deliciously savory. And could hear soft music, in the distance. It was an angelic female voice singing *All Alone Am I* and she wondered for a split second if the aneurysm had burst, she was dead, and this was the afterlife. If it was, there was an exemplary piano performance in heaven and the voice sounded like Alison Krauss. She felt Cookie's fur under her hand.

Guess I'm not dead.

She opened her eyes, gave Cookie's ear a stroke, and was rewarded with a lick across her fingers. It was daylight, but it didn't feel like morning. Looking around, she realized she was back in the guest room at Chloe's. The bedside clock said it was almost evening, a little before six.

Then it all came rushing back. The party, her grandfather, semi-waking on the floor of the mansion's library, Chloe helping her up, then out to the car. She vaguely remembered lying on the back seat of Chloe's SUV and falling into a dead sleep here.

She was suddenly alert and bolted upright to draw in a full breath. With the memory of what had occurred in the library came a sense of profound awareness.

I'm really doing it.

She rocked gently back and forth—this thing was overwhelming. But truth sang deep inside her. She knew it and felt it. She had wondered if Dr. Chin's recovery was a coincidence, but this time, with her grandfather, there could be no doubt. After she worked her way through the walls—whatever those were—it was the same feeling as when she healed an animal.

Chills ran up and down her spine and goosebumps prickled on her arms. It dawned on her: This skill gave her a new, powerful sense of purpose. And she realized she'd never had any sense of purpose. She squared her shoulders. No more denial, this was a reason to be, something she could do, to contribute, to justify her space on this earth.

For however long that was going to be.

———•• ◆ ••———

Chloe pushed the door open and peered around. "Ah, you're awake. You OK?"

"Yes, thanks." Eva took her handbag off the chair and gestured for Chloe to sit. "I'm crazy hungry—but talk to me first. How is he?"

"Mom called a couple of hours ago bursting with the news. Dad's much better. He stood and took a few steps. First time since the stroke. She said the drooping side of his face is not as pronounced, and he's much more active."

Eva shut her eyes for a minute, taking in the thrill of this new awareness. "That's great."

Her aunt shook her head. "Eva, to say it's great is a profound understatement... I don't know what to say about it."

"I'm finally believing it."

"That's a big step." Chloe raised her eyebrows. "But...?"

"It exhausts me so badly—how do I make it work?"

"You do have a lot to figure out."

"How do I work, pay bills, finish college? And what about the naysayers, the hate messages...?"

Chloe covered Eva's hand with hers. "I don't know. I'm still trying to get my head around it all. I can't imagine what you're going through. Give yourself some time to acclimatize." Her eyes filled with tears. "But it was an amazing experience. For me. When I sat there with you and Dad... it was a warm, peaceful place. Almost like being in deep water."

"I was finding it hard. With your father." Eva corrected herself. "With Grandfather."

"Then afterward, everyone wondered what was wrong and I didn't know what to tell them. Nobody knew, then, what you'd done, that Dad was much better."

"They do now?"

"I had to tell Mom," Chloe replied. "That Gleason article set them up, don't forget. And Roberts went into the library just after we left, to see if Dad wanted anything, and found him vibrant and talking. Asking for you. He said he'd had a dream that you were there."

Eva shut her eyes, remembering. "It was...." She ran out of words. "Let's just say it's a novel way to get to know someone."

Chloe's face relaxed and she smiled. "I'll say."

"What did Will say?"

"About the healing? Oh, he's flabbergasted, in Mom's words. The idea of sending someone to yoga to deal with insomnia or anxiety would elicit a mocking guffaw from my brother. He's the head of a company that deals in hard science, things that have been proven and re-proven and re-proven..."

Eva sighed. "No room for any metaphysical ideas."

Chloe grinned. "This'll bug the hell out of him. You can bet science has not yet found a way to test, or quantify, this type of healing." She stood. "I've got veggie soup on the stove downstairs. Want some?"

Eva swung her legs out from under the comforter. "Sounds great."

Famished, she downed two bowls of Chloe's soup, with chunks of Italian bread.

"Mom is planning a dinner party for the family for Saturday night," Chloe said. "To meet you properly. OK? You didn't really get to know anyone today. It was madness, too many people."

"And I got distracted by Grandfather..."

"Yes, you did!"

Eva grinned.

Driving home, Eva debated calling Michael but knew that would be a long conversation and she didn't want to pull over. Her fifteen-year-old SUV was way behind in the technology department, and she had long since managed to lose her Bluetooth earbud. Silly little thing. Someday she hoped to be able to join the modern world and have a car that allowed hands-free Bluetooth phone calls. *Have to save up for about twenty years, BG.*

She needed downtime in her haven, at home, at Jamie's. But she used this hour alone, driving home in the dark, to decompress. She listened to a Bach violin concerto and let it soothe her.

When she and Cookie arrived back home, late that night, Jamie was ready for bed. Padding about in her favorite bathrobe, she made Eva a cup of chamomile tea and fussed over Cookie.

They made their way to the living room, where Eva tucked her legs under her on the overstuffed couch and let out a long breath.

"You look tired," Jamie said. Her eyes narrowed. "But it's more than that..." Then a smile slowly lifted the corners of her mouth. "Oh, you've slept with him."

"Didn't know if I should tell you."

"Oh, Eva, I'm so sorry about the scene I made—"

"No, no," Eva cut in, trying to reassure her.

"Let me say this. I should have known better. Secrets never work out—they only harm the secret holder. And I'm good with Michael. Honestly."

"Here's to no secrets," Eva said, gamely, holding her tea mug in the air in a toast. "And yes, I'm tired, but it was mostly from the healing today." She brought Jamie up to date, telling her about the party and the healing in the library of the mansion.

"After your grandfather," Jamie asked, "were you wiped out like after you healed Mom?"

"Worse! Passed out and woke up in Chloe's cottage. Slept for ages. But how on earth am I going to make this work, when I can only help one person at a time and then I'm drained and useless for hours?"

"But you don't get tired like that when you heal animals. What's the difference? Feels like that's important, somehow. Don't you think? Wouldn't it help if we figured that out?"

"I don't know where to start," Eva said with a sigh. She pulled Cookie onto her lap as if the little dog's presence could help her think.

"Is the difference in you? Or in the person?" Jamie asked.

She pondered this. Shook her head. "Well, I don't do anything differently. I don't think." She closed her eyes and tried to relive the experience. "It's just there's no *resistance* in an animal. It's not work. People are work. So, the big question is, why?"

Jamie smirked. "Because so many people are a pain in the ass?"

"You may have something there," Eva said with a grin. "But surely you don't mean your dear mama is a pain in the ass."

Jamie held up a hand and rocked it back and forth. "You didn't hear it from me."

Eva laughed.

"Speaking of Mom," Jamie said, "I had to tell her. About what you can do. I had to. Anyway, I figured the secret was out, what with that blog. She wondered why she got better so fast. And why her asthma now seems to be in remission." Jamie's eyes were huge. "This whole thing is just..." She trailed off. "I don't know what to say."

Eva spoke slowly. "I know."

"But oh, boy, Mom had a hard time accepting the whole thing, science based as she is."

"Hang on, just because science can't explain it, doesn't mean it isn't real."

"Well, you know what I mean.'

"I just don't want people to think I'm a flake..."

"I don't know anyone who is less of a flake." Jamie watched her for a moment, her eyes misting. "Anyway, I truly thank you, from the bottom of my heart."

Eva sipped her tea and tried to brush it off. Jamie's thanks made her uncomfortable. Along with the entire situation. She'd managed to be invisible most of her life. Was her life now going to be a daily trek through others' awe and gratitude? Being gawked at? Being attacked? Being noticed and hounded? That would be her worst nightmare.

Jamie took a swallow of her wine. "Before I forget, Clare says hello. She's in California for a couple of days on business."

"Is that... going to work out, you think?"

"Hope so." Jamie smiled slowly. "So far so good. I'm not even reacting to her cat, oddly. I thought that was going to be an issue. Maybe I've outgrown that allergy. Anyway, we're just about through with the 'Wonder of Me' bullshit. You know, where you tell each other how great you are?" She grinned. "When she gets to know my faults, I hope she can get past them."

"What faults?" Eva asked. "You don't have faults."

"Sure I do. I'm impulsive, a loudmouth, I talk too much, don't think before I speak... I could go on, and on. And by the way, can you heal me of those?"

Eva smiled. "Those are what make you *you*, Jamie. That's what will make her love you."

Jamie grimaced, then grinned, her good nature always winning out.

With peace in the air, they sat in companionable silence for a minute or two. Eva had her friend back.

Chapter 23

Maybe she was overreacting. It seemed to Eva that the whole Gleason blog and the rumors of her being able to heal might blow over. She focused on her website work and boned up for two vet tech exams. They were such normal days she wondered if the reactions to the blog were just puffs of smoke, which would dissipate into nothing. There was no further mention on social media sites and the comments seemed to have stopped on GsGs.com. It was a huge relief—maybe it was going to be treated like a joke. She hoped people would believe it was just another fake story written to garner attention. After all, Roger Gleason did have a reputation for posting clickbait.

Her shifts volunteering at the shelter were quiet, too. She helped a rescued barn cat with serious skin allergies and a poodle mix someone had surrendered because they couldn't afford Lyme treatments for him. The poor thing was subdued and clearly in pain. She wanted to shout for joy when the dog responded quickly. An hour later he was moving about better and licked her face in what she could only assume was gratitude. Anthropomorphizing again, she thought with a wry grin.

This amount of healing, and the joy it brought, she could certainly handle.

"I seem to be staying under the radar with this. It's possible this whole thing will fade away," she told Michael on the phone.

"You could be right. I hope so." His tone was dubious. "Or this could be the proverbial calm before the storm. Once news gets out of your healing people? What's going to happen then? You said your grandfather's doctors were shocked? Upset?"

"That's what Chloe said. They felt sidestepped or something."

"Why am I not surprised? You know some MDs have massive egos."

"Well, it's been quiet. Maybe no one will believe it. I've got fingers and toes crossed."

Michael's tone lightened. "I have a surprise for you."

"A surprise? Give me a hint."

"Nope, no hints. You're too smart, you'll figure it out. Just wanted to let you know there will be a surprise the next time I see you...Which is when? When are you free? I'm on call Saturday and Sunday, and I know you're jammed with studying. How about Friday? Your exams done then?"

"Yes, one is Wednesday, and an essay paper is due Friday."

"Have you thought about the fact you might not even need your vet tech studies? You don't even need to diagnose—you just cut to the chase and heal them."

Eva could almost see him shaking his head. Was that threatening to him as a veterinarian? She hadn't thought of that. "Oh, but I need a license, to make a living at it. By the way, is Jerry still upset with me?"

"Not that I'm aware... why?"

"You haven't asked me to help at the clinic the last couple of weeks. I figured he was still angry. He had a right to be—I was wrong, even though the little cat recovered, and no one got sick."

"No, Jerry's on board now. And a few of us want you to come work at the clinic."

She drew in a breath. And waited.

"Just one doesn't..." Michael gave a light laugh. "Kurt is afraid if you heal all the animals, we won't make any money anymore. You know, on diagnostics, and treatments, etc. He said you might as well come work there and all the rest of us can stay home."

"Oh, Michael."

"To hell with him. He's always been an Eeyore. I tried to rib him out of his negativity by saying, 'We'd better not heal them too fast or we'll damage the bottom line.'"

"What did he say?"

"He didn't get the sarcasm. Nina tried to point out that word of mouth would have people lining up to bring pets to us. We would be busier than ever. That got everyone seriously considering it... But then they couldn't figure out how to charge for your services."

Eva didn't know what to do with any of that. There was silence. "Michael? You still there?"

His voice was low. "I wish you were here right now... I want to hold you..."

Her body responded and she found herself longing to be in his arms. His strength was enticing, not to mention his kisses. A fire started deep inside and grew at the memory of being close to him, in his arms, skin to skin. The fire, the connection. Desire flooded through her.

But some restraint was called for. She was determined not to fall so deeply into the vortex of that indescribable experience again. Not to lose herself; it made her feel completely out of control. Better to enjoy sex with this man but keep her heart and spirit guarded. She thought she could manage this thing and keep it light.

She said, "Come here for dinner Friday night. I'm not the world's best cook, but you have bought me dinner, like three times, and I want to pay you back."

"Nobody's keeping score, sweetheart."

"Still... I make a damned fine lasagna. Warmed up from Trader Joe's."

He laughed.

"It won't be your mom's lasagna," she said, "but..."

"Hell no, my mom can't cook worth beans. She can't even cook beans. My dad says Mom's cooking is so bad the flies chipped in to buy a new screen door."

Eva laughed out loud.

"It's my dad that makes a spectacular lasagna," Michael continued. "But I promise I'll never tell him about yours."

"I'd never live it down," she replied.

—— ••◆•• ——

As it turned out, Michael had been on to something when he said her peaceful days might be "the calm before the storm." Now, winds were beginning to swirl as word of the "miracle healer" began to spread. When Eva arrived at the shelter late one afternoon, Roger Gleason was waiting there again, and was rudely skeptical. He grilled her with questions like, "What did you give my nephews' cat?" And "Is this a scam and the other animals were not sick at all?" Then with a sneer, "Do you claim God gave you a 'gift?'" Determined not to let him rile her, she ignored him and his repeated offers of payment for an exclusive interview.

Besides the reappearance of Roger Gleason, two people were waiting in the parking lot, desperately seeking help for their pets. One was an English Setter with metastatic cancer. The other was a cat with a urinary tract infection that wasn't responding to antibiotics. With Jake's OK, she took the two animals and owners into the shelter's office to get away from Gleason, and to get out of the heat and humidity. With both animals, the healings were effortless for Eva. But she couldn't help wondering where this was going to lead. There were so many animals needing help.

Not to mention people.

Her thoughts were interrupted when Jake approached her, just as the last of the two pet owners was leaving.

"I'm sorry about Gleason, Jake, he's difficult."

"Trina called him a nutjob. Don't let him bother you."

That might be easier said than done.

"By the way," Jake said, "you've got quite a few emails in the general inbox... I printed them out for you."

They were addressed to her attention at the shelter's email address. The first was a request from someone in New Haven, asking if she could cure their cat of kidney failure. The next was from a woman in New Jersey who inquired where her office was and how to book online. And what her hours and fees were. Eva shook her head. "My hours and fees?" she muttered. "I can't charge *fees*."

"Why not?" Jake asked. "Think about it—how are you going to handle this? Correct me if I'm wrong, but healing animals is what you want to do, right? Once word gets out, and it looks like it already has, your day will be jammed with healings. If that's the case, how are you going to make a living? If you don't charge for this, how are you going to survive?"

"Yeah, I hadn't thought of that..."

He shook his head. "I can't believe this. Sounds like science fiction..."

Eva pointed to the printouts. "There are a couple more here... same kind of query. And here's a weird one, get this. It's a request, no, more of a plea, from someone in San Francisco (*San Francisco?*) to help their paralyzed cat. Can you believe this? They offer to fly me there, put me up, and give me any fee I want." She read on. "They suggest expenses and $10,000."

He glanced over from the notes he was entering into the computer and gave a low whistle. "That is one loved cat. Can I come? Tell them you need an assistant."

She grinned. "Oh, and here's a nice thank you from the two kids that brought me the old cat with arthritis the other day." She held the thank you card up so Jake could see it. "You know, Gleason's nephews. It's a bit stiff and formal. I bet their mom made them write it."

Jake said, "And there's one envelope addressed to you. It was in the mailbox, but I think it was hand-delivered."

He was right. There was no return address on the envelope, no stamp, no postmark. Eva ripped it open. When she pulled out the single sheet of plain white paper and saw the words, she gasped, and her heart missed a beat.

You're a scam artist. Only Jesus can heal. God will punish you.

———— ••◆•• ————

The elevator was descending, fast. Eva punched the buttons, hard, again and again, nothing worked. It dropped and dropped, then it suddenly sped out of the building, down a country lane, and raced along the side of a vast black lake. She could see out of the elevator as if one wall was a windshield, but somehow it remained an elevator. Beyond the lake lay an endless field of crushed lilies. She could smell them—the fragrance was overwhelming and sickly.

She couldn't stop this hurtling box. There was no steering wheel, no brake, no way to control it. A vast wood of enormous trees lay ahead, and she was hurtling toward it, completely out of control. She was paralyzed. And trapped.

She jerked awake, sweating and gasping.

The nasty letter and the online comments had gotten under her skin and were infecting even her dreams. Every time she closed her eyes, hoping for a bit more sleep, she saw the words from the hate letter and from Twitter: "Fake healer," "Scheming bitch," and "Scammer" floated across the blackboard of her mind.

When she finally managed to get back to sleep, inevitably she woke again and again, overheated, turning her pillow over to feel the cool side under her cheek. She checked the window A/C unit, but it seemed to be working normally.

She couldn't stop wondering where all the venom was coming from in these comments and posts. Were they from extreme religious groups? Or from doctors or scientists who were close-minded about anything that was spirituality or energy related? Or just from nasty people looking for a fight?

Why? Who am I hurting? I'm just being kind.

Would they prefer those two human beings and all those animals continue to suffer, perhaps die?

Chapter 24

When Eva opened her front door, Michael's heart sped up at the very sight of her. He grinned as the two dogs brushed past him and bustled into the foyer, happy to greet her and Cookie. The three dogs all sniffed each other eagerly.

"Oh, Michael! You did it!" Eva dropped to the floor to hug the pups. "I knew you were thinking about adopting the Golden, but Jeremiah too, huh?"

"Yes, Nellie's hip dysplasia seems to be at bay, thanks to you, and I can look after her if it returns." He grinned. "What am I saying? *You* can. And as for Jeremiah, just look at this face." He bent down and held Jeremiah's face in both hands. "I mean, just look at this sweet face." Jeremiah licked his hand. "The puppers seem to like each other," he added. "These two can keep each other company when I'm at work."

"Is this the surprise?"

"You pleased?"

"Oh yes, it's wonderful." Eva was still kneeling on the floor trying to cuddle three dogs at once.

"Wait a damn minute," Michael said, with his hands on his hips. "You hug the dogs first? Well, I guess that shows me where I fit in the scheme of things."

She laughed and he pulled her up and into his arms.

He gazed down at her face. That beautiful face. He slid her glasses off, ran his thumb along her cheek, then slowly kissed her, a long soft kiss that sent his pulse racing. "Good to see you, beautiful."

But he could sense something in her eyes. "What?" he asked. "What's happened?"

She reached for her glasses and grimaced. "I'll tell you over dinner."

"Tell me now. Please."

She led him to the kitchen counter where she scooped up the printouts of emails Jake had given her. Singling out the envelope with no return address, she handed it to Michael.

"To make matters worse," Eva said, "when I got home, I saw that word was now spreading across the internet, too. Someone had shared it on Facebook and Tiktok, and Twitter was trending the hashtags #MiracleHealer and #FakeHealer."

She grabbed her phone, opened it to one of the Twitter threads, and showed him.

It was not good. As he read, he was more and more shocked by the skepticism, anger, even vitriol in the comments. He kept reading, trying to find something to soften this news. "To be fair, there are some open-minded comments here...."

"Not many," she said, her face grim.

He kept reading. '*I won't be taken for a fool.*' Then '*Con artist.*' There were plenty of cries of '*Fake News*' and a few comments which simply read, '*Lock her up!*' Someone used all caps to shout *BLASPHEMER.*

She spoke softly, belying the obvious stress she was under. "The storm you warned me about could become a hurricane."

"What you're doing is important. *Really* important. And you're going to need help. We'll figure it out, sweetheart."

"We? That's kind of you, Michael, but it's my problem. I can't expect you to worry about this."

Michael studied her. She still didn't get it. What happened to her, happened to him. But he couldn't tell her that. Yet.

All evening Eva was distracted and worried, and he focused on bringing her comfort and pleasure. Even bliss...

She drove him wild. Just being near her kept him in an almost continual state of arousal. She was so wildly sexy. Understated, but undoubtedly the embodiment of sensual womanhood. He simply felt he could watch her forever. She didn't even know how beautiful she was or what she did to him.

Making love with her that night, he was attentive and gentle, focusing on her, which he found thrilling. To care that much. To be that connected. He knew, somehow, that their first time had been as magical for her as it had been for him. He couldn't explain it and he suspected she couldn't, either.

But now, she seemed restrained. Was it just stress? Or was she holding back from him?

———•••◆•••———

"Looking good, Michael," Tia said, gazing around his living room, where the woodwork now gleamed white, and half the walls were a beautiful gray-green color.

"It's coming along," Michael admitted as he ran the paint roller up and down the wall. He stopped and studied her for a moment. "And hey, love the hairdo... Mom said you were getting it cut. Boy, she wasn't kidding!"

"Well, it's been long hair since forever. So, when I saw a picture of Halle Berry with what they described as a 'spiked up pixie cut,' I thought, 'that's for me!'"

Michael eyed his glamorous sister. Only eighteen months older than he was, they had always been close. They even looked alike, so much so their mother called them her twins. He turned back to the wall with a roller full of paint. "Halle Berry, huh? Good choice, she's hot."

"She's old enough to be your mother."

"Don't care. Beauty is beauty."

Tia grinned, that grin that lit up her face. She ran her free hand through the new do. "And the best part is, there's no rhyme or reason to it, it's supposed to look this wild." She chuckled. "I should've done it years ago."

"Want to grab a paintbrush and cut in over there?" He pointed to the wall surrounding the fireplace.

She groaned. "How desperate are you? You know what a lousy painter I am." When he didn't chuckle, or even respond, she studied him. "What's up, Michael? You're preoccupied. Want to take a break and take the dogs out?"

He sighed. "Ok, sounds good."

He stretched, tucked the wet roller into a plastic bag, then turned to his dogs and to Tia's little chihuahua, Mabel. "Want to go for a walk?" The dogs all leaped up and raced for the front door.

As they headed down the lane, with the dogs on leashes, Tia asked, "Isn't there a state forest near here. With trails?"

"Yes, about a mile. Up for that?"

"Sure. When Mabel gets tired, I'll pop her in the backpack, she loves to ride in there."

Tia shoved her spare arm through Michael's and squeezed it. "Sweetie, what's up with you?"

Michael took a deep breath. "It's Eva... How do I say this? She blows hot and cold—she comes toward me, then backs off, then opens up and I see all the potential..."

"And here you are, fixing up your house for her."

Startled, he stopped walking and stared at her.

Tia cocked her head to one side. "Aren't you?"

"Yeah, I guess I am."

"A tad premature, don't ya think?"

They walked on. "You're right, it is premature," Michael admitted. "She's definitely holding me at arm's length."

Tia studied him. "I've never seen you like this. It's only been a few weeks. Does she feel the same?"

Michael let out a frustrated guffaw. "I thought she did... But maybe not. Oh, I don't know. She's guarded. I think she's going to vanish at any moment." He thought for a minute. "I think she's afraid, and I'm not sure why. Says she's never been in love before. She was with somebody for a couple of years but when he suggested they move in together, she backed out and broke it off. I don't see what she's afraid of."

"Everything you tell me about her sounds incredible," Tia said. "Her kindness and compassion. This gift, her beauty. She might be an old soul in a young woman's body, but this time around she's been damaged by grief and loss." Tia paused. "And the trauma is ongoing now with the invasiveness of the people that are asking so much of her."

"But I'm not asking anything of her. I just want to help her, to love her."

"That might be asking a lot... for her," said Tia.

Michael's mind was churning.

"She doesn't have much trust in the world, it sounds like," Tia said. "Having lost her mother and her aunt, Eva never transitioned from childhood to adulthood with her mother. She was just hitting puberty when her mom died and then suddenly, she was living with her great-aunt, who was much older. She had to grow up with a whole generation of influence missing in her life."

Michael hadn't thought of that. He walked quietly for a few minutes, his sister by his side, the dogs trotting along next to them.

"And then there's the aneurysm," he said slowly.

"What?"

He told her about the MRI, Eva's potential for a burst aneurysm, and how her mother had died. Tia stopped in the middle of the road and stared at him.

"She has so much on her plate," Tia said quietly. "So, she's afraid to love in case she dies and abandons someone... you, in this instance." She shook her head. "Knowing you could die at any moment would certainly change your outlook on life."

Tia and Michael stood facing each other on the quiet wooded lane, dogs sitting next to them, watching them.

As a car approached, Tia grabbed his arm and pulled him to the side of the road.

"That's what you get paid the big bucks for, Tia," he said. "Why you're a great therapist... Thank you."

"I'll send you my bill."

"Ha ha."

"Seriously, honey, be patient."

"Be patient," he muttered. "Be patient. A lifetime of hearing that..."

Tia chuckled.

Michael groaned. "I absolutely can't wait for the damn day everyone stops telling me to be patient."

Tia's chuckle turned to an outright laugh. "You do see the irony in that statement, my brother, don't you?"

He knew Tia was right. Eva was worth waiting for.

Chapter 25

"You look tired, dear." Dr. Chin gave Eva a hug, offered her a bottle of flavored water, then gestured for her to sit, in her vast, windowed office on the hospital's fourth floor. Although luxurious, with couches and chairs and a beautifully carved oak desk, it was somehow antiseptic. Well, it was a hospital.

"A lot on my mind. And not sleeping well," Eva replied. "Exam week..." She didn't go into the threatening letter and online comments. "What did you want to see me about?"

"Well, it seems I don't have asthma anymore." Dr. Chin's voice was full of wonder. "I've seen my chest x-ray and the lungs show no inflammation whatsoever. I understand I have you to thank."

Eva gave a tiny shrug.

"I've been driving Jamie wild asking how you did it."

"I wish I knew."

"I confess, it's been hard for me to accept. My background is pure science, as you know..."

Eva had to say it. "You're right. What I'm doing is *not* science. It hasn't been proven yet. What I'm doing... this thing that's coming through me has never been tested. Your science hasn't caught up with what I'm doing yet!"

Dr. Chin's eyes widened.

Eva plowed on. "And why is everyone so suspicious, so angry, so negative?"

There was silence.

"I'm sorry dear," Dr. Chin said slowly. "I didn't mean to insult you. I didn't say it isn't real. In fact, I think I may owe you my life."

"We'll never know. I'm just glad you're all right. You were so sick, and we were so worried."

Jamie's mother stared out the window and seemed to gather her thoughts. "I don't remember much—just a dream of floating in warm water. When I woke, I felt so calm. And I still feel different, somehow. Since then. More peaceful." She paused and smiled slowly. "Maybe this is how people feel when they've approached death and been given a reprieve. In any event, I don't know how I can ever thank you."

"I'm not sure thanks are needed," Eva said. "I didn't learn how to do it. This... skill... may not even come from me. That sounds weird. But it certainly isn't something I can take credit for."

"Well. What is it you kids say? 'I got nothin'." Dr. Chin crossed to her huge desk and perched on its edge. "I heard about your grandfather, as well. The whole thing is just... amazing." She paused. "And I hope you can do it again. For a tiny baby, eight months old, admitted here this morning. With meningitis and complications." Dr. Chin stared out the window. "Meningitis in babies has a high death rate, as much as fifty percent. It's confirmed, a Neisseria infection, he's had two seizures, and is in surgery now to drain the subdural effusion." She refocused on Eva. "Sorry, I drifted into medical lingo. We don't know if he's going to make it. The parents tried for ten years to get pregnant. Now they're frantic they might lose him. And if he does recover there could be lifelong neurological issues."

"Of course, I'll do my best."

Dr. Chin looked down at her phone. "OK, good, he's out of surgery and back in PICU. I'll take you to him." She headed for the door, leading Eva down the long wide hallway.

Eva asked, "Isn't there a vaccine now for meningitis?"

"Yes, and he did have his shots, but the vaccine is not 100 percent effective—no vaccine works 100 percent. There are rare cases. And the incidence is slightly higher in African Americans."

"How did you explain me?"

"I just told them you use therapeutic touch, and they were fine with it. I sensed they don't understand, but it doesn't matter..."

At the door of the PICU, Dr. Chin handed her gloves, gown, and mask, and after donning protective gear herself, led Eva in. There, like a tiny lone island in a sea of equipment, the baby lay in bed with tubes and wires protruding everywhere, his head bandaged. A gowned and masked woman sat next to the bed with her hand gently stroking the baby's arm, which lay outside the blanket. A nurse stood nearby checking vitals from various monitors.

Eva wished Dr. Chin had warned her what she was going to see. She had to take a deep breath to handle the surge of emotion from seeing the little boy alone in this sterile world. Fortunately, he was asleep, or still unconscious from the anesthesia.

Dr. Chin introduced Eva to the mother, and the tiny boy, Jaydn.

"Hi, Mrs. Rose," Eva said softly. The woman was masked, but Eva could see the fear and exhaustion in her eyes. Mrs. Rose nodded and turned back to look at her child, so still in the big bed.

When Dr. Chin disappeared to the hall, Eva spotted a stool at the side of the room and pulled it to the edge of the bed. The little boy was beautiful. Long black eyelashes rested against his perfect chocolate skin. She reached out and laid her hand on the baby's arm, so hot to the touch.

"Hi, Jaydn," she whispered.

Mrs. Rose said quietly, "It means 'God has heard.'" She looked up at Eva. "The name 'Jaydn.' And He did. We tried for years. So many years. He heard, and this little angel is the result." Her eyes filled with tears.

Eva wished she could scoop up the baby and hold him. Since that wasn't possible, she gently wrapped her hand around the small child's arm and lay her other hand against his body, over the coverings. She closed her eyes and wished she had music to open her to the vibration.

But there was no need. The connection was as fast and seamless as when she held a suffering animal. The energy was right there, available, unhampered. She connected, felt the familiar vibration and deep dark sensation, then there was the pure spirit, so fresh, so clean, yet extremely low in energy. She spent blissful minutes floating in the water with this little new soul, feeling him strengthen. She knew, when she finally brought herself back and disconnected from him, that he was better.

But she couldn't say that to Mrs. Rose. When Eva stood up, she saw the mother's eyes were shut, and her cheeks wet with tears.

Eva left the PICU to find Dr. Chin waiting outside on her phone. She finished her call and looked at Eva, expectantly.

Wary of sounding too confident, Eva said, "I think it worked. Guess we'll just have to wait and see."

Dr. Chin took a deep breath. Then shook her head in obvious amazement. "You just know?"

"Yes. I'm... starting to."

"And how are you—can you drive home?"

Eva realized with a start that she wasn't tired. There was no exhaustion at all. It felt just as it did when she finished helping a cat or a dog. She was peaceful and happy, not drained.

Back at Jamie's, she greeted Cookie and heard her roommate calling from the attic. Taking the stairs two at a time, she stopped in the doorway to the large attic area, where she found Jamie, arms deep in a box, amidst a sea of stuff piled on the plank flooring.

"You need help? What are you looking for?"

"Mom asked me to look for a box of photographs she's missing," Jamie said, "from when I was a kid. When Dad was still with us. When I asked her about it, she looked a little sheepish. Said something about wanting to spend some time with memories."

"Not like your mom to be sentimental."

"She says she 'rolled the dice with death.' Not like her to be dramatic either," Jamie retorted.

"I know, right?"

It was unbelievably hot and humid, even on this rainy day in August, so Eva set up a fan in the attic doorway. Needing more than the single hanging light bulb casting hard shadows, she used a flashlight to scan the contents of the attic. Countless boxes pressed up against an ancient bookcase, thick with dust, which looked as if it hadn't been disturbed in thirty years. A rolled-up rug was tucked next to an old beat-up screen, and a dozen paintings lined the wall. Some of this was Jamie's or hers, some Jamie had discovered when she bought the house. The old couple who owned it had passed away, and the attic had been overlooked by the cleanout crew.

Eva ripped open a box, which turned out to be full of files and tax returns, so she sealed it up again and kept looking. Eventually, she isolated two boxes of her own, containing photos and memorabilia belonging to Sophie or her mother, and carried those out to the hallway. She'd been meaning to go through those for years.

"Oh, cool, our yearbooks." Jamie wiped the dust off one and held it up. "Will I ever want to look at these stupid things again? Oh, and my tennis awards..." She dropped them unceremoniously back in the box. "I'd better not get diverted, or we'll be here all day."

Eva glanced up. "And die of heat stroke in the process." She gazed around again, using the flashlight to scan the writing on the boxes. Then she saw it, off to the side: a box with faded writing: PHOTOS 2000–2010.

"Jamie, look—I think I've found them." She pointed. "The dolphin pics might be in here, too. I'd love to see those again."

They hauled the boxes out to the hallway and by the time they'd carried them downstairs, they were dripping with sweat.

Jamie cranked the AC unit in the kitchen to its highest setting and began to sift through photos. "Oh, boy. My baby pictures. Mom will want these, for sure." She held another image up for Eva to see. "And look, it's you and me on the swim team. What were we, twelve? Before you had to quit?"

Eva nodded. She drained her glass of iced tea, then dug into a box of her mother's, containing prints of one of the many times her mom had taken her to the beach. There were happy smiling images of each other, then Eva found their attempt to automate the camera to take a shot of them both. They'd only managed to shoot their knees and feet. She grinned, but her smile quickly faded. She remembered why all these pictures had remained untouched for years. The lump of grief was like a stone in her throat.

Dropping the images back in the box, Eva pulled out half a dozen packets of pictures. This could take all day. But then a brightly colored object half-way down the box caught her eye. Pushing the envelopes aside, she drew out a book, covered by an image of a wide azure sea, purples and blues abundant. In elegant script it read, "Journal," on its cover.

Eva drew in a sharp breath and showed Jamie.

"Oh cool!" Jamie exclaimed. "Your mom's?"

"Must be."

Jamie dropped the pictures she was looking at and stood next to Eva to study the journal.

Eva's heart was pounding. Her throat closed. She lay the journal down on the table, and covered it for a moment with her palm, like she covered the emotion threatening to choke her. Searching through the box of pictures once more, she pulled out another packet holding pictures of sea creatures. Turtles, whales, and otters. And dolphins. She found the ones of the baby dolphin her mother had spoken of, the one she'd cared for the summer before Eva was born. Eva turned a photo over to look at the date. July 10, 1995.

"Look what I've found," she said to Jamie. "These must be from Mom's internship." She held the image up. "Look at that little creature... Mom said they named her Grace."

Jamie leaned over to peer at the image.

"Mom told me the little dolphin was released to the wild a few months later," Eva said.

"That's some nasty cut on her fin."

"Yes, from a boat propeller, they assumed."

Jamie started scrabbling through the packets of pictures in the box in front of her. "Wait a minute... I want to find the ones of us swimming with the dolphins. Oh, they must be here somewhere... Bless my mother, she kept printing out pictures for years, refusing to keep them on the computer. She said it just wasn't the same as being able to hold them in your hand."

Waving around a picture by thumb and forefinger as if it was dirty, Jamie muttered, "Here's *another* picture of Dad...Why does she keep these?" She groaned and dropped it back into the box. Digging deeper, she triumphantly pulled out another folder and studied the writing on the front. "Here they are!" She dragged her chair closer to Eva's.

There were scores of images taken by Jamie's dad that magical day, on the boat and in the water, with the dolphins. Eva could feel the excitement all over again. To be swimming with those wild creatures, the feeling had been almost visceral, and it now seemed to roll right off the photographic paper.

Jamie studied a photo. "Hey Eva, you've got to see this. This is the larger, older dolphin from that day. Where's that picture of your mother's baby dolphin?"

Eva sifted through the shots and found it.

"Look," said Jamie, the excitement clear in her voice as she compared the two pictures. "That older one had a big scar in exactly the same place as the little dolphin."

Eva drew in a sharp breath.

"Wow," Jamie said. "Could that possibly be the same dolphin?"

"This was twelve, almost thirteen years later..." Eva said. "But dolphins can live up to thirty-five years..."

"So, it could be her! Wouldn't it be amazing if we met Grace?"

⸺ •• ◆ •• ⸺

Cookie bounded across the lawn, leaping into the air to catch the tennis ball Eva had thrown. When Michael pulled into the driveway, Eva and Jamie were cheering the little dog, as she raced triumphantly back with her treasure.

"Just stopped by on my way to the clinic to see you off. Wish I wasn't on call this weekend," he said, as he plucked the tennis ball from Cookie's mouth and hurled it across the grass.

Eva glanced at her watch. She was leaving to drive up to the Hastings compound for the dinner party. In her honor. She suppressed a shiver. Part of her wished Michael could go with her but another part of her was glad he couldn't.

She filled him in on the healing of little Jaydn, on how easy it had been.

Michael listened. "And you're not tired... Maybe because it was such a tiny human being," he added with a grin.

Eva said, "There weren't any walls. You know, those big obstacles I hit?" She shook her head in frustration. "I have to figure out what those are." She turned to Jamie. "OK, time to hit the road. Cookie, you have fun with Jamie and Clare."

"She will, honey. I'll see to it. Cookie and I are best buds," Jamie said, tossing the ball again.

Michael walked Eva to the car. "Well, at least those walls, so far, have not been strong enough to keep you out..." He wrapped his arms around her. "Are you keeping *me* out?"

She chuckled and gave him a hug. Waving at Jamie, she threw her bag in the car.

Her chuckle was a cover. Michael's last words had struck a chord. A discord. Having made the conscious decision to hold back from him, she should have known he would sense it. And now she felt, what was it... guilt? Was she being unfair to him?

Lately, she had found herself thinking of him a hundred times a day. The time she spent with him was invigorating, stimulating, and yet somehow comfortable at the same time. That was new. And making love with him, well, she'd never known anything like it. Was it just incredible chemistry and attraction or something more?

How do I navigate this situation?

She had no clue how to handle the threatening letter and all those cruel online comments, either. Heading north on I-95, the rain started, and with it came a feeling of despondency, even gloom. Even the joy of healing that beautiful infant faded beneath the memory of those hateful words. The social media posts were offensive and annoying, but at least there was an unreal quality to anything written online. There was distance because it was virtual, and Eva believed most people who wrote nasty things online would never do it in person. Wouldn't have the nerve.

But the hand-delivered letter was another matter. It hit home and even frightened her because it was local. Someone had walked right up the steps of the shelter and dropped that letter in the mailbox. That person was nearby. That person was real.

Her mind was roiling.

I didn't ask for this. God knows I don't want the notoriety, the fame, or the responsibility. It's a curse.

She popped in her Abba greatest hits CD. But even their bright music didn't lift her spirits. Her mother had loved Abba, having sung along to them as a child herself. Switching to the radio, Eva found a classic rock station playing "Dust in the Wind," by Kansas. As beautiful a song as it was, it just seemed too depressing today. Even nihilistic. Eva clicked it off and opted for silence.

She hoped the beach would help. Pulling into the parking lot at Roger Wheeler beach, she saw rows and rows of empty spaces. It was a cloudy day with occasional rain showers, so the stretches of sand were almost empty. She found a huge piece of driftwood that made a great bench. Gazing out at the sea, she breathed in the rich, raw smell of the ocean, salty and tangy and fishy, all at the same time. That aroma seemed to be in her blood, from her mother, from her childhood.

She had tucked her mother's journal into her bag and now pulled it out. She scrolled through page after page of her mother's scrawl, feeling somewhat disconnected. Like she was out of her body reading the words in a play, in a novel. She read about Trish, her mother's colleague at the marine institute, about helping her father in his helicopter training school, about returning to college to get her degrees.

Then this entry:

July 6, 1995: New England Marine Institute

I had an amazing experience today. I have to write it all down, so I never forget it.

It was dawn, so cool and quiet at the institute. Although a warm day for the coast of Massachusetts, the saltwater held its usual icy chill as I slid into my waist to greet my two friends, the dolphins. Mamie nuzzled her beak against my belly, cackled, and grinned her huge grin, then Sugarloaf gently bumped his melon directly into my lower abdomen. It was so odd, it was as if they knew. But how was that possible? I've only been sure for a few days.

How ever will I manage? How do I get my Bachelor's, then a Master's in marine biology, with a child? Will Dad help? And how do I tell him?

Eva glanced up at the date again. That must be me. The dates are right. Her heart quickened and she realized she wasn't breathing. She drew in a long breath and returned to the pages.

I approached the tanks where we keep turtles, otters, dolphins, and even whales that need help, and there, in the small holding tank, was Trish, our staff biologist. This is the woman who usually makes me think of a honeybee or hummingbird with her super-charged metabolism. But at this moment she was standing motionless, holding the new little dolphin they rescued last night. The one so injured by a propeller that they were not sure she would survive. Only about two feet long, it was lying so still in Trish's hands. She carefully kept the baby afloat, blowhole out of the water, while she carefully reached for a bottle of formula and held the nipple to its stubby snout. There was no response.

I climbed down into the water and slid my hands under the small dolphin's body, taking over from Trish who disappeared into the building. I was alone with this tiny creature.

I studied her, little Grace. So small! And such a nasty cut in the baby's fin now held together by a clear line of stitches. Otherwise, the gray skin was flawless. Through the water, I could make out the distinctive yellow and gray pattern in the shape of an hourglass on her flank.

And a big eye watched me. I crooned and cooed sweet talk to the baby dolphin, but it remained still.

And then it happened. A strange stirring in my lower belly sent an icy sensation racing up my spine. It wasn't pain, exactly, just pressure, almost as if my insides were vibrating. It was like nothing I've ever felt. Or was this normal in the first few weeks? How would I know?

Then the little dolphin in my arms began to stir, almost vibrate, too, and the sensation of pressure in my abdomen grew even stronger. I was just opening my mouth to call for help, but then the baby shivered, relaxed, and lay motionless. A chill of dread washed over me.

I hollered to Trish to come quickly.

With that shout, Grace's tail began to sweep up and down, and I could feel its muscles bunching and tightening. I know I gasped, as with a burst of energy the dolphin pushed out of my arms. That frightening sensation down low in my abdomen faded and disappeared.

I held on to the ladder and watched, mesmerized, as Grace swooped around the tank. She gave a series of clicking sounds and when I reached for the bottle of formula, she pulled at it noisily. After demolishing the bottle, she took off around the tank again.

*When Trish came running, we laughed, and
whooped, and high-fived!
Indescribable. My heart was so full it ached.*

As Eva tucked the journal under her windbreaker, it started to
mist. Pulling the hood over her head, she stayed right where she
was. Watching. Thinking. The waves hitting the shore were
insignificant. She scanned the relatively still water further away
from land, but there were no white caps out there. And no dolphin
fins either.

She was trying to process what she had read. Her mother
healed that little dolphin? The connection to her mother was so real
at that moment, so visceral, she could almost feel her arms around
her. Smell her light fragrance of lavender shampoo. Hear her floaty
gentle laugh. She was a healer, too.

She wanted to talk to Michael. But she was alone. She had two
more hours before she was due at Chloe's and the world was her
own. No one knew where she was. In the past, she'd always loved
that sensation.

*I'm in charge of my destiny. No one is watching me or asking
anything of me.*

She breathed a deep sigh. Being alone had always been freeing
and peaceful. But now she couldn't find that feeling.

Chapter 26

It was time to stop them. "Enough with the grilling," Eva said, with a small smile, to soften the demand. "Please."

"Dear me, everyone," her grandmother said. "She's our guest of honor and we're making her uncomfortable!"

A maid, dressed in black with a white apron, filled Eva's glass with sparkling apple cider. Eva and the Hastings family were gathered in the great room of the mansion, where twenty-foot ceilings and giant windows created a breathtaking room filled with light. On one end towered a floor-to-ceiling fireplace of golden stone, and pottery planters filled with trailing greenery and creamy yellow calla lilies lined the outer walls. The color of the wood floor matched the blond leather settees and chairs and was broken up by gold and black rugs. The entire effect was stunning, if slightly imposing for a poor kid from rural Connecticut. Eva hid a surreptitious grin.

She was damp through and through after the beach, so she had showered and changed at Chloe's. Packing for the weekend, she'd worried about what to wear, but the choice was limited. With Chloe's advice, she'd packed her good black slacks and her only silk shirt and wore these with her mother's silver dolphin necklace.

Arriving at the Hastings mansion, her father took hold of her hands, kissed her cheek, then stood back, studying her. "It's hard for me to believe," he muttered, with a firm shake of his head.

She pulled her hands away.

He gave a small smile. "But look at the evidence." He turned to watch his father approaching.

Her grandfather's gait was a bit stiff, but the change was remarkable. This was a different man than the one she had knelt beside in the library.

He spoke slowly, but clearly. "Thank you, my dear Eva." He held her eyes for a long moment.

Eva studied him. There was now both color and life in his face, and it held next to nothing of the right-sided droop that was so apparent when she'd met him. And she felt she knew him, somehow. Warmth flowed from him as if they'd known each other for years. Like family. They had truly connected, as people so rarely do, she thought. And it seemed he felt the same. He smiled, held her eyes, and she felt touched, hugged, linked to him, somehow.

Her grandmother spoke. "My dear girl, we're speechless at what you've done."

"It's amazing to me, too," Eva said, quietly.

For the next hour the Hastings family fired questions about the healing: How did it work? What did it feel like? When did she learn she could do it? Was it from God? What about the blog from Gleason? And on and on. As she told the story, in detail, she realized a piece of her wanted them to be proud of her, to respect her. She answered their questions as best she could, but enough was enough.

Roberts, the butler, spoke from the arched doorway. "Mrs. Hastings, Ma'am, dinner is served."

"Saved by the bell," said Olivia, winking at Eva and draining her champagne glass. Eva wondered if this young woman, her half-sister, was always this glamorous. Olivia was an elegant sight in slinky silk slacks and matching tunic with silver chains and bracelets setting off the soft gray material. She looked and moved like a model, even though her movements were deliberate. The kind of measured movements someone employs to convince others she's not drunk.

"Thank you, Roberts," Angela stood and took Eva's arm. Her delicate perfume drifted up from her tiny frame. Magnolias and jasmine.

"I'm sorry about the goldfish bowl," Angela said.

"At least it's done," Eva said. "I guess I had to get it over with."

"You must admit it's astonishing—they're just trying to take it in, to understand it. As are we. William's blood pressure is normal," her grandmother added, "for the first time in months. Years, in actual fact." She patted Eva's arm. "And I promised Susanna I would make apologies for her. Surely you met her last weekend. Will's wife. She has a migraine and is unable to join us."

"Perhaps I can help her," Eva said.

"Oh yes, dear, that would be lovely," her grandmother replied, but Eva knew she was distracted, as the older woman ushered them all into the grand dining room.

A combination of savory aromas met them, reminding Eva she hadn't eaten since breakfast.

A voice spoke behind her.

"I asked Grandma if I could sit beside you," said Samantha.

Eva smiled. "That'll be nice."

Her youngest sister grinned as Eva slid into the seat. "You're going to be famous."

"Oh, I hope not," Eva replied, shuddering.

Samantha looked shocked. "Why wouldn't you want to be famous? I think it would be *awesome*."

"You must be a true extrovert if you think being famous would be great."

Samantha cocked her head to one side. "I guess I am. I'm studying acting and theater. I want to be on the stage. Don't know if I'll be good enough to get famous, but I'm going to try!"

Eva grinned.

From where she was sitting on Eva's other side, Chloe smiled her support. Jared, then Olivia (after refilling her champagne glass) took chairs on the other side of the long mahogany table. Seafood bisque was already served, and two maids came around offering warm rolls.

This room, if anything, was even more sumptuous than the Great Room. The long mahogany table held elaborate place settings, each of which included plates for every course and an arsenal of silverware. Flowers bedecked the table's center, along with burgundy-colored tapers in brass candelabra. Eva felt like she was in an updated version of Downton Abbey, minus the footmen. She couldn't imagine ever accepting this lifestyle as the norm.

Her grandfather stood, holding aloft his crystal wine goblet. He spoke slowly, but clearly. And he stood without swaying. Her grandmother gazed up at him from her seat at his right, beaming.

"Before we eat, I'd like to make a toast."

Everyone raised their glass.

"My speech is improved but is not yet easy. So, you'll be pleased to hear: no speeches." He cleared his throat. "A toast to a wonderful addition to a wonderful family." He lifted his glass toward Eva. "A sincere and loving welcome, to Eva."

He saluted his glass toward her and a chorus of "To Eva" filled the room, then came the clink of glasses.

Eva flushed. Fortunately, everyone turned their attention to the bisque, and the room filled with the sounds of clinking spoons, voices, and a distant soft piano. Eva wondered if they had hired a pianist for the evening just to accompany them from another room. She half listened to Samantha's chatter, noting as she talked, her young sister picked endlessly at the sides of her fingernails, tearing off bits of cuticle. She seemed unaware of this nervous habit. Eva interjected a comment now and then, while she covertly studied the members of her new family.

Her grandmother, dressed all in soft blue, was deep in conversation with Will, at the end of the table. Her demeanor was cordial and pleasant, but Eva suspected her grandmother was strong as granite deep inside, capable of handling anything, and certainly the rock of the family. Then it hit her that her grandfather was just the opposite. Eva had encountered wall after wall of steel, which she'd had to dissolve before she came upon and connected with the soft center, the essence of who he really was. Underneath.

Jared spoke little, seated next to Olivia, but Eva felt his gaze from time to time. When she met his eyes, invariably he looked quickly away. Olivia chatted with Chloe and downed more champagne. Eva noticed her grandmother eying Olivia, a frown forming on her face. A storm brewing there, Eva thought.

She heard smatterings of conversations:

Olivia's voice: ... "modeling ... I'll need to live in Manhattan. Found a wonderful loft apartment..."

Her grandmother's voice: ... "You know I believe you should run for office..."

Her father's voice: "And you should know by now I'd never bother with politics. Real power is never seen."

Jared's voice: "...the docs are annoyed with your recovery? Seriously?"

Her grandfather's voice: "Let them be annoyed—to hell with them. They work for me."

She spotted a menu card in front of her place setting. "Chateaubriand" was the main course, whatever that was, and unwilling to show her ignorance, she didn't ask. As the maids came around with steaming platters, she saw it was just roast beef. One mouthful and she realized it wasn't *just* roast beef. It was like nothing she'd ever tasted. Delectable, mouth-watering, and so tender. Chloe grinned at her expression and murmured that it was served with a truffle sauce.

Eva felt like a jigsaw piece cut from the wrong puzzle.

No one in Eva's circle of friends threw dinner parties like this one. No one. They usually got together in a potluck-style gathering, sitting around someone's coffee table, on the floor, or on beanbags. Eating chili, or tacos. Eva figured her generation simply embraced the messiness of real life and had abandoned perfectionism. But it did occur to her that perhaps they were just poor and didn't have a choice.

Chloe said, "So, are we going to give Eva the tour? She wants to see the greenhouses."

Will replied, "I can go one better. I want to show you around the business, Eva. Can you come up to Boston this week? And meet everyone? There may well be a place for you in the company..."

Olivia said, "What he really means is he's dying to study you. To figure out how you're healing people. To *test* you." She giggled. "You're a lab rat."

"Olivia, shut up. You're speaking nonsense." Jared's voice dripped with assumed authority.

Quick as a flash, Olivia retorted, "Better than you, kissing ass, lickspittle lapdog that you are."

Jared's face contorted with anger.

"For Chrissake, Livvy..." Her grandfather said.

Olivia continued as if he'd not spoken. "And anyway, how is it nonsense? You guys want to monetize her. Tell the truth, Dad."

Eva's father spoke with command. "*Olivia.*" She stared at him. "That's enough, girl."

Angela added, "And that's enough champagne. Marta, no more champagne for Miss Olivia."

Olivia's face turned red. "I'm fine, Grandmother."

Will said, "All evidence to the contrary. Now be still."

Olivia threw her napkin down on her plate and stood. "Excuse me, everyone, I'm going to bed."

Jared laughed. "At 8:30? Yeah, right. There must be brandy in your room." He laughed harder.

Olivia stormed out.

Angela said, "My apologies, Eva."

Jared was still chuckling. "Yes, so sorry, Eva. Didn't expect such dysfunction, did you?"

Will said, softly, "Jared. Stop."

Angela turned the conversation, deftly. "I will be delighted to show you the greenhouses in the morning, Eva. There's something I wish to speak to you about. I'm glad you agreed to stay—it would have been a long drive back for you tonight. I've put you in the Davenport suite—it has the best view across the water."

Coffee and dessert were served in the adjoining room, which they called the Hearth Room. This room was smaller, darker, with leather chairs, mahogany bookshelves with fluted columns, couches of wine-colored tapestry, and rich oriental rugs. Eva liked this room better; it was a cozy space, with another beautiful stone fireplace, and she could almost smell the wood fire burning in that hearth on a snowy night.

As Chloe poured coffee, Eva's grandparents and father approached. Angela took Eva's hand. "How can we ever thank you?"

Before Eva could respond, Will said, "Well, I can start by setting up a fund for your education. Tuition, books, whatever you need—"

Eva said, "But—"

"No, Will, your father and I have already done that this week," Angela said.

"Wait a minute," Eva said, firmly. "I don't want to be *paid* for helping Grandfather."

Her grandmother's voice was also firm. "Now, Eva, don't think that we're doing this because you helped William. No, you're our granddaughter." She took a highbacked chair and motioned the others to sit near her. "We didn't see you grow up, but we can be involved now. Does that make it easier to accept?"

Eva's throat closed up and she swallowed, hard. She sat on a buttoned leather settee.

Her grandfather spoke. "That's right, my dear," he said, quietly. "Your grandmother and I took care of your college fund. It will take longer to get a trust arranged. Maybe a month or two. Lawyers, you know—"

"Grandfather," Eva began, shaking her head.

"No, no. This is not gratitude. Not charity." He paused, in thought. "Although I do owe you my health, perhaps my life. But that's not why we're doing this. Our other grandchildren each have a trust, so it's only right and natural that we would want to do the same for you."

Eva spoke slowly. "But I'm not a Hastings."

"You look like me and you look like Chloe," said her grandmother. "It's obvious you're a Hastings, Eva."

Eva didn't know what to say to that.

Samantha spoke up. "Dad says you want to be a veterinarian, right, Eva?"

"That's right," she said.

"Not a doctor?" her grandfather asked, taking a cup of coffee from Chloe. "Why not study medicine? Choose a specialty. Cardiology. Or neurology. Good money in that. I have a good friend, the head of Neurology at New Haven Medical—"

"She wants to be a veterinarian, William," Angela said briskly.

"So she says," Will said. He turned to Eva. "Your boyfriend is a vet, so you want to be one as well, I assume."

Eva bristled. "Wait a minute—"

"Oh, is he supposed to be a secret?" her father asked.

Angela spoke firmly. "Now, Will, don't tease her."

He patted his mother's arm. "You're right, Mother. But there's no prestige in being a veterinarian. Why not be a doctor, like Dad says?"

"It's not prestige I'm after," Eva said. She swallowed the retorts that flew to her mind. She said calmly, "I love animals. All I've ever wanted to do is help animals."

"And what about people?" her father asked, slowly.

Eva took a breath, smiled, and said, "I can still help people... I don't need to study medicine to do that."

That stopped the conversation.

Chloe said, "Good point, Eva." She grinned. "You can't argue with that, Will."

Jared spoke up from across the coffee table. "You don't need to study medicine to help animals either, it seems. Why go back to college at all?"

"To get a degree. To be legitimate."

"Why? You're already better at it than everyone else."

Was that a sneer on Jared's face? Eva wondered how her brother could make something so positive sound so negative.

Chloe said, "You want qualifications, right Eva?"

"Right," Eva said. "Then I can legally make a living."

Jared said, "But if they're setting up a trust for you, why bother? You'd never have to work again."

Eva bit her tongue, once again filtering out a harsh response that wanted to jump from her lips. Before she could summon up something polite, her youngest sister spoke.

"Then why do *you* work, Jared?" Samantha's voice was steely. She put her coffee cup down, hard, on the table with a clang. "You're first in the office every day, last out, I hear."

Jared stared at her in silence.

"Oh," Samantha said. "I get it. Territorial, much? It's your business, your corporation, right? No usurpers allowed?"

Will spoke up firmly. "Enough of this. We're having a pleasant evening, let's not spoil it."

Chapter 27

When Eva finally bade good night to Chloe, who had shown her to the sumptuous Davenport Suite, she was exhausted. She longingly eyed the giant sauna tub in the adjoining bathroom but feared she'd fall asleep in it and drown. Once in PJs, she brushed her teeth and hair and slipped into the crisp white sheets. And what was that fragrance? She idly wondered if they used some sort of lavender rinse in the washing machine.

One deep breath and her whole body relaxed, as she let go of tension she wasn't even aware she'd been carrying. She'd survived the evening without disaster.

But she wanted to go home.

There was a soft knock at the door, then it opened. Samantha peeked around the door.

"Oh, good, you're awake," she said. "You're not sleepy, are you? I don't want to go to bed yet."

It was already quite late, and throughout dinner, Samantha's capacity for idle chatter had been astounding. Eva feared if she got started again she might not stop till dawn. But Eva didn't want to be rude, and she also sensed that her youngest sister received little attention from anyone else in the family.

Eva patted the bed beside her, and Samantha hurried over and flopped down next to her.

Samantha pursed her lips. "Olivia's jealous of you..."

"What?"

"It's true!" Samantha exclaimed. "The whole family's been talking about you all week. We've hardly talked of anything else. And earlier today I overheard Olivia saying to Jared, '*All week it's been Eva this, Eva that.*' Her voice was dripping with jealousy." Samantha laughed. "It's funny... My whole life I've endlessly heard '*Olivia this, Olivia that.*' Now that it's *her* turn, she's not the center of attention and she's pissed."

Studying Samantha, Eva was taken aback by the anger, even hatred on her younger sister's face. There were certainly some undercurrents of issues between her half-siblings. On second thought, that was an understatement.

"Olivia's a bitch," Samantha said, adamantly. "She's always been a bitch, now she's a drunken bitch."

"She must have some redeeming qualities."

"I can't find them. She's always been spiteful. When I was about seven, she cut the head off my favorite doll, Josie. Left it on my pillow." Samantha cringed. "Never apologized, but blamed Jared. But I know it was *her*..."

"Oh, that's creepy."

"I cried for weeks. Dad bought me a new doll, but it wasn't the same," Samantha said.

Samantha stood and strolled around the room, peering into Eva's travel case, and fingering her watch and necklace on the bureau. Over her shoulder, she said, "There's something wrong with Olivia. She's a complete narcissist." Giving Eva an odd look, she sat back down on the bed. "Do you know what narcissism is? I've been reading about it—I'm studying psychology. It's a good minor to have if you're majoring in theater and acting."

Samantha spoke quickly, almost tripping over her words, but Eva got the impression the girl was bursting to just talk with someone. Did no one ever talk with her?

Samantha's eyes flashed fire. She bounced up and down from her toes to her heels, excitement pouring from her, and chatted on about everything from Stanislavsky and Method Acting, to Chekov's *Three Sisters,* to a current Broadway production of *Sweeney Todd.*

"Sounds amazing," Eva said.

"But Dad says he won't pay for me to go to Juilliard or The Actor's Studio." Samantha sighed. "He wants me to study finance or law or something useful to the company." She grimaced. "So, I guess I can't go until I'm twenty-one, when some trust funds open up for me." Her chin jutted out. "Then I can do what I want."

"What do your grandparents say?"

"*Our* grandparents?"

"Oh, right, our grandparents... sorry. That's just weird, I've never had grandparents before."

"You don't have grandparents on your mom's side?"

Eva shook her head. "Died when I was young." She yawned. She didn't think she could stay awake another moment. "I'm fading, Samantha. See you in the morning?"

"Call me Sam. And yes, we always have breakfast on the patio in nice weather. I'll even try to get up, since you're here." She grinned, threw her arms around Eva, and hugged her for a long minute.

When Samantha headed for the door, Eva scooched down in the bed, thinking there was a rather desperate, needy quality to that hug. *Poor Sam.*

She was asleep in point five of a second.

---- •• ◆ •• ----

Eva dreamed the dolphin dream. Her favorite. The weightless sensation in deep water, the touch of their silky skin, the sense of joy in their presence, the larger dolphin's grin... Could that have really been Grace? She floated in the dream for as long as she could, but the cool morning breeze across her face brought her to wakefulness.

It was early. The window near the bed was cracked open and a cool breeze drifted in off Cape Cod Bay. *Were dolphins ever spotted here?* She hopped out of bed and went to the window. The was nothing between the house and the bay but rolling lawns and beds of flowers.

But it was the sunrise that made her gasp. There was nothing like a sunrise over water, and this one was spectacular. It was as if someone had swept a giant paintbrush on the edge of the sky so that a wash of peach and blue and gray filled the horizon. In its center glowed a half ball of golden light, with its fingers stretching far into the streaks of colors on either side.

The waves hitting the shore were insignificant. She scanned the relatively still water further from land, but there were no dolphin fins. She hadn't really expected to see them, but she always hoped.

Suddenly, she had to close that distance and be nearer the water. Throwing on shorts, tee, and flip-flops, she crept down the staircase and across the great room, through the French doors to the patio. But the water would have to wait. Eva spotted her grandmother strolling amongst the roses, carrying a wicker basket over her arm.

"I love an early morning walk in the garden," Angela said with a smile.

"How's Grandfather this morning?"

"He's good." Angela Hastings, a tiny woman, was somehow a big presence. Laying the wicker basket down in the grass, her grandmother pulled her into a hug. She looked up into Eva's eyes, and although she didn't speak, her eyes were misty. Eva bent over to hug her grandmother. She was struck again by the magnitude of what she had been able to do for them. As she pulled back, she was aware of Angela's effort to collect herself.

"So, what did you want to speak to me about?" Eva asked.

"Come, sit for a minute." Her grandmother led her to a wrought iron bench tucked against a bed of roses. "I'll get right to it. I have a friend whose husband is dying of pancreatic cancer. He's in hospice. Will you try to help?"

"Of course," Eva said.

"You know her—well, you know *of* her. She's the governor of Connecticut, Audrey Lambeth."

Eva's heart started to race. Such a public figure. How could she keep her healing under the radar if she helped the governor of Connecticut?

Her grandmother said, "Audrey's originally from Massachusetts, from right here in Plymouth County, and I've known her for decades. Her husband, Charles, is a retired federal judge. They have a home in Mystic, and she told me that is where Charles wants to die. It's heartbreaking. He's a lovely man, has donated millions to charity over the years..." Angela stopped herself. "Anyway, my dear, can she call you?"

Eva nodded.

Her grandmother reached for Eva's hand and squeezed it. "Thank you, dear. This must be... *strange* for you." Then her tone lightened. "I hope you slept well?"

"Great, thanks. Even though Samantha could have kept me up all night. I had to boot her out."

"She's a talker, all right. But means well, I think." Collecting the basket, her grandmother began to clip creamy yellow and apricot-colored roses as they walked along the grassy path between the garden beds. "Although she and Olivia haven't yet grown up enough to see the benefit of being sisters. They're at each other's throats much of the time." She clucked her disapproval.

"I noticed." Eva told her grandmother about the doll incident.

"Oh, I never thought it was Olivia, I thought it was Jared. Just teasing his little sister, trying to make it look as if Olivia had done it. He was jealous from the moment Olivia was born." She shook her head. "Although, I suggest you ask Chloe about it. She has a different take—she always thought it was Samantha herself. We never knew for sure."

Over her grandmother's shoulder, Eva spied Chloe approaching from the patio.

"Ask me what?" Chloe said. "Good morning, Eva, coffee's on the patio..."

"About Samantha... that doll business years ago," Angela said.

"Ah, yes. That was weird." They turned toward the patio. As Eva poured coffee, Chloe spoke softly. "Sam hasn't had it easy. In my opinion, all three kids suffered from the relationship, or lack of it, of Will and their mother. That was Will's first wife. She was a rebound relationship from your mother, I think, Eva. Married her way too fast... She couldn't, or wouldn't, stand up to him and became a shadow of herself over the ten years they were together. When she left, she and Will must have come to some sort of arrangement because she didn't take the kids." Chloe paused. "Of course, there's some question in my mind whether Samantha is even Will's."

"Tsk tsk, Chloe, now that's pure speculation," Angela said.

"Maybe..." Chloe replied. "Anyway, Sam certainly didn't have the attention she wanted from either her mother or Will."

Will pushed open the French doors and strode onto the patio, which put an end to the conversation, but Eva continued to wonder about her youngest sister. Being tough was a requirement to survive in this family, she suspected. And she didn't think Samantha was.

◆◆◆◆◆

Driving home, Chloe said, "So, you're coming into some money. Good news, huh?"

Eva couldn't decide. "Money does weird things to people." Without thinking, she added, "I get the impression Will never had to fight or work hard for anything. He was always surrounded by all that money, enabled as well as protected by it. Like green armor." Realizing what she had said, she said quickly, "Oh, sorry, Chloe—"

Her aunt brushed it off with a casual wave of her hand. "Don't worry. I know what you mean. It's true."

"As for letting them help me, taking their money, I don't know yet. I mean, it's amazing that my college expenses could be paid. I'm so tempted..."

"But?"

"But what will I owe them?"

"You'll owe them nothing." Chloe was adamant. "Will owes *you*."

Eva shrugged. "I guess. But he wants me to tour the company facilities. What if Olivia's right—that he wants to test me?"

"You know, Eva, would that be such a terrible thing?" She shot Eva a look, and quickly added, "Now, hear me out. It's so tiring for you to heal people, and I've heard you say, 'there's only one of me.' Well, what if testing found a way to mitigate that? What if there's something in your blood that could be identified, to help more people? Or even something genetic that could be learned? And anyway, what is there to lose?"

Eva unclenched her hands. "You might have a point. I think it's because Will is pushing for it... I don't know, it just rubs me the wrong way. I don't quite trust his motives." She sighed and thought for a minute. "What if he expects something in return for funding my education? Like he has with Samantha? She told me she wants to go to Juilliard or The Acting Studio, but Will won't let her."

"I know that's what she says. I doubt it's that cut and dried. Over the years I've learned to take what Sam says with a large pinch... Don't forget, it's Mom and Dad who sorted your college fund, not Will."

Eva thought about that. "Are you saying I won't have to make a deal with the devil?"

Chloe grinned.

"And also, there's the fact that they're not too keen on my studying to be a vet. Seems they'd prefer me to be some "prestigious" neurologist." She sketched quotation marks with her fingers.

Chloe saw Eva's grimace. "I know—shoot me now, right?"

They drove in silence for a few minutes. When the song playing on Sirius Radio switched to "In My Life," by the Beatles, Eva softly sang along.

Chloe asked, "How goes it with your Michael?"

"I don't know if he's *my* Michael," Eva answered quickly.

"He could be, if you wanted it, right?"

"I guess... but I'm not sure. He touches me, connects with me in ways I've never really experienced before. It's unnerving."

"Oh, but it's what we all long for. That kind of connection. And most people don't even know it. We're too busy hiding ourselves because we're shy, or embarrassed. Or afraid of getting hurt. Or worst of all, think we don't deserve it. I believe everyone is lonely, it's an existential condition of humanity."

"I just think I'm better off alone."

Chloe reached forward and turned down the sound just as the track changed to "Here, There, and Everywhere." She glanced over at Eva. "I'm not sure anyone is better off alone."

Eva glanced across at Chloe. Her aunt's face was serious.

"I've been in love," Chloe said. "Once. He was also a Michael. He was *my* Michael. But I always called him Micky. I knew we were doomed, but I seized each moment and held on tight, clutching at happiness like the fragile blown glass it is..."

"What was he like?" Eva asked.

"He was a musician, played the mandolin and guitar, with his heart in his fingers. He taught music at the high school, but his rapture was in playing. When he played, his soul soared. And the souls listening soared with him. That's partly why I decided to give scholarships to talented students. I love it, and I carry on in part to feel close to Micky. Let's see, how can I describe him? A Bach concerto would move him to tears, but he sounded like a demented crow when he sang. He was a blood-red tulip, he was bubbles of champagne. He belly-laughed like no one I've ever known. Taught me how. When he entered a room, the room grew brighter. He was my giggle, my heart, my guiding light. In some ways, he was my hero."

Her aunt was a poet. "Why was it doomed? What happened?"

Chloe took a long breath. "He was married, and I couldn't help myself. He couldn't seem to help himself either. We met when we could, for an hour at a time. But what an hour that was. His wife was ill, had been for years, with Multiple Sclerosis. He loved her, and she never knew. About us, that is. We went to great lengths to be sure she'd never know."

Eva waited. She knew there was more. There had to be.

Chloe was quiet for a minute or two, then said, "I felt tremendous guilt over loving him. He spoke of ending it dozens of times, but we were his happiness, his comfort, his rest from looking after Jennifer. But he loved her, and I certainly didn't want him to leave her—I didn't want my contentment, my completion to be at her expense. She needed him, and he needed to do the right thing. I loved him for it."

She sighed. "But we were human. We couldn't find the strength to deny ourselves the joy, the bliss we got from our stolen minutes together..."

Chloe's face stared straight ahead at the highway and her voice became expressionless. "He died, one icy February day. Six years ago. We'd spent two glorious hours together, then I drove him back to his car. As I left him, I had a bad feeling. A weird feeling... I stopped the car a couple of blocks away, feeling unsettled, and I almost turned back. Something was wrong. I brushed it off as absurd, but five minutes later, I heard the wail of an ambulance, then it raced by me. I knew. I just knew."

"Oh, Chloe."

"Everyone wonders why I don't date, now, find someone to love. My relationship with my Michael, my Micky, was the most wonderful fourteen years of my life." Chloe swallowed. "Nothing could approach that. I don't even want to try."

Eva's aunt turned off the highway, just as "Here There and Everywhere" ended and "Let it Be" began. She stopped at a red light and turned to Eva. Reaching for her hand, she said, "Enjoy each moment. You don't know what's around the corner."

"Don't I know it."

"I'm not referring to the aneurysm," Chloe said quickly. "Although I imagine it feels like the Sword of Damocles."

Eva squeezed her aunt's hand. "Thank you for telling me."

"You may wonder why I did," Chloe said. "I've been thinking about your Michael. I hope someday soon you can undo the wrappings around you. It's like you're mummified, sweet girl."

The light changed to green, and Chloe put both hands back on the wheel. "If Michael is right for you," she added, softly, "he'll be both the garden in which you grow, and the gardener that protects and nourishes you." She sighed. "Believe me, if your

Michael is anything like my Michael, that would be the best thing that ever happened to you."

Eva knew her aunt didn't expect a response.

Chapter 28

Monday morning turned out to be one of those ungodly hot and humid mornings, after a night where the temperature didn't drop below seventy-five degrees. Eva planned to work in her bedroom today, where there was an A/C unit. It was going to be a scorcher.

"Did you see the new Gleason blog yesterday?" Michael's voice on the phone was cautious.

Eva shook her head. "Jamie and Clare told me about it, last night. Suggested I avoid it—that made sense to me." She could do without more harsh criticism and cynical attacks.

"Yes, good idea. And there's another article in this morning's online New Haven Times. They say they reached out to you for comment."

Eva sighed.

"Yeah, they came to the shelter. I wasn't there but they left a message with Jake. I ignored it."

"Well, I've texted you the link."

"I'll look in a bit. How bad is it?"

Michael said, "Not *bad*. Amazed. A bit hyperbolic. It seemed like the whole hospital talked to the press. The mother of the baby with meningitis certainly did. The reporter used the word 'miraculous,' a direct quote from the mother."

Eva could hear him tapping on his laptop as he read from the article and scrolled down the screen.

"And the mom claims her fibromyalgia pain has gone, too," Michael added.

"What?"

"The mother feels no pain. Probably full of endorphins from her baby's recovery."

"Oh, right," Eva said. "That's probably what it is."

"She said you're an angel. That her baby went from the brink of death to perfectly well in a few hours. It's quite the article."

When she hung up, Eva peeked out the kitchen window. No one was there. Would press people find out where she lived? She was afraid it was only a matter of time.

But there was a bright side to the situation. This confirmed that she had helped the baby with meningitis, and with this knowledge came quiet exhilaration.

Eva led Cookie upstairs to collect her laptop. She turned the A/C up high, put on instrumental soft jazz, and for the next two hours, blotted out everything except the new website she was creating. Based on interviews with her client, a small firm of financial advisors, she worked in soft grays and blue, choosing a minimalist background with next to no decoration. Just light gray vertical lines to divide the main content from the menu bars. As a kind of nod to the pinstripe suit, she thought with a satisfied grin. She was almost finished adding the client's content, when she stood up to stretch and heard her phone dinging down the hall in her office.

It was a message from Governor Audrey Lambeth, asking Eva to call. Even though her grandmother had prepared her, she was still stunned to hear the crisp voice she'd heard so many times on TV and radio. Eva returned the call but only reached the office of the governor's Chief of Staff. While she sat on hold, she nearly succumbed to the desire to slam down the phone. Her palms started to sweat, as a hazy dangerous future seemed to stretch out before her.

What have I gotten myself into?

Then, there was the governor herself on the line.

"Ms. McGrath? Thank you so much, for calling back, and for agreeing to see my Charles. He is suffering from pancreatic cancer, which your grandmother may have told you. The outlook is... not good. In fact, he's just entered hospice." Her voice broke.

"I'm so sorry, Governor Lambeth."

"Thank you. And please, call me Audrey. Angela told me what you did for William, and that you might be willing to try... to help in some way. Can you come?"

Eva understood how this woman had reached the position of governor. The energy of her charisma and authority rolled right down the phone line. Or through the air, which was more applicable, seeing as it was a cellphone. In any event, this woman was powerful, and Eva wondered how anyone ever said no to her. Or if they ever did.

When she agreed to go to the Lambeth home in Mystic that same evening, Governor Lambeth offered to send a car. Eva started to demur, thinking she could of course just drive herself, but then remembered how exhausted she was after healing adults and gratefully accepted.

Hanging up, she called Michael. They'd planned to get together that evening, but this changed things.

"Oh, man, the governor? How cool is that?" Michael's voice was excited. "I'll come and be a bodyguard."

Eva had to chuckle. "The governor has a security detail—I looked it up. Twelve guys whose job it is to protect her."

"Not for *her*... for *you*."

"Well, how can I turn down that chivalrous offer? Thanks, Michael."

"A bit more exciting than grilled-hamburger-and-old-movie night I had in mind. And she's sending a car? I was going to offer to take you, but this is better. I hope it's a limo with champagne in the fridge." He paused. "I know you're thinking I should be serious in this situation, and I will be tonight. But her husband's illness is going to be a thing of the past. I believe you're going to take care of that, my sweet Eva. This is going to be the luckiest day of the governor's life."

———◆———

That evening, they pulled up to a large Victorian house, right on the water in Mystic, with a bronze plaque mounted on a stone column. Eva read aloud, "Lambeth House."

"Gorgeous," Michael said softly, for Eva's ears alone. "Victorian Italianate style, there's even a widow's walk, look." Michael pointed to the roof. Eva could see a raised and fenced rectangular structure built on the roof of the house. But the beauty of the house hardly made an impression on her. She swiped her palms along the sides of her pants, to dry them, then rubbed at the knot in her stomach. So much was expected of her. What if she couldn't deliver? What if it didn't work this time?

The young chauffeur eased the Town Car to a gentle stop, adjusted his cap, and hopped out to get Eva's door. She opened it herself, turning to thank him.

"I'll be right here when you need me to take you home, Ms. McGrath," he said with a smile.

Audrey Lambeth met them at the door, greeting them warmly, then led them through her home to the screened porch at the back, which overlooked spacious flower beds and a pond with a fountain.

"Charlie, Charlie, she's here. Honey?"

Charles Lambeth lay in a hospital bed, placed so he could look out across the vast lawns and garden. Eva had to suppress a gasp when she saw how thin he was. Gaunt even. His bony arms lay outside the white sheet, and he was so motionless it flashed through her mind that he was already dead. But no, his sunken eyes opened and met his wife's. Audrey Lambeth murmured again to him, telling him Eva McGrath was here, and had to remind him she was a touch therapist who was here to try to make him feel a bit better. Then Audrey gestured for Eva to take a seat next to the bed. Michael pulled up a wicker chair close to Eva, and Audrey sat on the edge of the bed holding her husband's hand.

As she gazed at this fatally ill man, Eva's heart fell. Along with her hope. Then Charles Lambeth's eyes found Eva's. She took his hand and was flooded with sensations. Compassion, empathy, pain in her upper abdomen, sadness... She smiled gently and asked him to close his eyes and imagine being in his favorite spot in the world. He whispered, "Telluride," and the corners of his mouth lifted in a small smile.

"He's a terrific skier..." Audrey said, softly.

Eva shut her eyes and felt Michael take her other hand. Waves of warm energy flowed into her from Michael, filling her with strength. She was reminded that the same thing happened when Chloe touched her during her grandfather's healing. Without thinking, Eva said, softly, "Audrey, please take Michael's hand." She felt, more than saw, Michael and the governor join hands. And with the circle complete, she felt the change. She could feel Audrey, strong, but with fear and grief staining her energy. And she could feel Michael. Also strong, so strong, fearless, but warm and kind and confident. All of which flowed into her. Combined, the energies were somehow greater than the sum of the parts. The depth of power startled her briefly, but then she basked in it. This was different, stronger, deeper somehow. The expanse of the circle grew until the energy encompassed her.

For a few moments, before she descended into the vast dark space of meditation and healing, she focused on the sound of the fountain, on the splashing, gurgling water. On the warm soft evening air through the screens all around her. The fragrance of roses. The sound of an owl hooting in the distance. From Charles, she felt the greatest weakness she could imagine.

The first wall was of steel. As she focused on it, she slowly understood that it was her *own* wall, not created by the man in the bed. That realization came as a bit of a shock, and it took her a few moments to refocus. Then the wall dissolved, and although there were several obstacles beyond it, they were not as rigid, yielding without too much effort.

He's nearly gone.

The healing itself took a long time. It was as if the man was already partially over to the other side. Eva floated, in the sensation of deep water and the others' energy. She waited patiently, but it didn't feel like waiting, exactly. Waiting implied the passage of time. This pool of energy existed outside of time, exempt from it. It was more akin to suspended animation, but with contentment, suffused with bliss, in this deep space.

She had no idea how long she was "under." How long the moment held. It could have been minutes, it might have been hours. When she surfaced from the gentle vibration and connectedness, she felt peaceful, hopeful. She knew this feeling.

That was the last thing she knew.

•• ◆ ••

Several hours later, Michael checked on Eva, where she lay on his bed, for what seemed like the hundredth time.

After Eva had collapsed onto the hospital bed, Michael scooped her up in his arms and reassured the almost frantic governor that "this happened" when Eva performed a healing. He carried her out to the car, laying her gently across the back seat.

The wide-eyed chauffeur muttered, "Oh my God, is she OK? Should I drive to the hospital?"

Michael shook his head. "No, home, please." He gave his own address to the driver, and climbed into the limousine, lifting Eva's head onto his lap. He left his number with the driver for the governor.

All evening he paced and yes, worried. He'd called Jamie to bring Cookie, who immediately jumped on the bed next to Eva. Michael and Jamie sat in the living room sipping wine, talking about the experience, and whether they needed to call a doctor. All Eva had said, almost in her sleep, during the ride home, was that her stomach ached.

"She'll need food," Jamie said. "What's in the house?"

Michael thought. "Pad Thai from last night."

"That'll do. And water, or tea," Jamie added. "I'll make a tray."

"Thanks, Jamie. I'm glad you're here."

"We have to look after our girl," she said with a smile, as she headed for the kitchen.

When Michael's phone rang, he was once more upstairs in his bedroom checking on Eva, seeing if she was awake. So, he learned of Charles Lambeth's improvement as he stood gazing at the beautiful, magical woman lying on his bed. With her little dog snugged up at her side. Phone back in his pocket, Michael stood, overwhelmed with thoughts, realizations, and emotions. It was the most inspirational and emotional moment of his life. By a long, long, way. This young woman, who he prayed would be his partner in life, was able to heal people on the brink of death. And he'd felt it, experienced it with her, felt the depth and the power of it. Tears sprang into his eyes, and as he heard Jamie behind him, he turned to her.

Wiping his eyes, he whispered, "That was Audrey Lambeth. She said her husband is better. He's sitting up, energy improved, groggy from the morphine, but hungry. And the pain has dropped by seventy-five percent."

Jamie wrapped her arms around him, and they stood in the doorway and wept.

••◆••

An hour later, Eva sat on the edge of Michael's newly installed whirlpool tub as it filled. She looked pale, drained. He pulled a pile of plush towels from the cabinet, then lit the candle sconces above the tub. The fragrance of lavender and vanilla filled the steamy bathroom. He pointed to the tub, its water moving in slow current from the jets at the sides. "Hop in. I'm going to get a glass of something... red wine, I think. You want some apple cider?"

"Thanks. And check if Cookie's OK?"

"She's the best—she stayed right with you while you slept. Now, all three of the pups are asleep in their beds in the kitchen, but yes, I will give them all your love."

Eva smiled and gave him a sleepy thumbs up.

When he returned, she was deep in the water and her eyes were closed. Her unique beauty struck him yet again. Would he ever look at her and not be mesmerized? Her long hair floated in the water beside her head, like a halo. She moaned softly as he slipped into the water across from her.

"Better?" he asked.

"Yes," she replied. She opened her eyes. "Tonight was..."

He watched her hunt for the words. Reaching for her hand, he squeezed it gently. "I know. I can't describe it. There was a circle of energy between us all. It was like... we were connected."

"Yes." Eva sighed and closed her eyes again. She said slowly, "You know, Michael, my whole life... or since my mom died, I've always felt like I'm floating in the middle of a vast lake. Alone. In a canoe. There's no light but the faint moonlight on the water. I have no oars, no sail, there's no shore in sight."

She paused, and he said nothing. She was beginning to open, to drop some of the tight bindings that were wrapped around her. He was loathe to say anything, in case it was the wrong thing, in case she closed up again. So, he just listened quietly.

"It's been like that for so long I'm not even frightened anymore," she said, softly. "I just know that as the tide and the wind will take a river, it will take me. And my job is... has always been... just to survive."

Her eyes opened and met his, those luscious brown eyes that held specks of gold.

"I never knew why I was here," she said. "But, discovering I can heal... Well, it's like gaining oars." She was quiet for a moment. "And binoculars. And sail and rudder."

"Don't stop there. A map. And I will throw in the outboard motor." He smiled and squeezed her hand.

"Thank you, Michael," she said. "Thank you for everything, tonight." She sighed. "This is absolute heaven. The pulsing of the water... and the temperature is just right. I feel like molasses. But it's late, it must be almost midnight."

Michael couldn't have cared less what time it was. She was here, and she might be letting him in. Letting him help her. At last.

"Good. Enjoy," he said softly. "But save me just a bit of energy, I have plans for molasses in a little while."

When she crawled into bed, he headed downstairs to lock up. He gave the dogs a few minutes outside, then locked up the house and headed back to the bedroom. He found her curled up in the fetal position, fast asleep. He slid in beside her, spooned her gently, and simply enjoyed her softness, her nearness.

And so much for doing things with molasses, he thought to himself with a grin. But her opening a bit to him was a step in the right direction. It made his heart ache to think of her description of being lost and alone on the lake.

Well, tonight he could be the canoe.

Chapter 29

Eva woke suddenly, hearing Cookie's bark. Sitting up, she saw the little dog standing with front paws on the windowsill, staring out at the front lawn. Eva heard someone shouting. It sounded like Jamie.

"Get off my property! For the last time, get off. Ten more seconds and I'm calling the police. Move it. I *mean* it. Ten... nine..."

It had been a week since Eva had helped Charles Lambeth and the media presence had been building. Eva rubbed her eyes and hurried to the window, where she saw several cars and a van, complete with TV broadcast antenna, parked on the road. A dozen or more people stared up at the house or called out questions to Jamie. This was the worst yet.

"Do you believe she really heals, Ms. Chin?"

"How does she do it, Jamie?"

"Have you witnessed a healing?"

"Has she always been a healer or did this just start?"

"Will she answer some questions?"

"What is it like for you, rooming with a miracle healer?"

"Is Eva your girlfriend?"

Jamie ignored their questions, just kept counting down. They did back up, until their feet were on the public road, and that's the best Eva and Jamie could hope for.

Eva recognized Roger Gleason among the small crowd. He seemed to have a permanent leer on his thin face. A female reporter, one of the Barbie doll types from network news, held up a microphone. She stood in front of the van, the side of which announced it was WCUX, a local media station. A male photojournalist aimed a long telephoto lens toward the window where Eva stood. She jumped back and yanked the blinds shut.

She raced downstairs, just as Jamie slammed the front door behind her.

"Pushy swine," Jamie said. "Pissing me off." She turned to peer out the side lights and sighed.

"What are we going to do about it?"

"Nothing we can do."

"Oh Jamie, I'm so sorry. I brought this down on you."

Jamie turned to Eva. "Oh, I don't know... It's kind of exciting. You're famous! I told them you'd gone away to stay with friends in Vermont, but I think they just spotted you in the window." She peeked out at the reporters again.

"And somehow my cell number is out—I had fourteen messages yesterday."

"Fourteen?"

Eva nodded. It was rare to get phone calls anymore, most everyone texted. She'd waded through the voicemails: a local New London newspaper asked her to comment on a story they were running. Left a number. Then a well-known health influencer on

YouTube inquired if she would be willing to sit for an interview. A slew of other journalists left messages. The thought of calling them all made her cringe. Then one from a 212 area code. Manhattan.

"There was even one from some guy at CNN wanting to arrange for me to come to New York City for a Sunday talk show."

"*National TV?*" Jamie's eyes were huge.

"Yes." Eva gave a small groan.

"You're not going to do it, are you?"

Eva shuddered. *As if.*

"Well, I hate to add to the pile," Jamie said, "but there's an article about the governor and her husband this morning in the Hartford Telegraph, too. Which mentions you. Wait a minute..." She dug her phone out of her pocket. Finding the page, she held it up for Eva to see.

"Governor's Husband in Miraculous Recovery Thanks to Local 'Healer'"

Eva scanned the article. It covered Charles Lambeth's battle with pancreatic cancer, hospice, mentioned Eva McGrath was seen leaving the Governor's Mystic home, and that Charles Lambeth had been on the mend since that evening. Doctors were refusing to comment, but a spokesperson for the governor's office confirmed his improvement and voiced astonishment.

Jamie said, "They put 'Healer' in quotes... but otherwise it's not derogatory."

"I don't even dare look at the comments." Eva drew in a breath and tried to smile. "All this before tea and breakfast. I call 'do over.'" She longed to go back to bed and start again. Turning toward the kitchen, over her shoulder she said, "The governor called me yesterday, apologizing about it leaking out. Someone from her staff must have talked... Anyway, the good news is she wants to meet with me about how to go forward from here with my… healing gift, as she put it."

Jamie turned from the open fridge, staring. "What does that mean?"

"She mentioned starting a foundation for me." Eva filled the kettle. "For support, for legitimizing me, for scheduling and connecting people that need healing."

Jamie's mouth dropped open. "That would be amazing."

"Chloe tells me the governor and her husband are wealthy, so they may even kick it off. But the governor also mentioned raising money for studies to legitimize healing—make me less of a target. By testing me. I know I was against it, at first when Will Hastings pushed it. But I've thought about it—it could be a good thing. If they can pin down exactly what happens when I heal someone, it could give me scientific credibility in the medical world. Anyway, we're meeting next week. A foundation could help me figure out how to make all this work."

"And give you resources!" Jamie exclaimed. "This would solve so many issues—the way things stand now, you just can't heal people every day, as tiring as it is for you, and keep up your website work…"

Eva sighed. "I know. And study. And get to the shelter. And help at Michael's clinic."

"And have a life," added Jamie.

I need to stop this roller coaster.

To that end, Eva decided, having finished her exams and papers, to take a break from online classes and her website-building business. She'd been hoping for some time off, some beach time, some play time. Some time to help at Michael's clinic and the shelter. But everything had changed. The clinic had only asked Eva for help once in the last couple of weeks, for a dog with diabetes. Furthermore, Jake had asked that she not come to the shelter for "a little while," as he put it, to "let things settle down." He told her the reporters and TV people were a constant nuisance.

Plus, the shelter was inundated with requests for healings. When Jake brought her a young cat with a nasty case of ringworm, at the same time he delivered an enormous pile of queries from all over the world. From as far away as Korea.

All she could do was shake her head at how fast word had spread online about her healing. Eva had no idea what to do about the countless requests. There were only so many hours in the day.

At least some good was resulting from all this publicity. With more awareness of the shelter's activity, people were coming out of the woodwork to adopt pets. Jake suspected they all hoped they could adopt one Eva had healed, and they all certainly wanted to lay eyes on her.

Eva missed the clinic, she missed the shelter, she missed Jake and her friends. She missed going to her yoga class for the peace of mind it gave her. She'd tried creeping into a session, and remained at the back of the room, hoping she would not be noticed. But two people spotted her, pointing and whispering, and a young woman approached her to ask if it was true, that she really could heal people. Before Eva could answer, the woman begged her to help her grandmother. Feeling overwhelmed, she grabbed her bag and raced from the class. Then felt guilty because she should heal if she could. Wasn't that right? She had to because she *could?*

And what if it came down to choosing *who* she would try to help? Some of the requests came with offers of money, sometimes great amounts of money. That couldn't be the deciding factor. It just couldn't be. Wealthy people should not be able to buy the best health care. Thinking about it made her skin crawl. She'd always believed that health should be unrelated to profit. That no one should suffer for being unable to pay for a doctor or surgeon. She'd wondered for years if Sophie might have survived had she been able to afford the best cancer treatment.

Eva was grinding her teeth in her sleep, taking antacids for a burning stomach, forgetting to eat, and finding it hard to meditate. Or relax. Or exercise.

Coming and going from Jamie's house felt like a perp walk. Eva held her hand or her bag in front of her face and scurried as quickly as she could to the front door. When the neighbor whose property bordered Jamie's to the back noticed the media circus, he suggested Eva hide her car behind his barn, then slip through the wooded lot, then past the hedge into Jamie's yard. So far it was working, but Eva didn't know how long that would last.

Reporters showing up every day got old fast, as did creeping around avoiding windows and asking Jamie to take Cookie out. Early one evening there were no reporters, miraculously, so she dared take Cookie for a short walk. But on her return, she spotted a van in front of the house. She hightailed it back around the curve of the road and crept in the back way once more. And Michael's house was no reprieve—the press had heard about their relationship and were showing up at his house, as well.

She needed a break from thinking about everything. A break from thinking, period.

At Chloe's suggestion, Eva decided to spend a few days with her in Rhode Island, as it seemed the reporters hadn't yet figured out their family connection. With Michael promising to drive up on the weekend, Eva packed up. Then she sneaked around to her car, Cookie following happily, and hit the road.

Chapter 30

On Monday morning, Eva, Chloe, and Michael headed to Boston for the promised tour of the Hastings Pharma facility. Being at Chloe's had been a great break; she spent three restful days helping Chloe in the garden, playing with the dogs, and watching Michael get to know her aunt. They took to each other as if they were old friends who just hadn't seen each other for a while. Eva couldn't help but smile. It came so naturally to Michael, as open and gregarious as he was. For a moment she was envious—how do people do that?

Most of the tour of the pharmaceutical company sounded like a corporate sales pitch. Eva let the buzz-words float by her, such as "Precision medicine," "Targeted solutions," and "Global quality R & D." She had to make herself tune back in, as her mind had wandered. Hastings' Chief Scientific Officer was droning on and on about the wonders of molecular and genetic profiling, then he ended with, "Our world-class medical care is designed to drill down into highly focused efforts to improve the lives of patients, employees, and our communities." *Blah blah blah.* Eva thought she could replace all of that with the words, "There's a pill for that." She mentally chastised herself for a lack of respect.

Bottom line, she wondered how all this related to her. She was fascinated by the clean rooms, the high-tech instrumentation, and digitalization, and she recognized the enormous value of vaccines, painkillers, advanced antibiotics, and other lifesaving drugs. But she felt removed from this world, wondering if any of the scientists there would accept her form of healing. But they recognized her. One female lab technician burst out, "Oh, I've heard of you—you're the miracle healer!" The technician, flustered, apologized and turned back to her tasks.

At the end of the tour, Will Hastings led them to the executive dining room, where a long, glistening table was set for eight. Waiters bustled around the room with wine and other drinks. The savory aroma of roast chicken floated around the room, and even though Eva was on edge, her stomach growled.

Jared was there, of course, smart in a gray suit and tie, and Samantha, in rumpled slacks and a blowsy shirt, arrived after the tour. Her hair was pulled back in a scrunchy, her chubby face scrubbed clean. Eva gave her younger sister a warm hug and invited her to sit next to her. Susanna, Will's wife, had arrived as well, having made the short trek from the townhouse in Boston. Eva found she couldn't make any inroads in getting to know Susanna. Once again meticulously dressed, if conservatively, in a light green jacket and skirt, she was as icy and polite as her suit, and as at the party a few weeks earlier. And as unreadable. Olivia was absent, again, off at some modeling engagement in the city and Eva wondered at that. Did her half-sister simply not care? Or was it a deliberate snub?

Will took his place at the head of the table, gesturing for Eva to sit at his right hand. Michael took the chair to Will's left, which meant he was directly across from Eva. Everyone settled into the remaining seats around the table, but Jared gave her a cold look. It occurred to her she might be usurping pride of place by sitting next to Will Hastings but couldn't find the charity to be concerned.

Tough cookies, Jared.

Lunch was served, and Eva began to relax, listening to Sam chatter on, on her other side, about her next trip to New York for a "fab" off-Broadway play.

Will said, "Eva, Chloe tells me you might be willing to submit to a bit of testing."

All heads turned to Eva.

"We need to talk about that," Eva replied. "As in blood work?"

"Of course, but I was thinking more along the lines of an MRI and EEG."

"No MRI." Eva realized too late she'd sounded adamant.

Will's eyebrows went up. "Why? There's nothing dangerous about an MRI—it's safe, with no side effects. It's just magnetic energy."

"Sorry, no MRI," Eva repeated. She felt Chloe and Michael watching her and knew they respected her privacy regarding the aneurysm. "As for the EEG, could you explain that?"

Will studied her, then shrugged off her refusal. "Electroencephalography or EEG is the process of measuring and analyzing electrical activity in the brain. Then it's compared to normal or average values."

"I've been researching healers," Michael said. "The results of clinical testing are few and far between, but there was a study using EEG, a few years ago, which seemed to show different brain waves in healers."

"I'd like to see that, Michael," Will replied.

"It suggested energy healers can actually shift brain states when they're engaged in healing. They tested all kinds of practitioners—Reiki, Shamanic healing, Quantum Touch, and the like." He had everyone's attention around the table.

Jared cleared his throat and spoke up. "If we do the EEG, we will need a signed liability waiver, Eva."

"No," Eva said again. "No liability waiver."

Jared's chin jutted out. "Excuse me?"

Michael said, "Any test that requires a liability waiver would be something you needed more information on, and to think about, right Eva?"

"Yes, that's right, thank you Michael."

"I'll take it from here, Jared," Will said. "Of course, Eva, there's nothing that needs a liability waiver." He turned to Jared who had tried to butt in. "No, Jared, we're fine."

Jared fell silent, plunking down his water glass, his eyes down, his jaw firmly set.

Will turned back to Michael, pursed his lips in thought, and Eva noted the baleful eye of a closed-minded skeptic. He said, "Michael, did this study confirm that the energy wave differences were possible, or probable, in the brains of the healers? Was there a control group, was it double-blind?"

"Didn't need to be. The healers in a resting state were the control. During the healing state, the energy of their brain changed. The results were astonishing. The healers shifted brain states across all frequency bands: Delta, Theta, Alpha, and Beta. The greatest was in global Alpha spectral power."

Michael stopped and looked around the table. "I'll just send you the study—I can see some eyes glazing over." He grinned. "Suffice it to say, healing is indeed possible, even probable. In simple terms, we believe healing information rides on an energy wave. And we have Eva here as evidence."

He met her eyes and smiled.

"Ah," said Will, "there's the age-old question of probable versus possible. As you know, hard science is steeped, stewed even, in probabilities. We have to be."

Eva saw Michael take a breath, and he glanced at her. She mentally wished him luck.

"Most of my life." he said, "I've struggled with the two concepts of probable versus possible. I've been intrigued by science, that world where everything is judged and defined by how *probable* it is, how likely it is." He paused and looked around the table. "But, for me, the mistake happens when those steeped in science think if something is *improbable* then it's *impossible* as well."

Will began to speak, and Michael held up his hand. "I get it, sir. Before you can put something in a bottle and sell it to millions of people you need to prove it's going to do XYZ every time somebody takes it. But too many times, those who've dedicated their energy to the scientific side of things have abandoned possibilities entirely."

Eva added, "Surely science must include curiosity? The curiosity of what might be *possible?* How else would anything new get discovered?"

Will scratched his chin. "Well... You think I don't believe you, Eva? You're both rather defensive. I've seen my father's improvement. I've heard about your governor's husband. I believe you. I want to know *how*. Don't you want to know how? What if this gift is something we can use to help millions of people?"

Michael's tone was conciliatory. "Sorry if I was adamant, Mr. Hastings. But I've encountered so much arrogance, even hubris in the scientific world. In my view, that world regularly forgets that when something new is discovered, invariably there's universal mockery, and the idea is completely discounted. Until it's proven again. Then again. Then suddenly everyone jumps on board."

"Right," added Eva. "The situation finally reaches a tipping point, and everyone accepts it's true."

"What's that old line about things being impossible until they're done?" added Michael. "Nelson Mandela, I believe. Anyway, I think that sums up Eva's healing gift."

Susanna spoke up. "Let's lighten up the conversation, please Will. Some of us feel a bit excluded." She smiled her frosty, distant smile.

"Of course," Will replied. Turning back to Michael, he said smoothly, "So, young man, are you going to be my son-in-law?"

Eva gasped. She felt the heat rush into her cheeks.

Quick as a flash, Michael replied, "Wouldn't it be great to have a veterinarian as a son-in-law?"

"I think it would be awesome,' Samantha said with a grin. "I love animals. But isn't it heartbreaking, even unbearable when you lose a dog or a cat?"

Will tossed a hand in the air, as if throwing away her remark. "Don't ask silly questions, Samantha."

It was Samantha's turn to flush red.

And what was with Will? Honestly, asking Michael about being his son-in-law. Eva wondered if her father was trying to unnerve her. Well, it sure didn't look like he had unnerved Michael. Not even slightly.

"I don't agree. Not silly, Sam," Michael said. "It really is, it's hard. But it's more heartwarming when we save one and that's what we do more often than lose one. That's become particularly easy since I met Eva."

Eva met Michael's eyes, those warm, deep eyes. She felt a shiver of pride. He was so smart, so personable, handling these people so well.

"So, Michael," asked Samantha, whose cheeks were still red. "What do you make of Eva's healing?"

"You folks used the word 'gobsmacked.' That's what I think of her healing. I'm gobsmacked." He smiled at Sam. "But on a more serious note, to me, the natural evolution of science is in the study of smaller and smaller amounts of energy frequencies, or vibrational energy. That's the realm in which Eva's healing operates, we believe."

"And it will be harnessable?" asked Will.

Michael's eyes were on Eva. "It is for Eva."

"Which is why Father wants to test her. Think of the millions of dollars... If he can harness her," Samantha said, a cool smile on her face.

Ahh, payback. Eva didn't say it aloud. Instead, she said, "I feel like a horse." She gave a wry grin and the mood lightened.

Will leaned toward Eva. "So, my dear Eva, will you do me the honor of having lunch with me, just the two of us this week? We have things to discuss. And we need to get to know one another."

Eva drew in a breath and met his eyes. This man created a prickliness in her that was unusual. "Possibly, I'll look at my schedule. But it's a bit far for me to come on a workday, all the way to Boston."

"I'm going to be in Providence this week, looking at a potential acquisition. Does that help? Meet me, say Wednesday, in Providence?"

She realized her hands, in her lap, were clenched. She was not looking forward to facing this man over lunch for an hour or two. But maybe he'd be different away from the rest of the family. She hoped so.

Chapter 31

After lunch, in the hallway outside the dining room, Eva drew Jared to one side. "Can I have a word, Jared?" She saw, or rather felt, his guard go up. "I'm not a threat to you, so why are you so hostile?"

He let out a cross between a guffaw and a chortle. "I'm not hostile, just realistic. If you want hostile, spend some time with Olivia and Samantha."

"Excuse me?"

"What you see is what you get with me. At least I'm upfront about the fact I don't trust you—I don't know what your game is yet."

"There's no game," Eva replied.

"So you say. What is it you want from us?"

"Isn't it possible I just want to know my family?"

"Well, take a good-faith warning. Watch out for my sisters."

"What do you mean?"

"Olivia will act like she doesn't care, one way or the other, and Samantha will try to be your best friend. But either one of them, or both, will stab you in the back when you're not looking."

"Why? I've done nothing to any of you."

"Don't be naïve. Or disingenuous. It's because Dad talks about you all the time."

Eva was stunned into silence. Then she found her voice and flashed back with, "You don't have to worry about me. I don't want into the company, and I don't want any of your inheritance, Jared Hastings."

"Generous of you, but it's too late for that. They've already written you in."

"Well, I'm sorry you feel I don't have a right to it— since I *am* your father's daughter. I'm your half-sister."

"Not proven," he whispered.

"Get your father to take a paternity test. It can be part of the blood work."

"I will,' he replied. His eyes were cold slits, his face hard, and the vivid image of a snake appeared in Eva's mind.

Eva lost control. "No matter. With the *welcome* I've received from you, and the dysfunction in this family, I'm not sure I want to be part of it anyway. Chloe is a delight, and I want to get to know *my* grandmother and grandfather. As for the rest of you... I may just take a pass."

Jared sneered at her. "Please do. The truth is, you're an embarrassment. You make us look like quacks, like flaky lunatics. I don't want you connected in any way to this company. Or this family." He spun on his heel and stormed away down the hall, with all heads turned to watch him.

Eva was left shaking and trembling. As Michael crossed to her, concern on his face, she wondered, a little too late, if anyone had heard her angry words.

—— ••◆•• ——

"Jared is possessive about the company, and your sisters are just jealous," Chloe said, in a matter-of-fact tone as she drove them all back to her cottage. "Frankly, they've all been grumbling and whining about you, but not in front of their father. Or their grandparents either, for that matter. Give them some time. They'll chill out when they realize you're not after their positions on the board. Or planning to usurp their dad's attention. I don't see you and Will getting real cozy, somehow."

"No, probably not," Eva replied. "But I'll give it a chance. He's my father, even though it doesn't feel like it. Or how I *imagine* it should feel."

Michael spoke up from behind them in the back seat. "You can't pick and choose relatives. Every family has an odd duck, an Uncle Charlie they don't know what to do with."

"This is hardly an odd duck. The kids are all at each other's throats, and my father, well, he's a narcissist. Pure and simple. He *sounds* as if he wants to help me. But I don't trust him. Sorry, Chloe."

Chloe shook her head. "You're right. He's difficult..." She slapped the steering wheel lightly. "Oh, I keep forgetting, there's something I've been wanting to tell you, Eva. I've been wondering if you're healing more than one person at a time."

"What do you mean?"

"Well, is it possible that when you're healing someone, other people touching you at the same time also have improvements in their health issues? You see, ever since you healed your grandfather, and I was there with my arm through yours, the eczema has cleared up on my forearms. And my dodgy knee, from an injury years ago, stopped hurting."

Eva stared at her.

Michael said, "And you think it's connected."

"Oh yes," Chloe said. "I had arthroscopic surgery on my left knee fifteen years ago and it's ached ever since. All those years, until that day in Dad's library. Now it doesn't." She glanced at Eva again.

Eva took this in.

"Nothing else adds up," Chloe said.

Michael's phone beeped, and Eva heard him answer.

"You know, Chloe, there are more coincidences like that," Eva said. "If they *are* coincidences. Not sure if I told you, but the mother of the baby with meningitis said her fibromyalgia cleared up after the healing session. And Jamie suddenly is no longer allergic to cats. She was holding my hand when I helped her mother."

Chloe glanced across and Eva met her eyes. She could see the excitement on her aunt's face.

"Damn, I'm sorry about that, Luke," Michael said into his phone.

When he ended the call, Eva asked, "What was that? Is Luke OK?"

"Yes. Just annoyed. The press has been pushy at my place, too, the last few days." For Chloe's benefit, he added, "He's my cousin. He pops in at my place when I'm gone and takes care of my dogs. He said the reporters are being a pain—some guy followed him home last night to see if we were there... I can tell you, Luke didn't take well to that. He has a temper. I've ordered a couple of security cameras and you guys should do the same for Jamie's house."

"Maybe security should be Job One for the new foundation," Chloe said.

Eva's stomach started to churn. "Security? You mean like a security guard? Following me everywhere?"

"It may go with the territory, honey," Chloe replied. "What about that nasty threatening letter you got?"

"Nothing further," Eva replied, hoping that was the end of it. "Just nasty online stuff."

Michael said slowly, "What do you two think of Eva giving a press conference, so some questions get answered? You know, the old offense-is-the-best defense idea. Meet it head-on. Do you think that would settle them down, and they'd leave her alone?"

Eva shuddered. "What do you think, Chloe?"

"I don't know. These guys are like paparazzi. You give them a taste and they'll want the whole meal. It could just fire them up."

— •• ◆ •• —

When Michael headed home from Chloe's, Eva strapped Cookie into her harness to drive home. Listening to instrumentals from Tim Janis, she focused on unwinding. She felt like a nomad. She wished she could go back to not knowing. Not knowing she could heal, not knowing her father, not knowing Michael.

Wait. Not knowing Michael? Well, he wanted so much more than she could give. Or should give. Besides, if she hadn't met him, perhaps she'd never have learned she could heal. Discovering she could heal drove a wedge between the past and the present. It was as if her life had tipped into a new place; it was divided into "Before Healing" and "After Healing." Her life was forever altered and she couldn't go back. A yearning for peace and anonymity washed over her.

I'll just have to figure it out.

She was going to have to find a way to schedule healings with time afterward for sleep and rest. The healing session with Governor Lambeth's husband took so much out of her she literally had to be carried out, by Michael. For these sessions she absolutely needed to have someone she trusted with her. She was also going to need time with animals in between since they seemed to restore her, to charge her back up. The next step was to figure out how to develop the skill, so it used less energy. The foundation could be a help with all of this.

She was looking forward to being home that evening. Jamie had texted she was off to Clare's, but she'd left plenty of her homemade Shepherd's Pie. All Eva and Michael had to do was reheat it and make a green salad.

Eva suddenly realized with a start that she and Michael had been together three nights in a row. This thing might be getting too close for comfort. Every time she lay, warm and safe in his arms, she realized she was deepening her connection to him. Lately, when she woke up alone, the first thing she did was look across at the other pillow, and felt surprised, even disappointed, when it was smooth, untouched. When he wasn't there. She was sure an emotional cliff loomed ahead and had no idea how *or if* she could avoid it. Maybe she should end it right now. But every time her brain decided to do it, her heart wouldn't let her.

Eva changed lanes as she neared the Stonington exit from I-95 and noticed the blue sedan that had been behind her for several miles also changed lanes. Glancing up at her rear-view mirror, she watched it follow her off the exit.

You're getting paranoid, Baby Girl. Stop it.

She assumed the car would head south, toward Westerly, but no, it proceeded to follow her north, away from the busier areas. She strained to see the license plate when she sat at the first light, but the car stopped too close behind her. And she couldn't see the driver's face, just a bright green baseball cap. She reached for the button with her left hand and locked the doors.

Eva had grown up in this area and knew the back roads well. Without signaling, she made a sudden left and accelerated sharply. Two seconds later, the car behind her followed, increasing its speed to catch up with her. Her heart started to pound. Telling herself not to blow it out of proportion, she reasoned it might just be someone from the media, who, having figured out the connection between her and Chloe, followed her from Chloe's house. But something made her turn toward North Stonington, away from her final few turns to Jamie's house. She drove into the village of North Stonington and parked right outside the State Police building in the center of town. Leaving the car running, she watched as the car behind her, a big gray SUV, carried on past and turned at the next street. Coincidence?

She took a few deep breaths, then hurried to the station entrance. She turned, stood there, and scanned the road for a few minutes, willing her heart to stop racing. No sign of the car. Maybe she should just head home? But wait, if it *was* a reporter, then why didn't they just stop when she did and try to engage her? Call out questions? That decided it, it didn't feel right. She pulled open the door to the station.

She spent twenty minutes inside, with an austere state trooper, sharp in her gray shirt with blue tie and gold emblems. Relieved the woman took her seriously, Eva calmed down and convinced herself it was just a coincidence, that she was making too much of it. She told the trooper she didn't want to make a report. Instead, the woman walked her to the car, waved off Eva's thanks, and even offered to follow her out of town, to be sure. By this time, Eva felt a bit silly, but as she drove home, she checked her rearview mirror countless times. No one followed her.

She didn't even tell Michael about the incident when he arrived that evening. He was excited to relay how he'd managed to lose a van from WZUR TV, by racing around back streets, taking quick left and right turns. Then he'd had to push through half a dozen media people outside Jamie's, but told them Eva wasn't there, that she had gone to Colorado for a few weeks.

"Didn't know I could lie so well. I'm pretty sure they didn't believe me," he confessed with a grin, "but what the hell, it was worth a try."

Eva thought telling her tale would be anti-climactic after that.

But she went online and ordered pepper spray. She hoped she'd never need to use it.

Chapter 32

Michael put the media circus out of his mind, and they ate in the kitchen at the back of Jamie's house, away from the prying eyes.

Michael rummaged in the freezer. "You said something about ice cream. Ah, coffee with chocolate chips, perfect. You want some? And tea or decaf?" He put on the kettle and glanced over to Eva. She was gazing out the window over the back lawn. "Yo, where've you gone?"

"Oh, my mind wandered... No, no ice cream, thanks." Michael noted she had hardly touched her Shepherd's Pie, had mostly pushed the food around on her plate. "But chamomile tea would be great," Eva added, fondling Cookie's ears beside her. She looked over at Jeremiah and Nellie, curled up in beds on the other side of the room, near the porch door.

"The dogs seem to make a great little pack," Michael said, following her gaze.

She nodded.

"Do you want me to come with you to the meeting with Audrey Lambeth tomorrow?"

"Oh, no thanks, no need," she replied. "The governor will also have a friend of hers, a non-profit attorney, there for the meeting. So, I'll get my questions answered."

He grabbed cups and teabags from the cabinet. While the tea steeped, he stepped out onto the back porch to peer around toward the front of the house. "Ah! Alone at last." He glanced at his watch. "10:30 and they've given up. Hooray, miracles do happen."

She smiled.

That smile floated his world. He crossed back to her, took her hands, and pulled her up. Enfolding her in a hug, he whispered in her ear, "Forget ice cream, I have a better idea. Something even sweeter. Let's have tea and then I'm going to take my beautiful woman to bed."

She stiffened, just for a second.

He pulled back to look into her eyes. "What?"

"Nothing, Michael."

"It's the 'my woman' piece, isn't it?"

"Well," she said defensively, "it's new to me, that's all."

"Get used to it," he said with a grin. When she didn't smile, he asked, "Don't you like the idea?"

"I don't know yet," she answered slowly.

Michael released her, gently, and studied her. "I think you do. But you seem to be in a battle with yourself about it. Us. Our relationship."

She sat back down in the chair by the table. "You're insightful. It's a little unnerving."

"Well, babe, fair warning, more unnerving stuff is just ahead."

She looked a question at him.

"I'm in love with you," he said.

Eva drew in a sharp breath.

"I love you, too, Michael," he said in a high voice. "You're the best thing that's ever happened to me! I want to marry you and have thirteen kids..."

Eva didn't laugh. "What does that mean to you? 'In love'?"

Aware of her eyes on him, Michael took the ice cream back to the freezer and brought their cups to the table. Pulling his chair closer to her, he swished the teabag back and forth in his cup, studying it as though it were terribly important.

"There are various levels of love, I think," he said, finally. "There's the crazy attraction stuff. Not sure that has much to do with love. It's hormones. Chemistry. That rapturous, addictive phase when you can't think of a thing but the person you're wrapped around. People think that's love, but it really only lasts a couple of years, usually."

"That's what I've always thought."

"Right. Then there's liking," he said. "I like, respect, and admire you. If we were just friends, it would still be an honor." He sipped his tea. "And then there's a piece that is somehow *choosing* to love. Because I like, admire, and respect you, I *choose* to love you." He smiled and took her hand, kissing the palm. "It's an easy choice, though, believe me."

"Oh, Michael."

As he looked deep into those gold-brown eyes, deep as a mountain lake, he lost his train of thought. He closed his eyes to collect himself and could feel her energy through her hand. It flooded him, filled him, and held a reminder of the incredible experience he had shared when Eva healed Charles Lambeth. That feeling of floating in deep water, that sense of connection, with its power, its depth.

He opened his eyes and found her studying him. "Then there's the piece of love I simply can't explain." He paused. "It's a love beyond choice, Eva."

She stared at him, and her eyebrows went up. Her brow furrowed slightly, and he tried to explain. "It's a soul-connecting kind of love. Where you'd walk through fire or deserts, or dig away a mountain with a spoon if you had to, to get to your beloved. It's a love that survives heartbreak, tragedy, age, infirmity. The love you see between two old people walking slowly through the park on a Sunday, holding hands."

He was lost in her eyes. But somehow found.

"That's love beyond choice," he said. "Fed by tenderness and understanding. Fed by compassion and kindness. Fed by time and the pursuit of dreams. It seems a force stronger than death itself." He found he was out of words. He waited for her response.

"Have you ever felt it?" Eva spoke so softly it was almost a whisper.

He shook his head. "My parents have it. My dad first saw my mom when she was eighteen, when she waitressed at a diner after her freshman year of college. He's four years older. So, at twenty-two, he told his brother she was the girl he would marry. His brother laughed. But my dad set about persuading her. It took him a few years, but Dad is nothing if not patient. And tenacious." Michael grinned then grew serious again. "Their love gave me a high bar to aim for."

Leaning forward, he slipped a lone strand of hair behind her ear. She reached up and pressed his hand against her cheek.

"I don't have a model for that kind of love, Michael," she said. "You know my history... and most of my friends' parents are divorced." She thought for a moment. "Those that do have parents who stayed together still wouldn't say their folks had that kind of relationship. It sounds rare. You're fortunate to have experienced it—or at least seen it—with your parents."

"I always believed it was an attainable goal. I've never settled for less, and I hadn't ever come near it."

The words "until now" hung in the air, and Michael decided to leave them there, unsaid. He'd said enough.

Chapter 33

No reporters met Eva when she arrived at the Lambeth's Mystic home.

"They gave up a couple of days ago," Audrey said, as she led Eva to the couple's joint office, a cozy room with back-to-back walnut desks and floor-to-ceiling shelves jammed with books. She poured Eva a cup of mint tea, then left the room at the sound of the doorbell.

Eva was stunned by the difference in Charles Lambeth. He was still thin, but his energy was different now, there was a boyish vibrancy to it. Dressed in a lightweight turtleneck and khakis, his skin glowed with ruddy color, his grip was firm. "How are you feeling?"

Holding both her hands, he said, "I'm great, thanks to you." A slow smile lit his face. "I thought I was on my way to my maker. I don't know how to thank you."

Eva smiled and squeezed his hands.

He said in a low voice, "And, lucky me, I can eat all the brownies and ice cream I want, now. My wife can't complain and make me eat healthy food."

"I heard that," Audrey said as she came through the door with a woman behind her. "I give up, Charles Lambeth. You're incorrigible."

Eva grinned at him. She felt as if she knew him well, felt at ease with him. As if, somehow, they'd opened up a connection that remained once the healing was done. She'd noticed something similar with Dr. Chin, and again with her grandfather. It was like a *pathway* had been opened. Yes, that was it. She had the benefit of a view right into their spirit. She *saw* them, that part of themselves they never showed to the world. It hit Eva that it was a little like studying an illustration when you've been told it contains a hidden image. You don't see it, then as you continue to stare at it, suddenly you do. You study a bunch of trees and leaves, and suddenly you see a giraffe. It's almost as if your eyes go a little out of focus and that's where the new image is. It was there all the time. And, of course, once you see it, you wonder how you couldn't see it before.

Audrey introduced her to the newcomer, their attorney friend and colleague. Nancy Grayson looked about sixty, but her movements and energy were much younger. Her calm, collected presence seemed to fill the room. Thin and wiry, Nancy wore casual jeans and a bright blue blouse and explained this was a work-from-home day. She also lived in Mystic and beamed with pleasure as she told them she'd walked from her house. Twelve minutes and no fossil fuels burned, she told them with a grin.

"I've known Nancy since college days," Audrey explained. "We served on some committee or other for Mystic, years ago. And she organized our foundation." Audrey handed Eva a card, which read, "The Audrey and Charles Lambeth Foundation."

Nancy gave Charles a hug. "Well, my old friend," she said. "Looks like you're going to stay with us after all!"

"Thanks to Eva," he replied. "She has a powerful gift and needs help with it." He turned to Eva. "I assure you, this foundation will be set up as per your wishes, it will be your baby. We'll help in any way we can, and our foundation will donate the funds to get it going. And we can help you interview the people to run it—Nancy and Audrey have good ideas, already."

Eva realized she was chewing on her lip and forced herself to take a deep breath.

Audrey studied her. "What's worrying you?"

"So many people... so many people ill, injured, needing help. How do I..." Eva trailed off with a sigh.

"The very thought of it must be daunting," Audrey said. "But look at it this way: If you only heal three people a week because you need to rest up after each one, there are *three* people helped, cured, saved. Many had run out of hope." She smiled at her husband. "It's huge, Eva."

Within an hour, they'd explained to Eva how foundations functioned, what was involved in the set-up, a little about fund-raising, and what the foundation could do for her. She agreed that conducting tests could legitimize her, if a scientific basis for her healing could be established. It could take what she did out of the realm of the supernatural or paranormal. She hoped it could give her credibility and standing in the medical community, something that seemed impossible at the moment. As for how many people she'd try to help, they set her mind at rest: If she could only work with one person a week, and that's all she could manage, they assured her that was fine. Healing animals would be a given. Public outreach and education were major parts of the plan. And they all felt a security plan for her was an absolute requirement, a done deal. As uncomfortable as it made Eva, she now recognized the sense in it. As for fees, they agreed with her idea: to ask people for a donation of whatever they could afford.

Nancy and the Lambeths had answered her questions without her even needing to ask them.

Charles said, "There's no hurry, Eva. But your grandmother told us you want to be qualified as a vet tech, then a veterinarian, to help animals. Now while that's an admirable aim, it isn't strictly necessary if you go about it this way."

Audrey said, "Angela and I talked at length last night about all of this. She and your grandfather are planning to direct monies from their foundation as well. So, you have everything you need to set this in motion."

———••◆••———

Before heading home, Eva parked by the water in Mystic and called her aunt to tell her about the plans for the foundation. As she gazed out over the calm waters of Williams Beach, she envisioned, just for a moment, the path ahead of her with bubbles of excitement replacing the pangs of trepidation that had been haunting her.

This is the way, and I can do it.

"Chloe, I just came from the most amazing meeting. This foundation is a godsend, and I'm so grateful to the Lambeths. And to my grandparents." She filled Chloe in.

"Sounds good," Chloe said, after hearing the details. "I have a foundation, for my music and scholarships, so I know a bit about it too, and if I can help in any way, I'd love to. And also, yay Mom! She told me last night that they'll get involved, at least to help finance the foundation."

"Do Jared or Olivia know about this?" Eva asked. "Or my father?"

"No, I don't think so."

"Best if we keep it that way."

"OK. Not that my folks' foundation is anything to do with them, or with their inheritance."

"But still..." Eva said. "There's enough tension."

"You're right. They won't find out from me." Chloe's voice changed in tone. "Oh, and by the way, some press showed up here yesterday, so our connection is not a secret anymore, honey. It was bound to come out. But not to worry, I have an idea for an escape for you."

"What do you mean?"

"I have a dear friend, Corinne West, who owns a cottage right on the beach between Westerly and Charlestown. I think it's near Quonochontaug or Weekapaug, one of those Rhode Island villages that end in "aug," anyway." Chloe chuckled. "She rents it out as an Airbnb, and her last booking for the season was last week. She was getting ready to close it up for the winter but said you could have it for as long as you need it. With the press knowing where you might be, it's time for some surreptitious sneaking about... don't you think?"

"Yes, absolutely. Can you lend me a short black wig and cheek pouches?" Eva gave a guffaw of laughter. "That's good of her, Chloe, but right on the water, I can't afford that."

"She said you can pay the heating bill if you insist. Aside from that she wants nothing in return. Anyway, you get a place to recoup your strength that no one knows about except you and me. And Corinne, of course. And she's not going to tell anyone. I've known her for years—she said it would be an honor to help. Her way of paying it forward."

Eva grinned. "What a treat—sounds wonderful."

"Oh, you'll love being there, sweetie. You open the door and there's the sand. Almost literally. The porch is 200 feet from the water. And it's decked out—everything you could want in the kitchen, updated bathroom with a jacuzzi, and it's beautifully furnished. You don't have to bring anything except groceries. I'll text you the address and where to find the key."

Chapter 34

Deep in thought about the foundation, and the offer of a cottage on the beach, Eva nearly overshot the turn. Parking behind the barn, while generous and thoughtful of their neighbor, was a nuisance. Traipsing around behind the barn, and through the hedge to Jamie's backyard had been inconvenient, but at least she escaped the media ghouls who seem determined to make her life a living hell. But now, as she planned to stay at the beach cottage for who knows how long, she'd have to make a number of trips to carry bags and boxes and her computer. Jamie had said she'd help, but still... Well, she guessed she'd just pack light or do it all in the middle of the night.

The press interest hadn't let up. If anything, it was growing. Her voicemail was constantly full of messages and Jake texted there were mountains of requests at the shelter. More and more websites and social media outlets had picked up on her story. The cottage was a much-needed godsend, and gratitude for Chloe and her friend Corinne flooded through her.

She ran upstairs to pack. As she grabbed her duffel bag from beside the bed, she spotted the large box of photos she'd carried down from the attic, the one with the dolphin pictures and the ones of her and her mother. She almost hauled it back to the attic, then wondered what other pictures there might be. Maybe of her father, when he was young? She could take it with her to the beach cottage but no, on second thought, she certainly wasn't going to carry that sucker all the way to the car. Glancing at the time, she figured it made no difference what time she arrived at the beach cottage. Might as well have a look now.

Unceremoniously, she dumped the box on the bed, turning it on its side and shoveling all the envelopes of pictures out on the duvet. Spreading them out, she saw they dated back to the eighties, and there were plenty from Eva's childhood, in the late nineties.

But something else caught her eye. Nestled among the envelopes filled with pictures was a stack of letters tied together with a ribbon. Handwritten letters, on what appeared to be personal stationery. Lifting the packet and flipping through the letters, she saw each one was addressed to her mother at their old house in Stonington. The return address read Patricia Silva, from Fall River, Massachusetts. Who was that? And why did her mother keep them all these years?

Eva scanned through until she located the oldest date stamp: October 25, 1995. When she opened the letter, a photograph fell out, an image of an older woman in a large circular water tank, her hand on the nose of a young dolphin. The dolphin was grinning at the camera as if posing. Eva flipped the photo over to read, "Grace says hello!"

The letter itself was in a spidery upright hand, precise but energetic. Filled with the dashes of a quick-thinking mind.

Dearest Marianne,

I do hope you're well and finding your way around in Connecticut. We miss you so much here — but I do understand why you had to go. You did the right thing — I guess there was nothing else for it. The police weren't going to be able to help — they didn't seem to want to, anyway! And he didn't seem fazed by the threat of a restraining order — as you said, he would have just ignored it.

Eva read the words again. "Restraining order?" *Wait, what?* Who was the woman talking about?

He's shown up here a few more times, hoping to catch you, and arriving unannounced. Oh, he's a charming son of a gun — but now he finally believes you don't work here anymore. I think. I hope. I'm so sorry you had to go through that, Marianne.

I hope you're feeling well and have found a good doctor and midwife — that makes all the difference in the world.

"Midwife"... Eva looked at the date again. So, her mother was pregnant when she moved down from Massachusetts. With her. Does this explain why her mom had moved, left college, and abandoned her dream of becoming a marine biologist?

Trish veered off into news about the other people at the marine institute, and her own family, her son, her grandson. It was cheerful and newsy. She closed with:

One of these days I must get down to Connecticut, I'd love to see you...

Fondly,

Trish

P.S. See how much Grace has grown? She's well and fit, now — we'll be releasing her soon!

Eva plowed through all the letters, which spanned about ten years, one or two a year over that time. Sometimes a letter was included inside a Christmas card, sometimes a birthday card. Of course, Eva realized she was only seeing Trish's half of the conversation. Besides news from the institute, Eva learned Trish had retired in 2010 and moved to Cranston, Rhode Island, to be near her son and grandson.

When Eva had read every letter, she gathered them together again and wrapped them up. Her mind was in a whirl. Had her father actually stalked her mother? So badly she had to escape and move to another state, dropping out of college and bringing up a child alone? A kernel of anger grew in her belly. She wanted to give him the benefit of the doubt. But who else could Trish be referring to?

Could she find this woman? Trish Silva? Hopping online and bringing up Google, it took about fifteen seconds to find Patricia Silva in Cranston, RI. She still lived at the same address.

Eva grabbed her phone.

"I'm looking for Trish Silva."

"This is Trish. Who is this, please?"

"This is Eva McGrath, Marianne's daughter..."

There was a pause.

"Eva? Eva! Oh my! What a delightful bolt from the blue you are this afternoon—is Marianne with you? We lost touch over the years..."

"Mom passed away in 2007."

Eva heard a gasp.

"Oh, no, I'm so sorry," Trish said. "That explains why I didn't get a reply to my last few letters. I'd hoped she was just busy—but after a while, when I didn't hear back..."

She talked like she wrote, fast, and with dashes, Eva thought. "Could I come to see you? Talk about my mother?"

"Well of course, dear, I'd love that. I'm retired, struggling with arthritis a bit, but I'm here."

Eva suggested the next morning and it was as easy as that. She was meeting her father at noon at a restaurant in Providence, and Cranston was on the city's doorstep. Before she faced her father, she would have a chance to get clear what happened twenty-six years ago.

───── •◆• ─────

Corrine's cottage on the beach in Rhode Island turned out to be only a twenty-minute drive from Jamie's. Eva gazed around the open living area with its linen-covered couches, woven throws, and rattan and wicker chairs. Chloe's friend had created a true haven. This was a high-class Airbnb for people who could afford to vacation right on the water. A large, shingled bungalow, probably built in the 1930s, it was completely renovated and included a canopied porch just steps from the sands of the beach. There were three large bedrooms, huge by Eva's experience, and she luxuriated in the space. All to herself. And her little cocker spaniel. The dog ran around exploring, then settled herself on the overstuffed couch in the living room.

"Hey Cookie, pretty good, huh?"

By midnight, she was tucked up in the pillow-top bed, windows open, and chatting to Michael on the phone, updating him about the foundation meeting. She didn't mention the letters from Trish Silva. She decided she'd wait and see what she learned the next morning, from Trish. And the lunch meeting with Will Hastings.

She told Michael about the cottage on the beach. "Lucky me. This place is just gorgeous. I must send the owner a fruit basket."

"But why don't you just stay with me?" Michael asked. "Then I can look out for you. The journalists have never seen you here, and they are hardly outside at all... it's sporadic."

"Thanks, Michael, but I really need a break."

There was a short silence. Then he said, "Of course, I understand. Well, I'll come see you and your new refuge tomorrow night."

Eva stroked Cookie, by her side, and let the crisp sheets and soft pillows envelop her. *I've died and gone to heaven.* Through the open window near the bed, she listened to the gentle surf touching the shore and drew in long breaths of fragrant salty air. She planned to get up early for a walk with Cookie on the beach. It was open sea to the east, with Block Island out there in the water somewhere. Where so many dolphins had been seen over the years.

Then off to Cranston, then Providence.

She sighed.

Don't think about it, tonight. Enjoy this room, the sounds and smells of the sea, and go to sleep, BG.

---- •◆•• ----

"I was so fond of your mother," Trish said.

Eva had easily found her way to the well-kept ranch house. Now she sat in the kitchen, studying Trish as she buzzed around preparing decaf coffee and selecting cookies to scatter across a plate. Not an ounce of fat on her, Trish's snow-white hair was cut short and wispy, and she wore a plaid shirt, khaki work pants, and leather flip-flops. Although wizened, and slightly stooped, Trish's energy seemed more like that of a thirty-year-old, than of a woman in her early eighties. Eva couldn't see any sign of the arthritis Trish had mentioned. The older woman seemed to be constantly on the move, pushing her purple-framed glasses up on her nose or shoving up her shirt sleeves. As if there was just too much energy to contain and it had to pour out somewhere.

Trish poured coffee into a heavy pottery mug and handed it to Eva, then sat across from her guest at the small kitchen table. "Your mother had so much drive—she was so excited about her studies and working with marine animals. Your mom loved them all. And she was so good with them... Dolphins, otters, turtles are returned to the wild, if possible. The institute always tries to limit human contact so most can be sent back to the ocean, but sometimes the animals are too injured to be considered releasable." She paused, deep in thought. A faraway look came over her face, and a small smile. "Did she ever tell you about Grace, the baby dolphin we rescued? The vet came and stitched up a nasty cut in her fin—but she lost a lot of blood and we thought she wouldn't make it. But the little dolphin recovered, and so fast. It was amazing."

Then her eyes met Eva's. "I'm getting way off the track," she said with a grin. "Your mother was a naturalist, very green-oriented. Not materialistic—not at all. When she found she was pregnant—and she learned who the Hastings family were—she was appalled that her baby might be influenced by that lifestyle and belief system... the 'entitlement of the oligarchy,' she called it. She abhorred that possibility—that would be completely against her nature. So, she broke up with him. Well, I have to say, that wasn't the only reason, she told me. He was also pushy, arrogant, and just 'not for her,' as she put it." Trish paused, to add cream to her own mug. "Turns out she was right to end it. But he didn't take it well—not well at all."

"Your letter said you were sorry she had to go through that," Eva said. "What did you mean? Go through what?"

Trish sighed. "You've met Will Hastings?"

"I have."

"What's he like now?"

Eva thought for a moment. "Superficially charming, but controlling underneath, self-centered. Even narcissistic. I figured money does that to some people."

Trish shook her head. "I think maybe he was born like that. Who knows? But he was certainly spoiled and enabled—that didn't help. There was a real kernel of nastiness in him. He stalked your mom for weeks, and she kept telling him 'No.' She told him it was over, but he kept calling and showing up at her apartment. He called the institute and showed up there a few times. I was worried, toward the end..." Trish pursed her lips. "I remember your mom saying, 'No one leaves a Hastings, I guess.' Marianne described his arrogance as 'the point where confident crosses the line into dangerous.' Anyway, she threatened to get a restraining order." Trish gave Eva a pointed look. "And he laughed."

"He *laughed*?" Eva took that in. "What about me... the fact that Mom was pregnant?"

Trish shook her head again. "She never told him."

"Is that why she quit school? Is that why she moved down to Connecticut?"

Trish sighed. "I'm sorry to have to tell you this." She paused, her lips tight. "It was the last time I saw her... That night, after he had shown up at the institute, only to be turned away yet again, he was waiting for her at her apartment. She'd worked an evening shift, so it was late, about 11:00. He got pushy about coming in to 'talk,' as he put it. Tried to force himself on her. She said no and pushed him away. He said all those things nasty men say, like 'You know you want it,' and 'You don't really mean no.'" Trish paused and took a deep breath. "It still makes me so angry I could spit."

Eva sat still, listening, with her skin crawling. This man was her *father.*

It got worse.

Chapter 35

As Eva parked in Providence and found her way to the Café Nero, she gave up trying to give her father the benefit of the doubt. Trish had laid to rest that possibility.

Will Hastings was late. At the small bistro, she sat gnawing on breadsticks and sipping soda water. But it didn't settle her queasiness. She glanced again at her watch. 12:40. When he finally breezed in, he casually tossed out the kind of half-apology you get from self-important people who don't think they owe you one.

"The meeting ran over," he said. "But Haverling Biotech is a great company. It could be perfect to expand our line of advanced pharmaceuticals, and great potential for genetic research and production. I could, of course, just steal away two of their top researchers, but on deeper review, the corporation in its entirety will be a great asset."

They exchanged a few inane pleasantries about her drive there, that it was a lovely mild day for late September. *Blah blah blah.* She was silent as her father ordered a beer and glanced at the menu. Her heart was pounding.

Then he studied her. "Your hair is up again. You know, you should wear it down more. It looks great like that. And I notice you wear no makeup. You're beautiful, but you might consider a bit of makeup to enhance that. Looks matter in business."

"I'm not in business."

"You could be."

She left that one alone.

Will checked his phone, then lay it down near his plate. "So, no boyfriend today?"

Eva shook her head. "He's working."

"He seems like a good guy."

"But he's just a veterinarian."

Will Hastings didn't pick up on her sarcasm. "He's smart," he said. "I like him."

"That's a relief." Again, the man was oblivious.

The waitress placed a beer in front of Will, he took a gulp. "Now," he said, "We need to talk about your undergoing some testing. I've organized it for next week. I'm sure for something so important you can be available." He must have read Eva's face because he added, "Now I know you aren't too keen... But we must learn *how* you're doing it. What the mechanism is. I'm sure you agree."

When she opened her mouth to speak, he leaned toward her and carried on. "Eva, I know you're eager to help people. And you're concerned about only being able to heal one person at a time. We can find out what it is you do, try to make it easier on you, so you can fulfill your destiny to help thousands of people."

Eva stared unseeing out the window. She was deep in thought, but not about the testing. Then she realized he was waiting for a response. "I'll think about it."

"I need to know—it's booked for next Monday." He watched her for a moment, his face perplexed. "And the next bit of business: I wanted to let you know I'm re-writing my will. You'll be an equal beneficiary with Jared, Olivia, and Samantha. I'm meeting with the lawyers in Boston tomorrow to finalize all the details." He again waited for her response, this time with a small, cool smile on his lips.

It's a blatant bribe. She suppressed a shudder. "Have you told Jared or my sisters yet?"

"Sure." He grinned. And shrugged. "It's not their money."

"Or Susanna? What does she think?"

"Not hers, either. The prenup is clear."

Eva kept her face expressionless.

"You don't seem too thrilled with this news."

She chewed on her lip.

His eyes narrowed. "What's up, Eva?"

Eva drew in a long breath. "Tell me about your relationship with my mother."

He flashed Eva a look she couldn't decipher. "That was a lifetime ago. Why do you want to rehash all that?"

"I want to know what happened."

"There's nothing to tell—"

"Why did she feel she couldn't tell you about me?"

"How do I know?" Will banged his palm down on the table so hard the silverware jumped. Several people glanced over at him, but he ignored them and carried on. "She should have told me. She *should* have. I was ripped off. I missed your whole life—your school years, your childhood." He glared at Eva. "I could have guided you a whole lot better than to a career as a damned veterinary technician."

Eva drew in a ragged breath. The fury inside her was heating to a fiery ball of lead in her chest. "You know, you say you want to get to know me better, but all you've done is tease me, criticize me, and mock me since we met."

He gave a small wave as if that idea were not even worthy of his attention.

Eva's hands were fists in her lap. "I wonder if you did the same with my mother."

Will Hastings laughed.

"You stalked her."

"What?"

She repeated it. "You stalked her. You bullied her."

He gasped. His eyes widened, and he paled. "That's a lie. What did she tell you?"

"Nothing at all. I was a child."

"Then what the hell are you talking about?"

"I've spoken with a colleague of hers at New England Marine Institute. I know what happened."

"It's nonsense. Whoever told you this is a liar. I did nothing to your mother. Just told her it was over."

"*You're* the liar. You were waiting for her at her apartment one night and got rough with her. You struck her in the face. And she fell into the doorway. You yanked her up, but she turned and nailed you with her knee. Thank goodness for that self-defense course she took in college. It paid off."

Will Hasting's eyes narrowed. Then his face relaxed and he let out a guffaw. "What a great story."

Waves of deception rolled off this man across from her and she couldn't bear another second in his presence. She stood so abruptly her chair fell backward to the floor with a clatter. Grabbing her handbag, she headed for the door.

She heard him call out from behind her, "Wait, Eva, what are you *doing*?"

She stormed out of the restaurant.

As she started down the sidewalk, Eva felt him grab her arm from behind. She twisted around to face him and yanked her arm away. "Don't touch me."

His face became conciliatory. "Come back in, sit down, let's talk. I would never hurt your mother. I liked her, why would I hurt her? We had fun together."

Just for the briefest of seconds, she wondered if she and Trish could be wrong, but then it hit her: that's the power of the narcissist, to make you doubt yourself. And they continue to endlessly lie. That's their M.O.

A female pedestrian on the street spoke up. "Are you all right, Miss?"

Will spoke sharply. "She's fine. We're just having a *private* conversation."

Eva gave a shaky smile to the woman. "I'm OK but thank you." The woman hesitated, but then turned, and continued on her way. Eva reached into her handbag and pulled out the pepper spray.

Will eyed it and backed up a small pace, his hands up. Then smiled, a condescending smile. "That won't be necessary. For God's sake, Eva, what's wrong with you?"

"What's wrong with *me*?" The molten lead inside her boiled over and the words came spitting out of her mouth. "You ruined her life."

"Not true," he countered, a calm expression on his face.

Oh, he thinks he has me under control now.

"I have pictures," Eva said in a low tone, almost a hiss.

"What are you talking about?"

"Pictures. My mother had pictures taken of the damage to her face. Her black eye. Where you ripped her shirt. The bruises on her arms."

That stopped him.

"Oh, no reply to that? Yes, I have pictures."

"It wasn't me, Eva, it must have been someone else. Maybe she got mugged. Poor thing."

"It was you."

"For chrissake, why won't you listen to reason?"

"Because my mother told her colleague everything. That you bullied her, you hit her. That you tried to rape her."

Will's face was ashen. "That's one hell of an accusation."

"She fought you off and escaped—in the middle of the night. She fled to Connecticut, to hide out with her aunt. She abandoned everything, college, her friends, her dream of becoming a marine biologist. Then brought me up alone, a single mother struggling every step of the way."

"That's crazy talk. She didn't need to run from me. Why would I do anything to your mom?"

"Because she said no. You just couldn't leave it alone when she told you it was over. For you, she was the 'one that got away.'"

Will started to speak but Eva cut him off.

"No one leaves a Hastings, huh?" She stared at him. "Well, watch this."

She spun around, strode off down the sidewalk, without so much as a backward glance.

Chapter 36

Still violently shaking, Eva drove south. She was halfway back to the cottage before she could begin to think straight. It was true, what he had done to her mother. And he didn't accept responsibility, just denied it, over and over again.

And this person, who had caused such harm, was her own flesh and blood. She was *of* him. How was that possible? Did he become that way from his upbringing? Or was he evil? And if so, was evil genetic?

She made up her mind. She was done with Will Hastings, and if the rest of the family wanted to know why, she was damned well going to tell them. But now she knew why her mother had cut him completely out of their lives.

Just as she opened the cottage door to let Cookie out for a walk, her phone dinged. It was a text from Jamie's mother asking her to call ASAP.

She connected. "Hi, Dr. Chin, what's up, you OK?"

Dr. Chin's voice was urgent. "Oh, Eva, thank you for calling back, we have a situation. It's one of our nurses, he's a patient here in the hospital. We're all so fond of him. He suffers from epilepsy, fell in his apartment, and hit his head. His neighbor found him, called an ambulance. There's brain swelling, so he's undergone shunt surgery. But the doctors aren't hopeful. How long he was unconscious is uncertain, so there could be irreparable brain damage. Little more we can do. Are you willing to try?"

Eva drew in a long breath. It flashed through her mind that if she was successful, she would have to endure hours of exhaustion again.

But this was a man's life.

"Hello?" Dr. Chin said. "You there, Eva?"

"Yes, sorry, on my way. I'll leave Cookie off at Jamie's, first, and be there as soon as I can."

Dr. Chin met her in the front lobby, led her through the maze of the hospital, and ushered her into the man's room.

Eva hadn't prepared herself for the scene. Enough movies and TV shows featuring ICUs should have ensured it wasn't a complete shock, but she was thrown a bit by the medical paraphernalia. The breathing tube, the IVs in the man's arms, the machines monitoring vitals with their signature beeping, the ventilator to his lungs whispering and sighing. It was all so cold and impersonal. And the man was alone.

Eva spoke softly. "Does he have family here? Are they on their way?"

"Our records listed a sister in Greenwich. We've left her a message and hope she gets here soon. His neighbor told the emergency personnel that most of his family is in India."

"His name?"

"Deepak Kumar."

Eva pulled over a chair to sit near the man in the bed. Dr. Chin squeezed her shoulder in thanks and left her, saying she'd wait in the hall.

The man lay motionless. Although of Indian nationality, his face was shockingly pale, as if his blood couldn't reach his face. His jet-black curly hair looked oddly incongruous against the wan skin. He was young-looking. She glanced at the chart. He was forty-nine.

"Hi, Mr. Kumar. I would like to call you Deepak, if that's all right. I'm Eva. I'm going to take your hand." It was icy. Glancing around, she spotted a closet where she found his clothes in a bag, and on a shelf, two blankets. She covered him with the blankets, and took his hand again, rubbing it gently to warm it.

Eva closed her eyes and tried to settle in. Still rattled from the confrontation with her father, she had difficulty achieving the connection, the vibration, the healing place. It didn't help that she had no emotional connection to this man. She didn't know him at all, and it occurred to her again that in previous healings, with people, she'd had the energetic input of others. Jamie, with Dr. Chin, Chloe with her grandfather, and Michael and Audrey with the governor's husband. Same thing with the baby—the mother was part of the experience. In every case, someone in the connected circle of energy had a deep emotional connection to the person Eva was trying to heal. Furthermore, Eva, herself, had a personal connection when healing Dr. Chin and her grandfather. It crossed her mind these were factors she needed to think about.

But first, this poor man. As she began to relax, haunting strains of violins crept into her awareness, and she recognized Pachelbel's canon playing through speakers in the ceiling. It was one of her favorite pieces of music, never failing to move her. The melody brought a stirring deep within her, and the vibration began. Faint, but there. She tried to open. To find the way to the connection. Slowly, the deep, dark sensation grew larger and larger, until it filled her mind. Water, warm and breathable, was all around her. In front of her, separating her from this man's energy, was a wall, which gave easily with her intent. Her wall?

Then she felt, directly ahead, another barrier. Stronger than the first. It didn't yield. She pressed gently, then harder. Then harder. Still nothing. She had to stop and take a breather. She floated in the water for a few moments, feeling this hard shell in front of her. It was a gray wall, with veins of black through it, solid, like dark marble. She opened, she pushed, she sent energy, compassion, understanding. Then in one big effort, she sent all the intent she could muster at one time, hoping to dissolve and break through it. Once more, nothing.

She brought herself back from the deep pool in which she had been floating and walked to the window. Staring out, blindly, she realized how fatigued she was, not only from nights of poor sleep, and stress, but from the task she was now failing.

No, she told herself firmly. *You're not failing.*

Taking her seat again, she drew in a long breath and settled into the vibration and darkness once more. She spoke to the man in her mind. "Let me in, Deepak. I can help you. Let me." With that, she pushed as hard as she could against this forbidding wall. Nothing.

Eva withdrew again, at least from the effort to break through. Sitting quietly, she focused on recouping her energy and just floating in the deep. She thought about it. She had nothing else. She didn't know what to do. But she stayed where she was, not willing to give up.

Suddenly, with no effort on her part, the wall before her vanished. It didn't dissolve, as she had experienced previously. It just disappeared as though it was never there. Just beyond, where the wall had been, was complete darkness. She probed it gently, but this wasn't peace, not bliss. A massive struggle was taking place, and she was buffeted by unfamiliar energies she didn't understand.

Then the connection ended, abruptly, and the feeling of struggle ended. The sensation faded, then evaporated. She reached out into the darkness, again and again, but there was nothing. No further wall to contend with, no spirit to connect to hers, nothing at all. She was left in a cloud of chilled air, and it hit her that she was alone. Floating alone.

Horrified, Eva froze. Understanding flooded through her. He had died. Right there as she had connected, the spirit gave up on the body and slipped away. He had died, as she was holding his hand. No one he loved or cared about was with him.

She shuddered, and lay her head down next to his body, on the hospital bed. The last thing she remembered was an overwhelming heaviness, shadows all around her, and a fierce headache.

———•••◆••———

When she woke, her first sensation was an icy chill. She sat up slowly, to find the room spinning around her. She stayed still, breathing quietly, and waited for the sensations to settle. *Where am I? How long was I asleep?* She glanced at her watch—she'd only slept half an hour. She was lying on a big couch in Dr. Chin's office. Shivering, she pulled the blanket closer around her. When she swung her legs over the edge to sit up, the room whirled again and once more she had to wait. She took a deep breath, but the headache caught her by surprise, and she gasped.

"Oh, you're awake, how are you doing?" Dr. Chin was at her desk. Before Eva could respond, she heard raised voices outside the office door. The door opened, and in burst a dark-skinned woman, dressed in western clothes but wearing the Hindu bindi, the red dot, on her forehead. Dr. Chin's young male assistant was close on her heels.

"Dr. Chin, I'm so sorry," the assistant said, "I told her you weren't available. She just barged ahead."

Dr. Chin rose from her desk and waved her assistant's apology away with her hand. "It's all right, Craig." As he disappeared, she said to the woman, "Do we have an appointment? How can I help you?"

"My brother, he's gone, and I wasn't here to be with him. But that woman was." She pointed at Eva. "I saw her!"

"You must be Nisha Kumar," said Dr. Chin. "I'm so sorry for your loss."

"Are you? You let a stranger—she's not a doctor, not a nurse—be there with my brother, and he *died*." She turned hard on her heel and pointed again at Eva. "I saw you there, with your head on his bed." Her voice rose even higher. "You *killed* him."

"Now now, Ms. Kumar," Dr. Chin said, "your brother had suffered tragic brain damage—"

"Don't you 'Ms. Kumar' me, I'm going to the police. Or filing whatever complaint I can... The nurses didn't know who she was, just some stranger, sitting and touching him?" Her voice was raised in near hysteria. "Who does she think she is—I wasn't even there. He died alone, without anyone who loved him..." Nisha Kumar's voice trailed off into a sob, and she covered her face with her hands, and the tears squeezed out from between her fingers and ran down her cheeks.

Eva tried to stand but the room was spinning. "Ms. Kumar, I'm so sorry—"

Dr. Chin held a hand up to Eva to stop her, grabbed a couple of tissues from her desk, and approached Nisha. "There, there, Nisha, come with me, we'll get you some water or a nice cup of tea..." With her arm around the woman's shoulders, Dr. Chin escorted Deepak Kumar's sister from the room.

Sickened, Eva lay back down on the couch.

Chapter 37

"Dr. Michael, you have a phone call. Line three."

Michael turned in the hall to see Roxanne leaning out over the reception desk.

"Who is it?"

"Said her name is Jamie," she answered, "and she said it's important."

He hurried to the break room. Why would Jamie call him at work? Was Eva OK?

"Jamie, hey, what's up?"

Her voice was tight. "It's Eva. Can you come with me to the hospital?"

"Hospital?" Michael's heart began to pound. "Oh, God, is she all right?"

"Don't know. She's wiped out after a healing. Mom doesn't think she should drive. Horizon General."

"Got it, on my way."

Dr. Chin was waiting for them in the hospital lobby when they arrived. Her face was tense.

Michael asked, "How is she?"

She explained as she led them to her office. "Eva was here at my request to try to help a patient, one of our own employees. He had a severe head injury. Afterward, she woke enough to get to my office to lie down, but I had to help her." She quietly opened her office door.

Eva sat on a couch by the window, and when she spotted them, she jumped up, but had to reach for the arm of the sofa to steady herself. A look of fear crossed her face. "Omigod," she said. "What's happening? Is everything all right?"

"We should be asking *you* that," said Jamie.

"Why would I not be all right? I'm in a goddamn hospital for chrissake."

Michael stared. This was a side of Eva he hadn't seen.

Eva stood. "I feel sick. I think I'm going to throw up." She headed shakily for the door.

"That way, Eva." Dr. Chin pointed to the door on the other side of the room, where Michael could see a sink.

Eva disappeared into the bathroom and closed the door.

Michael met Jamie's eyes. Her face was tense.

"That's not like her," Jamie said. "I don't mean just the nausea, I mean snapping at us." She shook her head and turned to her mother. "What happened?"

Her mother was quiet.

"Mom?"

Dr. Chin's lips were pursed. "I think she had a rough time, with this healing. It didn't work." She paused.

"Go on," Michael said.

Dr. Chin sighed. "The man died while Eva was trying to help him. His monitors went off and the nurses raced in. His sister had arrived by that time and found Eva semi-conscious beside his body. They brought in the crash cart and tried to revive him. But it was too late. He was gone."

"So, he would have died anyway, right?" Jamie asked. "Eva was just too late to be able to help?"

Dr. Chin nodded. "Right. And since then, the man's sister has been asking questions. She came here and accused Eva of killing her brother." She shook her head.

Jamie swallowed. "There's no way Eva contributed in some way to the man's death, is there?"

Dr. Chin answered, emphatically. "No. There's no way. Medically, it's not possible."

"Well," Michael said, "I don't think his sister is thinking 'medically.' She wants someone to pay."

"She's mostly struggling with the fact that he died alone, I think." Dr. Chin sighed. "She's torn between blaming herself for not getting here in time and finding someone else to blame."

Over Dr. Chin's shoulder, Michael saw the bathroom door open. Eva came out, looking pale and she stood wiping her mouth with a tissue.

Dr. Chin turned to Eva. "Are you OK? Any better?"

"I just want to go home."

The office door opened a crack and Dr. Chin's assistant peeked in. "Dr. Chin, Mr. Becker is here."

"Good, thanks, Craig. Hi Ben, thanks for coming." She introduced them to Ben Becker, the hospital's in-house counsel.

Eva said, "I didn't hurt him. I just held his hand, relaxed, and meditated. That's all."

"I know, I know, that's what Dr. Chin told me," Ben replied. He shook his head. "Well. I don't understand how you're doing it, but it's certainly not practicing medicine in any sense accepted by our medical or judicial system."

Dr. Chin asked, "What happened when you talked with his sister?"

"I've talked her down," Ben said. "I think. She doesn't have a case."

"A *case*?" Eva said, her eyes wide.

"You didn't diagnose, you didn't prescribe, you didn't 'treat' with any medical device or drug... You just held his hand. That's not practicing medicine. But you'd be smart to practice in Rhode Island, instead of Connecticut, where Safe Harbor Laws protect alternative practitioners."

Michael watched Eva, wondering if he should intervene. Eva looked like she would fall down, right there where she stood.

"In any event," the lawyer said, "you need your patients, or I guess I should say 'clients,' to sign a disclaimer, where they acknowledge you're not a medical doctor. And you need to sort out a business license. That's where there's legal risk."

"But I didn't take any money," Eva said.

"It's not a business," Dr. Chin added.

"If you want to charge fees—" Ben said.

Eva cut him off mid-sentence. "I'm not doing it anymore. I'm done. Done with healing people. Maybe done with healing, period." She turned to grab her handbag from the couch.

"Well, if you change your mind," Ben said, "I could draw up a disclaimer form for you."

Michael said, "With respect Ben, Eva is exhausted, I don't think this is the right time—"

Eva cut him off. "You and Jamie didn't need to come."

"But Eva—" Jamie didn't get a chance to finish that thought.

"No, no, I'm OK, I just have to get home."

"Thank you, Ben," Dr. Chin said, standing. He gave a little salute and turned for the door.

Michael said to Eva, "One of us can drive your car home, and—"

"No. I'll drive myself." Then she added, as if an afterthought, "Thank you anyway." She headed for the door.

Jamie muttered, "You're welcome." She exchanged a glance with Michael.

Back at Jamie's, as Michael and Jamie pulled into the driveway between several press vehicles lining the road, Michael said, "Damn. The buggers are still here." He spotted Cookie loose on the back lawn, so Eva must be out there, out of sight of the journalists. Ignoring the questions they threw at him, he found Eva on the back porch. Behind him, he heard Jamie call out "No comment" to the media's shouted questions as she followed him.

Eva turned and spotted them, held up her hand, and said, "I'm sorry Michael, it's not a good time. I need to rest and then get going. I'm just giving Cookie a few minutes outside."

He stared at her, more and more flummoxed by the minute. He shoved down a wave of irritation. "I came to get my car, Eva."

He saw her face flush. "Oh, right," she said.

Michael took another step toward her, but she held up a hand to stop him.

He heard a shout from the front of the house, from the press, and some laughter.

Eva let out a sound, almost a growl. "Why the hell won't they go away? For God's sake, will they ever let up?" She turned on Michael. "And why is everyone fussing over me? Telling me what to do?"

Michael was wordless.

Jamie said quickly, "Eva, for God's sake—"

Eva cut her off with a hand. "Michael, I can't do this anymore. I'm sorry, but this isn't going to work."

He felt slapped.

She continued, as if on a roll she couldn't stop. "It's too much right now."

"The healing?"

She nodded.

"And us?" he added, softly.

"And us."

He stiffened as anger flooded through him. He said, "Oh. You're going to vanish. When the going gets rough, huh?"

"How dare you," she shouted. "You have no idea what I'm going through. The weight, the responsibility. That man died, he *died*. As I connected with his spirit. I didn't help him, I couldn't help him..." She gasped as if someone had cut off her air supply.

"Oh, God..." She moaned. "Well, I tell you, I'm done. I'm not doing it anymore." She swayed and reached for the porch banister.

Michael ran to her and grabbed her, wrapping his arms around her. She was rigid in his arms. "Stop fighting me."

"I have to get going," she muttered.

"Where?"

"Back to the Airbnb—I need to go. I need..." She trailed off.

He pulled back to study her. "What *do* you need, Eva?"

She firmly shook him off. "I don't need anything."

"Well, I need *you*."

"Oh come on, what do you need me for?"

"Seriously? I love you. I need to look out for you, to help you."

"That's not need."

"Eva..."

"Anyway," she said, "you'd better prepare yourself, when I die, you'd be without me."

He stared at her.

She swallowed, waved her hand in the air. "You just need great sex. You can find that anywhere."

He felt a knot in his stomach and fury burned in his throat. "Don't do that—"

"I've got to go—"

"Don't do that either. God damn it, Eva, why do you either push me away or run?"

She took a deep breath. Her fists, at her sides, clenched so tight her knuckles were white. And she was visibly shaking. She straightened her shoulders. "Michael, I can't give you what you want."

At that, the tightly coiled ball of wire inside Michael snapped. Nearly exploding, he spun on his heel and headed down the porch steps.

Jamie had stood there silently watching this exchange. She shook her head. "Eva, this is not Michael's fault—"

"Don't you start." Eva whirled around and headed for the back door. "Come on, Cookie." The door slammed behind her.

Michael kept walking, around the house, heading for his car.

"Wait. Michael," Jamie called after him. "I'll talk to her. This is just not like her. The man dying... it hit her hard. She doesn't mean it."

He waved a hand in her direction. "She wiped me off like shit off a shoe. I have to get out of here."

Chapter 38

When the porch door slammed behind her, Eva raced upstairs to her bedroom, watched Michael drive away, and paced back and forth on the hardwood floor. She longed to head straight off to the cottage, but was exhausted and hurt all over as if she'd been in a boxing match. And lost. She groaned and summoned the familiar numbness to shade the ache inside. And the ache in her head. She rubbed her temples, wishing she had the energy to go downstairs for an ice pack.

She stretched out on the bed. When she closed her eyes, she relived the accusations from Nisha Kumar, then the last moments with Deepak, again and again. The shock of his death rolled over her, in giant waves, ugly and unchangeable.

She switched off her phone, and overcome by weakness, she succumbed to the odd sense of darkness that pressed down on her. The last thing she remembered was Cookie licking her hand and curling up at her side. Then she was out cold.

But even in sleep, murky images taunted her. She woke, gasping, having dreamt she teetered on a precipice, staring down. She stood on a tiny island, and a canyon fell away from her on all sides. Couldn't take a step in any direction... If she fell, would she ever land or just keep falling into an abyss, forever? In the distance, beyond the canyon, she could just make out Michael's eyes, narrow with anger and hurt. He spun away and vanished into the mist across the chasm.

She was shaking.

That's it. No more trying to sleep.

Splashing water on her face helped the dizziness, and the weird sense of darkness and depression began to fade. But she had behaved so badly—why had she been so harsh with Michael? And even with Jamie?

Eva hurried downstairs to find her best friend in the kitchen.

"Jamie, I'm so sorry. Please forgive me. I don't know what happened. I freaked out, I guess."

"Yeah, you did."

"I just went right off the deep end. I lost it. I took it out on you."

Jamie said slowly, "And you took it out on Michael."

"Yes, I guess so."

"Well, if you want his forgiveness," Jamie said, "I think some groveling will be called for. He was pretty angry when he left."

"This is no excuse, but I learned something about Will Hastings." She told Jamie about the letters from Trish and the subsequent confrontation with her father.

Jamie was thoughtful. She spoke slowly. "No wonder your mother didn't tell you about him." She shook her head. "That's awful, Eva, everything's just coming at you. Michael doesn't know any of this yet?"

Eva shook her head.

Jamie reached for a platter of chicken legs from the counter. "I roasted these—thought you might be hungry when you woke up."

Eva's stomach growled in response. "Sounds great, thanks."

Voices from the press outside. Eva checked her watch. 6:00 p.m.

"Yup. They're still here," Jamie said.

"It's been such a weird day, feels like the middle of the night."

"You didn't sleep very long."

Eva shook her head. "I'll go back to the cottage. It's quiet there—they haven't found me there." She dropped the chicken leg back on the plate, suddenly no longer hungry.

Jamie eyed her. "You know, you're going to have to find a way to keep eating through this."

Eva's head still ached. Elbows on the table, she rubbed her forehead with her fingertips.

"You serious about not healing anymore?" Jamie's voice was hesitant.

"I don't know. Maybe I'll just work with animals."

Jamie said, softly, "You don't like people much, do you?"

Eva lifted her head and stared at her friend. "It's not that... Well, ok, they do make me uncomfortable sometimes."

Jamie said, "Do I make you uncomfortable?"

She shook her head. "You're not people." When Jamie didn't laugh, Eva said, "You know what I mean..."

"You know the fact the man died was not your fault."

Eva searched for the right words. "Yes, I know. Of course. But... it's different, Jamie, healing people. It's much harder work. The exhaustion is overwhelming, feels like the flu. I ache all over after this one. And, besides, it's dangerous."

"How?" Jamie asked. "They might die?"

"And legal stuff."

"And threats."

"Yes." Eva sighed.

Jamie started for the door. "I'll be back in a minute. I forgot to pick up the mail. I've got to brave that crowd again."

In the kitchen alone, Eva tried to ignore the shouts from the reporters, as they called out questions. Then the front door slammed and she heard Jamie's quick footsteps approaching.

"They're so rude..." Eva said. She did a double-take when she saw Jamie's face. Tension had hardened her friend's lips into a straight line. "What?"

Jamie held out an envelope and tossed the rest of the pile of mail onto the kitchen table. "I hope this isn't..." Her voice trailed off.

As she took the envelope, Eva's heart jumped into her mouth. No stamp, just her name printed in Times New Roman font. No address. For a moment she couldn't bring herself to open it but took a deep breath and unsealed it. Plain typed, it was just a few words:

You've been warned.
Die, BITCH.

Jamie read it over her shoulder. "Oh, God. Wait, don't handle it." She whirled around to yank open a drawer and grabbed a plastic zip bag. Carefully handling the letter and envelope by their corners, she slipped them into the bag and sealed it up.

Eva stood stock still. Her heart began to pound, as adrenaline shot through her. Her nerves were surging like electrified wires.

"Sit, Eva." Jamie reached into her pocket for her cell phone. "I'm calling 911."

———•• ◆ ••———

"But he, or she, whoever it was, was *here*, at my home! They hand-delivered it!" Eva cried.

Officer Giordano, of the New London Police Department, leaned back in his chair, across the table from Jamie and Eva. Thin to the point of gaunt, this man belied the idea of paunchy police who popped donuts like lifesavers. He looked like he could use a few club sandwiches. Sighing, he rubbed his face.

"I'm sorry," he said, "at this point there's nothing we can do."

Disappointment flooded through Eva, and she could see Jamie clench her fists.

"Can't you protect her?" Jamie asked.

"We don't do that. However," he added quickly, "I'll have this dusted for fingerprints, and we'll check it against the criminal database."

"You can get fingerprints from paper?" Eva asked.

"Oh, yes, ma'am. Paper fibers absorb the oils and sweat from fingertips, so if the culprit is sloppy, we'll find them." He stood, signaling an end to the interview.

"So that's it?" Eva was stunned, feeling anger tighten her throat. "Is threatening someone not a crime?"

"Yes, it sure is. Threatening in Connecticut is a Class A misdemeanor with up to one year and fines up to $2,000. And if we catch him delivering another letter, we'll arrest him."

"So," answered Jamie, "you want him to deliver another letter... or worse."

"No ma'am, I didn't say that." He studied Eva. "My advice,' he said, "is that you're careful. Don't be alone if you can help it. Check your door and window locks. I didn't see security cameras, I recommend you get them, front and back. I'm sorry I can't tell you more. We'll be in touch if we have any luck with fingerprints."

When he'd gone, Eva peered out the window. The mob of reporters seemed to have grown. She recognized some of their faces, and the relentless Roger Gleason was there, as usual.

The police officer worked his way through them, speaking to a few. Eva couldn't hear what was said.

"Damn," she said, "On top of everything else, every news outlet in town now knows that the police were here."

Jamie said, her voice bitter, "I know. And it was a giant waste of time, anyway. I should've known better. You know, the Supreme Court says the police are under no obligation to protect us. Period. Their job is to show up after you've been raped, robbed, or murdered, and collect evidence for the prosecuting attorney. Then they try to catch the perpetrator, which doesn't always happen. Often doesn't happen." She stopped pacing and turned to Eva. "Did the pepper spray arrive?"

Eva nodded.

"Good. I hope you don't need it. But I think you should keep it with you. And the security cameras are ordered and I'll get them up ASAP." Jamie was quiet for a minute. "And you might think about getting a handgun and learning how to use it."

Eva just stared at her.

Chapter 39

"Come on Cookie." With the aching now receding, Eva headed toward the cottage, longing for the smell of the sea. And that soft pillow-top bed.

Jamie had argued with her about being alone, but Eva was adamant. She needed alone time, decompress time, and insisted she was safe. No one had seen her collect her car from behind their neighbor's barn, so no one knew where she was. They wouldn't be looking for her in Rhode Island. And now, she had pepper spray.

It seemed weeks since her meeting with Trish—was that just this morning?

Numb, driving on auto-pilot, Eva kept checking her rear-view mirror. No one was following her. But that knowledge didn't make her feel any better, any calmer. Her nerves were still sizzling.

What a long day this had been, with pressure from every direction. First, the confrontation with her father. Then Deepak's death. Then his enraged sister, with her accusations and fury and the media with their relentless questions. To cap it off, she'd yelled at Michael and ended their relationship. She had treated him so badly. No, she couldn't think about that now.

And then the death threat. As she plowed through all the unsolvable dilemmas, she kept coming back to those words, to the incomprehensible idea that someone actually wanted her dead. Her brain was in an endless spin. With no solution in sight for any of these insults to her psyche, they mercilessly pummeled her.

"Die Bitch!" The words rang in her head.

Who wants me dead?

A sudden, unbidden thought struck her, from out of nowhere.

Jared.

"No," she said out loud. Her heart, fueled by adrenaline, began to race.

Her own brother, even if only half-brother? She was really freaking out, to start thinking it might be someone she knew, someone related to her. Olivia. Or Samantha. Hell, she might as well suspect her grandmother. Or Will's stiff wife, Susanna.

"Get a grip, BG," she said aloud, as she tucked her car well into the driveway of the beach cottage.

She traipsed around the house, made tea she forgot to drink, then heated up a can of soup for dinner, which she found she couldn't eat. Cookie whined, padding around after her. She tried to watch a movie, but couldn't concentrate. Music didn't help, a hot bath didn't help. Her heart kept on pounding and the knot in her throat held fast.

She climbed into bed but couldn't drift off. She was exhausted, but not sleepy. Soon giving up, she threw on sweats, grabbed a warm fleece to combat the cool breeze near the water, and headed down the few steps to the sand. She stood gazing eastward. A seagull swept past, heading for wherever his home was for the night. A moth floated near her face. She drew in the moist air, with its sweet fragrance of sun-warmed grass and salt water. Lights from houses or streetlamps down the coastline twinkled, and stars speckled the sky. She could make out the clouds, and half of a nearly full moon peeked out, casting shimmering light on the water.

As Cookie explored the sandy beach, Eva gazed out across Long Island Sound in the direction of Block Island. She pulled the fleece tightly around her and dropped down to sit cross-legged on the sand. When Cookie trotted back to her, she tucked the dog under one arm and closed her eyes. She stroked her pup's ears and fondled the little muzzle. Her heart rose into her throat and her eyes burned. As if she'd spoken her love, the little dog licked her hand.

Out of nowhere, Shakespeare came to mind: "The slings and arrows of outrageous fortune." Yes, fortune was certainly troublesome, right now. Once more she attempted to think through her problems but couldn't focus. Her brain felt muzzy and weariness overtook her. Solitude wrapped her round in an icy prison. She snuggled Cookie closer.

You're back on your own, BG, said a voice in her mind. *That's what you wanted. Are you happier now?*

Her stomach churned. *Well, I will be again.*

The "other" voice said, *Fine. We'll go with that.*

She felt numb. And tight. Her legs and arms were tense and rigid, her fists were clenched, her rib cage felt encased in concrete. The sense of an unbreakable cage grew tighter and tighter, until she couldn't take a full breath. She heard again, in her mind, Chloe's words. "It's like you're mummified."

Eva moaned, and Cookie popped her head up to stare at her.

"It's OK, honey," she said, stroking the dog's head. Eva slid down on her side, her head on Cookie's body, and closed her eyes.

She hoped sleep would come, but it was not to be. Cookie squirmed out from under her head and took off running. Eva groaned, and sat back up, seeing her little dog worrying a ghost crab at the edge of the water, and barking. Shushing Cookie, she called her back.

Clambering to her feet, she kicked off her sneakers, and waded out into the water. It should feel cold, it was late September. *Why am I standing here in the icy water?* She could hardly feel the chill as small waves of the surf slapped against her legs.

Michael. In that instant, more real than memory, he was everywhere, before her, around her, above her. Those eyes, deep chocolate and sparking with fire. His smell, of soap, leather, and wood shavings added to the powerful sensation that he was there, real, physical, touching her. Her whole body responded as if she were in his arms. Those arms, encompassing her, his skin pressed against her. She was enveloped with warmth. She longed to let go, to release herself in that warm wild wet place of their mouths together. Wet and warm and connected. And not holding back.

But he was gone.

The concrete cage encasing her shattered into millions of tiny pieces and she heard a keening, wailing sound. It was coming from her. Doubled over, she began to sob, salty tears pouring down her face, flooding out to join the salt of the sea, taking with them her regret, her guilt, her grief, her aloneness.

Time stopped. Eva had no idea how long she stood, weeping, up to her knees in the salt water. Finally, drained, her breath slowly calmed. She brushed the tears off her cheeks and stood there, silent, just breathing in the still night air.

She stretched her arms out wide, feeling the tingle, the life, in her fingers, feeling the expansion of her chest as she sucked in a deep breath. She felt as light as a dandelion fluff. She laughed aloud.

Behind her, on the beach, Cookie whined.

"It's OK, baby," Eva called back to Cookie, "I haven't lost my mind." *Or maybe I have…*

As she turned back toward the shore, a light rain began. She jogged for the house, to dry off and change. Glancing at her watch, she saw it read 10:30 p.m.

Hope it's not too late.

———•••◆••———

As she hurried into the house, she didn't see the fins in the water, moving slowly back and forth, just off the shoreline.

Chapter 40

When he saw her, standing there dripping on his doorstep, his heart thudded in his chest. Had she come to berate him again?

"It's raining," she said.

"Yes."

"I'm drenched... Forgot an umbrella."

"I see that." He was paralyzed, staring at her.

"Can I come in?"

"Oh, Eva, I'm sorry, of course, I'll grab a towel."

He waited while she dried off and changed into one of his sweatshirts. He'd spent the evening feeling hollowed out to a shell. Completely empty. He understood that the stress of the man's death pressed hard on her, plus Jamie had called to tell him about the hand-delivered death threat. Now was when Eva really needed help. But when things got too rough or scary, instead of leaning on him, she leaned away.

He heard her approach behind him in the kitchen, where he was busying himself boiling the kettle and collecting mugs and teabags. Her arms came around him and he felt her face press against his back. Stiffening, he left the cups where they were and turned in her arms, to look down into those eyes.

"Michael, I'm so sorry."

"OK," he said slowly, "For what, exactly?"

"I spoke from a place of exhaustion and... I'm not even sure what. Deepak's death got into me and terrified me. In a way I can't describe. It was as if it stained my spirit—I didn't feel like myself."

"I get that." He waited, quietly watching her. Then, he said, "Why are you here? Have you changed your mind? Do you want to come back? To us?"

She hesitated, then nodded.

"I don't know if I can, Eva. You've shoved me away so many times."

"I've been alone, and chosen to be, for so long."

"You keep people at arm's length."

"Yes, for safety."

Michael sighed. "I did everything I could to make you feel safe."

She shook her head. "I thought I was safe with my mother. Then with Sophie."

Shock reverberated through him.

She whispered, "I didn't think I could survive... being left alone again."

His heart ached but his world expanded. He answered her whisper. "What's changed?"

Those sweet golden eyes looked up and met his. And held. "I love you, Michael."

He couldn't speak.

She held on tight, and then said, in a small voice, "And it turns out, losing you is worse."

"Worse than what?"

"Worse than the *fear* of losing you..." She paused. Then, "Can you ever forgive me?"

His answer was a long kiss.

"I'll take that as a yes..." she said, her voice shaking.

He pulled her close and held her. They needed to talk, but right now she was in his arms.

"I have so much to tell you," Eva muttered, into his neck.

"It'll keep." He led her up the stairs to his bedroom.

His mouth closed over hers and two tongues became one. He kissed her long, and longer, and longer.

———••◆••———

Arousal swirled. Every one of Eva's senses shivered with awareness every place where his skin touched hers. The smell of his breath, the feel of muscles of his back under her hands. Pulling him ever closer. Wrapped around him, hardly an iota of her skin untouched by his.

Their lovemaking was as natural and rolling as the smooth current in a river. She flowed with him, felt herself floating, coming to life in his eyes, where there were no fences, no walls. The energy between them grew and grew, with all the magic, the calm, the vibration of the healings, but with the additional element of fire. Of passion.

Heat and fullness in her lower body as they connected, became one body. Deeper and deeper into his eyes, she found and touched the lake, then sank into it. Nothing but a slow cyclone of energy, a giant ball of warmth and connection. He was above her, yet within her, all around her. Everywhere... together this world was a ball of sensuality. Deeper, deeper. Eddying into those eyes... all one.

Ever-growing heat in languid movement, now increasing in speed. Hips moving. Arms stroking up and down, fingers pressing hard into his back.

Higher. Hotter. Deeper. Closer.

A growing, expanding sensation, the darkness of the night sky bright with shooting stars.

He was the electricity that sparked the flame. And she was the universal womb, from which all life flowed.

When she slowly returned to an awareness of her separateness from Michael, Eva drew in long steadying breaths. She had visited another world, *they* had visited another world. The connection was with him, yes, but it was also with something greater. Greater than the two of them. This was a path to bliss, not just physical bliss, that her body provided. But was it just her body? There was something beyond the physical when she was with Michael. A recognition, a longing to go home fulfilled. Belonging. A shared path to the creator's feet.

She turned on her side to face him, inches from his face. His arm was wrapped around her waist, keeping her near.

Eva welled up, she wasn't sure why, and a tear dripped onto the pillow.

"I've never seen you cry," he said softly.

"I haven't, since my mother died, until tonight."

He gently wiped her cheek.

"I understood a few things this evening, there on the beach." She lay still, remembering. "And I have more news, but it'll keep," she said, an echo of his earlier words. She didn't want to think about her father, the way he had treated her mother. Or the death threat. She didn't want to bring all that darkness into this glistening space. She sat up. "I have to get back—Cookie's at the cottage."

"Why didn't you bring her?"

She looked away. "I didn't know what my reception would be..."

He gently turned her face back to him, so their eyes met. "You didn't?"

"Well, I *hoped* I knew what the reception would be."

"Ok, I'll come with you." He grinned. "Don't want to let you out of my sight... just yet."

"Oh no, you get a good night's sleep. You're on call early, aren't you?" She glanced at the clock on the bedside table. "It's midnight, you go to sleep. Come up tomorrow night. I'll cook you dinner."

"Oh goody, you have a Trader Joe's nearby?"

She laughed aloud. "I *can* put a steak on a grill."

───·•◆•·───

She headed out to her car, grateful the media had gone home, abandoned the siege. Plugging in her phone, to charge it, she realized it had been switched off all evening. Flicking it back on, she started back toward the cottage. She'd only gone a mile or so when her phone rang. Glancing down where the phone was sitting on the console, she saw the caller was Chloe. Chloe never called, she always texted. And it was late. Eva had a strange sensation in her gut, like butterflies. Something was wrong. She found a place where she could pull over to the side of the road.

"Chloe, everything OK?"

Her aunt's voice was tense, and she sounded breathless. "Oh Eva, there you are. Been trying to reach you."

"Phone was off, what's going on?"

"Will's had...your father's had a heart attack in his hotel."

"What?"

"A few hours ago." Chloe's voice cracked. "He's in the main hospital in Providence, I'll text you the address. I'm here now. Mom and Dad are on their way. The rest of the family too."

Eva took a deep breath.

"Eva, are you there?"

"Yes. Is he going to be OK? Is it serious?"

"He's in the ICU," Chloe said softly. "It's not good. He's in a coma, cardiac arrest, and they don't know how long he lay there..." She drew in a ragged breath.

"OK. On my way." Eva rang off.

Her hands gripped tight around the steering wheel as the car idled at the side of the road. She found herself rocking forward and backward. *A heart attack?* Her mind taunted her. A few hours after their words on the pavement he had a heart attack. This was her fault. A wave of nausea rolled over her and she climbed out of the car, pulling in fresh air. Out of her unkindness and cruelty she'd attacked him, verbally attacked him. The one thing she never wanted in her life was to harm another person. And this was her own flesh and blood.

Eva called Michael, who offered to go with her, but she asked if he could go up to the cottage to look after Cookie. Then she sped northward on I-95.

She had sworn she was going to have nothing more to do with Will Hastings. Because he had ruined her mother's life. But none of that mattered now. This man was her father.

Chapter 41

Jared's face was grim. "Dad was late coming down to dinner. And he'd been acting strange all afternoon. We had a series of meetings with the Haverling Biotech people... and he was distracted throughout. Said he was fine, but I knew something was up." Jared shook his head, his lips pursed. He shot a look at Eva, and she wondered how much Will had said to him about their lunch meeting. If he'd said anything at all.

"We decided to stay in Providence. When he didn't show up on time for dinner, I found him. He was in the adjoining room, flat out on the floor." Jared's voice broke and he turned his head away. "Don't know how long... Then it was fifteen minutes before the EMTs got there... I did CPR, and they got his heart started again, but..."

His grandmother rushed to pat his arm. "Thank God you were there, Jared. I can't imagine what would have happened if...." Her voice trailed off. She was pale.

The ICU family waiting room was soulless, impersonal, but at least they had privacy. When Eva arrived, her grandparents, and Chloe were already there, as was Jared. They told her Susanna was in San Francisco, visiting family, but was now on her way. As was Olivia, from New York. Samantha had arrived just after Eva and now sat with Chloe on a couch, with her aunt's arm around her. Samantha's eyes were puffy and red. The mood was somber, but

Eva noticed there wasn't the usual sniping at each other. It was as if, with their leader lying in a hospital bed, fighting for his life, the troops had tacitly agreed to a ceasefire.

Eva's grandmother turned to her and whispered, "Will you help him, Eva?"

Angela's voice sounded strained but controlled, and Eva could sense the effort that took. Eva pulled her close into a hug and spoke softly in her ear. "I'll try, Grandma, I'll try."

"Can I get in on this?" It was Olivia, hurrying in after her four-hour drive. Eva hardly recognized her. No make-up, hair in a ponytail, this was a different woman from the glamorous creature she'd met at the parties. Gone was the brashness. Also, noticeably absent were the effects of alcohol. This young woman was clear-eyed, quiet, but with a trembling bottom lip.

Angela turned back from receiver to giver of nurture, pulling Olivia into a warm embrace.

Eva's eyes stung. Family. Support. She was witnessing everything she'd missed, all those years.

As they waited, there was little conversation. Some held magazines but no one turned pages. Her sisters' eyes were fixed on their phones, but Eva doubted they could concentrate. She couldn't. Her grandfather kept disappearing to the hallway to make phone calls. The vending machines in the waiting room offered tea and coffee of dubious quality, but no one cared enough to make the trek to the café on the next floor.

The doctors were conducting tests, the nurse had told them, and there would be a report any minute. They'd had to wait for a cardiac specialist and a consult from the top neurologist on their staff.

"Dad's informed the staff and other family members," Chloe said. "Plus, he's organized a full-time nurse for Will, to augment the staff here at the hospital. And for when he gets out." She didn't add, "If he gets out." But Eva heard those words in her mind.

Chloe gave her an odd look. "You OK? I know you're upset about Will, of course, but is there something else?"

Eva spoke softly for Chloe's ears only. "Will and I... had words."

"When? What do you mean?"

Eva spoke in a whisper. She wanted no one else to hear this. "Yesterday. I met him for lunch. We never even got to food. I tackled him for the way he treated my mother."

"Oh... there's more to that, I can see." Chloe's eyes widened. "Oh, I get it," she exclaimed. "You're thinking somehow you caused this." She shook her head, vehemently. "Now, Eva, you can't blame yourself for his lifetime of poor eating, for stress, for loving his malt Scotch. And he only stopped smoking last year."

The door opened, and two doctors in rumpled white coats appeared, one studying his clipboard. Their faces were grim, and Eva's heart jumped into her mouth.

"Will Hastings' family? I'm Dr. Torres." He gestured to his colleague. "This is Dr. Hooper."

Her grandfather's voice shook. "I'm William Hastings, Will's father. Will he be all right, Doctor?"

"As you know, your son suffered a major heart attack and subsequent cardiac arrest," Dr. Torres explained. "Unfortunately, his brain was without oxygen for a significant period of time."

Angela gasped, her hand over her mouth. Chloe reached for her, wrapping an arm around her mother.

"He's stable," the doctor said. "He's in the ICU, on life support. That means a ventilator is breathing for him, and we are closely monitoring all his vital signs. We've run a battery of tests and I'm afraid all initial indicators are not good."

Olivia's voice was high and soft, her eyes huge. "What does that mean?"

Dr. Hooper replied. "The EEG is non-reactive. Other tests confirm this. I'm so sorry."

"Do you mean flat line, Doctor?" Jared asked. "Brain death?"
Dr. Hooper cleared his throat. "Yes. I'm sorry."

There were gasps, and Olivia moaned.

"I'm sorry,' the doctor repeated. "You folks will have a decision to make. Not immediately, you have time."

"Do you mean like turning off the machines?" Chloe asked bluntly.

"No!" Angela Hastings cried. "No! There will be no turning off of machines!"

As her mother's knees began to buckle, Chloe and her grandfather helped her to the couch. Angela appeared to have aged ten years, her face had crumpled in on itself, her eyes were half shut, and her mouth was open. She rocked back and forth, one hand holding tight to Chloe's and the other fisted on her chest. She moaned softly. Chloe sat next to her, rubbing her shoulder.

The door to the waiting room opened again and a woman, dressed in a suit and carrying a folder, stood in the doorway, looking around, as if deciding whom to speak to. This was not a nurse. As she approached them, Eva scanned the woman's nameplate. "UNOS, United Network for Organ Sharing."

Her grandfather had seen it, too. He didn't give the woman a chance to speak, even to introduce herself. "Get out!" he hollered. "You're a *ghoul*. For God's sake! *Go!*"

The woman scurried out the door.

The tension in the room was palpable.

As Olivia and Jared continued to talk with the two doctors, Eva heard more explanations that meant nothing to her, about brainstem reflexes, myoclonus setting in, and she switched off. She couldn't listen any longer, couldn't take any more in.

As the doctors quietly conveyed their commiserations once again and left them, a nurse arrived to take them, one at a time, to the ICU room. She explained they would need to be ready to move out of the way quickly if emergency staff needed to get to Will.

By now, Olivia and Samantha were both openly sobbing, Jared, was pale, his face rigid. Chloe stayed with her mother.

It was quiet but for the sounds of weeping. Eva looked around at her new family and found all eyes were turned to her. Even Jared's.

Her grandfather cleared his throat, then said, "Eva, go to him. *Please*, you go."

There were no objections.

But the appeal, the hope, the desperation in all those eyes haunted her.

The nurse led her down the hall to a private room. She pointed to the flat lines on the EEG machine and spoke kindly, but firmly. "I don't want you to get your hopes up. I'm sorry, but people just don't come back from an irreversible coma." She touched Eva's shoulder and left her.

Having so recently experienced the typical ICU set-up in Deepak's room, the tubes, IVs, and beeping monitors didn't shock her. But there was the man himself, so confident, so strong, normally filling a room with his energy. Now rendered helpless. And for Eva, it had been a long afternoon, indeed, a long couple of days. Exhaustion dragged at her, tried to pull her down. An hour's sleep in Dr. Chin's office was no help at all. Her eyes were gritty from fatigue.

To make matters worse, she was alone this time, without Chloe's energy, or Jamie's, or Michael's. She'd come to understand how valuable this contribution was to the healing process. But was it essential? Could she do it on her own? It struck her that she'd been alone when trying to help Deepak. And had failed utterly. Her mind was spinning out of control and her heart was racing. The last person she had tried to help had died. Right there while she held his hand.

What if I can't heal my father? Will they blame me if I fail?

She flexed her fingers and rubbed her hands to release some of the tension, then pulled a chair close to the bed. Sitting there quietly, she stared at her father's pale face, partially obscured by the breathing tube protruding from his mouth.

The last words they had said were hateful, hurtful, lies, or bitterness. How to cross that chasm?

What about what he did to her mother?

She shook her head, gazing at this man in the bed.

I need him to take responsibility, to apologize. So, I can forgive him.

But wait, Baby Girl, forgiveness is for yourself, don't forget. Setting down a burden. Not granting forgiveness just holds on to anger, which is exhausting.

So, am I stuck in my own ego? That I'm right? Or even holding on to some bit of power I think I have? Even if fabricated in my own mind?

There were no answers.

"Hi, Will." She couldn't call him Dad. Or even Father. She took his hand, massaged it gently. It was cold. "I don't know how to do this. I have to confess that upfront. And I don't know if you can hear me anyway." She paused. "I'm sorry I was harsh. But come back now."

She closed her eyes and said softly, in her mind, *Help me. Please help me.* As she waited, willing the vibration to start, a sense of calm slowly and surely took over. She left the fear, the guilt behind. The vibration began, and with it, confidence slowly grew.

I know how this goes. I know how. I can do it.

She let her thoughts drift to Jamie. Kind funny Jamie. To Dr. Chin. To beautiful Chloe, her aunt, but also a new friend and mentor in her life. To her grandmother, her grandfather, their generosity and support. To little Samantha. As her attention focused on each person, it was as if they'd touched her, and she experienced an opening, a sense of deepening into the space.

Michael. Dearest Michael. Heart of her heart. She'd saved the best for last. Love poured through her, filled her, and her awareness expanded to include animals. To include children, plants, trees, beauty... And music. Everything she loved.

She fed off this love. She would *use* this love.

The sensation of deep water surrounded her, and she floated, patiently, enveloped in the peace that was this moment.

Then, there was the wall. Right in front of her. Not too thick, not too hard, gray in color. She smiled inwardly at it, recognizing it as her own, and it dissolved with no further effort. She understood, now, what that first wall was.

You've been striding around in all that armor, Baby Girl, but when you dive into deep water, none of that is going to be of any value down there. None of it. It just weighs you down. Stops you even being able to swim.

In the end, healing was just essence meeting essence, at the purest spiritual level. That's why it worked.

Beyond that first wall, her own, now stood granite. Ice and black granite. She had no sense of what lay beyond that. And this was different than anything she had encountered before.

A wave of darkness, of dark energy, rolled toward her from the wall. She didn't shrink back. Almost as if she sat in a bubble of unbreakable glass, the energy bounced off it and she continued to move forward. Toward the cold stone. What was this black energy? She had no idea. She just knew it couldn't reach her. She was stronger than any murky energy rolling toward her. She touched the granite shield, again and again, with her own intent.

Let me pass. I want to help. Let me through.

She waited, focusing on this wall, unbothered by its efforts to keep her out. Unbothered by time, or the need for patience, or any fear of failure.

All of that remained behind her, residing in the memory and ego of her body sitting on the chair. Her spirit was beyond that, free of that, and was not going to take no for an answer.

And the wall started to weaken. Like the white or gray streaks in a sheet of marble, the icy granite formed cracks. The streaks widened, more and more, opening wider and wider. Further and further, it broke open, until the wall just fell down, in slow motion, revealing the open space beyond.

Eva approached and touched this openness gently. It shimmered, trembled, then slowly relaxed, performing a metaphorical stretch. Eva smiled, deep inside. This was the spirit that had been trapped inside her father. Could she set it free?

At least she could dance with it. Her spirit and the spirit behind the wall intermingled, flowing and blending together, just as gases combine, until indistinguishable. Together they created a circle of warmth and deep water and all-encompassing peace.

Chapter 42

When Eva woke, it was to an insistent beeping sound. It took her a moment to realize where she was. Her face was down on her arms, on her father's hospital bed. A hand was touching her hair— he was stroking it back from her face. Lifting up quickly, she saw his eyes were open.

Oh my God. She grabbed his hand and squeezed it. "Don't try to breathe, there's a machine breathing for you—hang on, the nurse will be here in a moment."

He gave a small nod. His hand felt strong and sure.

The nurse came rushing into the room, calling for help. Eva pushed her chair back into the corner of the room and watched as the room filled with professionals, who were checking the monitors and running her father through tests. The nurse who had escorted her to this room stood still, just for a moment, with her mouth open, staring at the wavy lines filling the EEG screen.

A doctor said, as he peered into Will's eyes with a small flashlight, "Welcome back, Mr. Hastings."

Will lifted a hand and gave a slight wave, then pointed to the breathing tube.

"Hang on, sir, we will need to check a few things. Wanting that tube out of there, huh? Give us a few minutes." Eva heard someone say they'd page the neurologist.

Eva mentally left them to it. She closed her eyes and realized she wasn't aching after this healing. Just weary.

She had done it. The relief washed over her in huge waves as she fell back to sleep.

When she next woke, the medical team was gone, and her grandmother was sitting on the edge of the hospital bed next to Will. The breathing tube was gone, and she could hear her grandmother speaking to him.

As Eva approached them, her father reached for her hand.

"Everyone has been in for a minute or two, Eva," her grandmother said, stretching an arm around Eva's waist. "But Will keeps asking for you." Angela's eyes were full of tears.

Will's eyes held Eva's and he squeezed her hand. Clearing his throat, he spoke in a cracking voice. "Stay. Stay for a while."

She had connected with this man, her father, she knew him now. Under all that bluster, that lack of empathy, that harshness, was a spirit. But this spirit differed from other spirits she'd encountered. It wasn't the spirit of a powerful man, it was the undeveloped spirit of a child. It had never been allowed to grow as it should have over the course of his life.

She could relate. She'd also been trapped behind walls, of her own making. But she'd benefited from connecting, essence to essence, with animals for many years. And now with humans. And with each of those encounters her spirit had grown.

She doubted her father had ever really touched another soul. He lived his life denying his spirit.

It was 3:45 in the morning by the time she left the hospital, texting Michael the news about her father, and that she was on her way back to the cottage.

She simply didn't want to wait around and talk about the recovery. Or see her family stare at her, or even cope with their gratitude. She was still floating in the mild fatigue and greater awe about what she had just experienced.

Healings would always be overwhelming, she figured, and tiring. In that deep place of healing, every little nano bit of her spirit was touching every bit of her father's, and she gave. His childlike spirit was full of need. So, she gave, gave of her own essence to him.

All the loving people involved in a healing gave, too. Subconsciously, she was sure, but they gave. She could feel it. There was power in this new knowledge, and she wanted to explore it.

And she needed to figure out, to face, why Deepak had died. It wasn't anything she did, of that she was now sure. Perhaps it was his spirit's time. Perhaps his spirit was done.

But now, she couldn't wait to get home to her borrowed beach cottage, and to Michael. She was only twenty minutes away from this temporary haven when the rain started. It had been drizzling off and on all day, but now the skies opened.

She was traveling slowly, since visibility was now reduced, when she saw the headlights looming up behind her. Way too close behind her. *Damn tailgaters.* People could be so stupid, she thought. She looked for a place to pull over, to let it by, but there was a marsh close to the road, almost no shoulder. So, she sped up a bit, hoping the driver would back off. Eva kept watching for a place to let him pass. The car sped up, keeping right behind her, so close it was almost touching her car.

Her heart leapt into her mouth. What if this wasn't just a lousy driver? What if this was the same car that followed her a few weeks ago? She couldn't tell. It was 4:30 in the morning, pitch black here on the rural road off I-95, and all she could see was the car's headlights, blinding her.

Middle of the night, and not another car on the road. She was on her own. And leading this person to the cottage wasn't an option. If he or she was just a journalist after a story, she didn't want them to know where she was staying, and if not... well, most of the nearby cottages were now empty for the winter.

For just a moment she was tempted to stop, get out, armed with her pepper spray, and face this guy down. But she abandoned that idea. She hated movies and TV shows where the female protagonist was brave to the point of moronic. Eva had received death threats, so stopping on a lonely country road in the middle of the night to face off with a stranger following her? No way.

With the words "Die bitch" emblazoned on her mind, she stepped on the accelerator, going as fast as she dared. She was going to have to outrun this guy. Forty miles per hour, fifty, sixty. The car stayed right on her tail. She didn't even dare pick up her phone and try to call 911 for help. She needed all her concentration and both hands on the wheel. The tires squealed as she took a curve way too fast. Her racing heart, fueled by adrenaline, pounded under her ribs.

When the rain lightened up, she hit a straight stretch, gave a quick glance at her phone. No signal. She had to get to the next town, to find cell reception, to find houses close together. To find a police station. She was unfamiliar with this area, just that there were two large chunks of state forest land—she could see endless woods on either side of the car.

She heard the acceleration of the car behind her, then it bashed into her rear bumper. *What the hell?* She took a chance and stepped on it, pressing the accelerator to the floor.

She was too late. The car behind her came hurtling up alongside hers and she saw the leering face of the driver at the wheel. She recognized that face. She could only watch in horror as he pulled the wheel toward her. He shoved his car into hers, and she felt as well as heard the crunch and shriek of metal each time the two cars collided. Between the wet road, the speed, the force of the collisions, and her shock, she lost control of her trusty old SUV and spun off to the side of the road, weaving precariously, then hurtled down a small ravine. The car rolled, and the last thing Eva knew was the pain of being punched in the face, the world turning upside down, and then blackness.

———•◆•———

"Where *is* she?" Michael said for the fourth time, to himself, as he looked once again at his watch. She should have been here an hour ago. His texts remained unanswered, his calls went straight to voice mail. He spoke to Chloe, who confirmed the time Eva had left the hospital. He promised to let her know when Eva safely arrived.

What happened? Did she just pull over to the side of the road to rest? Why didn't she call, if that was the case? The state police told him there were no reports of accidents in the area. But they did warn him of the dead patches in cell reception, due to the state parks lining Route 216.

Pacing back and forth wasn't helping. Finally, urgent to do something, he grabbed a rain jacket and his keys. Cookie whimpered. Michael told Jeremiah and Nellie they were on guard and said, "Come on Cookie."

As he headed away from the shore, he wondered if this was complete folly. He hoped it was as simple as trouble with the car—after all, it was an ancient old thing. But it was a lot of miles to Providence, and if she had run out of gas, or had some other car problem, she could be anywhere along the route.

Michael slowly headed north on 216. Suddenly something hit him. What if she had chosen to come down Route 2, through Charlestown? No, that wouldn't make sense, way too slow. But even still, he kept double-checking his phone connection to the car, so he'd hear if a text or call came through. She might arrive at the cottage while he was wandering around some rural road.

Even though it was lightly raining, he opened the front windows on both sides, so he could see more clearly. Cookie shoved her head out the window directly into the breeze and the moisture. He realized he'd forgotten to put her in her harness, but he didn't want to stop now. He kept his eyes peeled for cars at the side of the road or traveling in the opposite direction. But at 5:30 in the morning, no one was out on the road.

Just as he approached a wild-looking wooded area, Cookie suddenly started to bark. She jumped up to place her front paws up on the door panel, looking as if she might jump right out. He leaned over and grabbed her collar, but she struggled, still barking and whimpering.

"What's wrong with you, girl?"

Cookie was staring back, across the other side of the road, and becoming frantic. Probably a coyote, raccoon, or fox. But something made him slow down. As he did, the little dog hurled herself out the window and took off down the shoulder of the road, the way they'd come.

Michael made a quick U-turn and pulled over. Jumping out, he hollered again and again to Cookie, who had disappeared over a berm at the side of the road. Reaching through the passenger window, he grabbed a flashlight from the glove box and peered down into the swampy trench, like a small ravine. Beyond that lay deep woods. Was there something down there? He could certainly hear Cookie whining and barking. He followed the little dog down into the darkness.

There was the car, Eva's old SUV. The roof was caved in, the driver's door as well, and the entire car was covered with mud. Cookie was jumping, barking, and scratching at the driver's door.

"Eva!" he shouted. Heart racing, shoving down panic, Michael raced down the slope, sliding through several inches of mud, through rocks and weeds and tall grasses not yet knocked down by frost. Calling out her name.

As he neared the car, he could see Eva beating on the window with her hands. And ramming her shoulder into the door. The relief to see her moving poured through him—she was alive. No matter how injured she was, she had the energy to be shoving against that door.

"Eva, hang on, you OK?"

"Oh, Michael," she shouted as she pressed her forehead against the window, "I knew you'd find me."

"Cookie found you!" He tried the door handle. Jammed shut. Pulling, yanking, it wouldn't budge.

"I can't get out. And the seat belt's jammed."

They needed help. Michael glanced at his phone. No signal. Reaching back, he tried the passenger door behind her, but both doors were dented in. The SUV had obviously rolled down that embankment.

He stumbled through the mud to the other side of the car, where the passenger door wasn't as damaged. Jamming his foot against the back door for leverage, he yanked, again and again, until the front door finally opened with a loud creak.

He had to reach in just to touch her. She grabbed his hand, still struggling with the seat belt, and pushed the flattened airbag forward out of her way.

"Sure you're ok? Legs ok?"

"My face hurts—from the airbag, I think."

As she spoke, he yanked on the seatbelt, then hunted through her glove compartment, looking for something to cut with. Swiss =Army knife, perfect. He slit through the seatbelt and helped her climb over the center console and pulled her out of the passenger door. He grabbed her, she clung to him.

"Oh, Michael, he ran me off the road..."

Michael thought he'd heard wrong. "*What?*"

"He tried to kill me."

"Sweetheart, what are you saying? Who?"

"Roger Gleason! It was Roger Gleason. He followed me, rammed the back of the car, then rammed me from the side. I couldn't... the car wouldn't... then I was rolling." She sobbed. "Oh God, Michael."

Michael was speechless. He had to get to a phone.

Chapter 43

"You're sure? Seems like we should get you checked out."

"No, I'm sure. I'm fine,' Eva said. "My face hurts, and I have a small bump where I must have hit my head... But no broken bones and I'm not bleeding anywhere. Just an exhausted muddy mess, but no, no hospital. Believe me, I've had enough hospital to last me a while."

It only took fifteen minutes to get home to the Airbnb on the beach. She'd been so close, all that time. Michael had called the police, who agreed Michael and Eva could go back to the cottage, where the police would come to interview them after they checked out the accident site.

"I'm not looking forward to talking to the police..." Eva said softly. "A long day is turning into a long night." Cookie was on her lap on the front seat and Eva stroked the little dog. She relaxed her head back against the headrest, but when she closed her eyes, she relived that moment when Gleason leered at her and rammed into her car.

"Cookie won't let you out of her sight. Or out of her touch. I know how she feels," Michael said, reaching to squeeze Eva's hand yet again.

As she climbed out of the car, in the driveway, and started for the cottage door, she felt an ache, a sharp ache, in her head. It didn't surprise her that after an accident like that, after the adrenaline wore off, she'd get a nasty headache. But as she greeted Michael's dogs inside the front door, the headache grew.

"I need some painkillers," she muttered.

"Not surprising, sweetheart, I'll get them." Michael turned toward the downstairs bathroom.

"Thanks. I'll make tea." As Eva started for the kitchen she heard Cookie barking at the French doors at the back of the house. The dog jumped up on the door, whining, then the other two dogs joined in.

"What a racket! For goodness' sake, Cookie, what is it? What's out there?" Staring through the glass of the French doors, she suddenly grabbed her head as a stabbing pain shot through it. It was so agonizing she cried out.

At the same moment, she saw the fins, out there near the shoreline. The rain had stopped, the sky was beginning to lighten, and two dolphins were swimming just a few yards out into Long Island Sound.

Oh my God! Still clutching her head, Eva ripped open the door, and all three dogs burst out ahead of her. Trying to ignore the hot skewer in her head, she hurried down the steps, through the dry sand to the wet sand, and then into the water. Mindless of her shoes, or jeans or jacket, she waded straight out toward them.

The pain was unbearable, but the dolphins were here.

—••◆••—

"I found the acetaminophen," Michael called out from the powder room. "I'm sorry, but we need to get your head checked. You can't mess around with a headache after an accident. Especially you, Eva. I've called 911, they said they'd be here in about fifteen minutes."

Then he heard the dogs' frantic barking and Eva's cry. At a run, he raced to the open patio door, to see her, slightly hunched, holding her head, and knee deep in the ocean. He started after her.

And saw what she saw. Those fins moving in the water. Drawing in a sharp breath, he took the wooden steps two at a time. Eva stumbled forward, once, twice. Then, just before she reached the dolphins, Michael saw her fall. She collapsed, completely limp, and almost in slow motion, disappeared under the water.

Oh, God. He raced across the sand.

Keeping his eyes pinned on the spot she went under, Michael plunged in after her, his only thought to reach her. Heart in his mouth, he pushed through the rolling surf.

Then, he saw her, lifting up, out of the water. As he watched in amazement, her entire body floated there, horizontal, as if she were simply lying on the surface. He stopped and stared. She began to rotate, slowly, the water streaming off her body and hair.

Higher out of the water she rose, until two dolphins came into view, underneath her, the fins gleaming wet either side of her body. Sleek bodies head to tail, they continued to circle slowly, and she glistened as she rode them in the growing light of pre-dawn.

There was no danger. Michael knew it, and even the dogs stopped barking and just stared. Eva was turning, turning, turning, her eyes closed, her wet clothes plastered to her, while the dolphins held her safely out of the water. Not an offering, not a sacrifice, but a conduit for heaven's energy.

Long minutes held, and nothing moved but the gentle surf and the rotating dolphins. A glow of light was forming all around the dolphins, with her lying on them, and Michael gasped. This was not moonlight. Was it sunshine hitting the water right there? No, the sun had not yet risen above the horizon... And there was heavy cloud cover, anyway. Besides, this light appeared to be emanating *from* the circle of dolphins and woman, not shining down upon it. He shook his head. He was imagining the light. He had to be.

For thirty seconds he stood and stared, ready to dive in and grab Eva if she sank again, if they left her. But they didn't. Another thirty seconds, another minute. Shaking, his teeth were chattering from the chill of the late September water, and from an overwhelm of emotion. The shock of this image. Awe at the sight of dolphins holding his beloved Eva.

———••◆••———

Eva opened her eyes, saw Michael, and smiled.

Where had she been? A warm place, held, caressed by the touch of her friends, the dolphins. There was no sense of her body as she floated, no pain, no chill from the water. Currents of vibrations had lifted her from the searing headache, then blackness as she collapsed, to a world of glistening light. Rather than the deep dark place of her healing moments, this was a sparkling, euphoric place. No walls, no obstacles, just pure joyfulness. Even a bubbly sense of fun.

The dolphins gently separated beneath her, and she slid down into the water, reaching for a fin with one hand, running her fingers along the ragged scar.

"Grace..." she murmured.

The dolphin's head turned to Eva, mouth open in her trademark smile, and she clicked and whistled. Then pressed her body up against Eva's side. Eva stroked the animal, murmured to her, thanked her for coming, again and again. Then she wrapped her arm around Grace, over the top of her body, behind the silky head. She floated like that, eyes closed, holding the dolphin.

The vibration and deep space returned, as she reveled in the energy and heart of this wild being. Enthralled by the sweetness of the connection, her spirit rolled and flowed, played and danced with Grace.

But at last, she felt the movement of muscles under her arm and knew Grace was preparing to say goodbye. Returning to the awareness of her physical presence, Eva felt how chilled she was, how cold her hands and feet were.

But the headache was gone.

When she opened her eyes, she lifted her arm, and Grace moved away, just a little, turning to pull her head out of the water, open-mouthed, whistling. Eva gazed into the dark eye that stared at her, unblinking, and she smiled.

"Bye, Grace."

Grace responded by pulling up out of the water, rising vertically, and moving backward, away from Eva, using her tail. There were more clicks and whistles, then Grace shot away through the water, the second dolphin close behind her. Eva stood transfixed, watching them. About twenty-five yards away, Grace leaped high out of the water, high into the air, again and again, before finally turning to the deep sea, to join the rest of her pod.

Chapter 44

As Eva yawned and looked around, it took a moment to remember where she was. A hospital room. The doctors had prodded her for what felt like hours, finding nothing abnormal on a plethora of tests. She had finally dozed off to a light sleep while waiting for the results of the MRI. The neurologist on call had insisted on it.

There was a lingering sense of unreality about the last few days. But no headache. She felt well, rested even. She just needed some normalcy. Smiling to herself, she realized her normal parameters were going to have to change. Between the gift of healing, and the gift of Michael, normal looked different now.

Michael was just outside her room; she could see him through the door, with Jamie and Clare, talking quietly with the police officer and the detective. They had asked her a seemingly endless stream of questions and she had recalled every detail as clearly as she could of the "accident," as they called it. She informed them, in no uncertain terms, that it was no accident. It was attempted murder.

As she sat up, yawning, she saw Jamie and Clare hurrying toward her from the hallway.

"Geez, Eva, you scared me to death," Jamie said as she hugged her. "I just got the text from Michael—we came straight away. What a nightmare!"

Clare added, "Michael brought us up to date. I can't believe you went through that. It doesn't make sense —is the guy insane? I thought he was a journalist."

Jamie let out a guffaw. "Nah, paparazzi type. You know, hyperbolic headlines. And a religious zealot to boot. You could be right, he's simply insane. But whether insane or evil, they have to nail that son of a bitch."

"Absolutely," said Michael as he came back into the room. "And there's something else, Eva. While you were asleep, the detective was notified that they found a tracking device on the floor of your car."

So that's how he knew where I was. Eva shuddered.

"Thank God, he never found you at the cottage, alone," Jamie added.

"Oh man," Clare said, with a grimace. "That's terrifying."

"And they found a fingerprint on the tracking device," Michael said.

"Can he slither out from under this?" Jamie asked.

"Guys, I saw him," Eva said. "I *saw* him! Does eye-witness identification mean anything?"

"Could he claim it's your word against his?" Clare asked.

Eva said, "He can try. But there must be paint from my car on Gleason's. Don't you think? That will confirm it."

"The police did mention that," Michael said. "Nope, he's toast. The bastard. The guy's looking at a whole slew of charges. Misdemeanor to felonies, right up to attempted murder."

The neurologist appeared in the doorway. "Well, Ms. McGrath, good news. Everything is fine—you'll be pleased to hear the MRI is normal. Nothing to concern us, so we can let you go home. I'm sure, after the night you've had, that's where you want to be." He smiled.

Eva hesitated, for just a moment, but she had to know. "What about the aneurysm, Doctor Hart?"

His eyebrows shot up. "Aneurysm? Am I missing something here?"

"I was diagnosed with an aneurysm when I was eleven. They called it a Familial Intracranial Aneurysm. The neurologist told us it was located at the base of the brain."

The doctor pulled up glasses from the leather cord around his neck, then fiddled for a few moments with his electronic pad. He studied it carefully. "No, there's no aneurysm."

"Could the MRI have missed it?" Michael asked.

The neurologist shook his head. "No. This is a nice clear scan. Eva, you do not have an aneurysm. Perhaps a mistake in the first place, they may have had a poor image, or read the MRI incorrectly. That was a long time ago, what, about fifteen years? Technology's come a long way since then."

Eva sat, stunned, and hardly heard the doctor saying he would get the nurse to start the release papers. She did hear Jamie gasp.

Jamie was almost jumping up and down, excitement pouring off her. She grabbed Eva's hand. "Eva! That's incredible!"

Eva was still trying to take it in. When? Why? How? She didn't for one second think the original MRI was poor quality, or they'd read it incorrectly.

The aneurysm she had, was now gone.

She met Michael's eyes and knew he was thinking the same.

"Grace," Eva murmured.

He nodded, his eyes shining.

Epilogue

Six months later

Jamie's big grin lit up her face. "Damn, girl, look at you! You look amazing."

Eva's hair flowed down in long creamy waves, over the shoulders of the coffee-colored dress and gold scarf. She grinned.

"And you're so tall," Jamie continued. "Craning my neck, here. Are you wearing *heels?*"

Eva lifted a foot off the floor and posed to show off her brown suede boots. High-heeled boots. "Oh, yes, I've got height and I'm going to use it. I'll take all the advantages I can get."

Jamie grinned. "And I can't believe you're giving this speech. Who are you and what have you done with Eva?"

"It's a big day—I've been working toward this for months."

Eva was waiting, with Jamie and Michael, in a small anteroom in Hartford City Hall, for Governor Lambeth to introduce her to the press. They had chosen the historic old building for its impressive three-story marble and granite atrium.

"It's full, I mean *packed*," Michael said. "There must be 200 press people out there. And you should see the crowd out front. Looks like thousands, in the streets, jamming up traffic."

When they left her to join the crowd in the hall, Eva peered out the front window to the street below. The invitation to the press had gone out only a few days ago, but word must have spread, for she could see a vast throng of people in all directions. An unusually cold day in late March, they were wrapped in winter jackets and scarves against the chill wind. A few members of the crowd held signs, and she was glad they were too far away to read. The protesting and even outrage had continued over these months, and although Eva didn't understand it, she was trying to get used to it. Today she hoped there would be no disturbance. One of her main goals with the foundation was to be able to validate her healing and silence some of the critics and naysayers, who seemed to shriek daily about her work.

Police officers created a comforting presence at the edges of the crowd, and those invited had been checked and cleared by security personnel before being allowed to enter the building. Eva was adapting to the idea of her own, almost constant security detail. Today this was Frank Ricci and Bob McCormack, who stood outside her waiting room. She knew they were scanning the crowd for threats.

At least Roger Gleason was no longer a threat. She'd woken in a sweat from nightmares for weeks, reliving the moment he'd slammed into her car, and the terror as she rolled down the embankment. When apprehended, he had melted down, ranting that he was compelled by a "higher moral duty" to kill her. His attorney had entered an insanity defense.

Eva refocused on the speech ahead. She had prepared her notes, rethinking and editing countless times over the last few weeks. So much to tell the media, about healing, yet she had to be careful not to delve too deeply into details, and to keep her talk succinct. Sharp. On the money.

As she waited for the governor, Eva let her thoughts drift back to the most recent in-house test, conducted six weeks ago at the foundation's new headquarters in Waverley. The trial was set up specifically to ascertain if more than one person in a healing circle benefited from the energetic connection. Twenty people formed a large circle, holding hands.

Most of these volunteers had health problems they wished to address. One was a young man who suffered severe hay fever and allergies to cats. Another was a woman who experienced such harsh episodes of anxiety and depression that it severely affected her life. Then there was the elderly woman with debilitating arthritis. The musician, Kip Ryan, described his occasional migraines but said they didn't happen when he was performing regularly. He figured it was the endorphins from singing. One woman, herself an asthma sufferer, had also brought her elderly Chihuahua, now lying on her lap, who suffered seizures. The very thought her little pet might be helped had filled her eyes with tears.

Only one woman had no current health issues to share. Annette, who was a homeopath, had also trained as a nurse. She had suffered as a much younger woman from Chronic Fatigue Syndrome but had recovered through the use of a homeopathic remedy. Explaining to the others that homeopathy works in an energetic capacity, she was completely open to the concept of energy healing. Also, Chloe and Michael both joined the group, although they couldn't define specific health or pain problems. Eva simply wanted them there, for support.

As Eva settled into this expanded healing circle, she quickly found the dark warm space to which she was now accustomed, and focused on each person, one at a time. The energy of the woman next to her was the most available, and she had to reach a bit further with her mind to access the next person, then the person after that. Just as she was beginning to think this would be a twenty-person healing session that would exhaust her beyond measure, the energy began to swirl and combine. The sensation of being underwater deepened. The daisy chain became a circle of energy of people to whom she was physically connected, now energetically connected.

She waited for twenty sets of walls she would have to dissolve. Instead, she experienced one vast, grayish cloud, in front of her, which she touched with her energy. It slowly drifted away, upward and outward, leaving clear energy in front of her. And all around her.

And there was light. Soft cream-colored light. Usually, she was in deep darkness. Was this goodwill a cascade of intent from twenty people combined? She had no idea and spent no more time pondering it. She was vastly content to float in the warmth, in the sensation of water and light.

After a time, a sound brought her back. It was a clicking sound, like toenails on a tile floor. And that's what it was. Opening her eyes, she spotted the little chihuahua prancing at his owner's feet. The volunteers began to stir, take deep breaths, and open their eyes. The group spontaneously broke into laughter seeing the little dog dancing about.

"Oh, Tootsie, you darling!" The woman glanced up at the rest in the circle. "He's acting like a puppy again! He hasn't trotted around like this in years. Look at him!" She laughed aloud and the little dog leaped back into her arms, jumping up to lick her nose.

Eva suddenly realized that not only was she not twenty times more exhausted, she was not fatigued at all. Was she getting better at it? Or was it that when enough people combined their energy, she directed the collective energy rather than using up every ounce of her own?

Over the weeks since this healing circle, the members reported improvements to the foundation's scientific team. Plus, they described a sense of inner knowledge, a wisdom they felt they'd somehow gained from the experience.

She shook her head in amazement once again. The implications were exciting, to say the least. How many people could be healed at once? Could she hold hands with 500 people in a concert hall and have them all benefit? 1000? Was it limitless?

Eva was drawn back to the present by the silence in the atrium beyond her waiting room. The crowd had quieted, and she heard Governor Lambeth welcoming the press contingent and introducing Eva's new foundation, based in Rhode Island for legal reasons. She spoke at length, explaining its concepts and charter: to conduct research, support, and educate about energy healing, and to provide an online scheduling system for Eva. She described the recent tests and their positive results.

"Now, enough from me," the governor said. "It is my true honor and privilege to present to you the woman you've been waiting for. As you know, she did indeed heal my beloved husband of pancreatic cancer and has helped countless people—and animals—in the last months. Ladies and gentlemen, Eva McGrath."

Although her heart rate picked up, Eva was not as nervous as she expected. She climbed the few steps to the raised platform, constructed so that speakers could be easily seen and photographed. Laying her papers on the podium, she thanked the crowd for their applause. Gazing up at the Corinthian columns, the balconies, and the soaring glass ceiling, she was filled with awe.

How on earth did I get here? Speaking before hundreds of people in this historic building, introducing the impossible magic of healing. *But this is not just what I do, this is who I am.*

My destiny.

She'd written a speech, but now, looking out at the sea of expectant eyes, she decided just to wing it, not read from prepared words.

"I have been blessed with the ability to heal," Eva said into the microphone. "I am often asked if this gift is from God. The answer is simple: I have no idea. I'd love to think it is, but that sounds so self-important. But I believe we will find that we all have this ability. This way to reach each other with energy."

She paused, settling into the moment. "Let me tell you a little about it. At first, it just feels like a deep meditation. Before I reach the deep place where I believe the healing takes place, I encounter what appear to be gray or black walls. And I've figured out what they are. They're the walls people create between each other. Walls of steel. But animals, and babies, don't have them. You know why?"

Her eyes roamed over the others in the crowd, some looking thoughtful, some confused, but all silent and listening. "Babies haven't yet encountered tragedy or heartache. And as for animals, they're guileless, so guided by their instinct that they're always open, simple, and uncluttered."

"Those obstacles I encounter are barriers we build over the course of our lives. We hide behind those walls, protecting ourselves from pain. Yet, ironically, those walls insulate us from the very thing we need to *alleviate* the pain. Connection to other people. And I believe we all yearn for that connection."

She stopped to let them process that idea. She studied the journalists in the first few rows. Some faces were hard with skepticism narrowing their eyes, but some seemed open, even encouraging.

It's a start.

Eva let her eyes rest on Jamie, Chloe, and her grandparents at the side of the crowd. And nearby were Samantha, Olivia, and her father. She had reached Will Hastings, connected spiritually with him, during his healing, and their relationship was on a somewhat different footing now. Chloe put it down to his brush with death. Maybe, Eva thought. Or maybe it was down to breaking through that granite wall. She doubted narcissism could be cured that quickly, in one effort, but he did seem quieter, more thoughtful. And kinder.

Olivia was warming to her, somewhat, and Eva believed she was going to have a good friend in Samantha. As for Jared, she didn't think she'd ever get close to him but figured she wasn't missing much. He hadn't come this morning, citing some pretext. She knew she'd have to work on some goodwill where he was concerned.

And there was her Michael, at the front of the crowd, his smile warm.

Her heart opened. The tingle of vibration began and just for a moment Eva felt the familiar sensation of deep water, the blissful peace, the connection with everything there is.

"Those walls of steel are pride, trauma, fear," she said. "Behind the walls is where our true spirit exists. And that's where healing is. In the connection we make beyond the walls."

•• ◆ ••

Audrey Lambeth and Eva's security guards stayed close by her side as she posed for pictures, shook a few hands, and answered questions. Floating on bubbles of exhilaration and achievement, she was nevertheless more than ready to escape when she felt Michael grab her hand. He led her back to the anteroom and enfolded her in a long hug.

"You were magnificent," he murmured. "Congratulations. I'm so very proud of you."

Eva threw her head back, wanting to laugh aloud with the pure joy of it. She reveled in the moment. The bubbles inside were sure to spill out everywhere or else lift her off into space.

He pulled back. "Wanna blow this joint?"

"Definitely," she said with a grin.

"Good. I want you to myself for a while," he said softly.

"What do you have in mind?"

"Somewhere private. There's something I need to ask you."

Her heart quickened. She glanced around. "We're alone here. What is it? You OK?"

"More than OK. I'm great."

"So, what is it?"

"Marry me, Eva?"

She shot back, immediately. "Yes!" Then added, almost as a sigh, "*Please....*"

The surprise on his face turned to joy as he lifted her off her feet and whirled her around. He set her down but didn't let her go. "Why did you say yes so fast?"

"Well, Dr. Lowery," she said with a grin, "it turns out you've ruined me for being alone."

Michael kissed her hand. "You're welcome."

The End

Did you enjoy this novel?

If you did, would you consider popping on to Amazon or Goodreads and leaving a review? Thank you!

Acknowledgments

My heartfelt thanks are entwined with admiration for my editor, Mark Carey, who juggles timelines, character arcs, and myriad other details while simultaneously running it all past his inner grammar Ninja. He combines his talents as a wordsmith with his sensibilities as a philosopher. Thank you, Mark, from the bottom of my heart.

My gratitude also floods out to my wonderful copy editors, beta readers, and dear "friends with suggestions": Gary Warner, Laurie Seymour, Jim Paradis, Cheryl Kareff, Deb Whitman, Gemma Jones, Diana Carroll, Marsha Campaniello, Thelma Tracy, Jeannie Tolson, Cheryl Prottsman, Temmer Darigan, and Jan James.

Your support means the world to me.

About the Author

Diane began her career in the UK as singer/songwriter on BBC TV. At 20, believing her first talent was acting, she had headed off to England, determined to study acting at the Royal Academy of Dramatic Art.

But life can take some funny turns. Before she could arrange an interview, she was "discovered," playing her guitar and singing to a small, New Year's Eve party at a hotel in Bath. A BBC television producer was there, a screen test followed, and the result was a network primetime series of variety specials! *The Diane Solomon Show* was a great success, and she quickly became a regular on British TV. She recorded five albums, appeared on countless TV and radio shows, hosted documentaries, and starred in musical theater productions. After heading four UK theater concert tours of her own, she toured with Glen Campbell on three European tours, and opened for a major Kenny Rogers' tour.

Then, after 15 years of traveling the world as an entertainer, the dreaded Chronic Fatigue Syndrome destroyed her career. She struggled for almost eight years, years of wading through half a life, finally regaining her health with the help of a homeopathic remedy. This launched her into new studies and a second career as a homeopath and nutritionist.

Now focused on writing, Diane lives in beautiful New Hampshire with her husband, Mark. She writes, edits, researches, designs, and builds gardens, always seeking more knowledge, more understanding, and more creative flow.

Diane Solomon has written seven books, published by Eloquent Rascals Publishing:

- A new series of health eBooks: "Healing Therapies that Work: *The Natural Treatment of Allergies and Healing Therapies that Work: The Natural Treatment of Ear Infections.*
- A middle-grade time-travel fantasy series called The *Ravenstone*, written with her husband Mark Carey. First: *The Ravenstone: The Secret of Ninham Mountain,* and the sequel: *The Ravenstone: The Twain.*
- *88 Guys for Coffee,* a humorous women's novel about online dating.
- *Chronic Fatigue Syndrome: A Guide to the Homeopathic Treatment of CFS/ME*, to hopefully help others afflicted with this dreadful disease. It quickly became the best-selling book in the homeopathy section.

More books are on the way!

For more information about Diane and her other books, check out her website, DianeSolomonAuthor.com. Or on Facebook: Diane Solomon Writer

Printed in Great Britain
by Amazon